# FROM THE VOID

## BOOK II
### OF THE
## ON THE VERGE
#### SERIES

# R. J. JOJOLA

For those we've lost along the way.

# ACKNOWLEDGMENTS

Thank you, so much, to everyone who has been a part of my journey thus far. First, to the amazing fans who make doing this so worthwhile. Your love and praise for *On the Verge* has brought it to life in a whole new way. Secondly, to my friends and family who have given me so much support in pursuing my writing dream. And lastly, the amazing team of people who have helped to take this series, and *From the Void,* to the next level. They include: my insanely talented cover artist, Rafa Teruel (rafater.com), my always instrumental and nurturing editor, Elizabeth Keenan, and of course, my dedicated beta readers.
None of this is possible without you.

# CONTENTS

# VOCABULARY

## STINTING (VERB):

*Rogue Skill.*

\* The act of temporarily slowing time in order to move to a new location. Usually to avoid or dodge an enemy. To a foe, outside the Rogue's perception, the Rogue appears to disappear and reappear in a new location.

## SHIFTING (VERB):

*Elven Skill.*

\* All elves are known as *shifters*. They can *shift* (transform) or take on the form of other entities. Samissians, Ellosians, and Ornz may only take the form of animals.

\* Jassokians, however, may take on the form of the elements; such as wind, earth, fire, water, and even smoke. They are *elemental shifters*. Since this skill can take decades to perfect, most only chose a single element.

# MAP OF MIRILAN

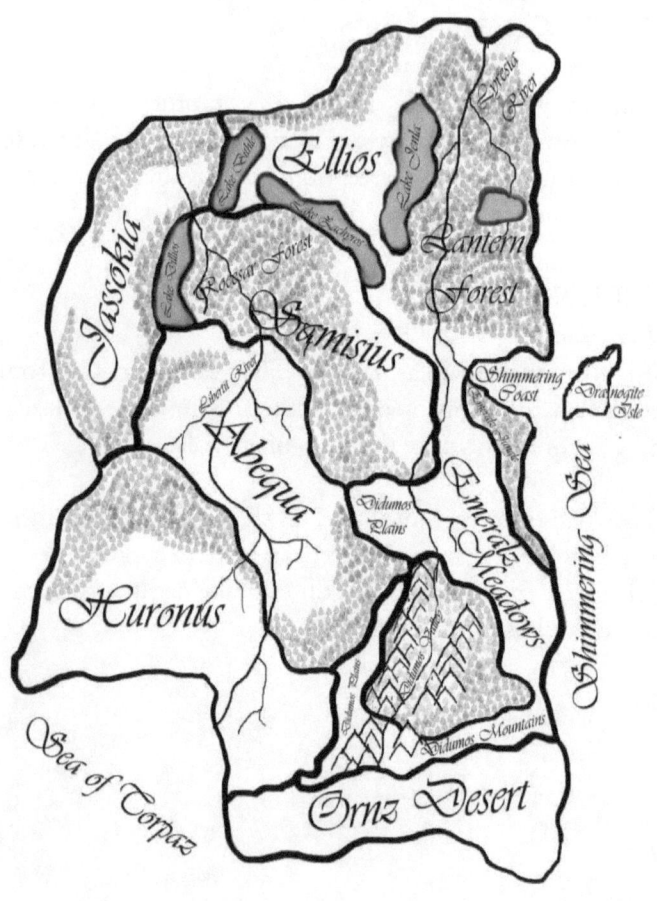

# CHAPTER I
## FATHER

The sound of wings cutting through the night air woke Samuel from his half sleep. He slid slowly upright on his top bunk. In the light of a full moon, an owl perched in the sill of his open window.

"Hooo... hooo..." The owl called. Its eyes glowed red in the darkness of the bedroom.

Samuel leaned over the side of his bunk to make sure his sister had not woken. Raelle lay fast asleep in her bottom bunk. In her arms, she held her dog Pip close. Samuel could hardly make out her fluffy black fur in the darkness. Next to him, Sasha stirred on top of his sheets. She stood and wagged her tail before stepping over the covers to greet her master. Samuel stroked his companion and gently eased her onto her side.

"Go back to sleep, girl. I won't be gone long. You stay here and look after Raelle and Pip."

Sasha rested her head on the blankets as her master had instructed. Samuel caressed her silky, brindle fur until she closed her eyes and drifted off to sleep. He quietly crept across his bunk and slunk down the latter onto the wood floor. The armoire's hinges creaked as he opened it. Samuel cringed and turned toward Raelle. Still, she and Pip snoozed hard underneath the covers. Samuel swiftly grabbed his clothes and boots that were piled up at the bottom of the cabinet and closed the door. He silently slipped into his attire. Once he finished dressing, he climbed through the window and landed softly atop the thick valley grass.

The owl flew up onto the branch of a nearby tree. "Hooo... hooo," it called. "It is tiiiime my princcce." The raspy voice of the bird slithered through its narrow, claw-like beak.

Samuel shoved his feet into his boots. In the light of the moon, he followed his avian companion down the grassy knoll in front of his family's humble cottage and into the woods. He swore he could see glowing pairs of red eyes whispering all around him. Samuel closed his eyes and did a double take. The whispers ceased and the eyes disappeared. All that was left was the owl that had woken him and the familiar array of wilderness that surrounded his homestead.

"Yessssss. Young Rooogue," the owl spoke. "Yesssss, Prince. Heeee is coming. Heeee shall bring you home."

Samuel paused when he reached the edge of a moonlit clearing. In the center, the shadow of a winged humanoid figure sat mounted atop a massive beast. As Samuel moved closer, he began to make out the daunting form of the enormous mount. The behemoth stood on all fours, at least a meter taller than he was, and had the face of a giant rat. The striations of its muscles bulged from its hairless, grey physique. Black razor-back hair started in between its meter-long bull-like horns and rode along its spine, all the way to its fat, spike-covered tail. Drool dripped onto the ground from behind its long canines. The monstrous mount's long, sharp claws stabbed into the forest floor, the weight of its massive body pressing the claws deeper into the soft earth with each passing moment.

"Yem prepim misit yut fralam?" The winged figure's eyes glowed orange as it spoke from atop its beastly ride. "Yem prepin commast im rezind ortan ire trupir isk yut fralam, im yut kistor?"

"I am ready," replied Samuel. "I have waited for this day for many years. I will not let him down. I will not let our kingdom down. I will make him proud."

"Then you shall have what you seek, prince Jowellia," the figured growled. "Tomorrow, on the anniversary of your birth, at sundown you shall fulfill your destiny." The figure bowed atop his mammoth beast. "We shall reconvene here at that time."

Samuel nodded. "I will be here."

***

Samuel spent the anniversary of his seventeenth year completely alone in the forest. It was especially lonely without

Sasha at his side, but he had no other choice but to leave her behind for now. Samuel found himself contemplating the events of his life thus far. Today, he would mourn the death of his younger brother Browden for the last time. And when it came time for the daylight to make room for the night, he would meet the caravan that would rescue him from his prison in the valley. He waited anxiously for the moment to arrive.

As the sun began its final descent into the west, Samuel sat in the clearing where he had met the winged messenger the night before. *I will come back for you, Raelle.* He rested his head against the base of a large pine. *I promise. I will not forsake you.* The ring in his pocket felt warm as he reached in to grab it. Samuel slipped the white gold band onto his finger. The cerulean gem set in the ring's center glowed bright against his knuckle. He closed his eyes and connected with his Lyre. *He is near. I can feel it. He will make me whole once again. Return all that was stolen from me and Raelle.*

With the sun setting behind the trees, the blue glow of Samuel's Lyre gem radiated like a beacon of hope. With his acute sense of hearing, Samuel picked up the sound of cracking branches and crunching grass beneath the feet of his liberators. *They're close.* His eyes pursed shut and his heart thumped wildly. Each moment that passed drew him ever closer to freedom and vengeance. He was on the verge of greatness.

Samuel sensed the energy of another bounce sharply off of his. When he opened his eyes, large brown irises met his gaze. It was almost like looking into a mirror.

"Stand, my son." The stranger offered Samuel his hand.

Samuel's lips could form no words as he studied the man in front of him. The man's long blonde hair was the exact same color as his. And his nose was almost an exact replica of Samuel's. The man's distinct mouth and aged skin were the only things that set them apart.

"My father. My king." Samuel bowed in reverence.

"I have waited seventeen years for this, my son." The man

embraced him.

Samuel buried his face in his father's shoulder, soaking it with tears. "I have longed for this day for so long, Father." Samuel stepped back to view him once more. "I have been patient, just as you requested. These five years felt like a lifetime to me."

His father smiled. "I've searched for you every day since they took you from me. When I sensed your nightmare five years ago, I was overwhelmed by hope. I sent my minions to find you, and they did. Your mentor tells me you have done well in your training."

"Yes," said Samuel. "He has told me the same. He says I'm ready to return to our kingdom. I'm ready to defeat our enemies and bring peace to Mirilan."

"Indeed, my son, indeed." His father stared into his eyes. "You are of pure blood. You are of royal blood. You are my son. You are the most elite of our elite. And to prove your worth, I have brought you a gift." Samuel's father reached into his pocket. He opened his hand to reveal a white gold chain that housed an ornate amulet with a black gem. "This gem is the key to your power. Your royal Lyre blood will be magnified by its energy. Your power will be unlimited, your stamina unattainable, and your skills unmatched." His father placed the gem-laden necklace around Samuel's neck. "You are the very definition of our elite, Samuel."

"Thank you, Father." Samuel bowed.

"One more thing before we leave." His father pulled something else from his pocket. "For your transition to be complete, you must drink this." He handed Samuel a small vial of black liquid. "It will render your royal Lyre blood all the more powerful when combined with your new gemstone."

"Whatever you ask of me, I will do." Samuel popped the cork from the vial. He raised it to his lips and poured the bitter liquid into his mouth. It felt warm as it trickled down his throat and into his stomach. "It is done, Father." The trees began to spin all around him and the ground escaped him.

A distorted smile crept across his father's face as a Minotirr stepped into view. The Minotirr reached toward him with his armored claws. Samuel's vision went black and he collapsed to the forest floor.

# CHAPTER 2
## WAKING THE DEAD

The robust smell of freshly cooked meats wafted into Samuel's nose. He stretched his stiff limbs as he sat up in the bed of an unfamiliar room. When he opened his eyes, they were met with the brilliant blue gaze of a complete stranger.

"Welcome home, my prince," the young woman said as she strolled over to his bed. With elegance and grace, she sat down next to him.

Samuel found himself speechless. The scantily clad woman had stolen the air from his lungs. He breathed hard as he studied her beautiful face, all the way down to her belly button, and over the curvature of her hips.

The young woman smiled with full lips and stroked her long black hair. "I am Naruncia. I am one of your chamber maidens. I've brought you breakfast." She picked a red fruit from the ornate silver tray.

Samuel did not blink as she leaned forward, exposing much more of her cleavage. "Open up," she said as she draped the vined fruit over Samuel's lips. He gazed into her hypnotic blue eyes and plucked the red fruit from the vine with his teeth. Inside his mouth, the berry burst with flavor.

"We will need to keep you well fed to keep your strength up, Milord."

"Yes, thank you," Samuel replied.

Naruncia continued to feed him meats and fruits until Samuel had his fill. "I hope you found your meal satisfactory, Milord."

Samuel cleared his throat and sat up straight. "It was delicious." The food was helping, but still, he felt incredibly weak. "Where am I? How long have I been asleep?"

Naruncia swept back a piece of Samuel's dirty blonde hair from his face. "You arrived here one week ago. You are home,

Milord. You are in the Rogue palace of Huronus. These are your royal chambers."

*I've been asleep for a week?* Samuel's eyes wandered the room. The silver walls of the chamber were painted with ornate black designs that seemed to shimmer in the morning light. Elaborate black sconces held blue candles at each and every corner of the room. The dark wood of his bed looked almost black against the light blue silk sheets that covered him. Samuel folded back the pastel linens and dangled his legs over the floor. As he pressed his feet into the smooth surface, the cool white marble felt soothing to his tingling toes.

"Please, allow me to help you, Sire. You've had a long journey." Naruncia stood and slipped her arms underneath his. "Would you like to see your view?" She smiled.

"Yes, please," said Samuel. On his trembling legs, he shuffled across the polished floor to the open palace window. A cool breeze carried an unfamiliar scent into the room and Samuel lifted his keen nose. "It smells salty, yet fresh."

Naruncia grinned. "Welcome home, Prince Jowellia." She pulled the sheer blue curtains apart to reveal the most spectacular view Samuel had ever laid eyes upon. "*This* is your kingdom."

Samuel looked out upon a bustling city of white marble streets and blue waterways. Below him, on either side of the palace, a waterfall cascaded down into a shimmering pool that fed into the city's many canals. Brilliant structures of blue marble and white stone lined the streets and seaways. Some of the structures were so tall that their domed roofs looked as if they might touch the clouds. Boats and carriages carrying men and women in all shades of blue attire decorated the city's marble and water grids. The dazzling vista overwhelmed Samuel as he took it all in. But it was what lay just beyond the city that truly stole his gaze. A glistening, blue body of water without visible end spewed a fresh salty scent into the air as it crashed into the sandy seashore. As it continued to bombard his senses, Samuel also felt Naruncia's hands creep over his naked shoulders and onto his bare pectorals. He let every ounce of air escape his lungs.

"It is beautiful isn't it, Milord?"

Samuel shuddered at Naruncia's hot breath against his neck. "Yes, it is the most incredible thing I have ever seen. So much so that I don't believe it."

"It is real, Milord, I assure you. And it is all yours." Naruncia draped her fingers across Samuel's arm and over his chest. She gracefully shifted in front of him as she ran her hands down his abdomen and over his most intimate region. "Even *I* am yours."

Samuel hyperventilated in silence as Naruncia pressed her soft lips to the bottom of his neck. He shivered as the kisses traveled up to his chin and made their way to his mouth. Never before had he been with a woman in this way.

Samuel combed his fingers through Naruncia's hair and took her in his arms. His body throbbed as she pressed her chest against his. Naruncia slipped her tongue in between Samuel's lips. Samuel's grip tightened around her round bottom. Her legs straddled his hips and he carried her to his bed. With his finger, he gently pulled one of Naruncia's silk straps over her shoulder and down her arm to reveal the treasure beneath. He pressed his mouth to the precious bounty and examined it with his hand. His body ached with pleasure.

Grasping the blue gem at the center of her cropped blouse, Naruncia exposed all of what Samuel so desired to see. She did the same with his linen pants before opening her blue silk skirt. As they connected fully, the gem in Samuel's ring and Naruncia's necklace blazed blue light. Samuel cringed as the black gem of his necklace surged a wild, hot passion through him. Finally, he had found his strength, his power, his desire, his destiny.

*** 

Samuel woke from his nap to find Naruncia fast asleep under the covers of his giant bed. He covered her exposed skin with the sheet before finding his way to the water closet within his chambers. A sink made of silver with a matching spout sat in front of a large ornate mirror. Samuel pumped the metal lever next to the spout several times before water poured into the basin. He splashed the cool liquid from the sink over his face. He felt as if he were in a dream. Or maybe he had just woken from a nightmare. Either way, being anywhere but his prison in the valley felt surreal. *You've waited long enough. You're home now. This is where you belong. These are your people, your blood.* Thoughts of his sister weighed heavily on his mind. He sighed deeply as he pressed a blue linen towel to his face. *I will come back for you, Raelle. I promise. I never wanted to leave you behind, but I had no other choice.*

When Samuel exited the washroom, he found Naruncia dressing on the edge of his bed. "You're fully rested, I see." She smiled and made her way toward a set of extravagant double doors. "This is your wardrobe, Milord." She opened the spacious closet and bowed. "You may wear anything you like."

Samuel stepped into the closet. His eyes could not blink. His mouth gaped at the elegant pants, shirts, cloaks, boots, and shoes that surrounded him. "There are so many options I fear I may not be able to make a decision."

Naruncia laughed, "Allow me to help you, Sire. What sort of things do you usually like to wear?"

"Well." Samuel shrugged. "I usually just keep it simple."

Naruncia giggled. "Then simple it shall be." She made her way through the large collection of garments and stopped at the back. "Here we are. *Simple,* just as you requested." Naruncia handed Samuel a pair of grey leather pants and a pastel blue linen shirt.

Samuel slipped into them and Naruncia handed him a black leather vest with a hood, along with a pair of matching black leather boots. "Thank you, Naruncia."

"Is there anything else I may do for you?"

Samuel smiled as he approached her. He took her in his arms. With a gentle hand, he brushed a long lock of black hair from her face and looked into her blue eyes. "Yes, you may call me *Samuel.*"

"Of course." Naruncia curved her lips and brushed a finger across his. "Anything else?"

"Actually, yes," Samuel said before kissing her forehead. "I would like to see my father. Can you take me to him?"

"Yes, Milord. I most certainly can." Naruncia laughed. "I mean, Samuel." She stroked his face with her hand. "I can take you to him now if you'd like."

"Yes, please." Samuel followed his new companion out of his chambers and into the hallway. Unlike his bedroom, the walls were not silver, but blue. It looked as if they were made of glass that had been purposefully broken and the pieces glued back together like a strangely cut gemstone. The bright light of the summer sun penetrated through the glass, making the walls glisten like the sea.

Samuel and Naruncia made their way down to the end of the hall and stopped at a giant pair of double doors. They were crafted of a silver metal and textured with blue glass and gemstones. Naruncia grasped the mermaid-shaped handles and closed her eyes. The blue gem in her necklace glowed as she used her Lyre to open the entryway.

Inside, they found Samuel's father sitting at a white and blue marble desk with ornate silver legs. He stood as Samuel entered.

"My son, you are finally awake." The king approached Samuel and embraced him.

"Yes, Father, I feel very rested."

"I trust Naruncia has done a splendid job tending to your needs?"

Samuel glanced at her. "Yes, she is perfect."

"I knew you would approve. Naruncia is of pure Huronian blood. Her family is nobility. She wishes to honor them by pledging herself to her prince."

"She is wonderful, Father."

"There are others as well. They have all pledged themselves to you. Each one of them is of pure Lyre blood."

"Thank you, Father."

The king motioned to Naruncia. "Please, leave us."

Naruncia curtsied. "Yes, Your Majesty."

10

The king walked behind his desk, where a marvelous buffet was set with ornate glassware. In the center sat a decanter filled with green liquid. The king poured two small glasses.

"Come. Sit. We have much to discuss." The king found his way to a love seat across from his desk. He set the drinks on the short table in front of him and sat down on the blue, velvet cushion.

Samuel met his father on the small couch. The king handed him the beautifully decorated glass of green spirit.

"A toast, to the return of my beloved son." His father lifted his glass. "May we begin to avenge your suffering and imprisonment."

"Thank you, Father." Samuel raised his tumbler and touched it to the king's. The cool green liquid eased his nerves as it flowed into his stomach. "However I can serve you and my nation, I will." Samuel hung his head. "If only Mother were alive to see my return."

"Your mother would be incredibly proud of you. To see you rise once again after all you have been through. Her spirit smiles upon you and blesses the great journey ahead."

"Indeed. The journey ahead, what does it hold for me?" Samuel asked anxiously. "What do you have planned for my future? How may I serve our grand king and elite nation?"

"I have spoken to your mentor," his father said. "And he believes that you are ready to lead our armies into battle. He asserts that you have excelled beyond his wildest dreams. You have done much work and shown relentless dedication over the past five years. I imagine it was incredibly difficult to keep your training a secret from your captors and your sister for so many years."

"Yes, it was, especially from Raelle. I love her dearly. She has always been there for me when I needed her. It was difficult not to let her in. I know she has suffered because of it. In fact, it is one of the reasons I sought you out today. I would like the chance to return to the valley and bring her home. She is all alone now with our captors. She too must come take her rightful place in our kingdom. She too is a Huronian Rogue."

11

"You are right, my son. Raelle *is* one of us and should be returned to her kingdom. My original plan was to help her escape after your return. But I am afraid... " The king looked down.

"What is it?" Samuel grasped his father's shoulder.

"I hate to give you such somber news, but Raelle has been killed. I knew she would go looking for you, so I sent one of the Minotirr to help her escape once she reached the clearing. But after you disappeared from the valley, Marista and Lorndan caught on to our plan and murdered Raelle before my Minotirr could get to her. Your captors did not wish to see Huronus restored to its former glory. They knew how much we needed her."

A lump formed in Samuel's throat. He tried to swallow it as he closed his eyes. When he opened them, tears glossed over his gaze. "No, this can't be. I would've felt it, I—"

"I am so sorry, Samuel. It is true. I was devastated when I heard the news. I too loved her deeply. For the first three years of her life, before she was taken, she was my world. Now, she is gone." The king looked to the floor, his head weighted with sorrow. "My Minotirr came upon her just as your captors set fire to your homestead with Raelle inside. They were too late. My Minotirr slayed your captors and brought back what was left of your sister. Her body is waiting in the crematorium. If you need, I can take you there. You may wish her farewell before the funeral and coronation ceremony commences this evening."

"Yes, please." Samuel blinked back tears. "What about the dogs? What about Sasha?"

Lochran sighed. "I'm afraid they too were victims of Marista and Lorndan. We found their bodies along with Raelle's. My—"

"I hate them!" Samuel cut in. "I hate Lorndan and Marista for what they've done. If your Minotirr had not finished them, I would have gladly done it myself! I'm sure they kidnapped my brother Browden as well. Poor boy, he never even got the chance to meet his parents before his passing."

"Yes, you are right. He was stolen from the king and queen of Abequa. Lorndan murdered them as well. He hated that they wanted to stand with me, and with Huronus. So, he killed them and took their infant son."

Samuel's hands shook as hot Lyre rage surged through him. "By the Architect, I hate them so much! I swear I will avenge Browden and Raelle. I will avenge you and our nation. I'm ready to lead our armies into battle. I am prepared to do whatever it takes to avenge our people, our nation, and our family."

"And so it shall be done." Lochran held Samuel's arm. "Huronus offered Abequa protection after the tragedy. They are now one, under my rule. But now, I offer Abequa to you. You shall not only be the reigning elite general of my troops, but the *new* king of the *new* Abequa. In an hour's time, we will be traveling there for your coronation. Raelle's funeral will precede it."

"Yes, Father." Samuel nodded.

"Shall we proceed to the crematorium?" The king stood.

Samuel wiped the tears from his face. "I'm not sure what seeing her like that will do to me. Maybe I shouldn't go."

"It is up to you. I will escort you if you're prepared. But if you are not, then you need not go." The king pulled something from his pocket. "Instead, I offer you this. My Minotirr found it among the burned wreckage of your homestead. I believe it belonged to Raelle." Samuel's father handed him a beautifully decorated silver brush. Strands of his sister's auburn hair were woven into its white bristles. "Yes," replied Samuel. "This did belong to her." His mind drifted to a memory of his sister.

"I love looking at the stars." Raelle brushed her hair as they lay atop a blanket in the grass beside a clear lake in their valley. "The vastness of our universe is so beautiful. Who knows, maybe one of those stars is home to a world like ours. Maybe the inhabitants of that world are doing the exact same thing that we are now."

Browden tugged on Raelle's long hair. "You sure do have a wild imagination, Sister." He laughed.

Samuel sat up. "I don't know. Maybe she's right. I mean, why should we be so special? There have to be other worlds out there. If not, then our universe is a lonely and desolate place."

Raelle pressed her hand to Samuel's cheek. "I can always count on you to see reason, Brother." Raelle smiled. "And I can always count on *you* to keep it interesting." She pointed at Browden and tossed her brush just before jumping over Samuel. On the other side, she tickled their surrogate brother, planting tiny kisses all over Browden's face. They laughed...

The pleasant memory brought a short-lived smile to Samuel's face. He shook his head. "She was a wonderful person. The loss of her life is a great loss to Lerim."

The king grasped the brush in Samuel's hand. "You know, it does not have to be this way."

Samuel raised his brow. "What do you mean?"

"I mean..." the king grabbed the black gem of Samuel's necklace. "That she does not have to stay dead. There is a way to bring her back. This black gem I gave you is a very rare stone with a very rare gift. With it, you can commune with the guardians of the black realm. Specifically, the guardian Azmodil. With his assistance, you can bring Raelle back from the dead. Using a small piece of your own soul, she will return with a new body. We do not have to be without her."

Samuel gripped his necklace. "A piece of my own soul? Isn't that dark magic?"

"It depends on how you look at it. I do not see this sort of ability or phenomenon as *dark*. I see it as a chance for a miracle—a chance to return our beloved Raelle to the living world. Do you not find it unjust that she will never see her homeland and she will never bask in the warm rays of the Huronus coastline?"

Samuel sighed and rubbed his forehead. "Yes, I do believe it incredibly unjust. And I miss her very much. I know she would love it here. Lorndan and Marista took everything from us, including a chance at a real life here in Huronus."

"Then we must try to bring her back."

"I don't know. Many would consider this sort of thing to be unnatural. Don't you think? I'm not sure that even Raelle would want to come back this way."

"My son." The king grasped Samuel's shoulders and looked him in the eye. "What better way to avenge your sister's death than to try and offer her a brand new life? A life of joy. A life without suffering. A life of safety and betterment."

"My heart is telling me to do it," Samuel said. "I know Raelle deserves a better life than what she was given. Tell me what I need to do, Father, and I will do it. I need my sister."

The king reached into his shirt and pulled a chain from his neck. On the necklace hung a key. Samuel's father used it to open a drawer at the center of his desk. He pulled a rolled parchment from the drawer before closing and locking it again.

"This is all you'll need." The king handed the parchment to Samuel. "Follow the instructions very carefully. You will need Raelle's brush, your Lyre harness ring, and your necklace. You must repeat the ritual each night before you go to bed. Once it is finished, Raelle will appear in your chambers. Her soul will reside within her new shell. Before long, she will be with us once more."

"Yes, Father. It will be done." Samuel tucked the parchment into the pocket of his leather vest.

"Go now. You must prepare for your coronation. If we are to bring Raelle back, then we must not have a wake."

"I agree," replied Samuel. "See you in an hour."

"Samuel," Lochran called. "This must remain between us."

"Yes, Father." Samuel bowed and closed the doors behind him. His hands trembled as he made his way back to his chambers. Inside, he found a young man waiting for him.

"Good afternoon, Milord." The young man bowed.

"Good afternoon."

"My name is Rulsan. I will be helping you prepare for your journey to Abequa." Rulsan stepped toward the door. "But first we must travel to the royal armory and get you fitted."

"Armory? What would I need armor for?"

"For the coronation, of course." Rulsan grinned. "It's tradition."

"Of course." Samuel shook his head. "Sorry. Let us go to the armory then."

Samuel followed his servant down the blue glass hall. Rulsan used the Torpaz gem from his necklace to unlock an ornate silver door. "This way, Milord."

Samuel entered the doorway onto the top of a white marble staircase.

"The armory is in the basement level," Rulsan explained. "Follow me."

Samuel trailed Rulsan down six flights of stairs until they were met with another door. Rulsan opened it and led Samuel inside. All around him, the walls were decorated with an array of daggers in all different shapes and designs, each laden with blue Torpaz gems, the stone of Samuel's people. They walked through the weaponry chamber and into the next room where sturdy mannequins garbed in different shades of blue Rogue armor lined the walls. Each getup looked tailor-made and had a unique design.

"This way, Milord. Your armor is back here in the royal armor chamber."

Samuel followed Rulsan into a back room, where he found a mannequin dressed in elaborate dark blue Rogue armor with a black hood. The designs sparkled with Torpaz gems. Samuel inhaled the scent of freshly made leather as he ran his fingers across the material and examined the metal studs that decorated it.

"This is for me?" Samuel grinned.

"Yes, Sire."

Samuel looked up at the strange, black mask that covered the mannequin's nose and mouth. The mask itself had a mouth of sharp metal teeth. At first glance, it looked slightly disturbing, but as Samuel studied it further, it grew on him and made him feel powerful.

"I hope you are pleased, Sire."

"Yes, I am, truly."

"Then we shall begin."

As Rulsan dressed him, Samuel heard faint screams, cries, and roaring echoing through the armory. "What is that?"

"What is what, Milord?"

"That sound. The screaming and crying, and—

"Oh, that is nothing," Rulsan chuckled. "We are one floor above the dungeon. You are probably just hearing the cries of prisoners, criminals, traitors, and slaves."

"Slaves?" Samuel winced.

"Yes, slaves. The people of this nation who do not possess Lyre. After their uprising with the Inclusionist movement, your father felt it necessary to keep them under control. To keep our people safe. To keep our elite blood brothers and sisters protected from their anarchy."

"I see." Samuel swallowed his uncertainty. "So these people are dangerous?"

"Yes, Milord. Incredibly."

"My father is a great man to keep his people safe."

"Indeed Milord, indeed he is."

# CHAPTER 3
## ABEQUA

Fully armored, Samuel stepped into a metal-plated carriage. Inside, his father sat with a dark figure. It was a woman, dressed in all black, with a large black headdress.

"Welcome, my son."

"Thank you, Father." Samuel sat on the opposite side of the carriage. He tried to get a look at the woman's face, but a long, sheer black veil made it difficult.

"Samuel, this is my companion." The king pointed to the obscured woman. "She does not have a name. She lost it long ago."

"Hello." Samuel lowered his head.

"Do not bow to her. She is beneath you. She is nameless and voiceless. It was her punishment for forsaking our Grand Architect and her people."

"Yes, Father."

The king called out to the driver who set the carriage in motion. But unlike any other carriage Samuel had ever seen, this one did not have horses or wheels. Instead it seemed to hover over the ground as it moved along.

"How does it work?" Samuel wondered aloud.

"It uses a special soil gem, which can only be found in Ellios. The gem uses and transforms energy to power other things. I do not know exactly how it is done. It is a technology developed by the Ellosians. My spies went to a lot of trouble to get their hands on it."

"I see. Well, it is incredible. I never thought such a thing possible." Samuel looked down to see the woman's withered hands shaking in her lap. Even though he could not see her face, he could feel her staring at him through her dark shroud. His eyes were drawn to hers as well. Samuel froze inside her penetrating gaze. A whisper echoed inside his mind.

*Samuel. Samuel… Open… your… eyes…*

"What is that? Who is that?" He looked around the carriage.

The king scowled. "What is what, Samuel?"

"Someone is calling my name. Don't you hear it?"

"It was probably just the people of the city chanting your name. They are very supportive of their prince and the soon to be king of Abequa. Do not be nervous. I understand this is a great deal to take in. But do not allow your nerves to get the best of you."

"I'm sorry, it just felt like she..." He looked over at the concealed woman. Her hands were now still as she gazed out the carriage window. "Never mind." Samuel shook his head. "I must be nervous. Only a week ago, I was living in a valley with my captors. Now I'm to be presented to an entire kingdom and made their king? It's a lot to take in."

"It is indeed." The king locked eyes with Samuel. "But you *will* get used to it. You must embrace it. You are of royal blood, pure royal blood. You are an elite, my son."

"Yes, Father," Samuel replied. But still, the woman in black ensnared his gaze.

***

Samuel was not sure when he had fallen asleep or for how long, but when he woke, his ears were suddenly bombarded by the sound of excited voices. Outside the carriage, they were chanting loudly.

"We've arrived," his father announced.

As Samuel stepped from the carriage, his knees trembled within his elaborate armor. All around him, joyful cheers and screams sounded off like sirens. Samuel's anxiety transformed into excitement at the sound of his name being chanted by an enormous crowd.

"The prince has returned!" Samuel heard his father's voice bellow behind him. It instantly silenced the crowd. In their reverence, they fell to their knees and bowed. The king then raised his hand high. "Rise, loyal elites of Abequa and follow your new king into the arena!"

Samuel did his best not to blink as he followed his father through the column-lined streets of Abequa. Each building, archway, and column was carved of dark grey stone and accented with garnet-colored marble. Massive carved stone statues of muscular warriors in heavy armor stood at the corner of every block. As they got closer to the giant doors of the coliseum, the largest of the dark stone warrior statues towered over them and up into a patch of low lying clouds. Abequan guards in suits of chainmail armor pulled down on levers fixed to the wall behind them, opening the enormous iron doors of the arena.

Inside the stadium, two more Abequan guards met Samuel, his father, and the woman in black. Their caravan of Huronian security trailed behind. The Abequan guards led the king and Samuel up a long ramp. All around them, empty steps of the coliseum waited for people to take their place among them. At the top of the incline was a large, covered balcony, set in the middle of the arena steps. Inside the balcony sat four thrones. One of them was already taken by Samuel's mentor.

"Samuel. King Jowellia." His mentor stood. "It is a pleasure to see you both together."

Samuel embraced his mentor. "Sornin, it's so wonderful to see you outside the Didumos Wilderness. For so long I had to hide all the magnificent things you've taught me. Now, I'm finally free to prove myself. I have you to thank for that."

As they took their seats, Samuel felt the excited energy of his mentor and the crowd that trickled in.

"You have done well, young prince." Sornin smiled and grasped Samuel's hand. "You are one of the best, brightest, and fastest learners I have ever had the pleasure of training. You and your father have much in common."

The king patted Sornin on the shoulder. "We were both truly blessed to have such an elite trainer. You are as good as they come, Sornin."

"Thank you, Sire." Sornin bowed his head.

As they sat and conversed, Samuel felt the woman in black's eyes boring into him. He turned his head to look directly at her. She sat next to his father at the end of the row of thrones. She immediately looked away. A shiver shook Samuel's body.

The sound of guards allowing people to pour in and fill up the coliseum stands snapped Samuel out of his trance. As soon as everyone found their seats among the steps, the coliseum doors closed and Samuel's father stood. The king slowly raised his hand out to the side and up into the air. The noisy crowd immediately quieted.

"Great warriors of the Abequan Elite, today we celebrate the homecoming of my son, Samuel Jowellia. As you all know, not long after his birth, he and Raelle were kidnapped and taken into hiding. In the process, they murdered my older sister, Shellere, our beloved queen, and her husband Dalan, the king of our great nation of Huronus. They destroyed my wife, Samuel's mother. They shattered our family. And they did it all in the name of the Inclusionist movement. This blasphemous group of mages functions under the delusion that all of us are created equal. They wish to dilute, and desecrate the bloodlines of this great continent by allowing the marriage between those who are born with Lyre and those who are not. They spit on our Grand Architect's name. Only we, the Elite, hold true to the will of the Architect. We know that it is his choice and his choice alone who shall be born of the Lyre."

The king paused and moved closer to the edge of the balcony. "But Huronus was not the only nation affected by this ludicrous and irreverent movement. Abequa too lost its rulers to the bloodthirsty and violent acts of the Inclusionists. They killed your Queen Jeanahn and King Sonee Vilgare. Their son's trusted mentor, Framin Macta, kidnapped their young son and took him into hiding. He took your young prince Chrishtan and warped his mind, leaving the people of Abequa without a true leader."

The king turned and motioned for Samuel to stand. He got up from his throne and met his father at the edge of the balcony.

"Today..." The king took his son's hand and raised it high. "We take back what is ours. Today, we the Elite, reclaim our blood right, and once again put a pure Lyre Elite on the Abequan throne!"

The cheers of the Abequan elite reverberated through the coliseum. Samuel could feel the sound swallowing him up.

"Lochran! Lochran! Lochran! Lochran!" The immense crowd chanted the king's name in unison.

Lochran shouted over the horde. "And welcome your new king, my son, Samuel Jowellia!"

The masses roared with pleasure. Samuel reveled in their validation. For the first time in his life, he had found the sense of purpose that he so longed for. He was no longer lost and unfulfilled. An enormous smile came over Samuel's face. He stood proudly next to his father and they both bowed to the people of Abequa.

Lochran raised both his hands in the air and quieted the Abequan people once more. They heeded the king's signal and took their seats on the steps. "We shall begin our coronation by honoring the Abequan tradition of the Royal Warrior Clash. Samuel has come prepared to honor your tradition with his skills in the coliseum."

Samuel turned to his father. "I have?"

"Yes, my son. You most certainly have." Lochran squeezed Samuel's arm. "You have been training for the past five years for this. All the time you spent with Sornin in the valley wilderness, training your Lyre, it has all prepared you for *this* day. You will earn your place as king by showing the Abequans what pure, Rogue, Lyre blood can do. This is how you will earn the loyalty of the people, and *your* new kingdom."

Samuel tried to swallow his apprehension. "Yes, father."

Lochran formed a half-smile. "Very good."

Sornin stood and pulled something out from behind his seat. "I have brought you something, my young apprentice." Sornin opened an ornately carved black wooden box to reveal two beautifully crafted Rogue daggers.

Samuel removed the blades from the box. His eyes opened wide as he studied the perfection of the edges and the intricate designs on the hilt. The Torpaz gems radiated a stunning blue light as he pressed the handle into his palm. "Thank you, Sornin. Thank you, Father." Samuel bowed. "They're perfect. I will not let you down."

Lochran slid his hand over his son's cheek. "You are a Jowellia, of pure Lyre blood. You are my son. I have the utmost faith in you and your gift."

"Thank you, Father." Samuel's heart began to race. He wanted nothing more than to prove to his father that he was worth rescuing. But also, that the betrayal of his sister had not been in vain. In the arena, he would obliterate his doubts and fears, avenge his sister's death, and take back the life that was stolen from him.

Sornin grasped Samuel's shoulder and smiled. "It is time, my prince. I will lead you to your place for the Warrior Clash."

"Yes, Sornin." Samuel followed his mentor down a staircase behind the thrones, through a narrow hallway, and onto a large, octagon shaped platform. Under Samuel's feet, the podium was decorated with red and black marble tile with the Abequan crest laid into them.

"I have great faith in you, Samuel." Sornin pressed his lips to Samuel's forehead. "May the Architect bless you on this day and reveal to the people of this nation the greatness within you, which I have already been blessed to witness."

Samuel embraced Sornin. "Thank you. I shall prove myself worthy of this day. I promise."

Sornin stepped back off the platform and reached for a lever on the wall. He pulled down hard, and the podium slowly began to rise. As Samuel pulled his mask over his nose and mouth, his hands shook and his knees quaked. He had no idea what awaited him in the arena. He had never engaged in combat outside his training. He prayed to the Architect to give him strength. He would either defeat the Abequan warriors in the ring and become king, or perish in the arena and let his father and his people down.

As terrified as he was, he convinced himself that he would allow nothing to get in his way. *It is my time. I will fulfill my destiny.*

At the top, Samuel found himself in the center of the arena. He could barely make out the people in the crowd as the light of the sun waned behind the coliseum walls. Suddenly, large Diamoz lights lit up all around him within the black marble floor of the arena. Samuel's heart jumped as six other platforms jutted up around him. Each podium held a robust Abequan warrior. The combatants' platforms were all set at different heights that were much taller than Samuel's.

The eager crowd cheered. Samuel's hands shook violently as they grasped the daggers sheathed on either hip. He closed his eyes and focused on his Lyre as he drew upon the energy within and around him. He honed in on one particular sound that eased the trembling of his hands.

"Samuel! Samuel! Samuel!"

The Abequan elite were rooting for him. He drew upon their energy. No longer trembling, Samuel drew his daggers with confidence and raised them into the air. Brilliant, blue light beamed out from the jewels of his elaborate Rogue armor and weaponry.

The coliseum rumbled and reverberated with the energy of excited screams and cheers of the Lyre-blood elite. Samuel looked around at his opponents, none of their Lyre gems shined as radiantly as his. *I was meant for this. The Architect has blessed me. It is my time!*

Samuel focused as hard as he could and felt his Lyre energy surge violently through him. Thick rays of light beamed out even brighter from every single jewel that adorned his weapons and armor. The crowd roared as his opponents shielded their eyes from the blinding light. *I am the chosen.*

Samuel immediately stinted, disappearing from his place and reappearing on the tallest platform next to him. Before the warrior knew it, Samuel was at his side. He crossed his two daggers together at the warrior's throat. He uncrossed them to slice the gladiator's gullet clean open. Blood gushed from the wound. The warrior's incapacitated body fell from the platform and crashed to the floor. The crowd cheered wildly.

A second warrior jumped from his platform to the podium where Samuel stood. He swung his enormous sword toward Samuel's neck. Samuel dodged the blow and disappeared. From his stint, he reappeared behind a female gladiator on the podium below. He sliced at the tendons on the back of her leg, but she brought down one of her short swords to block it. Samuel dodged her blow to his side and reappeared in front of her. With immense force, he kicked her backward off the platform. She flew a couple of meters before falling toward the coliseum floor where she landed on her agile, warrior feet.

Samuel leapt after her. The two of them lunged, jumped, swung and dodged at each other for a few moments. Suddenly, Samuel heard four separate thuds all around him. The other four warriors had bounded from their podiums to attack him. He was surrounded. Samuel dodged and stinted away from the blades coming at him from all sides. But there were too many of them. Even if he slowed down time, there still was not enough space to exit.

*No, I must not give in. I am the chosen. I will not be defeated. They took everything from me. I will not lose it again. I've worked too hard to get back here just to be killed.* Rage flowed through him as he channeled his Lyre into the black Opalz around his neck. He suddenly felt his skin grow warmer. An energy like he had never before felt was building within him.

Blinding light discharged from his gems once more as Samuel released his energy. Only this time, it was accompanied by a resounding and thunderous scream. Shrill and deafening sound waves screeched from the depths of Samuel's throat, blasting each of his foes back at least twenty meters. Samuel swore he had felt a bomb go off at his feet, but he hadn't. *What have I done? Is this the power gifted to me by the Architect himself?*

Samuel searched for his enemies. Two of the warriors lay unconscious near the bottom of a podium. Their helmets were bent, bloodied, and broken, crushed by the impact of being blown into the platform. The woman and one other male gladiator lay on the floor of the coliseum with their hands over their ears. They were trying as best they could to recover from Samuel's deathly blow. Samuel attempted to recharge his Lyre before sprinting, with Rogue speed, toward his adversaries. Close enough, he tried to scream once more, but his Lyre was not yet charged enough. Instead he stinted, disappearing, and reappearing over the warriors. In an instant, he crushed the woman's throat with his boot. Then he spun around to catch the other warrior before he could leap away. Samuel reappeared in front of the gladiator, shoving the blade of his dagger through the warrior's chin and up into his brain. Like a towering tree in a hurricane, the large brute of a man fell hard to the coliseum floor.

The crowd cheered and chanted Samuel's name. He ran and leapt from the ground to the top of his center podium and bowed to his supporters. But he stopped when he heard the sound of metal and gears grinding. On the far ends of the coliseum two enormous gates drew their metal bars upward. Armored soldiers with swords and shields poured in. Samuel heard his father's voice over the commotion. The people quieted to listen.

"And for the final round, my son, and your new king, will defeat an entire brigade of armed soldiers! Soldiers and members of the Inclusionist Movement who have been rounded up and brought to us by our Elite Huronian military. They are all yours, my son!"

Samuel looked down to the line of soldiers marching into the coliseum. There had to be at least a hundred of them. He felt a sudden jerk underneath his feet as all the platforms, including his own, lowered to the ground. There was no escaping the armed men and women who were coming for him. Samuel stood his ground at the middle of the arena. He closed his eyes and focused his Lyre. He drew upon the energy of the charged crowd and the rage within him. His body throbbed as his Lyre melded with the Opalz stone and back into his extremities.

As Samuel opened his eyes, numerous infantry closed in on him. Only a few more meters and they would surely have him. Samuel squeezed his daggers. *Raelle still needs me. I must avenge her death. This cannot be the end for me.* The thought of his sister's suffering at the hand of their faux parents enhanced his fury. With the men surrounding him only a meter away in every direction, Samuel leaned toward them. Light blasted out from his jewels followed by a colossal shriek that shook the entire stadium.

Samuel spun in all directions, pushing out his deathly sound waves until each and every soldier fell to the ground seizing. The seizing continued until blood seeped from their noses and ears. All around him, dead soldiers with bloodied faces littered the coliseum floor.

Samuel gazed up into the stands as he stinted in and out of the injured throng of soldiers, finishing off any survivors with his daggers. The crowd held their hands over their ears. Once the ringing had subsided and their hearing had returned, the entire stadium roared.

Once he had finished off all the soldiers, Samuel saw his father and his mentor walking down to meet him. They greeted him at the center podium. Lochran raised his hand high and the podium began to rise. He then grasped Samuel's hand as Sornin seized the other. They lifted their champion's arms high.

"Abequan Elite! I present to you, your new champion. Your new king, Samuel Jowellia!"

Instead of the cheers and chants that Samuel was anticipating, the crowd was silent. All at once, they fell to their knees and bowed to their new king.

"I present to you," Lochran continued, "the Elite Echo!"

Tears slipped from Samuel's eyes as the masses stood and clapped. They called out for their new king and chanted his mantra. "Elite Echo! Elite Echo! Elite Echo!"

# CHAPTER 4
## RECONCILIATION

The buzzing of the crowd followed Samuel and his family as they made their way toward the Abequan palace. Enormous red doors awaited them at the top of the castle steps. Two guards opened the colossal entry with the red Rubiz gems of their Lyre rings.

"This way, Sire." Sornin guided Samuel. "We must remove your armor and get you changed before dinner."

Samuel parted ways with his father and the woman in black. He followed his mentor up a back staircase to a royal Abequan chamber. Inside was a large sitting room with a small fire crackling in the fireplace. Sornin opened a set of double doors at the back of the room to reveal an attached boudoir.

"These will be your chambers, Sire. As king of Abequa, you will reside here."

"Thank you," Samuel replied. "But you don't need to call me, *Sire*. You may call me Samuel, as you always have."

"Yes, Samuel." Sornin bowed just as a knock came at the door. "You may enter," he called.

The garnet doors opened to reveal four young Abequan women. Each of them wore long garnet-colored dresses that covered only the most necessary parts of their top half. Gold bands spiraled around their arms and necks. Like the silk of their dresses, their dark hair and lips harbored a deep red hue. They did not blink as they strode into the room. At Samuel's feet, they bowed in reverence.

"These are your chamber maidens." Sornin presented the women. "They will be at your every beck and call. Whatever you need, whenever you need. Right now, they will be assisting you in the removal of your armor and changing into something more appropriate for dinner. I suggest something much more formal than you're used to. Your father will be expecting it. He intends to show you off."

"Yes, Sornin."

Sornin bowed and closed Samuel inside his quarters. The Abequan maidens began removing Samuel's blood spattered attire. Samuel had not realized it before, but underneath his armor he was trembling. As soon as his knees were free of their gear, they buckled. Samuel fell into the strong arms of one of his maidens.

"You must lay down, Sire." A stunning maiden with golden eyes held him tight.

Samuel's arms and legs quaked as the four young women led him to his bed in the next room. Samuel fell into it as if he had fainted. Helplessly, he laid back into the pillows against the headboard. He could not seem to catch his breath. With one of his hands, he attempted to swipe the hair from his eyes. His hand shook violently, he could barely lift it. He stared at it as his vision faded in and out of focus.

"W—wh— what's happening to m—me?" Samuel hyperventilated.

"You must recharge your Lyre, Milord," the golden-eyed maiden answered. "You have used a great deal of it this night."

"But I have used my Lyre plenty of times and never felt this way," he strained to speak.

The golden-eyed maiden seemed to glare at the black stone around his neck. "It is your new ability, Sire. Though it allowed you to triumph in the coliseum, it has taken much from you." She pulled a vial of black liquid from a pocket on her draped dress. "Here, you must drink this. It will help you to regain what you have lost while you meditate and recharge." She removed the cork from the vial and pressed it to Samuel's quivering lips.

"Th—thank you. Miss...?" he muttered.

"Volshira, Sire."

"Thank you, Volshira."

"You need not thank me," she replied. "It is my sworn duty to protect and care for you."

Volshira smiled at her king before turning to the maiden next to her. "Barnashda, would you please fetch the basin? We must get our king clean before dinner."

"Yes, Miss." The maiden bowed.

She returned with a washbowl and several linen towels. Each maiden took a cloth and began washing their king. Steam rose from the warm, wet towels as they slid along Samuel's naked body. He closed his eyes and gathered his thoughts in meditation, causing his extremities to tingle with renewed Lyre energy. He was not sure how long he had been meditating, but when he opened his eyes once more, he found himself alone with Volshira.

"How do you feel, my king?" She pressed her dark red lips to Samuel's forehead and sat on the bed next to him.

"Almost as good as new," Samuel lied.

"Almost?" Volshira ran her thumb and fingers across her king's brow line, down his nose, and over his lips. The Rubiz jewel at the center of her golden headdress emitted a dim glow as her hand journeyed down Samuel's neck and over his chest, all the way to his stomach.

Volshira's golden eyes mesmerized Samuel. His hand brushed the curvature of her shoulder and traveled down through the peaks and valleys of lean musculature that lay underneath her tan warrior skin. Samuel slid his hand over her carved abdomen before pulling her close. Unlike Naruncia, Volshira felt solid and strong in his arms. She grasped the back of his head and pulled him closer before locking her lips hard against his. Her well-built legs straddled and squeezed his aching hips. She took full control, sending Samuel into complete ecstasy. Burning hot Lyre raged through him. He felt alive once more.

As their erotic escapade came to a finish, Samuel felt completely recharged, his strength reborn and his power resurrected. He leaned in for a long and intimate kiss with Volshira. As he backed away, his eyes were drawn to the black gem housed at the center of her elaborate, gold, choker necklace.

"I see you have one of these as well." Samuel tilted his head and lifted his talisman from the chain around his neck.

"Yes." Volshira caressed the black gem of her necklace. "It was a gift from your father, for my devoted assistance and loyalty."

"I see." Samuel sat up. "And how is it that you assisted him?"

"I have gone to great lengths to retrieve information regarding our enemy without being detected. This gemstone is my reward. But it is not my only reward." Volshira kissed her way up Samuel's neck and bit down softly on his ear. "He also gave me this post with you. I am your royal guard and companion. It is my duty to serve and protect you and only you, Sire."

"Well, then I should consider myself lucky." Samuel smiled. "To have such a remarkable creature like you all to myself is the true reward. And please, call me Samuel."

"Of course, Samuel." Volshira kissed him once more before leaving the bed. From the wall, she grabbed a hanging ensemble. "This is your clothing for this evening's coronation dinner."

Samuel's eyes grew wide at the lavish coat and pants that Volshira laid across the bed.

"Not quite what you're used to?" She chuckled.

Samuel laughed, "No, not at all." He shrugged. "I spent most of my life wearing the same shirt and pants until they were so worn my mother would make me burn them. But…" His expression transformed and a scowl replaced his smile. "…she was not my mother. She was my captor."

"I'm so sorry." Volshira rushed to him. "It was not my intention to bring up hurtful memories. I just—"

"It's not your fault I'm upset," Samuel interrupted. "It's theirs." He grasped her hand and squeezed it tight before kissing it. "Shall I get dressed, then?"

"Yes, Milord," Volshira replied with a smile.

Samuel allowed Volshira to help him dress in his new and extravagant attire. He had no doubt that the ornate blue and garnet color scheme was meant to symbolize the coming together of Samuel's home nation of Huronus with his new nation of Abequa. Even though he felt silly in the fancy getup, he also felt proud to be the one to bring the two nations together. He was one step closer to helping his father bring peace and righteousness to the continent.

"You look strapping." Volshira squeezed his arms.

"Thank you." Samuel grinned. "Will you be joining us for dinner?"

"I'm afraid not." Volshira shook her head. "I was not invited."

"Well." Samuel pulled her in close. "I'm inviting you. You are my companion, and I want you there."

"As you wish, Milord."

"It's Samuel," he whispered, before pressing his lips against hers. They stopped at the sound of a gentle knock at the chamber doors.

"Samuel, are you ready for dinner?"

Samuel recognized the muffled voice. It was Sornin.

"Yes, we'll be right there," he answered.

"May I come in?" Sornin called.

"Yes, sorry. Please come in." Samuel made his way out into the sitting room and opened one of the doors.

"You look fantastic, my liege." Sornin smiled broadly as he entered the room. "You truly were born for this. I have never seen a more magnificent king."

Samuel laughed. "You're too kind. You're making me blush."

"We must head downstairs now, Milord. Everyone is waiting for you."

"Then by all means, we shall go now." Samuel locked arms with Volshira and followed Sornin down to the grand dining hall. Like the halls of the Huronus palace, the towering walls of the Abequan dining room were constructed of what looked like shattered pieces of glass that had been pieced back together. Though unlike the Huronus walls, the glass was the color of soil. When the light of Diamoz lamps gleamed through, it looked as if they were in a room made of smoldering coals.

As Samuel made his entrance, the voices that echoed throughout the dining hall stopped. All guests seated at the enormous table stood and bowed their heads in reverence to their new king. Lochran pulled out the largest chair at the head of the table for his son.

Samuel cleared his throat. "I've brought a guest, Father."

Lochran raised a brow. "Yes, I see that. What a wonderful surprise." He took Volshira's hand and kissed the back side. "How lovely it is to see you, Volshira."

"Thank you, Milord." She curtsied.

Lochran scowled for a moment. "I trust you will find a more appropriate dress for our next dinner."

"Yes, Milord." She looked down. "I'm very sorry. The invitation was unexpected and—"

"It's fine." Samuel cut in.

"Of course." Lochran nodded. "Mishtan?" He called to one of the servants. "Mishtan, would you please bring an extra chair for our unexpected guest?"

"Yes, Milord. Right away."

It did not take long for the servant to fetch Volshira's chair. "Where would you like it?"

"Right next to mine, thank you." Samuel answered before his father had a chance to speak. As soon as Samuel sat down, the rest of the table joined him at their seats.

Lochran raised his glass. "Let us toast to our new king, my son, Samuel Jowellia."

The Elite Abequan nobility raised their glasses high. "To the king," they toasted.

As soon as the salute was through, Abequan servants brought out large platters of meats, fruits, vegetables, and desserts. It was more food than Samuel had ever eaten in his entire life. As he sat at the table conversing with his father, his mentor, Volshira and some of the other Abequan Elite, his eyes kept returning to the woman in black. She sat in silence next to his father, her plate untouched. He shuddered at the feeling of her penetrating stare through her veil and into his soul. Samuel could not understand why he was so drawn to her. Amidst all the other voices in discussion, it sounded as if her voice was calling out to him. *Samuel, open your eyes*, it said. But her lips did not move.

"Can you hear that?" Samuel asked Volshira.

"Hear what?"

"That voice. Someone's calling to me."

"You've had a very long and arduous week, my liege." Volshira rubbed his back. "I'm sure you're exhausted. It's probably just your mind playing tricks on you."

"No, I swear my father's companion, the woman in black, the one who's staring at—

The woman's chair was empty.

"She was right there, staring at me."

"Well, she's not there anymore." Volshira eyed the woman's empty seat. "Lochran must have dismissed her. I think it is time you call it a night. It will do you some good to get some rest."

"I for one, couldn't agree more." Lochran cut in. "I am very tired as well." He stood. "Ladies and gentlemen, thank you for joining us this evening and celebrating the arrival of our new Abequan king. The king and I are both exhausted and will be departing for the evening. But please do not feel that you must leave. I have arranged for music and drinks in the ball room. So please, stay and dance the night away. We bid you farewell and good evening."

All of their guests stood to bid Lochran and their new king goodnight.

"Thank you all for such a grand evening," Samuel said, smiling.

His guests bowed.

Samuel locked arms with Volshira and followed his father out of the dining hall and into the main foyer. "Will you be staying with us tonight, Father?"

Lochran shook his head. "I am afraid not. I have a great deal of business to attend to in the early hours of the morning and believe it best to head back to Huronus tonight."

"I understand," Samuel said. "When will you be returning? I would love for us to spend some time together."

"I will return at the end of the week. As I said, I have a

great many things to take care of in Huronus. But I look forward to my return and our time together. I've waited a very long while to be able to do that."

"Yes, Father."

Lochran leaned in to embrace his son. He whispered into Samuel's ear. "Do not forget, you have a task to complete. You must avenge our beloved Raelle." He slipped Raelle's brush into Samuel's hand. A piece of parchment coiled around the its handle. Lochran backed away. "Volshira, I expect you will take good care of my only son?"

"Yes, Milord." Volshira bowed.

"Then I shall see you both at the end of the week. I bid you goodnight." Lochran smiled and turned to leave.

"Goodnight, Father." Just as Lochran exited through the red doors of the Abequan palace, the sound of music echoed out from the dance hall.

"They'll be up dancing and drinking all night," Volshira said. "Are you sure you do not wish to join them?"

"Yes," said Samuel. "I'm sure. I'm still not feeling quite myself yet. My whole life was spent sheltered in a valley. I think I need to take it slow when it comes to socializing."

"I suppose you're right." Volshira took his hand. "I didn't think about that. It would be quite overwhelming for you. Especially with that crowd."

Samuel laughed. "You would know better than I."

"Indeed." She grinned.

Samuel squeezed Volshira's hand. "I suppose this is where we say goodnight. What will you do for the rest of the evening?"

"Me?" Volshira asked. "I'll be posted outside your room. It is my duty, after all, to make sure my king is safe and secure. It will be myself, along with one other. So, if you should need anything, I'll be right outside the door."

"Then you had better go slip into your uniform, my dear." Sornin's voice echoed behind them.

"Yes, Sornin." Volshira bowed.

"I will escort our young king back to his chambers while

you do so."

Samuel and his mentor made their way to Samuel's suite. "Will you not be staying up all night dancing, Sornin?"

"Absolutely not." Sornin furrowed his brow. "It is not our way to engage in frivolity."

"You mean the way of a Lyre mentor?"

"Yes, that is what I mean."

Samuel shrugged and looked down. "Well, that doesn't sound like much fun to me."

"It is satisfying in its own way." Sornin patted Samuel on the back. "But that does not mean that *you* cannot participate in the frivolous merriment."

"I know," Samuel sighed. "I just don't think I'm quite ready for that yet."

"I understand," Sornin said. He motioned toward the male guard posted outside Samuel's room. "Goodnight, Samuel."

The sentinel opened the doors and Samuel entered.

"Goodnight, Sornin." As soon as the doors closed behind him, Samuel released a lengthy sigh of relief. From the moment he had woken to Naruncia that morning, he had been surrounded by people. It was something he was not used to. And it kept him in a heightened state. Alone in his new chambers, he felt his first sense of reprieve. His chest no longer felt tight. His jaw no longer clenched. And he breathed more freely. After removing his formal garments, Samuel dug through his gigantic closet and found a soft pair of grey linen pants. He then plopped onto his enormous and cozy bed.

On one of the pillows, Raelle's brush sat motionless. Samuel's gaze was drawn to it. After a moment, an apparition of his sister took the brush's place.

"Now what?" The apparition smiled as she lay on her stomach, gently kicking her legs. "King of Abequa, how are you feeling? I know you must be overwhelmed." With a big grin, Raelle turned over and sat up.

Samuel smirked. "You always know me so well. It's hard to hide anything from you."

"Well," she laughed, "you are my brother. I've known you your entire life. I love you. I miss you."

"I miss you too." Samuel pressed his eyes shut and a tear trickled down his cheek. "I'm so sorry, Raelle."

"Sorry?" She scooted closer. "Sorry for what?"

"For letting you down. For shutting you out. For leaving you. For everything. I—

"You know you're not sorry," Raelle whispered. "You know you wanted this to happen. You wanted it all."

Samuel opened his eyes to see his sister glaring at him. Her eyes were no longer green and white. They were completely black.

"Raelle? What's going on?" He backed away. "You know I didn't want any of this."

"Do I, dear brother? How could I?" She crawled eerily toward him. "You lied to me. You left me. You killed me." Her head twitched and her voice became sinister. "Just like you killed Brow."

"No! I didn't kill him. It was an accident. I—I—

"You got what you wanted, little brother. And now look at you. You are king. The king of Browden's nation! It seems to me that you got precisely what you desired. Leaving the rest of us dead in your wake."

"No, Raelle. Please!" Samuel scooted backward until he fell off the bed. Raelle followed. Slowly, she pulled something from her nightgown. It was a Huronian dagger. She stepped onto the floor and stood over her brother. Her face leaned over his and she drew the blade up to her throat.

"Raelle, please. You must understand, I—

Raelle sliced clean through her gullet. Blood poured from her gaping wound, splattering all over Samuel.

"Raelle, no!" Samuel screamed and hyperventilated. He struggled to wipe the mess from his blood soaked eyes. When he opened them, he was still on the floor of his bedroom. But he was not drenched in blood, just a great deal of sweat. Focused on trying to catch his breath, he tried to rise but slipped down again. His knees shuddered as he got up from the floor.

"Get it together, Samuel," he whispered. "It's not real. It was only a nightmare."

But the terror felt very real. Samuel crawled back onto his bed and over to his sister's brush. He plucked it from the pillow and his eyes began to well. Tears flowed freely as he held the brush in his hands. "I will not forsake you, Raelle. I will return you to this world. I will give you a better life than the one our captors stole from us, I promise."

Samuel knew what he had to do. He slid the parchment from the brush's handle. He unrolled it to find written directions and an incantation. As the paper instructed, he pulled several hairs from Raelle's brush. He placed them inside a trinket box he found on the table beside his bed. Next to it, he eyed a glass votive. He removed the candle and broke the glass against the wall. With a shaky hand, he collected one of the larger shards from the table. He used the fragment to make a small incision in the tough skin on the inside of his hand. He gently squeezed his lacerated palm over the inside of the trinket box. Blood trickled over the strands of his sister's hair until they were completely submerged. From the parchment, Samuel recited the incantation.

*Korlinar isk spironir.*

*Waltin isk ire drilom im Minotirr.*

*Hortem ire renchid cartimir isk mid.*

*Splicas fem tor lormi isk mid im splicas fem tor spirona is mid.*

*Grommid om uni i fracom.*

*Saskmid isk uni i rigim.*

*Plesarmid om uni tis dominor.*

*Mista i hortas cerpant isk uni, grommid om uni tor rigim empetra tis ire infint dominor im infint cerpastin isk ire ud grommid.*

*Ovtermid ire spirona isk ire virtom om uni, Gesp Royalm ire drilom.*

*Gesp Desmont isk ire Oblitora.*

*Azmodil, corontis isk spironir.*

*Notizt tor sacrim isk mid.*

All of the sudden, the blood inside the trinket box burst into flames. It quickly burned out, leaving the charred imprint of two hands with eerily long fingers at the bottom. Samuel felt his skin turn hot and sweat drip from his brow. After closing the trinket box, his quaking hands could barely place it back on the night stand. As Samuel made his way to the washroom inside his chambers, his knees joined in the unsteady dance. Using his Lyre, he brought light to the Diamoz stones mounted on the walls. He had only enough to offer a dim glow. Samuel leaned heavily into the marble counter of the washroom. His weak and aching muscles made it difficult to pump the lever of the basin. Only a small amount of water drizzled from the faucet. Samuel's unsteady hand reached again for the pump. His arm immediately recoiled away at the reflection in the washroom mirror. His eyes were completely blacked out and an enormous and ominous shadow with glowing red eyes stood behind him. Samuel spun around to see no one in the room with him. Growling whispers suddenly infiltrated his ears.

"Azmodil, Azmodil, Azmodil…" they chanted. Samuel's body grew heavy and his head became light. The counter was within reach. He grasped for it, but it was no use. The weight of his lean, muscular frame crashed to the cold, hard floor.

# CHAPTER 5
## REPRISAL

"Milord? Samuel?" A familiar feminine voice called to him. "Samuel, please. Please wake up."

He opened his eyes to see the blurry figure of a young woman with garnet hair. Samuel was far too weak to keep his heavy lids from closing. He could still hear her and felt her palms press firmly against his chest. A bolt of Lyre energy surged from her hands into his body.

Samuel's eyes jolted open and fresh air rapidly moved in and out of his lungs. "What's happened? I don't—

"It's all right." Volshira comforted. "You're going to be all right."

Samuel looked around to find himself back in his royal bed. Volshira sat next to him, fully armored. "I found you on the floor of your washroom. You were unconscious. I brought you back to your bed."

Samuel's breaths slowed. "Thank you. I—I don't know what happened. The last thing I remember was..."

Volshira leaned in. "You were what?"

"Nothing, it's not important."

"Please, don't shut me out. I may be able to help you." She softly brushed her hand over his face. "I care for you, Samuel. I know that must seem strange, but I feel connected to you. I did not anticipate this would happen, especially not this quickly, but it has. I'm sorry if I'm—

"No." Samuel gently grasped the hand she held to his cheek. "Don't be sorry." Samuel sat up and tugged on Volshira's armor. "It seems unfitting that you should spend your nights posted outside my room. I wonder if it's possible for you to spend your nights here, inside my royal chambers. You are my companion, after all. You should be by my side at all times. I'm sure we can find someone else to take your post."

Volshira smiled. "You are the king. I will spend my nights

and days with you if that is what you wish, my liege."

"I believe you already know the answer to that." Samuel slid the gold-plated armor from Volshira's forearm. His lips found their way to the back of Volshira's hand. "Will you stay with me, this night and every night?"

"Of course," Volshira said fervently. "It is an honor. I will be here for you in any way I can. And if you're willing to share with me, I'd really like to know what left you in such a state as this?"

Samuel looked down. "It's my sister."

"Your sister? Your sister was here?"

"No, it's not like that. You see…" Samuel shifted his eyes downward and he bit his lip.

"Yes?"

"You must swear never to tell a soul of what we speak."

"Yes, of course."

"My sister was killed. The same people who took me from Lochran, all those years ago, they took her too. But they killed her before I could get back to her and bring her here."

"So you are overcome with grief? That is why you fainted?"

"No… I mean yes, I am, but that's not why you found me on the floor. It's because I'm trying to bring her back."

"Bring her back? What do you mean?"

"I mean to resurrect her. I want to give her another chance at life," Samuel explained. "She deserves it."

"And you're using your Lyre to do this?"

"Yes, my father has given me the tools I need in order to do so. Tonight, after following through with the ritual and invocation, I must have fainted. It must have drained my Lyre. The last thing I remember is shutting the box and returning it to this table."

"I'm so sorry." Volshira frowned. "That must have been incredibly taxing. I understand the pain of losing a sibling. My brother too was killed. I miss him very much. I understand you trying to bring your sister back. It is admirable of you to sacrifice a piece of yourself in order to give her a new and better life."

Samuel wrinkled his brow. "How do you know what I must sacrifice?"

"Everyone knows that the cost of life *is life*," answered Volshira.

"It must be common knowledge to you. For me, everything is new and foreign. My whole life trapped in a valley, sheltered from the outside world. It was something Sornin did not mention in his teachings."

"I don't expect that he would." Volshira shook her head. "It's not the kind of information one is formally taught. It's information that is discovered by the young and the curious. Told to them in foreboding legends and learned from reading forbidden books. But now, I see it is more than legend."

"I truly hope so," Samuel sighed. "Or else I'm doing this for nothing."

Volshira took Samuel's hand. "I don't think your father would lead you astray. He cares a great deal for you. If he says it will work, then I believe it will. And I'll be here, from now on, to help and take care of you during your attempts to bring her back. I swear it. No harm shall come to you whilst I am near."

"Nor shall it to you, whilst you are in *my* keeping." Samuel pulled his companion close and kissed her. He slid a gentle hand up her arm to the buckle of her shoulder plate and unfastened it. With Samuel's help, Volshira removed all of her armor until she was completely bare. As her soft skin smoothed against his, he had never felt such passion. He ached for her. She was the most incredible being he had ever encountered and she belonged to him, and only him. The thought alone was arousing.

*** 

For the fourth morning in a row, Samuel woke as a king next to his strong and stunning companion. Each and every night, she had eased his pain after invocation and brought him back to life. Samuel knew that without her, he would most likely not be able to continue with his sister's resurrection. The process was excruciating and only intensified with each and every attempt. But Volshira's touch, passion, energy, and care kept him alive.

Samuel moved closer to her and ran his hand across the back of Volshira's naked shoulder. He swept her long, red hair away from the back of her neck and replaced it with a trail of kisses.

"Good morning, my king." Volshira turned over and greeted him with her golden gaze.

"Good morning." Samuel smiled.

"Today is the day." She kissed him.

"The day for what?"

"The day your father returns. Remember?"

"Yes, of course." Samuel wrinkled his face and pursed his lips. For some reason, the thought of seeing his father again did not please him the way it used to, but he did his best to keep it to himself. "I'm looking forward to it. I have much I would like to discuss with him."

"And don't forget." Volshira poked his nose with her finger. "You must ask him about this resurrection process. How long does it usually take? I fear it's beginning to take a toll on you."

"Yes, I'll ask him."

A knock came at the door.

"Samuel?"

"Yes, Sornin?"

"May I come in, Sire?"

"Ugh…" Samuel looked under the covers to see his and Volshira's bare bodies. "Give me just a moment." Samuel chuckled before having a good row with Volshira beneath the silk sheets.

"Stop it." She giggled. "We must get ready."

"All right, all right." Samuel laughed as he slipped into his grey linen pants. "You're right. But you'll have to dress me. I'm no good with the formal wear, as you know."

"Of course." Volshira flashed a crooked grin as she got dressed.

"May I come in, Sire?" Sornin called once more.

"Yes, please. Come in, come in."

"Thank you, Milord." Sornin rushed inside. "Your father

should be here within the next hour or so. It would be best for him to see you hard at work in your executive chambers. I know this week has been difficult because you haven't been feeling well, but it is important that Lochran see you doing your imperial duties when he arrives. I have taken care of most of the items on your desk and docket for the week. But I left a few odds and ends for you to accomplish while he is here."

"Thank you, Sornin. I don't know what I'd do without you. You truly are a blessing from the Architect." Samuel embraced his mentor.

"You are very welcome, my king. Now get dressed as quickly as you can, and I will meet you in the executive chambers."

"Yes, Sornin."

Volshira set out an outfit for Samuel and watched him as he dressed. "I know you feel silly in your royal garb, but I rather enjoy seeing you in it. It suits you."

Samuel grinned. "Whatever you say, Shira. I still feel peculiar in it."

Volshira approached him. "You are a king. You are *my* king. You must embrace it."

Samuel shook his head. "I know. You're right, as always. And once my sister has returned, it will be much easier for me. I'm sure of it."

"Yes, Samuel," Volshira said as she synched the scabbards around her waist and inserted a short sword at either hip.

"Do you really think you're going to need those?" Samuel asked.

"Every moment I'm with you, I'm on duty. It's my responsibility to protect you. You know that. Not just when we leave the palace."

"I understand." Samuel seized Volshira's bottom and drew her close. "As long as you're with me, that's all that matters."

She engaged him in a long, fervent kiss. "*You* are all that matters," she whispered.

***

Samuel had been in his executive chambers working for almost an hour when his father finally arrived.

"Sire, may we come in?" Sornin's muffled voice came through the immense doors of the chamber.

"Yes, of course," Samuel called. He looked over at Volshira for reassurance.

"It'll be all right," she replied assuredly. "Your father will understand your need for answers."

Samuel's hand held a quill and shook as Sornin and his father entered the room. He placed the quill back on his desk and stood to greet his father, whom he barely knew.

"My son, how are you settling in?" Lochran embraced Samuel with both arms.

Samuel sensed his father's love for him. He could feel Lochran's Lyre merge steadily with his. "I'm doing well, Father. The kingdom is amazing. I feel blessed every single day that you've chosen me as its ruler."

Lochran smiled through his lips and rested his hands on Samuel's shoulders. "It was fate. It is the Architect who has blessed you with this opportunity. I thank our creator each and every day for bringing you home to me. So, how have you been settling into your new position? It seems like you've been keeping up nicely."

Samuel glanced over at his mentor. "It's been a bit of an adjustment, but I'm doing my best to keep up with it."

Lochran laughed. "Well, it seems like you're doing a fantastic job. I cannot lie—I half expected to come in here and see you swamped with your duties."

"I would be if it weren't for Sornin. He's been incredibly helpful."

"I see." Lochran turned to Samuel's mentor. "Sornin, Volshira, could you two give us a moment? I have some things I need to discuss privately with my son."

Sornin and Volshira bowed before exiting, shutting the doors behind them.

Finally, Samuel was alone with his father. He had longed

for these kinds of moments for most of his life. But he could not understand why he felt so anxious. He could not stop trembling.

"Have a seat, Samuel."

"Yes, Father." Samuel sat down on a sofa at the center of the room.

His father continued to pace in front of him with his gaze to the floor. "I am very proud to see all that you have accomplished since becoming king. I knew you would not disappoint me. The royal blood of our Elite Lyre family does run through your veins after all."

"Thank you, Father."

"Sornin tells me that you have taken a liking to Volshira."

"Yes, I have. I care for her very much."

"She is a member of one of Abequa's oldest noble families. She would make a more than suitable wife for you. It would be the final step in joining our two nations. The child she would bear would be the first mixed blood faction maybe ever."

Samuel's breaths drew closer together. "Marriage? Do you think I'm ready for that? I'm only seventeen, and I've only just barely come out into the world."

"You are an adult and a king. The world cannot wait for you. As king, you must keep your kingdom and your people appeased. And this requires proof that you are moving forward. I believe that your marriage to an Abequan elite is just what we need to show the Abequan people that you are truly embracing them and their culture. Now, I know the thought of being promised to only one woman for the rest of your life is a scary idea, but you are the king. You may have relations with whomever you please, even after your wedding."

"No, it's not that. I care for Shira a great deal. The thought of being with another has not crossed my mind since I met her."

"Then what is it?"

"It's just, everything is moving so fast. I think I need more time to adjust before jumping into another ceremony. I—

"It is your duty," Lochran growled, "to keep up appearances and go outside of your comfort zone. That is what it means to be king. If you do not wish to be king, then I can find someone else."

"No." Samuel swallowed hard. "I *do* wish to be king. All I've ever wanted is to make you proud. I'll do whatever it takes. I'm sorry."

Lochran sat down next to his son. "I understand that all of this is overwhelming, but you will acclimate."

"Yes, Father."

"Now, how are things coming along with your sister?"

"Actually, to be honest, I'm not quite sure."

"What do you mean, you're not sure?"

"I mean, I don't think it's working. I've done exactly as the parchment instructs, but still made no contact with Raelle, and she has not returned in any magnitude. Most of the time I cannot even remember what happened. The only proof I have of the process is the way I feel afterward. The whole thing is taking a serious toll on me. Yesterday morning, I felt so debilitated that I couldn't even leave my bed. Shira tried to revive my Lyre, but it was useless. By the time last night came around, I was still too weak and unable to do the invocation. I think—"

"No, Samuel." Lochran's voice was cold and commanding. "What *you think* and how you *feel* has no bearing on this. You're going to have to be stronger than that if you wish to avenge your sister. No matter how debilitated you think you are. You cannot stop. Or else, there is no hope for Raelle. Are you going to give up on her so easily?"

"No, I—"

"Then do not think about the pain, and do not stop. That is all there is to it."

Samuel hung his head. "Yes, Father. I'll do what I must."

Lochran's scowl shifted to a crooked grin. "Very good. Which leads me to your next task."

"What is it?"

Lochran stood and walked toward the window. "It has

come to my attention that the false prince of Abequa has received sanctuary in the elven nation of Ellios. His name is Chrishtan Vilgare. I have been hunting him for years. He is a rebel of the Inclusionist Movement. His mentor, Framin Macta, kidnapped him when he was a boy and filled his head with horrid thoughts of pure Lyre bloods marrying and procreating with those that are not of Lyre blood. Although he is the son of the late Abequan king and queen, his mind has been twisted. Inevitably, Chrishtan sided with his mentor. His parents sided with me. And when his mentor, discovered this, he arranged for your captor, Lorndan, to return to Abequa to kill the king and queen and take their newborn son, Browden."

Samuel stood. A wet gloss coated his eyes. "I mean, I feel blessed to have had Browden in my life, but not at the expense of him being with his own parents. If he had never been brought to the valley, he would still be alive. He would be a prince of Abequa. Lorndan stole that from him. This Framin Macta and Chrishtan Vilgare, they also took that from him."

"Yes, they did." Lochran turned back toward Samuel. "They stole Browden's future, just as they stole yours and Raelle's."

Samuel gritted his teeth. "I can't imagine wanting my parents dead. All these years, all I wanted was to be with my real parents. I don't understand how this Vilgare could be so twisted." Samuel clenched his fists as anger and frustration surged through him.

Lochran left the window. "I told you, it's because his mentor brainwashed him. And because of it Chrishtan became a rebel leader of the Inclusionist Movement."

Samuel stood and slammed a fist into his desk. "Then we must draw him out and defeat him. Clearly, he is a sick man. To wish death upon one's own parents is appalling. I understand he was manipulated by his mentor, but even so."

"Yes, he is a very disturbed young man with very dangerous beliefs. He and many others have been indoctrinated with these obscene values. We must put a stop to all of them, starting with Vilgare."

48

"It shall be done, Father." Samuel bowed.

Lochran smiled broadly at his son. "I have no doubt that you will be able to defeat this blasphemous warrior. His defeat will bring great honor to me and to the people of Huronus and Abequa." The king squeezed his son's shoulders. "I trust in your abilities and the power of our elite bloodline. Tomorrow, you shall lead our troops to Ellios and draw out Chrishtan Vilgare."

# CHAPTER 6
## LOSSES

Inside his horseless carriage, Lochran's mind reeled with thoughts of what was to come. Tomorrow, his son would take Ellios and finally rid him of Chrishtan Vilgare. From across the carriage, he felt his companion's glare spear through her black veil and into his heart.

"Why must you do this, my love?" Lochran asked. "I assure you I know what I'm doing. There is no need to be upset with me. I thought you would be pleased with Samuel's return."

The woman said nothing.

"It's a shame we cannot talk, the way we used to. But you made your choice, and now we are both suffering the consequences. I know you must see that now. All that has happened is *your* fault. Now Samuel and I must clean up *your* mess."

The woman in black scooted to the opposite side of the carriage and reached for the door handle. Lochran grabbed her. With ease, he threw her into the carriage wall. His hand clutched her throat as he pinned her into the seat. "No!" he snarled. "You do not get to leave. You do not get to die. You will stay here with me, and you will watch as Samuel and I rectify all that you have set into motion." His grip only tightened and his companion began to choke. "I would kill you right now if I didn't think it was precisely what you wanted. No, I will not grant you that escape. I intend to watch you suffer for your betrayal." Lochran removed his constricting hold from her throat. "Do you understand?"

Still, the woman said nothing.

"That's what I thought," Lochran sneered. "After all the sacrifices I've made for you and our people. You are still a deceitful and ungrateful woman."

The memory of Lochran's first sacrifice invaded his thoughts, and he couldn't help but recall the whole episode.

***

"My precious, Bruelle." Lochran held his mistress close. "You have been so good to me and of great value."

"Yes, Milord. And I will continue to be." Bruelle swept a hand over Lochran's cheek with affection.

"Yes, you will." Lochran gently grasped her pregnant belly. "And our child is of even greater value."

"Yes, our child is truly a blessing." Bruelle looked down. "I only wish we didn't have to keep it a secret."

Lochran brushed the hair from her eyes. "You know that is the way it must be. I am king of Huronus now. I had a wife, the pure-blood queen. If ever anyone knew of my indiscretions, especially with someone like you, who is not of the Lyre, I would be looked at as a hypocrite. And we can't have that, now can we?"

"But you are the king now." Bruelle shook her head. "You can do whatever you please."

"Of that, my dear, you are absolutely correct. But I have appearances to uphold. It is not what I *actually do* that is important. It is what I *appear to do* that is important. Just as I have *appeared* to care for you."

"*Appeared* to care for me?" Bruelle stepped back. "What do you mean?"

"I mean precisely that. Caring for you is simply what I have *appeared* to do, not what I have actually done."

"I don't understand, Lochran, we've—

Lochran lunged toward her. Both of his hands squeezed firmly around her throat. "Did you truly believe that someone of *my* blood, of *my* position, of *my* standing would ever care for such a pathetic being such as yourself?" His voice grew menacing and his laugh malevolent.

"I—I—"Bruelle struggled to speak.

"I loved my wife. I could *never* love you. You are a pathetic, weak thing that is here only for me to prey upon. That is the only purpose of those without Lyre, to serve those of us who are above you. You are nothing. You are *livestock*. And you will be treated as such." Lochran crushed Bruelle's throat until she grew limp. He then scooped her flaccid body into his arms and laid her on the chamber bed. He felt for her pulse. It was faint, but still present. He pressed his ear to Bruelle's pregnant belly. He felt the energy of the being inside. His keen ears picked up its tiny heartbeat. "Hazale will be pleased."

Lochran opened the chamber door to see two of his Minotirr. "She is ready. Please take her down to the altar room and have her prepared. I will meet you there shortly."

"Yes, Sire," they growled.

Lochran shut the door behind him and headed to the back stairwell. He descended three flights to the basement of the dungeon. The echoes of blood-curdling screams infiltrated his keen ears. The cries of his human slaves being branded for his possession brought a smile to his face. Every single man, woman, and child of Huronus who was not of pure Lyre blood was now property of King Lochran Jowellia.

Lochran made his way down the cell block filled with conspirators and traitors. At the end of the hall, it came to a T. At either end of the T, were two larger, secluded cells. Lochran traveled first to the south end. The cell guard immediately bowed to him.

"Open the door," Lochran commanded.

"Yes, Milord." The guard used a metal key to open the cell.

Lochran stepped into the chamber. Inside, he found a nearly naked woman lying on the floor, garbed in lacerations and bruises. "Oh darling, how I've missed you."

The woman trembled violently at the sound of Lochran's voice.

"Please, turn around, my love." He approached her. "I wish to see your beautiful face."

The woman did not heed his request.

"Oh, come now." Lochran moved closer. "Do not be so stubborn. Or I shall have to force you."

The quivering woman with black hair turned to face him. Tears spilled from her deep blue eyes.

Lochran stepped in front of her and squatted down to her level. "Open wide."

The woman opened her mouth as Lochran instructed. Inside, was a wadded bandage. Lochran slowly pulled the long dressing from the woman's mouth. "There, it should be fully healed. Now, that's better, isn't it?" The missing bandage revealed a stump where the woman's tongue had been.

"Guard!" Lochran called. "Would you please notify the maidens that we are ready?"

"Yes, Sire. Right away." The guard left.

"You will be leaving your cell tonight and joining me for a very important ceremony, which means you will need to look your best."

It did not take long for the maidens to arrive with linen towels, a bowl of steaming water, and a black dress with accessories.

"Please, ladies, make sure she is presentable. My darling, I will see you at the ceremony." Lochran left the woman's prison chamber and headed to the opposite end of the corridor. There, he found another large cell. Inside, was another woman in similar condition. She was already in the process of being scoured by the maidens.

"You're cleaning up nicely." Lochran stepped into the cell.

The woman with auburn hair hyperventilated before opening her petite mouth. "Leave me be. I don't want to leave this cell. I would rather die in here than leave with you."

"There there, don't be angry. I've come to invite you to a very important ceremony. Here, let me help to remove these bandages." Lochran slowly unraveled the dirty dressings from around the woman's head and eyes. "Open them. Let's take a look."

"No, get away from me! You know I can't, you monster!"

"Do it now. Or I will have to take out my frustrations with your friend at the other end of the hall."

The woman tried to open her eyes, but her lids only

wrinkled up and down over empty eye sockets.

Lochran examined her. "Yes, they've healed up very nicely."

The woman spit in his face.

Lochran carefully wiped the saliva from his cheek and backhanded her across the face. "Is that any way to treat someone who is giving you a second chance? I don't think so. So ungrateful." Lochran backed away. "Ladies, when you are finished here, please inform my guard and he will handle it from there."

Lochran left the cell and walked down the hall to another flight of stairs. Already on the basement level, these steps took him even deeper underground. At the bottom of the stairwell, his feet slid across the blue marble of a long hallway. Sconces of Diamoz stones lit the black marble walls of the corridor. In the middle of the walkway, Lochran paused to admire an enormous canvas. Painted onto it was a forest of red leaves. Within it, owls watched from the tree tops as children laughed and played with their parents. Once finished admiring the artwork, Lochran walked to the end of the passage where he opened two massive black doors and entered into the altar room. Inside, six Minotirr surrounded the stone altar. On top of the altar, a very pregnant Bruelle lay unconscious, covered by a black sheet and surrounded by black Opalz stones.

"Thank you, my faithful companions. I believe I can take it from here."

The Minotirr bowed and stepped back from the altar. A knock came at the door.

Lochran pointed at one of his Minotirr. "Irlast, would you please see who is at the door?"

"Yes, Milord," Irlast hissed with his forked tongue. The Minotirr opened the doors to reveal the two women from the secluded cells. Both of them were now garbed in all black with large black headdresses. The woman who had been deprived of her tongue was covered by a veil. Next to her stood the woman with no eyes. Her headdress came down over her face to form a mask without eyeholes. It stopped just above her top lip.

"Ladies, please make yourselves comfortable. We are just about to begin."

The guard left them and two Minotirr escorted the women inside. "What do you want with us, Lochran?" the masked woman pleaded.

"What do I want *with* you?" Lochran asked. "I want nothing *with* you. I believe you both decided that you wanted nothing to do *with* me quite some time ago. You see, what *I* want is *for* you, not *with* you. I want for you both to suffer. I want you both to see the horrid tragedies you have caused." Lochran chuckled. "Well, *you* cannot see anymore, can you? My apologies. I want you both to understand intimately the pain and suffering you have caused. I want *you* to *listen* and I want *her* to *see* what your actions have driven me to. We have lost Samuel and Raelle and that is *your* fault. You both must live with the consequences."

Lochran approached the woman with the veil. He lifted the sheer fabric over her headdress and clenched her face tightly in his hand. "But *I* do not have to live with what *you* have done. I refuse to accept that Samuel is gone. And I will stop at nothing to find him."

He let go of the mute woman's face and walked toward the altar.

"That is why I invited you here tonight. Tonight, Ire Oblitora's princes, Maraz and Hazale, will grant me the ability to communicate and eventually discover the whereabouts of Samuel and Raelle. You both are fools to think you could keep them hidden from me. But you see, my dearly beloveds, this all comes with a price. Nothing is free in this world. And the price for this particular ability is hefty. As you know, Ire Oblitora, the Destroyer, is a collector of souls, as are his princes Maraz and Hazale. In order to find my son, I must make payment to both of them."

Lochran walked over to the altar and exposed his comatose and pregnant mistress. "Which is why I have two souls to gift to them this night."

The mute woman gasped and covered her mouth.

"What is it? What's he done?" the blind woman cried.

55

The veiled woman rushed toward Lochran, moaning and groaning. His Minotirr restrained her.

"What's going on? I cannot see!" the masked woman implored.

Lochran laughed. "You do not need to see, my dear. You need only listen."

The woman in the mask breathed hard. "Whatever you're doing Lochran, please do not hurt anyone."

"But that is how we get what we want in this world, isn't it? We hurt people. You should know all about that. You have done plenty to hurt me. Now, I'm trying to undo what the both of you have already done."

"But we never killed anyone!" yelled the masked woman.

"You need not think of this individual as some *one*, but some *thing*. You may think of her more as a resource, like the meat we eat from our table. She is not of Lyre blood; therefore, her life is worth as much as any animal for slaughter."

"Your mind is twisted, Lochran," the blind woman shrieked. "You cannot possibly believe that!"

"Oh, I most certainly do, because it is true. And if everyone else did too, then my father would still be alive right now. I would not have been raised by some filthy scrub without an ounce of Lyre in his blood."

"He loved you, Lochran," the blind woman pleaded. "He took care of you. It's not his fault fath—

The sound of Lochran's slap to the masked woman's face echoed through the altar room. "You do not speak to me of my father! Do you understand me? Or you will lose your tongue in addition to your eyes."

"Minotirr, it is time!" Lochran stepped back to the altar. Bruelle's body lay motionless and half alive. Lochran lifted his dagger from its sheath.

The veiled woman tried to get at Lochran once more. She moaned as she struggled in the restrictive arms of the Minotirr.

"Lochran!" the masked woman screamed. "Whatever you're doing, please stop!"

56

"Silence her!" commanded Lochran.

Two Minotirr restrained the masked woman and covered her mouth.

"Thank you. Now I shall begin." Lochran lowered his blade to Bruelle's neck. With precision and ease, he sliced her throat open. He observed with delight as she choked on her own blood and her life slipped away. Her blood flowed out from her wound and over the altar.

"Ire Oblitora, king of the Void. Collector of souls and destroyer of all that was and will be. I gift unto Maraz, your Prince of Nightmares, *this* meager soul. She now belongs to your Void, and your Void alone. Please, hear my calls. Reward my boundless loyalty. Enter this world, through me. My stones open the door so that you may return to your Void with this gift."

Lochran's head and neck snapped backward and rolled around his shoulders. Finally, it settled back into the upright position. His head twitched from side to side as he studied the dead maiden before him. In a pool of his sacrifice's blood, Lochran saw his own reflection. His eyes looked like black Opalz stones as he spoke in a new and malevolent voice.

"Invasamid disposa tor spirona. A rezindac isk uni, A empirat isk porisit, empiratir. A ire Oblitora!" It was the voice of his god, the Destroyer.

Lochran bent over the altar and sipped the new blood from its stone. With a red stained face, he looked out at his Minotirr. "It is time for our final sacrifice."

The Minotirr nodded in unison. The veiled woman struggled in their strong arms. She shook her head violently as Lochran lowered his dagger over Bruelle's pregnant belly. He sliced open her dress to expose her skin. "I offer now this blood of my blood, my offspring. A piece of me that now belongs to you, Hazale, warden of the Lantern Forest."

Lochran sliced into Bruelle's abdomen with his dagger. He reached inside. With his hand he removed the almost full-term fetus. Using his dagger, he severed the umbilical cord. The miniscule baby wailed in her father's hands. From a nearby table,

Lochran grabbed a blue silk blanket and wrapped the child.

"I hear a child," called the blind woman. "What are you planning to do, Lochran?"

Lochran ignored the blind woman and motioned to one of his Minotirr. His servant opened a small door on the chamber wall to reveal a large owl with glowing red eyes. "And to you, Hazale, warden of the Red Lantern Forest, I give to you, the blood of my blood, my offspring. Her soul is yours to devour in payment for the assistance of your Red Owls. I sacrifice unto you."

"Lochran, no!" the blind woman wailed. "Please! Think about what you're doing! You can't—

"I can and I will!" Lochran roared.

At Lochran's signal, the owl flew into the room. Lochran raised his infant daughter toward the ceiling. Her shrill shrieks echoed off the marble walls. They grew more intense as the owl swooped in, digging its talons through the blanket and into lifted it from Lochran's clutch.

"And ssso it shaaall be doooone," the owl whispered as it carried the baby back toward the shaft in the wall whence it came.

The veiled woman struggled and squealed in horror as the owl disappeared up the shaft, never to be seen again. She dropped to her knees and wept.

"What have you done?" her masked counterpart cried. "What have you become?"

Both women writhed and sobbed in the arms of the Minotirr.

Lochran slid his feet across the floor to where the women mourned. He stood tall in front of them. "Now you know how I have suffered. Now you can feel the pain that I felt when you took them from me. Each and every day, for the rest of your pitiful lives, you will feel that pain."

The masked woman shook her head. "You're a monster."

Lochran smirked. "Yes, I suppose you're right. I have become a bit monstrous, but I couldn't have done it without you and the people who murdered my father. So I suppose I have you all to thank."

The masked woman stood. "You have no one but yourself to blame…"

*****

The sudden jolt of his carriage coming to a halt put an end to Lochran's flashback. He found himself back in the present, parked out front of the Huronus castle. His coach opened the door and Lochran stepped out. His veiled companion in black followed closely behind. Once inside the palace, they made their way up three flights of stairs to Lochran's private dining hall. As always, the table was set for three. Lochran took his seat at the head of the table. His veiled companion sat adjacent to him. Lochran stared at the empty seat across from her, which had also been arranged with table settings.

"Mishtan," Lochran called to his servant. "Mishtan, where is my other pet? It is time for her to come to dinner."

"I'm afraid she is refusing to dine with you this evening, Milord."

"Refusing?" Lochran uttered a sarcastic laugh. "What do you mean, *refusing*?"

"Sire, she would not come out of her cell."

"You will drag her out of there kicking and screaming if you have to. She knows better than that! We will have dinner together every evening as we always have."

"Yes, Sire." Mishtan bowed before leaving the room. "I'll inform the guards."

Not much time had passed before two royal guards entered the dining room. Tangled up in their arms was a wriggling woman in a mask and headdress. Like the veiled woman at the table, she too was dressed in all black.

Lochran stood. "Now, now, my dear. Don't overexert yourself. Come and enjoy this dinner with us."

The woman's struggle declined, and the guards sat her in her place at the table.

"Now that's a good girl. Shall we eat?" Lochran clapped his hands. "Mishtan, we are ready for our first course, thank you."

Mishtan did as Lochran asked, and servants began bringing in the food. For the veiled woman they brought out a puréed dish. Lochran and the masked woman received steaks. With a large knife, Lochran carved into his rarely cooked meat. Blood pooled around it on his plate. He crammed a piece into his mouth and chewed it noisily and forcefully.

The masked woman pushed her plate away.

"Is there something wrong with your food?"

"I've lost my appetite." The masked woman grumbled.

Lochran held his knife firmly in his hand. "And why is that?"

"I'm just not hungry."

Lochran jammed the knife into the dark wood of the table. "You will eat! And you will spend time with your family. Today is no different than any other day."

"Yes, it is."

"What are you talking about?"

"I know what you've done. I know Samuel is here. Or, he was here."

Lochran scowled. "How do you know that?"

"I felt him. But I did not feel Raelle. What have you done with her?"

"I'm afraid that is none of your business. You washed your hands of Samuel and Raelle when you took them from me! Now…" Lochran attempted to calm himself. "You will eat this dinner with us, like a good girl, and you will not utter another word about Samuel or Raelle. They are no longer your concern. Do you understand me?"

The masked woman pulled her plate in front of her and ate a vegetable from it.

Lochran sneered. "That's a good girl."

The masked woman chewed and swallowed her food. "He *will* discover what you've done. And when he does, you will have to answer for all of it, Lochran."

Lochran stood. "I said, not another word!" He left his seat and landed a blow on the masked woman's face. Her head hung unconscious over her shoulders.

The veiled woman looked down, trembling in her seat.

"Now." Lochran smiled as he sat back down. "Let us eat dinner in peace. Tomorrow, we celebrate the demise of Chrishtan Vilgare."

# CHAPTER 7
## ATTACK ON ELLIOS

Samuel's rage thundered and his mind reeled. Breaths ripped in and out of his lungs at an alarming pace. His dilated pupils followed the rest of his troops as they fled in terror. He ran after them with immense speed. *They will pay for what they've done to Raelle. They will all pay.* The enormous thud of a female warrior landing hard on her feet in front of him caught him off guard.

"Samuel, stop!" Volshira screamed. Her breaths imitated his. "What are you doing?"

"Get out of my way, Shira!" Samuel sidestepped his love.

Volshira mimicked his movement. "No, I won't until you tell me what's happening! Look what you've done to our troops. This is madness! Lochran will be—"

"I don't give a damn about Lochran. He lied to me!"

"Samuel!" Volshira shook him by his shoulders. "What are you talking about? Lied about what?"

"My sister. She stopped Vilgare from killing me just now. She's alive. At least she was alive, until one of our men shot her!"

"You mean, that woman? That was your sister?" Volshira shook her head. Her breaths were loud and hard. "Are you positive? It doesn't—"

"Of course I'm sure!" Samuel roared. "Now get out of my way!"

"I'm afraid I can't do that, Samuel." Volshira pressed her palm into his chest. "My loyalties lie with the king. And I am certain that if you give him a chance to explain, you will see that this is simply a misunderstanding. It is possible that he too was fooled. Duped by our enemies. Do not rush to such conclusions. You must see reason. No one knew that was your sister. It was a mistake!"

"A mistake that may have cost my sister her life!"

"Samuel, please. Calm down. I know we can work this

out. Just please, do not harm any more of our troops. We need them."

"No! I will not stop." Samuel continued to dodge Volshira. "They will pay for what they've done."

"It was two men, Samuel! No one else did anything."

"Shira, if you do not get out of my way, I swear—

"What? You're going to kill me too?"

"No, but I will do what I must."

"Then you'll have to kill me, because I'm not letting you harm any more of our people. Killing them is not going to bring your sister back!" The sound of her swords leaving their scabbards rang in Samuel's ears. He swiftly lifted his leg and landed a hard, fast stomp to Volshira's chest. The blow sent her meters from where she once stood. Samuel did not blink as Volshira skidded over the grass "Stay out of my way, Shira!" he yelled.

Volshira found her footing and stood tall. "I do not wish to fight you, Samuel. But I will do what I must!"

In a split second, Samuel stinted, disappearing and reappearing at Volshira's back side. From behind, he wrapped his arm around her neck. The chokehold was snug. The trembling of his hand forced his dagger to vibrate against her throat. Droplets of blood trickled from the tiny cuts.

"You are a fool, Samuel." Volshira could barely speak. "Open your eyes and see reason! I love you." She did not struggle, but pressed her eyes shut.

Samuel's body shuddered and sweat poured from his face. The Rubiz gems of Volshira's armor and Lyre ring began to glow.

"Come home with me, my love," Volshira whispered. "Let me take care of you." Samuel's dagger continued to quiver against her throat. "Let me help you, Samuel. I love you..."

Volshira's gems blazed bright red light and Samuel released his hold. He dropped to his knees. Unable to catch his breath, he struggled to stand. It was no use. Volshira caught him in her arms.

"What's happening to me?" Samuel hyperventilated.

"You're overexerted." Volshira lifted his head. "We've got

to get you home."

"No, I can't leave now," he cried. "I must stay with Raelle."

The ground rumbled and shook beneath them. Volshira's eyes grew wide. Samuel turned his weak head to see what had caused her dreadful expression. From the Ellios lakes, mechanized combatants three meters tall stormed the brown soil beaches. In their midst, Ellios soldiers marched forward, fitted with metal, mechanized weaponry and attachments.

"By the Architect." Volshira's mouth gaped open. "I've never seen anything like it." She grabbed Samuel and tried to pull him to his feet. "We must go, now!"

Samuel struggled to pull his arm from her grip. "No, I won't leave my sister!"

"You don't have any other choice. They'll kill you if you don't go now! You're Lyre is drained. You don't have the ability to fight! Our men will offer us only enough time to barely escape." Volshira pulled a metal horn form her utility belt. She pressed her lips to the narrow end and blew. The sound of the siren brought more Abequan and Huronus troops out from the camouflage of the forest. They marched toward the mechanized elven enemy.

"You'll never make it to Raelle alive. Please, we have to leave now if you want to live!"

Samuel looked back at the metal army headed in their direction. The ground shook as the skies filled with enormous birds.

"What's happening? The birds, what are they doing?"

Volshira finally lifted Samuel to his feet. "Those aren't birds! They're Samissian air raiders!"

"What?" Samuel gazed up into the sky.

"Samissians, they're shape shifters. They can take on animal form."

Samuel's eyes followed the avian raiders overhead. From their talons, they dropped strange bronze balls.

"Samuel, run!" shouted Volshira.

But Samuel could barely move, let alone run.

Volshira looked around for a solution. It was too late, and the metal ball hit the ground. The intense and incapacitating energy of the overcharged soil gem inside blasted Samuel, Volshira, and their surrounding troops into chaos. Samuel watched in fright as shrapnel pierced through soldiers and horses all around him. As he lay on the ground checking his own body for metal pieces, his ears rang with immense pressure and pain. The gritty taste of Ellios soil and grass permeated his mouth. Suddenly, someone pulled him up from the torn up Ellios field and onto the back of a horse.

"We're going home!"

He could barely make out Volshira's voice over the sound of energy blasts from the mechanized army cannons. As the horse's motion pilfered the remaining air from Samuel's lungs, it became more difficult to breathe and even more difficult to see. Samuel struggled to save his consciousness, but it was no use. The darkness fell.

***

Samuel fell helplessly through the black abyss. His arms and legs kicked and flailed as he plummeted through the nothingness. He tried to scream, but nothing came out. His lungs were empty. He was empty. He felt just as barren of life as the Void through which he fell. It seemed never ending, a nightmare from which he could not wake. Accepting his fate, he closed his eyes and allowed the darkness to swallow him.

A painful blow from hitting an indescribable surface put a violent end to his descent. Samuel welcomed the intense pain of the collision. It reminded him that he was still alive. Samuel pressed his hand against the floor and attempted to sit up. Vomit spewed from his mouth. Another piece of evidence that he was alive. But still, he felt dead, devoid of life, absent of soul. He attempted to catch his breath, but there was none to be had. This was not a place of replenishment. It was a place of punishment. Samuel's arms gave way, and his face met with the strange surface once more.

"Welcome to the Void," a menacing voice hissed above him.

Samuel lifted only his head from the floor. "Who are you? What do you want?"

"You know precisely who I am." The sinister voice scratched from the entity's throat. "We had a deal, remember? *Ovtermid ire spirona isk ire virtom om uni, Gesp Royalm ire drilom. Gesp Desmont isk ire Oblitora. Azmodil, corontis isk spironir.*"

Samuel painstakingly sat up. His limbs shook violently. *The incantation.* Samuel's knees buckled in his attempt to stand. "Azmodil?"

"Yessss," the demon growled. The immense shadow that stood over Samuel was even blacker than the abyss. "You promised me a soul. You do not get to go back on that promise."

The demon's disturbing inflection evoked an indescribable fear within Samuel. "I—I—I gave you a piece of me—I—

"Yesss, you did. But it is merely a deposit of payment for your request." The gigantic silhouette moved closer. "You did not complete your recompense, and the soul you promised me was taken back."

"The soul I promised you? Not part of my own?"

The demon's grotesque face and glowing red eyes met with Samuel's. The scorching hot steam of Azmodil's putrid breath burned away at Samuel's skin. "Don't play dumb with me, Rogue. You let her get away. You told them where to find me!"

Samuel's empty breaths felt like rapid kicks to the chest. "Told who? Let who get away? I only wanted you to bring my sister back."

"Who do you think I am, boy?" Azmodil clutched Samuel's throat with his burning hand.

Samuel tried to scream, but only silence shrieked within the Void.

*** 

"Samuel! Samuel, please!" Sornin's voice echoed inside Samuel's demonic nightmare. His eyes jolted open to see his mentor's troubled face.

"What happened? Where was I?" The burns on Samuel's neck and face throbbed like the violent beating of his heart. *But it was only a nightmare, how could it have burned me?* His lips quivered and his eyes welled. "Please, someone tell me what's happening to me!"

"Samuel, calm down." Sornin helped his apprentice to sit up. "It's all right. I'm here." From the night stand, Sornin grabbed a glass of water and poured blue liquid from a vial into it. "Here, drink this."

Samuel downed the fluid as if he had not had an ounce of water in months. "Thank you. May I have more?"

"Of course." From a silver pitcher, Sornin poured more cold water into the glass. "You may have as much as you like."

The pain of his burns seemed to drift away with every sip. "What is that stuff?" Samuel touched his neck. The burns no longer hurt.

"What *stuff?*" Sornin replied.

"The blue vial. It's incredible."

"It's Torpaz blood, siphoned from the blue Torpaz gem of our people. It's a remedy for Rogue ailments and a recharge tonic. Surely Volshira and your other maidens have been making sure you receive it."

"No, I've never seen it before. They've been giving me something else."

Sornin put Samuel's empty glass back on the nightstand. "Something else? Do you know what it was?"

"I know that it doesn't help the way this does. It comes in a vial, like that one. But it's black."

"*Black,* you say? Well, I shall instruct your maidens to bring you the Torpaz from now on."

"What is it, Sornin? What is the black remedy?"

"It's not important. They were probably just confused. Abequans don't necessarily know the ways of our Rogue people. How are you feeling now?"

"I feel as good as new. I never felt this way with the other."

67

Sornin grinned. "I am relieved that you are well again."

"Sornin?" Samuel looked into his mentor's eyes. "What's happening to me? I was trapped in a horrific nightmare. Nothing like I've ever experienced before. In my dream, I was burned, and when I woke, I still had burns."

"When they brought you to me, you had the burns. I assumed you were burned at Ellios."

"I don't recall getting burned at Ellios. I'm telling you, Sornin, the dream felt real." Samuel shivered. "Thinking about it makes me feel ill. It was Shira that brought me, was it not? Ask her. She'll know."

"No, it was not Volshira. She did not return with you."

"But—she—how can that be? She is the one who dragged me out of there."

"I'm not sure." Sornin shook his head. "She may have gone to report to your father in Huronus."

Samuel's mind wandered into flashes of his skirmish with Volshira. The memory of Raelle's incapacitated body, pierced by an arrow, followed in its place. The power of the Opalz stone forced Samuel's simmering rage to an intense boil. He clenched his teeth and squeezed his fists. "I hate this!" He threw his water glass, shattering it into pieces on the floor. "I thought I was doing the right thing! I thought I was fulfilling my destiny. I trusted him. I believed him. I loved—"

"Who?"

"My father."

"But your father was not there."

Samuel gazed up at his mentor with wet eyes. "No, you're right. He wasn't, but he should have been."

Sornin shook his head. "I'm afraid I still don't understand."

"My father wasn't there. But Raelle, she *was* there."

Sornin's eyes grew wide. "Raelle? But how? She was killed. It couldn't have been."

"It was her. She saved my life." The tears poured from Samuel's big brown eyes. "She saved my life, Sornin." Samuel looked down. "And I left her. I left her all alone in the valley with those people. I kept everything from her. Thinking I could—

"You only did what you thought was right." Sornin took Samuel's hand. "You thought you were protecting her. I know you intended to return for her. You did the best you could."

"I failed her!" Samuel sobbed.

"We all thought her dead. If she's alive, then how have you failed her?"

"I killed her, Sornin."

"*You* killed her?"

"Not directly, but it was a soldier from *my* army. The army *I* led to Ellios. The shot that killed her came from *my* men. If only I had—

"You cannot do that, Samuel. You cannot live your life on *if onlys*. Would haves, could haves, and should haves are a fool's game. The past cannot be altered. Your decisions cannot be undone. Dwelling upon them will not rectify what has already come to pass. Your suffering and guilt will atone for nothing."

"The entire reason I trained in secret and left the valley is because I thought that once I finally returned home to Huronus, everything would make sense. That my suffering would end, that I could make things right again." Samuel pursed his lips and bit down hard. "But since returning, I feel even more conflicted than before. Everything seems so out of control. I don't know who to trust. I was told Raelle was dead. And after I found her alive, I was forced to hand her over to a sworn enemy in order to save her life. A man my father detests. But Vilgare cared for Raelle, I could sense it. I saw it in his eyes. In that moment, I trusted it. It was easy. But how could I trust a sworn enemy of my father? If Father was wrong about Raelle, then maybe he was wrong about this Vilgare as well."

"Your father loves you, very much," Sornin said in a comforting tone. "I do not think he knew that Raelle was alive. And he most certainly did not know she was in Ellios. The body that the Minotirr brought back was thought to be hers. As far as Vilgare, he is an incredible warrior mage. He is a master of his art and his Lyre. It is possible that he was able to manipulate you into trusting him. Or, he might truly care for your sister. But either way, he is a troubled young man."

"Yes, my father has told me. He has told me a great many things." Samuel's gaze journeyed to the night stand and stopped at an ornate box. He took the box from the stand and opened it. Inside, he found four handprints branded into the wood along with a piece of parchment. With hesitation, he plucked the incantation from the box. "Here." Samuel handed it to Sornin.

"What is this?" Sornin grasped the paper.

"I was hoping you could tell me."

Sornin unfolded the incantation and began to read. His eyes grew with a fearful revelation. "Samuel, how did you get this? Where did you get this?"

"That's not important. I just need you to tell me what it is."

"But—

"Please, Sornin, just tell me."

"Yes, Milord," Sornin sighed. "It is a Turning Request to the demon Azmodil."

"What is a *Turning Request?*"

"The demon Azmodil is one of the six princes of the Void. Like all other demons, he feeds on the souls of the living in order to thrive. But he does not kill his intended victim. He turns them wraith. The wraith, or physical body of the victim, then remains under the control of Azmodil or one of his human disciples."

"And how does this work, exactly?"

"Samuel, why do you want to know this? Turning someone is one of the darkest, most infinite punishments you could bestow upon a person."

"Sornin, this is not a request," Samuel snarled.

"All right." Sornin swallowed. "There are five hands that must be laid upon the victim and their soul before the transformation is complete. Azmodil burns, or brands, his victims with his five Torrid hands. Two above the heart, two below the heart, and the last over the heart. Then, and only then, is the transformation complete."

"And what about the individual doing the turning? Does anything happen to them?"

"Yes," Sornin replied with serious concern. "Which is why I do not wish for you to participate in this act. The turner must also sacrifice a piece of their soul. But Azmodil does not devour it—he keeps it instead as collateral. That piece will remain with him for all eternity and at any time can be used to call upon the turner. He appears to them in their dreams. He tortures them. He uses them."

"And what if the turner changes their mind? What if they do not complete the process?"

"Then Azmodil will systematically sever pieces of the turner's soul until they are nothing. Once the entirety of that person's soul is trapped inside his keep, then he can take full control of the turner. Their body becomes his vessel in the living world."

"So then he traps them in the Void and uses their body here on Lerim?"

"Yes. Samuel I beg you—

"I'm not going to do it, Sornin."

"Thank the Architect." Sornin held up the incantation. "Then what do you plan to do with it?"

Samuel took the parchment from his mentor. "Burn it."

"Very good."

"When do I see my father again?"

"I am not sure. He hasn't—

"Tonight, I will visit him tonight," demanded Samuel.

"But, Milord, your father is not inclined to –"

"Tonight, Sornin!" Samuel bellowed. "I do not care if I inconvenience him. We have much to discuss and it cannot wait."

"Yes, Samuel." Sornin stood. "I will make the arrangements."

Samuel threw the bed covers from his body and stepped onto the floor. "Afterward, we ride for Ellios. We're going to get Raelle back."

71

# CHAPTER 8
## DEMON

The enormous red sun that set in the west cast a rosy hue over the land. The sound of galloping hooves that echoed off the Huronus outer wall seemed to wake the guards from their day dreams. Samuel and his mentor stopped just outside the gates.

"Who goes there?" demanded one of the guards.

Samuel and Sornin removed their hoods.

"Prince Jowellia." The guards bowed. "We were not expecting you."

"I must speak with my father at once." Samuel moved forward on his painted mare.

"Yes, Milord." The two guards opened the enormous and elaborate gates of Samuel's home kingdom.

Samuel charged over the city's drawbridge and through the marble streets toward the palace. Huronus elites stopped and stared as the prince and his mentor raced by on their horses. At the bottom of the castle steps, they swiftly dismounted and ascended to the doors. The guards parted and opened them. Samuel and Sornin rushed through the stunning citadel and up six flights of stairs. They navigated through narrow, ornately decorated halls until they were met with the doors of Lochran's executive chambers. Samuel swiftly opened them to find his father sitting at his desk, drinking a glass of green spirit.

Lochran peered at them with a furrowed brow before standing. "Samuel, I was not expecting you. I was informed of your—

"Did you know?" Samuel cut in.

"Have you come here to interrogate me?" Lochran winced. "It is *I* who should be interrogating you, my son. You allowed that wretch Vilgare to defeat you and then killed half of my men."

Samuel stepped forward. "And do you know *why* that happened?"

Lochran shook his head. "The *why* does not matter."

"Because Raelle was there." Samuel saw the blow in his father's eyes.

"Then you succeeded in bringing her back?"

Samuel sighed and shook his head. "No, she has been alive this whole time. And you've known it all along."

"How dare you!" Lochran snapped. "You accuse me of lying?"

"Why were you trying to turn her, Father?" Samuel stepped forward. "Or better yet, why did you manipulate *me* into turning her? Were you too much of a coward to do it yourself? Was the cost too high for someone as mighty as you?"

"Why you insolent little—

"Is that true?" Sornin's mouth hung wide open. "Did you give Samuel that incantation?"

"What I do with my own son is no concern of yours, Sornin." Lochran raised a hand. Suddenly, without laying a finger on them, his chamber doors slammed shut.

Samuel closed in on his father. "Why were you trying to turn Raelle?" he yelled. "Tell me!"

Sornin grabbed Samuel by the wrist. "Calm down. You do not wish to engage with—

"No!" Samuel roared. "I want answers, and I want them now!"

Lochran chuckled. "You are a fool, Samuel."

"Yes, perhaps I am. I was a fool to believe you!"

Lochran sneered. "That dirty-blood scrub is *not* your sister."

Samuel shook his head. "But you said—

"I know what I said, boy. And I only said it because I knew how much you cared for her and I needed your cooperation."

"Sornin." Samuel turned to his mentor. "Is this true? Raelle is not my sister?"

Sornin nodded. "Yes, it is true. I—

"Then who is she?"

Sornin sighed. "She is your cousin and the rightful heir to the Huronus throne."

Lochran cleared his throat. "That is only half true." He scowled. "She *is* your cousin, but she is no heir. Only those of pure Lyre blood can claim the throne. My older sister's husband was a filthy half-blood! It was she that took you away from me, Samuel!"

"What are you talking about?"

"My sister had you kidnapped! It was she who conspired to have Lorndan and Marista take you away. And your false sister, Raelle, has the dirty, conniving blood of my sister running through her veins. I could not allow her to get in the way. *You* are the pure blood heir to this throne, not her!"

Sornin stepped closer to Lochran. "All the things you've told me over the years. They were all lies..."

"It doesn't matter what I told you, Sornin," Lochran growled. "Your place in this world is to do whatever I command of you. You are here to serve me. You are a mentor. That is your job!"

Sornin stood tall. "I do not serve any *man*, Lochran. I serve the Lyre. *That* is my job. You have become twisted over these years. I knew you were in pain. Your whole life, I saw it, felt it. But I convinced myself that one day, your rage would quiet. I thought that becoming a father would tame the beast within you. After they took him from you, I assured myself that once Samuel came home, you would find solace in taking care of your son. But I was wrong. You do not want peace. You only want to use him in your quest for vengeance and power. All these years I believed the words you told me because you were my apprentice. You were in *my* care. I raised you, I love you. But my love has blinded me from seeing the truth. I have failed the Lyre. That is clearer now more than ever."

Lochran glared at his mentor. "So then you see why *I* have chosen not to love. I do not wish to be weak, like you. I do not wish to be blinded by it, like you. I have loved before, you know that. And what did it get me? Betrayal, suffering, and loss. Even my own son defies me. You see Sornin, it is *I* who see clearly. I do not see the world through the guise of love. I see its raw and predatory nature. I refuse to be prey any longer. I am a predator. I am the beast. And from the Void, I will be reborn again. It is a pity that you won't be around to see it."

Samuel stepped in front of Sornin. "You will not lay a hand on this man."

"You forget your place, Samuel," Lochran scoffed. "You belong to me. I have clearly given you too much. It is time you learned your place. I did not wish to punish you, because in truth, I do love you. But I cannot allow that love to blind me to your impudence."

"Sornin has been more of a father to me than you ever could be." Samuel held back his tears. "You are twisted, Father. I see that now."

"You see nothing, boy!" In a flash, Lochran slapped a metal collar around Samuel's neck. With his other hand, he divided Sornin's throat with his dagger.

Samuel and his mentor both fell helplessly to the floor. Samuel was completely paralyzed. He groaned as the blood of his partially decapitated mentor pooled all around him. Samuel closed his eyes and when he opened them again, his father stood over him.

"You have been a very naughty boy, Samuel. And for your recklessness, you shall be punished. Only when you come to your senses and realize that my vision is the *only* vision, will you be released."

Samuel gained the smallest bit of energy in his arms. He used it to reach for the collar. He tugged, but it was in vain. His strength was tarnished. It felt as if all of his Lyre had been blasted into oblivion.

"It's no use, Samuel," Lochran snickered. "The soil gem inside that collar works in conjunction with black Opalz. Instead of giving energy, it steals energy. You are no more powerful than the average human. But only once you have decided to see reason, and take your place by my side, as my son, will I free you. Hopefully, you learn your lesson before Azmodil collects the entirety of his debt. You see, I am the only one who can pay that bail before it is too late."

Samuel crumpled his nose with disgust. "You are no father." He stared into the blacked out eyes of a stranger. "You are a demon."

"I may be a demon," Lochran replied arrogantly. "But I am still your father, and you will show me respect." He forced his son's mouth open and poured black liquid inside. Within moments, Samuel found himself lost in the blackness once more.

# CHAPTER 9
## FOR HER

The dim light of the Diamoz sconces cast a gentle glow over Raelle's pale face. Chrishtan raised his head from where it rested in his arms. He wiped away the hair that stuck to his tear-stained cheeks.

"I'm so sorry, Raelle," he whimpered. "I should never have let my guard down. I didn't..." His sniffles turned to sobs. He squeezed Raelle's cold hand in his. "We tried, we really did. We did everything we could. But it was too late. *I* was too late." Chrishtan buried his face in Raelle's long locks of auburn hair. His lament echoed inside the walls of the mortuary. On either side of him, Raelle's small dogs, Pip and Sasha, shared in his sorrow.

"I'm so sorry, Brother." Cohlen's voice lifted Chrishtan's head.

Chrishtan turned toward his brother. "How could I let this happen?"

"You didn't *let* this happen, Chrishtan. The fighting had ceased. Everyone thought it was over. A female warrior made the call. I saw her. It was a dirty move."

"Did you see her face?"

"No, she had her helmet on. I'm sorry."

"My own people turned against me." Chrishtan pounded his fist into his forehead. "They killed Raelle. Why should I ever go back? They can clean up their own mess!"

From the hallway, Chrishtan heard Oleevar clear his throat before stepping into the room. "Those Abequans, the Lyre Elite, they are not your people. They are power hungry, greedy Lyre-bloods that only care about themselves.

"Yeah, Chrishtan." Cohlen rested a hand on Chrishtan's shoulder. "Think of all your people who left Abequa. The ones who fled. The people you helped rescue. If not for you, they would still be enslaved by Lochran, or worse. You set up those refugee camps for your people, along with the Huronian Inclusionists, and they are grateful for it. Do not turn your back on them so easily. What happened to Raelle is a tragedy, but it is not the end. More will suffer and die if you give up now."

"Cohlen is right." Oleevar joined them on the slab. "Not to mention, you were able to defeat the Elite Echo. My mechanized army sent him and his troops running back to their kingdoms with their tails between their legs. You showed your people and ours precisely how strong you are. The Elite Echo is on the run."

"His name is Samuel." Chrishtan turned to face his brothers with wet eyes. "And he *will* be back."

"And when he does," Oleevar said, "we'll be ready!"

"He won't be back to fight," Chrishtan retorted. "He'll be back for Raelle."

"The Huronians cannot have her," Oleevar sneered with arrogance. "They lost that privilege when they betrayed her family."

"He *is* her family," Chrishtan retorted. "The only family she has left."

Cohlen grimaced. "What do you mean?"

"Samuel Jowellia, the Elite Echo, is Raelle's younger brother."

Oleevar shook his head. "I thought her brother was murdered."

"That's what Raelle thought, too." Chrishtan shifted onto his knees. "She found his body in the forest. But when I revealed the Echo's face—

"So that's why Raelle ran out there," Cohlen interrupted. "Everyone thought she ran out there after you, but–"

"Precisely," said Chrishtan. "She was trying to save her brother, and she did. And in return, she lost her own life. There is no justice in this world." Chrishtan closed his eyes and squeezed out his remaining tears. "Hope seems to slip away with each and every moment that Lochran remains in power."

Cohlen embraced his surrogate brother. "You are the hope, Chrishtan. Remember what Jenladra told us. *We* are the hope."

Oleevar joined in the embrace. "Cohlen is right. We are the hope. And we will take that power back and disperse it effectively. No one individual should have so much power. The only way to have peace is to ensure that the power is shared, just as it used to be.

Cohlen rose with confidence. "We will return peace to Abequa and Huronus. In Raelle's memory, we shall prevail."

Chrishtan stood and wiped his wet face. "I don't know what I'd do without you two. You are the best brothers anyone could ever ask for. I wish Raelle had gotten a second chance with her brother. What are we going to do about Samuel? Does anyone know what happened to him after I took Raelle?"

"Well," Oleevar sighed, "he proceeded to take out half of his own army with that echo ability. Then, rumor has, it that he was seriously injured and taken away on horseback."

"He's probably back in Huronus now." Cohlen rubbed his chin. "Do you think we still have a chance to turn him? If we tell him the truth, then surely he should see reason."

Chrishtan shook his head. "I'm not sure. Maybe if Raelle were still alive, but without her it will be much more difficult. I'm sure Lochran has filled his head with an intricate and unnavigable web of lies. After all, he already has half of Mirilan thinking that Framin killed my parents and brainwashed me. I can't even imagine what he's told Samuel."

Cohlen hugged his surrogate brother "Whatever it is, Chrishtan, we will figure it out and we will make him see reason."

"I agree," said Oleevar. "He is still young, and impressionable."

"And filled with rage," Chrishtan added. "He's unpredictable. But he *is* Raelle's brother, and I know he meant the world to her. So, I will do what I must."

"We will do it together." Cohlen smiled. "After all you've done for me, for everyone, you know we will stand by your side, no matter what."

"Now come, Brother," said Oleevar. "Let us get you out of these clothes and a hot meal into your belly. It's been an entire day since you've eaten anything, or left this room. I'm sure you haven't slept."

"I know." Chrishtan frowned. "I just don't want to leave her alone. She said she never wanted to be alone again. I just can't..." he choked.

"She is not alone, Chrishtan," Cohlen said, his voice filled with warmth. "She is with the Architect."

"I know you're right. I just can't bear to..." Chrishtan's tears came once more.

"But Chrishtan," Cohlen said. "You have the Opalz stone, remember? You can travel into the Verge."

"That's right." Chrishtan's frown dissipated. "You're right. So maybe we can see Raelle again."

"And..." Oleevar paused in thought. "So can Samuel. And Raelle can convince him to become our ally, once and for all. Then Lochran won't stand a chance."

"That just may work." Chrishtan grabbed Oleevar and Cohlen and kissed them both on the forehead. "You really are the smartest elves I've ever known."

"I won't argue with that." Oleevar smirked. "Come now Brother, it is time to get some rest. If we are to avenge Raelle, you must be at your peak. In the meantime, I shall come up with a plan."

"Your plan had better involve you getting to the Lantern Forest to see the Lady of the Realm," Cohlen chimed in. "You still haven't received your gift as Chrishtan and I have."

"Yes," said Oleevar. "I suppose you're right."

"We still need to get Lanadia of the Ornz Desert and Karaleste of Jassokia there as well," Chrishtan added. "The more of us who can enter the Verge, the better our chances of defeating Lochran."

Oleevar sighed. "Lanadia will be difficult, but not impossible. Karaleste though, is a different story. The Jassokians have signed a treaty with Huronus. It is a treaty of peace. They too agree that Lyre-blood humans should not breed with those who are not. They're—

80

"Elitist bastards," Chrishtan cut in.

"That's one way of putting it," Oleevar replied. "Their connection to the Grand Architect seems to put them above the rest of us. They've isolated themselves from the rest of Mirilan because they feel that we are not as enlightened as they. I would have to agree that they do have an incredible gift."

Chrishtan shook his head. "We've talked about this before. I don't care what their affiliation is. They're no better than the rest of us, as far as I'm concerned. And hoarding their abilities is no gift at all. They could be out here saving lives. Instead, they sign a treaty with the one man who spits on the very idea of the Grand Architect. He preaches hate. Lochran is a disciple of the Destroyer."

"Indeed." Oleevar nodded. "But it is under the guise of the Architect and that is all that matters; what he appears to do, not what he actually does."

"Well, I for one don't trust the Jassokians either," Chrishtan said angrily. "They may appear to be high and mighty, but maybe they're dabbling with the Destroyer too. No one comes or goes from that place. How do we know what they're up to?"

Oliver folded his arms. "That is an interesting theory. One that I had not considered before. But there could be some truth in it."

"I sure hope there isn't." Cohlen scowled. "And if there is, then we will expose them and Lochran." He raised his voice. "Once we're through, every sinister deed he has done will be known to all the people of this continent."

"Which means," Oleevar grasped Chrishtan by the shoulders and looked him in the eye, "we will need a sound plan of action and a strong Chrishtan."

"You're right." Chrishtan looked down with tear-filled eyes. "And I want to be that for you, for everyone." He struggled to find his composure. "I ju—I feel like, without her, a p—part of me is mi— it's missing."

"I understand," said Oleevar, patting Chrishtan on the back. "But you must find your strength *for her*. And like Cohlen

81

said, we will see her again, in the Verge."

Chrishtan nodded and his two brothers led him out of the mortuary. Chrishtan looked back once more to see that the dogs had stayed behind with Raelle. "Pip, Sasha, it's time to come with me now. We must say— His mouth refused to form the word. *Goodbye.*

# CHAPTER 10
## MORE TIME

Night slowly crept in as Chrishtan lay in his chambers. He did his best to keep his food down, but still his stomach burned and churned with grief. He closed his eyes and attempted to meditate, but his mind would not quiet. Inside his head, the hateful reverberation of Raelle's voice echoed, *Don't you touch me! I'm trying to save my brother!* The piercing sound and image of the arrow as it stopped Raelle's heart played mercilessly on. The harrowing memory attacked his skills of meditation. *How will I ever connect with Raelle in the Verge if I can't quiet my mind?* The sound of his own sobs startled him. "I can't be without her. I feel so empty."

Chrishtan jumped at the sight of a silhouette in his doorway.

"Chrishtan?" a female voice accompanied the figure.

Chrishtan squinted to see the shadow of a woman with long hair. "Raelle? Raelle is that you?"

"I'm so sorry." The woman stepped into the light of Chrishtan's fireplace. "I heard how much she meant to you."

"Shira?" Chrishtan stood. "Is it really you? I thought—

Volshira draped her arms around Chrishtan's large frame. "It's me. I'm home."

"But you were killed. They dragged your body away. You were—

Volshira's golden eyes looked into his. "I almost did die. But instead of finishing me off, they kept me alive. They held me captive, but I was able to escape."

"It's been over a year, Shira." Chrishtan swallowed his disbelief. "How did you do it? How did you get away?"

"I was patient. I let my Lyre guide me. I endured a great many things that no woman—or man—should ever have to endure, but I did it." She smoothed her hand over his cheek. "The only thing that kept me going was the thought that someday I would return to you. And I have."

"It's my fault, what happened to you." Chrishtan looked down. "If I had stayed hidden, Lochran wouldn't have threatened anyone. He may never have come after our refugee camps. They never would've taken you or hurt you. I couldn't bear the thought of your death, among others, being on my hands. I left that day. I swore that no one else would be hurt or killed because of me." Tears slid steadily from Chrishtan's eyes. "I should have known better. I've only been home for a day and already someone I care for deeply has been killed. It's entirely my fault. I'm cursed, Shira. The Architect has cursed me."

"No, you're not cursed." Volshira embraced him once more. "You're a king, the rightful king of a nation that Lochran wants for himself. *He* has done this to you, to all of us. *He* is cursed, not you." She grasped Chrishtan's face gently in her hands. "You are a beautiful person, Chrishtan Vilgare. It's why I loved you, all those years. I understood why we couldn't be together, because you were protecting me. But I didn't need protecting. I needed *you.* You're not cursed, just stubborn."

"Then why does it feel that way?" Chrishtan grimaced. "Every time I get close to someone, something awful happens to them. All I ever wanted was—

Volshira's lips cut him short. She grasped his hair in her hands and pulled his face to hers.

Chrishtan felt the connection between them reignite. But it wasn't what he wanted. "Shira, I'm s—

"Ssssh," she whispered in his ear. "It's all right. I'm here. Allow me to heal what ails you. Let me fix what is broken. I can take care of you." The Rubiz gems of her Lyre ring glowed red. They seemed to ignite Chrishtan's.

"Volshira, I—

An indescribable rapture came over Chrishtan and his words escaped him. With a strong arm, Volshira pressed her palm into his chest and pushed him into his bed. With her coaxing, he lay back on the sheets. Her dark red lips caressed his. Her muscular legs straddled his hips. A tug of war ensued within his mind. *You need her, you want her. No, I don't, I love Raelle. Raelle is gone. Nothing you can do will change that. You deserve love. You deserve happiness. You need Shira. No...*

"Yes," Shira whispered. "I'm all you need. I can be your savior, your love, your queen."

Once again, ecstasy took hold. The soothing energy of Volshira's Lyre seemed to wash away his aching stomach, his weakness, his suffering, and his reason. They all drifted away with each whispering word.

"Together, my love," Volshira continued. "We will take back Abequa. We will take back what is ours. Together, we will rule. Together, we will bring order to Mirilan."

Chrishtan lifted her from his hips. He took her in his arms and exchanged positions. With a gentle ease, he leaned over her and pressed his body into hers.

"I can be whatever you need, whatever you desire," whispered Volshira.

Chrishtan closed his eyes and met her lips with his. When he opened his eyes once more, it was Raelle who smiled back at him.

"I've missed you." Her green eyes looked deep into his.

"I love you." A tear trickled down from Chrishtan's eye before pressing his lips to hers.

"I love you too..."

***

Chrishtan woke alone, naked in his bed. The pillow next to him looked used, but no one else was there. His head harbored a gentle throb and his body a slight tingle. Something was off. From the floor, he grabbed his green linen pants and headed toward his chamber door. The second he opened it, Pip and Sasha came running in.

"All right, all right. Come here you mutts." He grinned.

They jumped and licked and cried until he gave them what they wanted, pets. "You guys are too much." A twinge of pain came over him, accompanied by the painful memory of

Raelle's death. His stomach quickly returned to its knotted state. He wished he could lie back down in his bed, fall asleep, and never wake up. *No, I must stay strong, for Raelle. Or else all of this was for nothing. We'll figure out a plan.*

From down the hall, Chrishtan heard his brothers' voices in the dining room along with one other. *It must be one of the palace maidens.* Chrishtan entered the dining room in nothing but his linen pants where he found his brothers seated with a female guest. Her back was to him and a hood covered her hair. The color of the woman's dress reminded him of the green one Raelle had worn less than two days ago. Chrishtan pictured her face inside the hood.

The woman stood and revealed herself. "Someone still likes to sleep late." Volshira smiled.

Chrishtan froze. *It wasn't a dream.*

"I have returned, my love," Volshira said, bowing deeply at Chrishtan.

"It must be fate," said Oleevar. "You, Cohlen, and Shira have been returned to us."

Chrishtan did not move.

Oleevar approached him. "I know, it was difficult for me to fathom as well, but Volshira is home and she is safe."

"Chrishtan?" Cohlen pinched his arm. "Are you all right?"

"Yes." Chrishtan shook himself out of his daze. "I'm sorry. ... Shira... did you come to my room last night?"

Oleevar, Cohlen, and Volshira harbored the same confused expressions.

"No." She shook her head. "I've only just arrived." She stood and pulled out a chair. "Here, sit. You must be in shock after everything that's happened."

Chrishtan froze. *I must be dreaming...* Volshira had never pulled out a chair for him, or anyone else for that matter, in her entire life. She had never been one to coddle or nurture. She had always been a direct and, assertive woman. If you could not pull the chair out for yourself, then you did not deserve to sit.

"I'll have them bring in some food for you," Oleevar's

voice brought him back.

Chrishtan cleared his throat and sat in the chair Volshira had presented. "Thank you." *Am I the only one who thinks her strange?*

Volshira grasped Chrishtan's hand and rubbed it with her thumb as she sat down next to him. "I'm so sorry for your loss. Olee told me everything. How much you cared for her. I can't imagine how difficult it must have been for you. Especially after..."

Chrishtan's mind wandered. *Compassion? This is not like her. Usually she'd be telling me to get over it and move on so we can save Abequa. I know she loved me. She had her own way of showing it, but never like this.* Chrishtan did his best to snap back to the present. "Shira, I thought you were dead. I saw you—

"I know, I know. But they didn't kill me. They kept me alive. Part of me did die whilst in their captivity. Especially when they told me you were dead as well." She pursed her burgundy lips. "But when I heard you were alive, the thought of seeing your face again got me through, I..."

Chrishtan tuned out again. He had heard this all before, last night in his chambers. *I must be losing my mind.* He rubbed his face with his hands, as though he was still half-asleep. *Did I dream it all? Am I still dreaming? Is Oleevar not taken aback by her peculiar kindheartedness?* The thought made him feel even more flustered. *How am I the only one bothered by this? Am I the crazy one?*

"Chrishtan?" A hand waved in front of his face. "Are you all right?" asked Volshira.

"Yes," Chrishtan answered, trying to bring his focus back to Volshira. "I'm fine. I just—I swear that you..."

"That I what?" Volshira's brow furrowed.

"Last night I had a dream that— ugh— and you're so different. I..." Chrishtan rubbed his forehead.

Oleevar pulled a clueless Cohlen by his shirt. "We'll let you two have a moment."

"No, I—

87

Chrishtan tried to stop his brothers. His mind raced and his thoughts bombarded him like a crushing waterfall. The overwhelming confusion pained him. It even scared him. Volshira scared him. This was not the woman he remembered. How was Oleevar so blind to this?

"It's fine. You two need to talk." Oleevar cut him off with a wide eyed expression.

"No, really. Olee, I—

Oleevar shut the dining room door before Chrishtan could finish. The idea of being alone with Volshira terrified him.

"Look at you." Volshira's hands caressed his face. "Always trying to remain strong despite everything. I know this isn't easy for you." Her golden eyes looked deep into his. "There's no need to pretend that you're fine. We all know you're not."

A heavy sigh fled from Chrishtan's lungs. Volshira's touch felt eerily familiar. But it was not the familiar touch he remembered so deeply from the past. Instead, it mirrored the energy from the previous night's dream. The warmth of a lustful flame ignited within him. His breaths grew more rapid and beads of sweat collected on his forehead.

"It's going to be all right now. I'm here." Volshira used a soft and sympathetic tone as she wiped the moisture from his face.

Chrishtan used every bit of energy and strength he could to put out the carnal flame. *What is wrong with me? What's happening to me? This isn't like me. I can't stand it!* He closed his eyes and attempted to meditate. Volshira brushed a finger over his lip. Instantly, his hand shot up and clutched her wrist.

"Don't!" The sound of his own irate voice startled him.

"I'm sorry, I..." Volshira swallowed and Chrishtan continued to squeeze her wrist. "Chrishtan, please. You're hurting me," she cried.

Chrishtan let go. "I'm sorry, Shira. I don't know what came over me. I..." His disturbing outburst frightened him. "I don't know what's wrong with me."

"I do," Volshira sighed.

"You do?"

"Yes." Volshira's hands gently massaged Chrishtan's thighs. "You're so stubborn that you never know when to quit. You've been through enough. Stop trying to fight your feelings. Stop trying to control your emotions. If you do, they will only come out as rage or anger. You must face your grief head on. It is what I learned in Lochran's horrible prison. You must not deny your feelings, your urges, your *self*."

Volshira's hands on Chrishtan's thighs only made him feel more tense. She had never been so affectionate before. But in spite of Volshira's odd behavior, Chrishtan willed himself to stay calm. He sensed that she genuinely cared and convinced himself that she really was trying to help him. Deep in his heart, he still cared for her too. He understood that Volshira had suffered more than he knew. Whoever she was now, had to be a result of that suffering. All because she had tried to save him.

"I'm sorry, Shira. I know you must think I'm being insensitive to what happened to you. I'm doing the best I can to stay strong. But the truth is, I blame myself for what happened to you." Tears began to well in his eyes. "I'm so sorry."

Volshira took his hand. "What happened to me, to Raelle, to your family, none of that is your fault. You must understand this."

"I'm trying." Chrishtan shook his head. "Really, I am. But I feel so sick inside. Like I want to crawl into a hole and never return. I know I'm grieving Raelle. I'm sad, I know that. I'm beyond sad, I'm a wreck." Tears slid from his blue eyes. "But there is something else. Something is wrong with me. I feel like I'm outside my body looking in. Everything feels wrong. My Lyre is off somehow. I had this incredibly vivid dream last night and you were in it."

"Your dream may have been a premonition," said Volshira. "Listen, I know that it's a lot to deal with. Raelle's passing and my return. For as long as I've known you, you've taken the entire world and held it on your shoulders. That's why I fell in love with you, because you are a strong, good, compassionate warrior. You were everything I wasn't. You tried to protect me by keeping me at a distance, but I think you've taken care of everyone else for long enough. It's time for you to take care of yourself. Do what feels right for you."

The clash of thoughts, fears, and grievances inside Chrishtan's mind drowned out Volshira's words. "I can't do that." He shifted in his chair and gazed toward the floor. "I must get Oleevar to the Lantern Forest."

"What?" Volshira winced. "Why?"

"It's not something I can explain to you." He looked her in the eye. "It is something that we royal-blood children were burdened with long ago. It's up to us to save Mirilan. That's the way it is. It's *our* fate, and *our* fate alone."

Volshira shook her head. "You don't have to go through all of this alone, Chrishtan. If you'd just let me in, I can try and help you."

"You can't help me!" Chrishtan raised his voice. "No one can help me. I must help myself. Jenladra said, it was up to me and Raelle to lead the others. Now Raelle is gone!"

Volshira grabbed his wrist. "Chrishtan, please!"

He tore Volshira's hand from his arm and stormed out of the dining room. His feet thundered through the palace corridors as he marched to his chambers. He slammed the door behind him. In the grand mirror next to the doorway, he saw his reflection glaring back at him. He barely recognized himself. With his brute strength, he pulled the gigantic mirror from the wall and smashed it onto the floor. Shards of glass scattered over the black marble tile of his chambers. Each splinter reflected parts of his image back at him. To Chrishtan, the broken reflection was much more accurate. It showed how he truly felt inside. He was in pieces. *This isn't me. I'm not this person. What's happening to me?*

A knock on the door startled him. "Chrishtan?" Oleevar's voice called from the other side of the door. "Please, you must let me in."

Ashamed of what he had done, Chrishtan did not wish to open the door.

"Please, Chrishtan." Oleevar's voice muffled through the

door. "Let us help you."

"Us?" Chrishtan clenched his teeth. "Who's *us*?"

"Me and Cohlen, your brothers, for Architect's sake!"

Chrishtan did his best to tiptoe around the sea of mirror shards and over to the door. He unlocked it and let his brothers inside.

Cohlen closed the door behind him. "Chrishtan?" He frowned. "What's happened?"

Chrishtan could not look at his younger brother. His shame would not allow him. He returned to his bed and sat down, rubbing his face with both hands. "I don't know. I'm not the warrior I used to be. I've lost control of my Lyre."

Oleevar calculated a safe route around the glass and over to Chrishtan. He stood in front of his surrogate brother, grasping the warrior's shoulders. "Chrishtan, you are human, and you have taken on too much."

Chrishtan cringed at his *human* label.

"You have endured much more than any other human, this I know for certain." Oleevar expounded. "There is nothing wrong with you. You haven't slept. You've hardly eaten. Your body and mind are telling you to take a break. You must get your strength back if we are to make it to the Lantern Forest and reconnect with Raelle."

Cohlen eased forward with a somber expression. "All of this is overwhelming for all of us. Here I am, back in Ellios, with a family that I hardly know. I barely recognize them. At first, it terrified me, but now I know I'm home. I know my family loves me. And none of that would be possible without you, Chrishtan. Together, we will triumph over the Destroyer. But you must allow us to help you. I allowed you to help me, now I'm returning the favor. Olee and I will do whatever we must to help you regain your strength. We love you. And I know Raelle loves you too. Even though she is no longer with us here on Lerim, I can still feel her love for you. And once we return to the Verge, you'll feel it too."

"He's right." Oleevar sighed. "Allow us to help you. We will support one another to get through this incredibly dark time.

There is still hope. And I know that hope lies within you, within all of us. In the Verge, we will all be together again and we will find a way to defeat our enemy. But we cannot do that until you have recharged. We will wait as long as we must for you. If it takes ten days or a thousand days, we will wait until you are well again."

"But we can't do that." Chrishtan frowned. "We must get to Raelle's brother. If we wait too long, it may be too late."

"We can cross that bridge when we get there. It is more important that you get well." Oleevar removed a vial from his pocket. "Here, I brought you this." He shook the orange liquid.

"Orange?" Chrishtan grimaced. "You know I can only have Rubiz blood."

"That is Rubiz blood." Cohlen smiled and sat down on the other side of Chrishtan.

"No. That looks orange to me." Chrishtan made a face.

"Of course it does." Oleevar grinned. "Because it is a new concoction I, myself, engineered and perfected." Oleevar handed Chrishtan the vial.

"What is it?" Chrishtan studied the liquid.

"It's Rubiz blood laced with just the right amount of Chocaz."

"Chocaz?" Chrishtan asked. "The stone we use to power our technology?"

"Yes," replied Oleevar

Chrishtan's eyes grew large. "That does not sound safe."

"Oh, I assure you it is," said Oleevar. "You see, like all other Lyre stones, Chocaz can be bled as well. And when you mix the proper amount with the blood of your faction's gemstone, it has tremendous healing effects, both physically and mentally. The pure energy of the Chocaz shocks your body and resets your Lyre. Now, it won't make you forget about the things that have happened. But it will help to ease the grief, separating your emotions from your logic. You will be sad, but you will not have the physiological effects of your sadness. Your trauma will become a memory, and no longer a condition. Unless of course an event triggers that trauma, then you'll have to do it again."

"I'm going to try and pretend I understand what you just told me." Chrishtan eyed the orange liquid once more. At this point, he'd do anything to stop the anguish and confusion from tearing him apart. "But I trust you, so I'll do it." Chrishtan took the vial and removed the cork.

Before he could lift it to his lips, Oleevar parried with his hand. "One more thing. It will force your body into a coma for at least twelve hours."

Cohlen grinned. "You could use a nice long nap, Chrishtan."

"Yes, I suppose you're right," Chrishtan said, defeated. "I'll toast to that." He raised the vial high before pouring it into his mouth. His throat tingled as the energized liquid made its way into his stomach. Almost immediately, he began to feel the elixir's effects. As his eyes grew heavy, he could barely make out what Oleevar was saying.

"I'm going to take one of your room keys with me." The elf's face moved in and out of focus. "I don't want anyone coming in here and interrupting the process. It could have terribly negative effects on you. I'll see you when you wake up."

Just before everything went black, Chrishtan felt Cohlen affectionately squeeze his hand.

*Goodnight, Brother.*

***

A knock at the door woke Chrishtan from the depths of his restorative slumber.

"Chrishtan?" A muffled voice called through the door.

Chrishtan gazed out his window and noticed that it was now night. *What hour is it?* He walked over to the sill and opened the window to let in a cool breeze. As he gazed out, the position of the moon told him that the sun would be rising in only a few hours. *I've been asleep for over sixteen hours?*

"Chrishtan?" The person behind the door called once more.

"I'll be right there," he answered. With his arms out wide,

he mustered a deep stretch. A calming sigh left his lungs. His chest no longer felt tight, and his mind had quieted. For the first time in almost two days, he felt some relief. *I guess Olee really does know what he's doing.* He shook his head. *What am I saying? Of course he does.* Under his breath, he released a soft chuckle. Shuffling his feet across the cool marble floor, he reached the door and unlocked it. He opened it to find Volshira waiting patiently on the other side.

"I'm sorry to bother you. I know you're still recuperating, but I can't sleep." She fiddled with her fingers. "I feel so alone in that room."

Chrishtan saw something in Volshira's eyes that he had only ever seen once before, on the day he met her over fifteen years earlier. It was the genuine fear and sadness of a young girl who had just lost everything. Chrishtan felt horrible. Whatever they had done to her. Whatever torture she had endured, had reverted her back to her ten-year-old self. A feeling that Chrishtan knew all too well.

"It's fine." Chrishtan stepped back and made room for Volshira to enter. "Come in."

Volshira forced a weak smile. "Thank you."

Chrishtan eyed her somber expression once more. "What is it, Shira?"

"It's just... I feel really bad for upsetting you earlier. It wasn't my intention. I just hated seeing you like that, in so much pain. I wanted to—"

"It's not your fault." Chrishtan closed the door behind her. "I don't know what came over me. Grief I suppose. But Oleevar has taken care of me. I'm feeling much more stable again. I'm sorry if I hurt you or scared you. That wasn't me. You know I'd never—"

Volshira laughed through her pain. "Hurt anyone? Yes, I know you, Chrishtan. You are a kind and compassionate man. We all do insensible and inconceivable things when we're in such pain and anguish as you were. I'm still not quite myself after..." Her voice trailed off.

Chrishtan motioned for her to sit with him on his bed. She did as he instructed. His arms greeted her and he held her close. "I'm so sorry, Shira. Truly I am. For everything."

She reciprocated his hug. "It wasn't your fault. We've all been through a great deal." Volshira relaxed her embrace.

Although his eyes were closed, Chrishtan could still feel her passionate gaze on his face. When his eyes opened once more, they were met with Volshira's golden stare.

"I've missed you so much," she said.

Chrishtan swallowed hard at the sound of desperation in her voice. He had never known her to show such vulnerability, even when she was just a girl. And as a woman, she had always been a strong, steadfast, and intimidating figure. If she wanted something, she went after it. If ever someone crossed her, she took care of it. She never needed anyone to take care of her, to coddle her. Even when she expressed her love to him in the past, it had been in a domineering fashion. *What have they done to you, Shira?*

"I've missed you too." He brushed her bangs away and kissed her forehead. "But we're together again. You're safe here. You know you'll always have a home in Ellios."

"I don't want Ellios to be my permanent home." Volshira groaned. "I want to return to Abequa. I want to return to my rightful home. Don't you want that too?"

"Yes." Chrishtan shook his head. "Of course I do. But—

"But what?" Volshira tucked his messy hair behind his ear. "Let's gather the troops, you and I. We can march them to Abequa and take back what is ours. Together, like we always talked about. I wish to be your queen, Chrishtan. I love you. You know that I—

"It's not that simple, Shira. We can't just storm Abequa and take it back. This is no longer a war of men. There are other entities at play now. War alone cannot save our nation, or us."

"Then what? What will save us? Do you have a plan?"

"It's incredibly complicated. It's like I told you this morning. It's a task that can only be carried out by the remaining heirs. Inevitably, sending troops to both Abequa and Huronus will become part of that, but not yet."

"What is this '*task*' you speak of? Let me help."

"I'm sorry." Chrishtan looked away from her anxious gaze. "I can't do that right now. It's of the utmost importance that it's kept a secret."

"Do you not trust me?" Volshira craned her head to find his eyes. "After everything we've been through?"

"Yes, of course I do." Chrishtan pursed his lips. "But it's just the way it has to be. The heirs and the heirs alone have the ability to take back Mirilan. But that does not mean that I won't need your help on the battlefield when the time comes. It's very—"

"I nearly died trying to protect you, Chrishtan." Volshira's voice escalated. "I was locked in a dungeon and tortured for over a year. The only reason I was able to make it through was the thought of getting back to *you*. I thought maybe you would see how much I love you. Now here you are, trying to protect me again. Keeping me on the outside. If you truly loved me, you would let me in." Tears fled her golden eyes and slithered down her tan cheeks.

"Volshira, I…" He held her close and combed his fingers through her burgundy hair. "Of course I care for you."

She forcefully pushed her way out of his embrace. "But you are not in *love* with me anymore, are you? Did you *ever* love me?"

Chrishtan looked down. "Of course I loved you, I—

"It's her, isn't it?"

"What?"

"Raelle." Volshira shook her head. "You barely knew her, and yet you loved her? More than you ever loved me? You love her still?"

"Well, I—

"She is not Abequan." Volshira stood. "*She* is Huronian. She is no warrior. She is *Rogue*. Her family is responsible for all of this. You can't possibly—

This was *his* Volshira. The one Chrishtan knew so well. The woman who *always* got her way. Even if by force or manipulation. It was always an argument.

"*She...* is gone!" The elevated volume of Chrishtan's voice sliced through Volshira's words like a guillotine.

"I'm sorry." Volshira lowered her head. "I shouldn't have..."

"I'm not going to sit here and lie to you. I did love Raelle. I still do love her."

"So you no longer love *me*?" Tears streamed down Volshira's disenchanted and fuming face.

"We have an incredible history." Chrishtan paused and took her hand. "I will always love you."

Volshira leaned in with her luscious red lips. "Come back to me, my love," she whispered.

"I'm not ready for—

Volshira's lips cut Chrishtan's protest short. "Please, Shira." He gently pushed her away. "I need time." Chrishtan's mind reeled. He had never seen Volshira act so desperate before. He was torn. He knew that her current and pitiful state was the result of his carelessness. It was his fault she had been dragged away and tortured and his feelings for her still echoed within his heart. *Something just doesn't feel right. She needs time. I need time... and I need Raelle.* Chrishtan's mind traveled back to that night on the beach. In that moment, he had been completely and utterly connected to Raelle. He had never felt anything like it in his entire life. In that moment, their Lyre had joined them as one. On the other hand, his affection for Shira was ever-present, but far different than his love for Raelle.

"We don't have time," cried Volshira. "We only have now. Our world is collapsing and we need each other. We must put the past behind us so that we can move forward. Together, we can restore Abequa to its former glory. Please Chrishtan. I love you. I need you." She leaned in again and a passionate kiss ensued.

Both Chrishtan and Volshira's Lyre rings illuminated with vibrant red light. Once again, Chrishtan felt a hot, volatile lust burn through him. *You need her. You want her.*

Volshira pushed Chrishtan into his bed and spanned his hips. "Let me be your queen." Her scorching whisper seethed into his ear. "Let me take care of you."

Something inside him snapped. His Lyre raged through him like a wildfire, reigniting his emotions, his trauma, his grief. A flood of memories burst through his recuperative dam.

"No!" He threw Volshira onto the floor. Flashbacks of his life's tragedies up to Raelle's death pierced through his mind and his heart. "Just leave me alone!" His blue eyes drowned in a pool of despairing tears. "You don't understand, Shira. And you never will. No one will!"

Suddenly, Chrishtan's door flew open.

"Is everything all right in here?" Oleevar stood wide eyed in the doorway. Cohlen was not far behind.

Chrishtan gazed down at Volshira on the floor. She glared up at him with livid and dejected eyes. Chrishtan turned and went to the window.

"Are you all right, Shira?" Oleevar helped her up off the floor.

"I'm fine, thank you." Volshira sniffed and wiped her tear-soaked face.

"How did you get in here?" Oleevar questioned.

"Chrishtan let me in, of course."

"I see." Oleevar continued. "Chrishtan, are you all right?"

"What do you think?" Chrishtan hunched over where he stood at the windowsill. His mind reeled with the noisy confusion and misery of his entire life's experiences. Raelle's death had forced his childhood trauma to resurface, blending the new trauma with the old. It was as if he could not discriminate between the two, creating one tormented mess of agonizing pain. Just like when he was a child, his body trembled and his breaths rattled. The touch of Cohlen's hand on his shoulder caused him to flinch.

"It's going to be all right. We're going to figure this out."

Chrishtan said nothing. His mind was too disheveled to collect a coherent response.

Oleevar joined Cohlen next to Chrishtan at the window. "Just tell me what happened. How did you feel when you woke?"

Chrishtan tried to swallow his feebleness. It took a

moment for him to find the words among the vehement clash of thoughts inside his brain. "I felt fine. I was still aware of Raelle's death. I was still grieving. But it was as you said I would feel. I was sad and aware of the loss, but I was in control of all else. And then..." Chrishtan's tortured gaze lifted and turned to Volshira.

Oleevar sighed. "Shira, I think it may be too soon for you two to reconnect. I know that you have been through a great deal and so has Chrishtan. It may be best for you two to take some time apart."

Volshira looked down. "I understand." Her face drooped in a somber expression that forced a tear from her eye.

Chrishtan hated that he had hurt her. He wanted to help her. He still cared for her. But something about the way he felt when they were together made him feel sick inside. He needed time.

"You don't have to be alone, Shira." Oleevar approached her. "Cohlen and I will keep you company while Chrishtan heals." He took her hand. "Anything you need, please do not hesitate to ask."

Volshira nodded regretfully.

"Cohlen, would you please escort Shira wherever she'd like to go and keep her company? I need to speak with Chrishtan and figure out a way to help him."

Cohlen flashed Oleevar a grim look and then another at Volshira. He looked as if something was weighing on his mind, but no explanation accompanied his skeptical expression.

"Yes Olee, of course. All I want is for Chrishtan to recover. I'll do whatever I can to help."

As Cohlen and Volshira left the room, Chrishtan's gaze returned to its downward plight.

"What's going on, Brother?" Oleevar probed.

Chrishtan rubbed his face with one hand and clenched a fist with the other. "I wish I could tell you. I really do. But I can't explain what's happening to me. It's like the Red Lanterns all over again. All that fear and agony I experienced when we came home. The nightmares, the agitation, the sadness, the loss, the grief, all of it. It's like everything I have done to try and move beyond it has returned tenfold. And somehow, my Lyre is being disrupted by it."

Oleevar shook his head. "I've never heard of Lyre being disrupted in this way. Not by situational variables or human emotion such as this. Never to this degree. There must be something else at play here. Another variable we have not accounted for." Oleevar sat down on Chrishtan's bed. "It may be this Opalz stone."

Chrishtan sat down and joined his brother. "It's a possibility, but I've been wearing it the entire time. The rage, this uncontrollable, unpredictable fury and..."

"And what?" Oleevar's face wrinkled.

"Nothing..." Even speaking of his unwarranted lust for Volshira made Chrishtan feel vile inside. It all began with his vivid and carnal dream the night before her arrival. *It felt so real. Volshira felt so real. Raelle felt even more real...* His mind flashed back to the dreamscape.

"No." Oleevar's probing voice chased the dream away. "Not *nothing*. I must know everything if I am to help you."

"I don't want to hurt her. After everything she's been through because of me. But I..."

"Are you talking about Volshira?" Oleevar asked.

"Yes."

"Yes, I too noticed that much of this began once she arrived here. I think her return is far too much for you to handle right now. Even when you two were together in the past, you did not see eye to eye on a lot of things. I know you loved her, but you fought quite a bit. She can be quite a bit to handle for anyone. But it still doesn't explain the disruption in your Lyre. Is there anything else you need to tell me?"

The troubling memory of his dreamlike encounter with Volshira returned. The light of their Rubiz stones glowed brightly in their lustful embrace. Chrishtan had never experienced anything like it. It was as if her Lyre had sparked a carnal rage within his, as if she could manipulate it. He tried to shut the lustful memory out of his troubled mind. The shame and guilt he felt over the experience outweighed his obligation to Oleevar's inquisition.

"No," answered Chrishtan. "Just that when she is around, I feel the most disrupted. I think I just need more time."

"You're sure that's all?" Oleevar questioned, his eyes still searching for the truth. "There is nothing else going on?"

Chrishtan paused and looked down. "Yes," he sighed. "I think I need to give myself more time to get through this loss before Shira and I reconnect."

"If that's what you truly believe, then I will do whatever I can to make sure you get that time." Oleevar reached into his pocket. "And also, I have more Chocaz blood to expedite the process. Unless of course you do not feel that it was helpful before."

"No, it was."

The pink hue of the rising sun slowly crept in through Chrishtan's window.

Oleevar cleared his throat and Chrishtan could feel his brother's hesitation. "One day from now will be the third day since Raelle's passing, which means her funeral will be held that evening. *And so it shall be that on the third day, all grievances shall be syndicated until they are no more. From grievance end, the soul of the departed shall be reborn in sanctuary. Grieve no more and celebrate life lived. Lose not, grieve not, fear not, for rebirth shall unite us once more.*"

Oleevar's scripture quote did not ease Chrishtan's pain. He knew that it was tradition to hold services on the third day after passing. But he was not ready to say goodbye to Raelle. *Whoever wrote those words must have known something we don't. Three days is nowhere near long enough to grieve. Especially when so many have fallen.* "Of course I will be there."

"Good." Oleevar rose to his feet. "Now let's see if we can get you feeling better before then."

Oleevar handed Chrishtan the small flask filled with orange liquid. Once again, Chrishtan removed the top, drank the fluid, and lay down on his bed.

"I will make it clear to *everyone* that you are not to be

101

bothered," Oleevar said as he moved toward the door. "No interruptions or unexpected guests." His brother's image gradually faded away and Chrishtan slipped back into his Lyre-induced coma.

***

Everything played out in slow motion as the alarming sound of the arrow whizzed past Chrishtan's ear. He watched helplessly as it breached Raelle's armor and penetrated her chest. Her green eyes rolled back into her head before she collapsed into her brother's lap. Chrishtan scooped her incapacitated body from her brother's arms. Her small frame felt like nothing in his warrior hold. Still in slow motion, Chrishtan ran to the Ellios Gates. He hollered at the guards to open them.

"Here!" Zeell hollered as he mounted a hovercraft and pointed at the empty space on the seat behind him.

With Raelle in his arms, Chrishtan hopped onto the vehicle, and together they sped toward the palace. Once inside the healing paddock, Chrishtan found shaman and healers awaiting their first casualty.

"Please!" He rushed inside and laid Raelle down on the first slab. He looked around the room wildly at the healers. "Help her! Somebody!"

The men and women in the room crowded around Raelle, pushing Chrishtan aside as they worked urgently. Chrishtan looked on fretfully as they tried a number of healing practices, but to no avail. Abruptly, the commotion stopped. The healers and shaman stood like they were frozen in time. Their heads hung motionless over Raelle.

"What's happened?" Chrishtan cried. "Why have you stopped? Help her, please!"

All at once, their heads snapped unnaturally into the upright position. Each of them glared at him with eyes like polished black stones. Still they said nothing.

Chrishtan swallowed hard and his body started to tremble. Suddenly, light vanished from the Diamoz fixtures.

Complete blackness engulfed him. Chrishtan froze. The eyes of the Shaman now glowed red. He listened closely to the slight echo of their voices that were now chanting in the old language. With each moment that passed, they grew louder and their eyes glowed brighter. Intense dismay came over him as Raelle slowly sat up, her eyes swirling like a luminescent pool of blood. In her hands, she held a crown. It glowed with red Rubiz gems and oozed with bright red blood. As Raelle made her way toward Chrishtan, her feet slid through the crown's mess of gore.

Chrishtan stumbled backward into the door. It knocked the wind from his lungs. He was trapped. Raelle placed the gruesome crown on his head. Chrishtan felt the blood drip onto his face. With a mouth full of razor sharp teeth, Raelle grinned. Her lips stained with blood, she leaned in to Chrishtan. He tried to turn his head away, but she grasped his chin with her claws. Her lips met with his and the metallic tasted of her kiss was unbearable. With her painful clutch rendering his face immobile, Raelle finally spoke.

"The blood of all shall be none, save one. The blood of the one shall resurrect all and obliterate one. The stone of the one true ruler resurrected."

***

The sound of something in his room startled Chrishtan from his nightmare. It took him several moments to catch his breath and calm his nerves. *The morning is almost here with the third day. Raelle's wake...* As he sat up, his eyes took a moment to adjust to the white light of a crescent moon that poured in through his window. In front of it, a shadowy figure gazed out into the night.

"This place sure is beautiful," the figure said. It was the voice of a woman.

"Who are you?" asked Chrishtan. "Show yourself."

The woman stepped into the light of the moon. Her long auburn hair hung down over her breasts, almost to her navel. Her sheer blue nightgown flowed in the breeze. The enchanting hue of her green eyes sparkled in the radiance of the night.

"Raelle? Is it really you?" Chrishtan's trauma jolted him back into consciousness. The anguish of her death hit him like a felled tree. Each and every breath grew more rapid and his eyes glistened with tears of distress. "This must be a dream," he sniffed.

"This is no dream, my love." A smile crept over Raelle's lips as she approached the bed. "I am real. This is real. *We* are real." She sat down next to him. The soft skin of her hand brushed over Chrishtan's cheek. "Let me take care of you, my love. I am your queen and you are my king. Let us be together for all of eternity."

Chrishtan gently grasped the hand that held his face and brought it to his mouth. He kissed it and inhaled her scent. "You smell different."

"I have been reborn." Raelle crept closer. "I *am* different, but I am also the same."

"But how?" Chrishtan asked.

"It doesn't matter now," she said smoothly. "All that matters is that we are together."

Again he felt it, the intense carnal desire. He wanted Raelle. He needed Raelle. As Chrishtan gazed into her glistening green eyes, logic abandoned him. His emotions took the reins and he pulled her closer. She met him half way, caressing his lips with hers. Holding her firmly in his arms, he gently laid her on the bed. His hands combed through her long silky hair while his hips pressed deep into hers. His passion was hot and his desire unwavering.

"I love you, Raelle," he whispered.

"I know." She smiled and reached down toward Chrishtan's hips.

Suddenly, he felt it. His breath fleeted in one heavy gust. An immense pain in the left side of his ribcage engulfed him and Raelle's green eyes transformed into a pair of deceitful golden irises. Below them, Volshira's devious lips smirked. She quickly pulled the enormous knife from Chrishtan's ribcage and out of his heart.

"I will not compete with a memory for my rightful place.

I will be Queen of Abequa," Volshira decreed. "And *you* and that dirty blood wench will be nothing but a memory."

Chrishtan wheezed. He could feel hot blood pouring from the wound. Volshira haphazardly pushed him off of her, and his slack, incapacitated body lay motionless. Chrishtan had not the breath to utter a single protest. Hovering over him, Volshira's face faded in and out. Her mouth moved rapidly, chanting a diabolical incantation in the old language of their people. With all of his might, he tried as best he could to hold on to his life, but it was no use. With Volshira's last word, Chrishtan let go.

Volshira's sinister voice echoed inside his beleaguered mind. "A prince for a prince. Tis Azmodil, ire demit pem paraso…"

# CHAPTER 11
# REBIRTH

Raelle opened her eyes. With a gasping breath, she sat upright on the slab where she lay. As the air entered her lungs, it felt as if she were taking her first breath after holding it far too long. All around her, potions of different colors lit up the shelves along the bronze walls. Jars of herbs and plants filled in the remaining spaces. The dim glow of the Diamoz lights made it difficult to see anything else.

*Where am I?* she thought.

"Hello?" Her voice was feeble and almost inaudible. "Is anyone there?" Raelle's eyes searched the dimly lit room. "Chrishtan?" Still, no one answered. Raelle looked down and noticed that she was garbed in a beautiful blue silk gown. She felt the subtle pressure of something on her head. With a trembling hand, she reached up to feel a halo of flowers. Her body felt clean and an attractive floral scent blanketed her skin. With halting legs, she pressed her feet to the stone cold floor and attempted to stand.

"Chrishtan?" she called. "Olee? Is anyone there?" Raelle's mind began to race and re-kindled her fear. Once again, she was all alone. Only this time, she had no idea where she was.

The startling sound of a creaking door behind her caused her to lose her footing. One of her hands just barely gripped the slab next to her in time and ended her descent. She wobbled again and steadied herself.

"Who are you?" She heard a voice call from behind her. "How did you get in here? Get away from her!"

Raelle spun around to see Cohlen and Oleevar standing in the doorway. Two small dogs followed behind them. Unlike the two elven men, the dogs did not question Raelle's presence. They rushed toward her with their tails wagging and whimpered wildly until she picked them up. With their little tongues they lapped away the tears from Raelle's face.

Oleevar stepped forward and raised his hands. With his Lyre, he brought more light to the Diamoz fixtures. As he studied Raelle's face, the dogs growled at his confrontational posturing.

"It can't be." Oleevar shifted his inquisitive gaze away from Raelle and over to the slab whence she came. He stared at it for a moment and then shifted back to her. "How is this possible?"

Cohlen had not moved. It was as if he had seen a ghost. "Raelle?" he murmured.

"Yes?" Raelle set the dogs on the floor. She could barely speak.

Cohlen finally moved in close enough to touch her. "It *is* you." He grasped her hand.

Oleevar shook his head. "But this is not possible. We did every test we could think of. You were gone."

*Gone?* Raelle began to panic. *Where did I go? Where am I now?* "Aagh!" Raelle winced. Her muscles felt cold and stiff. Her mind was still very foggy. Nonetheless, Raelle did her best to swallow her fear and find her composure. "Will someone… please… calmly…tell me what the hell is going on?"

Oleevar drew in a bulky breath followed by an equally long sigh. His hands covered his mouth as he sat down on the slab where Raelle had once lain. "It is difficult to say…"

"Difficult to say?" Raelle shook her aching head. "I went to bed last night, and when I woke up, I found myself trapped in this dark tomb. So please, *try* to explain *something* to me, anything."

"All right." Oleevar stood and uncovered his mouth. "Let's start with you and what you remember. Then we can try and explain it the best we know how."

Raelle rubbed her face with both hands. The uneasiness she felt from Oleevar and Cohlen reignited her anxiety. She sensed that something horrible had happened, but she did not know what. It made her stomach turn. Raelle blew out every ounce of air she could before taking another deep breath. "I remember coming here to Ellios with Chrishtan and Cohlen. I remember meeting you and your family. I remember going to bed and waking up in the middle of the night. Chrishtan woke me from my nightmare. He let me sleep in his room so that I'd feel safer. I must have fallen asleep quickly because the next thing I know..." Her gaze shifted to her slab.

Oleevar stood. His face pulled into a deep frown. "So you don't remember anything else?"

"No." Raelle's voice and hands shook as her worries amplified. "Should I?"

"Raelle..." Oleevar took a deep breath and released. "That was three days ago."

"Three days ago?" Raelle gasped. "I've been asleep for three days? But how?"

Cohlen looked down and shook his head. "You weren't asleep."

"Raelle... look at me." Oleevar took her quaking hand. "Three days ago... you were killed."

Raelle pulled away. "What? How?" She shook her head and frantically searched her mind for a memory, a hint, something, anything to help her understand what they were saying. "But— I don't – Then how could I be here now?"

With a somber expression, Cohlen sat down on one of the slabs. "Three days ago, we were attacked. The Huronians came looking for Chrishtan. Lochran sent his new general, the Elite Echo. He challenged Chrishtan to a duel. Chrishtan had nearly defeated him when you ran out onto the battlefield to save—

"Chrishtan!" Oleevar interjected. "You saw that he was in danger. He asked you to stay behind, but you went anyway. When you ran out, you were shot. We tried everything we could to save you, but the arrow stopped your heart on impact."

Cohlen shot Oleevar a peculiar look.

Raelle couldn't decide whether their explanation was making her feel more or less confused. But there was one thing she knew with absolute certainty, she cared for Chrishtan. She needed him. "And Chrishtan? Is he all right?"

"He survived the attack," Cohlen explained. "He was devastated at losing you. We all were."

"Where is he now? I must go to him." Raelle thought that surely Chrishtan could provide her with some clarity. Just being near him always seemed to make her feel better. His energy. His scent. His touch. His smile. It made her feel safe and secure.

Raelle started walking toward the door on unsteady feet. Oleevar grasped her arm as she passed him. "He is in an incredibly fragile state right now. We can't just go bursting in there. When he does finally wake and he is more stable, I will take you to him and we will calmly try to explain to him what is going on."

"And what exactly *is* going on?" Cohlen asked. "There is no explanation for Raelle's return."

"On the contrary little brother, I believe there is," Oleevar countered. "And I think it has something to do with this Opalz stone."

Raelle paused. "What do you mean?"

Oleevar cleared his throat and sat down next to Cohlen. "You see, our scriptures were written during the time of the Opalz stone, when it was more than just a myth. The scripture states, *And so it shall be that on the third day, all grievances shall be syndicated until they are no more. From grievance end, the soul of the departed shall be reborn in sanctuary. Grieve no more and celebrate life lived. Lose not, grieve not, fear not, for rebirth shall unite us once more.* It was a reality then and it is a reality once again. I believe our Lady of the Realm has offered it to us as a means to restore order to our great continent."

Cohlen rubbed his forehead. "So, in the beginning, these were meant as a literal translation? And this whole time our cultures have viewed them as something more metaphorical? Reincarnation of the soul instead of a literal rebirth?"

Oleevar grinned. "Precisely, Brother. So in theory, after three days, anyone in possession of the Opalz stone, *will* come back to life once more. I believe this is how Raelle has returned to us. But, there is only one way to be sure."

Cohlen raised a brow. "And that is?"

"Asking the Lady of the Realm in person, of course," Oleevar answered.

"Right, of course," said Cohlen.

Suddenly, a sharp pain struck the side of Raelle's chest. "Aaagh!" She collapsed to the floor.

"Raelle!" Cohlen rushed to her aid.

Oleevar followed behind. "What's happened?"

"Aaggh." Raelle winced in pain. Her lungs felt like they were collapsing. "I don't know. Something's wrong."

Cohlen gasped and clutched his chest. "I feel it too."

"What is wrong with you two?" Oleevar frowned.

"Something's wrong with Chrishtan. I can feel it." Cohlen shuddered.

"Feel it?" Oleevar's eyes grew wide.

"Ever since I returned from the forest, I've had this connection with him."

"I feel the same." Still clutching her side, Raelle stood with Oleevar's help. "I feel something horrible happening to him!"

Cohlen and Raelle both ran to the mortuary door, leaving a confused Oleevar in their wake.

"But you're going to need the k—"

Raelle heard Oleevar holler something at them as they rushed out of the room.

Raelle and Cohlen raced to the back stairwell. The dogs followed closely behind. Raelle's feebleness made it difficult to scale the surplus of stairs. With each passing moment, her pain and fear intensified. Once they made it to the royal floor, they rushed to Chrishtan's chamber door. Raelle pressed the handle, but the door would not open.

"It's locked!" She felt a pounding panic rising in her chest.

"I forgot," Cohlen said, his breath coming in short bursts between words. "Olee, he has the key."

"Ssssh." Raelle put her hand on his mouth. "I hear something."

"What?"

"Voices." Raelle put her ear to Chrishtan's door. "They're coming from inside."

Cohlen shook his head. "But Chrishtan was alone in there."

Raelle bent down to the keyhole and looked inside. What she saw made her heart sink.

"What is it, Raelle? Who's in there?"

She said nothing as Chrishtan took the red-haired woman in his arms. Raelle could not believe what she was seeing. They kissed passionately as Chrishtan laid the woman on his bed. Raelle's lips quivered as the man she loved made love to someone else. As they did, she could hear the woman chanting, but was unable to make out the words. Raelle wanted more than anything to look away, but something else caught her eye. The crimson-haired woman was reaching for something attached to her leg. *A knife!*

"No, no, no!" Raelle cried and the dogs immediately began barking.

Cohlen grabbed her arm. "What is it?"

"She's going to kill him!"

"What? Who's in there?"

"I don't know who she is!"

"What are you two hollering about?" Oleevar's voice called from down the hall.

"There's a woman in there," Raelle shrieked. "She's going to kill him. Hurry. Open the door!"

Cohlen peeked through the hole. "It's Volshira! Oleevar open it now!"

Oleevar ran to them and pulled the key from his pocket.

"Hurry, Olee!" Cohlen cried.

"I'm trying!" Oleevar fit the key into the slot. With a swift turn, it clicked and he threw the door open.

Inside, the stunning woman with long burgundy hair stood over Chrishtan. In the midst of the dogs barking, Raelle could still hear her chanting eerily in a language she had heard once before, but did not understand. The dogs continued to bark viciously as Volshira spun around. When she dismounted

Chrishtan, Raelle gasped at what she exposed. Chrishtan lay lifeless on his bed in a growing pool of his own blood.

"Shira!" Oleevar cried. "What have you done?"

Raelle rushed toward Chrishtan's incapacitated body.

Volshira lunged forward, stopping Raelle dead in her tracks. "You!" Volshira snarled. "This is your fault. Finally, I'm going to rid the world of you for good!"

Raelle did her best to avoid Volshira's hand, but the warrior was much too quick and Raelle much to drained. Volshira's warrior grip crushed Raelle's throat and slammed her into the marble floor. With her other hand, Volshira grasped at Raelle's ring finger and tried to remove her Opalz infused ring. "This time, it will be permanent!" Volshira snarled and threw the ring across the room.

All of the sudden, Oleevar transformed. He was no longer an elf, but a large grey panther. In his enormous feline form, he leapt onto Volshira's back. He dug his immense claws into her shoulders. Volshira cried out and let go of Raelle. Raelle crawled across the floor toward her ring. As soon as it was securely on her finger, she turned around to see Volshira pull her enormous knife from the band around her leg. She stabbed it into Oleevar's feline ribcage. A pain-stricken roar sounded sharply from his panther throat.

"No!" Cohlen shrieked and he too morphed before Raelle's eyes. But his transformation was no animal. As he hyperventilated, his hands shook violently. His skin became pale and veiny. His fingernails turned to long, sharp, claws and his blue eyes were now black. A demonic screech radiated from Cohlen's mouth that was now filled with rows of razor sharp teeth. Raelle covered her ears and watched in dismay as Cohlen's wraith form jumped into the air toward his brother's attacker.

Volshira pulled the knife from Oleevar's chest and dove into the massive window sill. As she jumped from the window, Cohlen lunged at her with impossible speed. Half way out the window, Cohlen's long serrated claws clutched Volshira's long crimson hair. From the middle story of the palace, he dangled her struggling body over the ground.

"You will pay for what you've done." He hissed and raised a white arm that pulsed with protruding purple veins. In an instant, he swiped his claws across the side of Volshira's face. Fresh red blood seeped from her deep wounds, and shredded skin now hung from her cheek.

Suddenly, Volshira swung with her knife, severing Cohlen's wraith fingers that gripped her hair. As he fell backward into Chrishtan's room, Cohlen shrieked once more like a demon from the Void. Black blood oozed from his fingerless hand as he wailed.

"What in the name of the Architect?" Oleevar's eyes gaped open at his brother's frightening phantom form. Now returned to his elven figure, Oleevar struggled to stand. With one of his hands, he covered his bleeding wound.

Raelle turned back toward Cohlen. She watched as his wraith hand gradually grew a new set of fingers. Once fully healed, Cohlen shifted back to his elven form and his unconscious head hit the marble floor.

"Oleevar." Raelle rushed to her friend. "Are you all right?"

"Yes, the wound is not lethal as long as I keep pressure on it. She missed my major organs."

Before Oleevar could finish his explanation, Raelle rushed to Chrishtan's side. The dogs did the same. They licked Chrishtan's face to try to wake him.

"No, please no." Raelle pressed her head to his chest. She heard nothing. "No, no, no!" she cried.

"Move aside." Still holding his own wound, Oleevar pushed Raelle away from Chrishtan's side.

Raelle cradled Chrishtan's head in her hands. She knew that losing Chrishtan, on top of everything else she had gone through, would surely break her. He was all that she had left. She sobbed loudly and watched in trepidation as Oleevar did everything he could to restart Chrishtan's heart.

The elf carefully examined Chrishtan's fatal injury. "I'm so sorry, Raelle." Tears welled in Oleevar's golden brown eyes. "He's gone. The knife stopped his heart immediately, and even if it hadn't, he has lost far too much blood."

A waterfall of tears cascaded down Raelle's face as she eyed the blood-soaked blankets. She smoothed her hand over Chrishtan's face and through his hair. "I'm so sorry. If only I'd gotten to you sooner." Raelle attempted to speak again through her sobs, but her words were indiscernible. She embraced Chrishtan's cold body and pressed her lips to his. Her sobs grew so loud that it sounded as if she too had been stabbed. Raelle allowed the grief to take over. It engulfed her like flames and the anguish burned through her. Inside, she too was dying. Without Chrishtan, she was once again alone in the world. Chrishtan had understood her, accepted her, and appreciated her for who she was. He had saved her in more ways than one. But now, Chrishtan was gone and Raelle felt more empty than ever.

Oleevar left the bed to shut and lock the chamber door. As he did, Cohlen began to stir. The dogs jumped from the bed to greet their waking friend. Oleevar offered his brother a hand and helped him up from the floor. Raelle's moans drew Cohlen's distraught gaze. As Cohlen approached the bed, he harbored a look of intense devastation. He sat down next to Raelle and embraced her with both arms. She reciprocated his hold and buried her head in his chest.

"I can still feel his pain," she sobbed.

"I know," Cohlen sniffled. "I know."

The sound of Oleevar's voice lifted Raelle's head. "Yes, it is true that our brother has been taken from us." He attempted to stop his own tears. "But if my theory is correct, he *will* return to us, just as Raelle has. He is still wearing his ring."

For a moment, the hope that Chrishtan still might return to her allowed Raelle to calm some of her nerves and ease some of her grief. "I hope and pray that you're right." She shut her eyes tight and squeezed out her remaining tears. "But something feels horribly wrong. It's as if Chrishtan's suffering is still alive within me."

Cohlen released his embrace and looked in Raelle's eyes. "I can feel it, too."

"You can?" asked Raelle.

"Yes," Cohlen answered. "When he rescued me from the Void, it's like he gave me a part of himself. Many of the memories I have are his memories. Most of the things I know, I learned through his experiences. The things I see in my head are through his eyes. It may be the same for you."

Raelle cringed. "It's like I can feel what he felt. It's almost unbearable."

"Listen, you two." Oleevar approached them. "I don't mean to trivialize what you are going through, but we need to come up with a plan and fast. No one, I repeat, no one, can know about this. We must keep it a secret. If word got out about the power of this stone and its immortal properties, there are people who would kill us to get it. Which means we must go through with Raelle's rebirth procession as planned. Even mother and father cannot know about this. We want it to be as believable as possible."

Raelle's brow furrowed. "Rebirth procession?"

"Yes, when someone dies, after three days we hold a ceremony. We celebrate the life that was lost and say our goodbyes. Then, we float the body out onto the lake on a bed of kindle. Once in the center of the lake, an arrow is launched and the body is cremated. Their body and Lyre is then recycled back into the soil at the bottom and their soul is *reborn* inside the Architect's light."

Cohlen turned to his brother. "But how are we going to go through with the ceremony when Raelle is still alive?"

"Well," Oleevar said with a shrug, "we're going to have to replace her body with someone else's."

Cohlen stared wide-eyed at his brother.

"Don't worry." Oleevar patted his brother on the back. "I'll take care of it."

"And Chrishtan?" Cohlen asked. "What do we do about him?" Cohlen looked doubtfully at Chrishtan's motionless body.

"We find a replacement for him as well. Then, we

announce his murder to the city and hold a ceremony. It will give people more fuel to rally behind us. In the meantime, we hide him somewhere until he is resurrected. Then, we proceed on our journey to the Lantern Forest."

"Whatever you say." Cohlen sighed and shook his head.

"Look, Cohlen." Oleevar crossed his arms. "I know this may make you uncomfortable, but it's something we must do. Proceeding with the ceremony will ensure our security. Once word gets out that both Raelle and Chrishtan are dead, it will keep Lochran off our backs for a time. He will see it as a victory. He'll let his guard down. We let things go quiet, giving him a false sense of security. Then, when he least expects it, we strike."

Raelle wiped the wet mess from her face. "It makes sense," she agreed. "I'll do whatever it takes to avenge my family and Chrishtan."

Cohlen glared at his brother. "See, Olee, *she'll* do whatever it takes to avenge her *family*."

Raelle was not sure what Cohlen meant by that, but she could sense the tension between them. There was something they were not saying. "Is everything all right with you two? Something I should know about?"

"Yes, of course, we're fine." Oleevar answered. "Nothing else you need to know."

Cohlen said nothing, but he pursed his lips.

"You're sure?" Raelle was not entirely convinced. *If Chrishtan trusted them, I should be able to as well… right? I sure hope so, because they're all I've got now.* The thought made her feel sick inside.

"Yes, of course I'm sure," answered Oleevar, but his brother just rolled his eyes. "Now Raelle." Oleevar continued as if everything were fine. "You're going to need to stay hidden until we leave for the Lantern Forest."

"Of course," said Raelle. "I'll do whatever it takes to help Chrishtan."

"I have the perfect location." Oleevar turned toward the door. "I'll take you there now." He paused and removed his hand from his wound. Blood had seeped through his clothes and covered his hand. "Come, hurry. I must get this stitched up."

Cohlen, Raelle, and her two dogs followed Oleevar through what seemed like miles of long corridors and passageways. After a long period of sneaking around corners and avoiding palace staff, they finally stopped in front of a large painting. On its canvas was the glowing city of Ellios underneath an enormous full moon. Oleevar raised the Chocaz stone on his necklace alongside the Emeralz of his Lyre-harness ring. As Oleevar moved the gems closer to the top of the painting, the lights of the city began to glow until they were blinding. At their brightest, Raelle heard a loud click. Oleevar opened the painting as if it were a door and stepped inside.

"This way," he motioned. "I'm taking you to my secret lab. I develop my greatest concepts and designs here. No one else knows that it exists, except for the two of you now, of course."

They followed Oleevar down a spiral staircase made of bronze, held together by oversized bronze nuts and bolts. At the bottom of the stairwell, they were met with an equally sturdy bronze door. Oleevar pressed his thumb into the lever and closed his eyes. Raelle watched intently as his Emeralz stone illuminated the doorway.

*Someday soon, I'll be able to call upon my own Lyre,* Raelle thought. *And once I'm able, I will avenge my family.*

Oleevar opened the door to reveal a circular room filled with soil samples, Lyre gemstones, glowing liquids inside transparent bottles, and other bizarre items. Oleevar immediately opened a drawer and removed a needle and thread to stitch his injury. While he sewed, Raelle observed all the strange gizmos and gadgets. She could have never imagined most of them. Some of them made odd noises in their unfamiliar processes. Along the walls, Oleevar had posted diagrams, notes, and concept drawings of notions that Raelle knew she would never be able to understand. Even though the room had no windows, bright Diamoz lights illuminated it in a way that made it seem as if the sun were pouring in.

In the far corner of the room, Raelle eyed a cozy bed of green sheets and fluffy feather-stuffed pillows. *Olee must spend a great deal of time down here,* she thought. *He's really gone out of his way to make it feel cozy.* Raelle made her way toward the bed and sat down atop its comfy surface. Pip and Sasha eagerly wagged their tails before hopping up alongside her and rolling all over the blankets.

"Please, feel free to make yourself at home." Oleevar winced as he snipped the last stich. "I only ask that you do not touch anything. I have many important projects I am working on down here." He shifted and pointed to a hallway. "There is a washroom over there, which has both cold and warm water. Another one of my many advances. Either Cohlen or myself will bring you food and drink whenever you should need it."

"Olee…" Raelle cleared her throat and did her best to hold back her tears. "Who was that assassin? She knew who *I* was."

Oleevar swallowed hard and looked at Cohlen. They exchanged regretful glances before both looking down.

Raelle raised her voice. "Who was that assassin?" she repeated.

Oleevar let out a long breath and finally spoke. "Her name is Volshira and she's not really an *assassin*, per se."

"Per se?" Raelle scowled.

"She is, or I guess I should say *was*, a friend of Chrishtan's… and of ours. She was like a sister to us in many ways."

Raelle shook her head. "Then *why* would she kill Chrishtan?"

"I don't know," Oleevar said, harboring a look of bewilderment. "And frankly, I'm still in shock over the whole thing. Until two nights ago, we thought her dead. She had been killed over a year ago trying to protect Chrishtan. Her body was never found."

"I told you something was not right," Cohlen said to Oleevar. "I felt it. I felt what Chrishtan felt. I didn't know the woman. The only gauge I had of her were my feelings and

Chrishtan's memories. But you reassured me that it was fine. That she *could* be trusted. So, I dropped it."

"Honestly, Brother, you're right," said Oleevar. "Something was up. And in the beginning, when she first arrived, I felt it too. But then, something happened. I suddenly felt at ease. My suspicions faded and I formed an overwhelming sense of trust and security with her. I felt almost bonded to her. After all, she was like a sister to us. But now that I look back, she was acting incredibly strange. Not like herself at all. But for some reason, I did not care. I did not question it. I did not see it. It was as if my mind was in a fog. But I see it now, clear as ever."

"There is more to this that you're not saying." Raelle said, flustered. "When I saw the two of them in Chrishtan's room. They were—

Raelle choked up. She could not bring herself to say it. She had witnessed the man she loved making love to another woman. "He was in love with her... wasn't he?" Raelle did her best to hide the pain, but her quivering lips and wet eyes could not lie.

"Yes," answered Oleevar. "At one time, very much so. They were incredibly close. But they never saw eye to eye. They were complete opposites. And after a time, Chrishtan pushed her away, but Shira never gave up on him. Not for a moment."

"Then— Then *why* would she kill him?" Raelle strained to ask. She needed answers and she needed them now. Her entire world had been turned upside-down once again. Everything she thought she understood. Everyone she thought she knew. The clarity she thought she had found had been shattered into a million pieces and she needed to put it back together. "You say she was acting strange? How? If she cared for him so much... he was such a good and solid person. Why would she—

"He is," Oleevar interrupted. "You're right. And I think that was part of the problem."

Raelle tilted her head. "What do you mean?"

"Shira was always such a tough and severe woman," Oleevar explained. "I think she blamed it on her family being killed during Lochran's insurgence. And I think that is what drew

Chrishtan to her in the first place." Oleevar paced. "Like him, she was Abequan. She was one of *his* people. And like her, he had lost his entire family. I think he felt that he needed to save her. But I'm not sure Volshira wanted to be saved. I think what she wanted was vengeance. They argued about it a great deal when they were together."

Raelle swallowed and looked down, "How long were they together?"

"Ever since we were kids. It continued to get more serious as we aged, but Chrishtan also put more distance between them as he matured. They could not see eye to eye on their philosophies. Chrishtan was never a man of vengeance."

Raelle shook her head. "He never mentioned her."

"Meeting you was probably the first time he felt that he was completely over her," Oleevar rebutted. "You helped him move on. I believe it was something he desperately longed for. He took Shira's death pretty hard. He felt guilty for distancing himself from her. It may have been difficult for him to talk about."

"So, I was a replacement? A tool to help him get over her?"

"No, that's not what I'm saying." Oleevar paused his pacing to shrug. "I just think that meeting you and falling for you helped him to see that he and Shira weren't meant to be. That he was meant for more. That Shira's vengeance was not the only road to salvation and saving his people. He could finally say goodbye to her forever."

Raelle released a long breath and rolled her eyes. "That's really not helping."

"Look." Oleevar lowered his brow. "Although Shira grew up with us, she became a tyrant. In my opinion, she manipulated Chrishtan into loving her. She guilted him constantly. And when he put distance between them, I think it made her feel like she had lost some of her power. And she needed power, Chrishtan's power, so that one day she could take her revenge on Lochran. Chrishtan was and still is the rightful heir to the Abequan throne. Through him, she could inevitably gain power and position. So in spite of him distancing himself from her and their many disagreements, she remained incredibly loyal to him. She would protect Chrishtan at any cost. And like I said, up until a few days ago, we all thought her dead."

Raelle got up from the bed. The thought that Chrishtan's death could have been prevented frustrated her. "If you knew all this about her, then why did you not keep a closer eye on her after her return? Cohlen said he felt uneasy about her."

"It's like I said," Oleevar retorted. "I can't explain it. It was as if my mind was in a fog. Maybe even under someone else's control. Maybe hers. But I have no idea how that is possible. Not to mention, if I hadn't seen her kill him with my own eyes, I'd never believe it. She may have been a difficult woman, but she always loved Chrishtan. She always put him before herself."

A twinge of resentment stung Raelle. The fact that Chrishtan had such a history with a woman like this made her feel as if she never knew him at all. "Well if she ever cared for him at all, I don't see how she could do what she did. If murdering someone you care for is your only way of gaining power, then that power isn't worth it."

Oleevar shrugged and returned to pacing. "I'm not sure what her intentions were in coming here. I'm not sure she intended on killing him. I know she cared for Chrishtan very much. Something may have happened that made her feel like she had no other choice."

Cohlen inhaled a sudden, sharp breath. Raelle noticed the color drain from his face. "I hate to say this, but I think she was set on eliminating Raelle."

Oleevar raised a brow. "What do you mean?"

Cohlen bit his lip in contemplation. "During the attack on Ellios, a female Abequan warrior gave the order to shoot Raelle. I saw it. I mean, I couldn't see her face because she was wearing a helmet, but it must have been her. I truly believe it was."

"It could have been," Oleevar said.

"But, how could she have known who *I* was?" Raelle asked nervously.

"I don't know," Cohlen replied. "Maybe because of your br—"

"It—it doesn't matter," Oleevar cut in. "Speculating about unknowns is not going to give us any real answers. The Huronians came here to destroy us. Weapons were fired, Raelle took an arrow. These things happen. We need to focus on the here and now."

Cohlen scowled at his brother, but said nothing. He crossed his arms and looked down, avoiding both Oleevar and Raelle's gazes. Once again, Raelle felt an uneasiness between them.

"Is there something I should know? Something else someone failed to mention?" she asked. "You two are acting very strange." Raelle felt a gnawing in the pit of her stomach. She was almost certain they were keeping something from her. Her trust in everyone continued to waver. And it all began with what she had seen through the key hole. It humiliated her. She felt silly and naïve. Her whole entire life, people had kept things from her. *I thought Chrishtan was different... did he not trust me? Do Olee and Cohlen not trust me?*

Cohlen glared at his brother, but still said nothing.

Raelle raised her voice. "What is it that you're not telling me?"

"Nothing," Oleevar finally answered. "We're fine. Just some brother stuff we need to work out. That's all."

Raelle furrowed her brow. She could tell he was still holding back, but she did not wish to waste any more time pushing the issue. Maybe it was something between brothers, but still she hated being on the outside. "I see. Well, I hope you do work it out because there is a great deal depending on us."

"Yes, you're right," agreed Oleevar. "Which is why we must stay focused and not allow our *feelings* to get in the way." He made a face at Cohlen as if to scold him.

Still Cohlen did not respond.

Oleevar approached Raelle. "It is pertinent that you stay hidden," he said, his voice weighty. "Please, do not leave my laboratory. If you need anything, either Cohlen or I will get it for you. In the meantime, just rest and take care of yourself. You're going to need all your strength for our journey to the Lantern Forest. Cohlen and I will take care of everything else. We will tell our parents about Chrishtan, show them the scene and proceed with all of the rebirth procession arrangements. Tomorrow, we will switch the bodies and bring Chrishtan here. I have a temperature controlled and sealed room where his body can remain intact while we wait."

Although Raelle was still unsure whether to trust Oleevar, she nodded a silent agreement. She had no other choice. Unlike the naïve girl who left the valley, Raelle now knew with certainty that it would be impossible to take on her enemies alone.

Oleevar took her hand. "You're sure you're up for this?"

"I have no other choice," Raelle answered. "I'll do what I must to help Chrishtan and the people of Mirilan." The thought of the boys leaving caused her to shiver. All though they had kept something from her and made her feel like an outsider, it did not pain Raelle as much as the thought of being left alone again. *I have to do this for myself and Chrishtan. For my people. Olee and Cohlen will be back to check on me. It'll be fine. I'm safe here...*

"Raelle?" Oleevar reiterated. "Do you need anything?"

"No... um... I think I have everything I need for now. Thank you."

"I do have a little something for you." Oleevar walked over to one of the bronze cupboards and opened it. Inside, Raelle saw vials of all sizes filled with a rainbow of different color liquids. From the top shelf, Oleevar grabbed a swampy green one.

"Here we are." He made his way back and handed her the vial. "This will help ease a bit of your pain, both physical and mental. You'll take a nice long nap and wake up feeling much better, I promise."

Cohlen nodded at Raelle and smiled as if to say, *It's all right. Go ahead and drink it.* He then helped Raelle and the dogs get tucked into bed while Oleevar straightened up a few things around his lab. Eventually, they said their goodbyes and bid Raelle goodnight.

With the boys gone, the silence ate away at her. It amplified the fact that she was truly alone. Raelle had lost the last person who had sincerely meant something to her, Chrishtan. In spite of his deceit and unfaithfulness, she still cared for him. Maybe even loved him. She resented the power he had over her. Tears fled her heartbroken eyes and whimpers slipped from her pursed lips. Memories of her first encounters with Chrishtan flashed into her mind. The meddlesome and handsome stranger who had refused to leave her alone. The man who nursed her back to health in spite of not knowing her or owing her a thing. His sly and attractive smirk. His sarcastic and teasing nature that reminded Raelle so much of her brothers, Samuel and Browden. The confident way he carried himself. The touch of his hand. The roughness of his beard as it rubbed against her cheek. The soft caress of his lips that made her feel more alive than ever before.

*He will return and explain himself.* Raelle tried to reassure herself, but it did not help. Instead, the image of Chrishtan's lifeless body atop blood soaked sheets shook her mind. Memories and visions of all that had happened to her and her family were not far behind. Raelle's whimpers soon evolved to sobs that vibrated deep within her throat. Fear and panic smothered her like the fire that had once engulfed her family's home. Images of dripping blood, mutilated bodies, and the murderous Minotirr played on and on. Without Chrishtan, she was truly alone with only her disturbing remembrances to keep her company. Raelle knew that if she could not take control of her thoughts and learn to meditate, she would surely come undone.

Raelle popped the cork from the vial Oleevar had given her, and swallowed the swampy fluid. It tingled as it ran down her throat and into her empty gut. She lay her head back down on the pillow and pulled Pip and Sasha close. Once again, Raelle felt as if she were back inside her nightmare, confused, alone, and afraid.

\*\*\*

Cohlen followed his brother in a brisk pace down the hall.

"Olee!" Cohlen called. "You must slow down. We need to talk."

Oleevar did not stop or turn around to address his brother. "I don't have time for this, Cohlen. I have important things to attend to before Chrishtan's return. You know that. Your job is to take care of Raelle until then."

Cohlen ran up behind his brother. With a firm grip he seized Oleevar's arm. "No, Olee. I'm not doing this." He spun his brother around.

"Look, Brother." Oleevar flashed a patronizing grin. "I understand that you and I need some time to talk. I've missed you too. And I'm thrilled that you're home. And I'm sure you want to talk about your new ability. I can see how shifting into a wraith can be rather frightening, but right now we have some other incredibly pressing matters to take care of."

"Yes, I understand that." Cohlen looked in his brother's eyes. He wanted nothing more than for his brother to validate him. But just like when they were children, Oleevar only saw him as a naïve little boy who would never be as smart as his brother. Or at least, that is how he made Cohlen feel. "I'm not as dense as you think I am. Yes, I am disturbed by my new ability, but I will come to terms with it, somehow. But what I really want to know is why we're lying to Raelle."

"About?"

"Oh, come now, you know precisely what I'm talking about. You lied to her about her brother." Cohlen couldn't believe his brother was pretending that he hadn't lied to Raelle.

Oleevar averted his gaze. "I did nothing of the sort. I did not even mention him."

*Now he's lying to me, too?* "Exactly." Cohlen released a frustrated breath. "You made no mention of him or the situation. You told her that she ran out there after Chrishtan."

"Well, that is why she went out there... originally." Oleevar squeezed his brother's shoulders and gazed into his eyes. "It is not yet the time to tell Raelle about her brother. You saw how she reacted the last time she found out he was alive. He is a distraction to her. When it comes to him, she shows no rational thought. She would put her life and ours in danger again if she knew he was still alive."

"But she has a right to know."

"Yes, you're right. She does," said Oleevar. "But now is not the time. Raelle is weak. She is untrained. And she's exceedingly vulnerable. If she found out about her brother, she'd leave here right now and go to Huronus to try and rescue him. I cannot allow her to do that in her current state. She must train her Rogue skills first and learn to properly harness her Lyre. Then and only then will she stand a chance to save her brother and not to mention, stay alive long enough to help the rest of us."

"Now that you've told me about your plan, it makes sense," Cohlen said. Even though he saw the logic of Oleevar's plan, something still bothered him. "But I shouldn't have had to force you to talk to me about it. You've never respected me, Olee. If we are to be a team, then I must know everything you're thinking and planning. And maybe, just maybe, I can offer some input of my own. I'm grown now, just like you. And I expect to be treated as such, with your respect."

"I understand." Oleevar said ruefully. "And I am sorry. This is just the way I am. It's the way I've always been. I assure you that you're not the only person I treat this way. But, you are my brother and I love you. So I will make a special effort to try and be more respectful and communicate more efficiently." Oleevar hugged his brother. "I've missed you, Brother. And I cannot express in words how having you back has made me whole again."

His brother's words brought tears to Cohlen's eyes. "Thank you, Olee. I love you. And I know that if we stick together, we can do this. All of it."

Oleevar ended their embrace. "We *will* do this, Cohlen. And once you and Raelle have completed enough training, we will get her brother back. I already promised Chrishtan, and I'm promising you now. But we are no good to Samuel until we are all strong enough to endure the worst in order to get to him and the other heirs. Until then, he will have to make his own decisions and choose his own fate. We've all had to do it."

# CHAPTER 12
## CHOICES

Samuel's pounding head resuscitated his consciousness. He tried to sit up, but his shaking arms were far too weak. With his blurred vision, he could barely make out the woman walking toward him. With gentle hands, she helped him sit up on the cot and lean against a cold stone wall. Samuel squinted hard enough to see that the woman had long black hair and bright blue eyes. She held something in her hand. It was a cup. She handed it to Samuel, and he slowly drank the cold water. With each second that passed his vision gradually returned to him and revealed that he was now locked in a dungeon cell.

The black-haired woman sat down next to him. Samuel eyed the wrinkles and lines of her face. She was at least twice his age. With her hand, the woman caressed Samuel's cheek. Her glossy blue eyes looked deep into his. Tears quickly began to fall over her high cheekbones. Suddenly, the woman leaned in and embraced Samuel with both arms. She keened out deep sobs. Samuel had no idea who the woman was, but he felt a strong need to comfort her. It was as if she had been holding in her sorrow for years. Samuel reciprocated her embrace.

"It's all right," he consoled. "It's going to be all right. Sssssh."

When their embrace ended, she held Samuel's face in her hands and gazed into his eyes once more.

"Who are you?" Samuel did not blink.

The woman pointed to her mouth and shook her head. Behind her, he saw a familiar black dress and veil hanging on the wall.

"My father's companion?"

The woman nodded. *Yes.*

"You were trying to communicate with me at dinner, weren't you?"

The woman nodded again. *Yes.*

"You were trying to warn me."

*Yes,* she nodded. Then she pointed to Samuel and back to herself. Finally she put both hands on her heart.

"What are you trying to tell me?"

The woman made her motions once more. Only this time she pointed back to him before making a cradling motion with her arms.

"Me and you... and a baby?"

The woman smiled and nodded. She tried to mouth the words. *You.* She pointed to Samuel. *My.* And back to herself. *Baby.* She made the cradling motion once more.

The realization crushed Samuel like a toppling stone wall. "I'm... your... baby?"

The woman smiled and nodded profusely.

"But if you're my mother, why can't I sense it?"

She pulled up the sleeve on her left arm and then his. Hers harbored a nasty scar. Samuel's looked as if it had recently been cut open and stitched. He had not noticed the throbbing pain until now.

"What did he do to us?" Samuel examined the wound. "He put something in there, didn't he?"

His mother nodded.

Samuel grimaced. "It disrupts our Lyre—

Like a blow to the head, Samuel's headache returned in a shock wake of pain throughout his entire body. "Aagh!"

His mother gasped and he could finally see why she was unable to speak. Her tongue had been completely removed. It horrified him. She held him close and tried to massage his head.

"Why? Why did he do this to you, mother?" Samuel cried. "He lied. He said you had been killed—

It hit him once more, like a bomb had gone off inside his head. Suddenly, he lost control. His body began to shake and quickly progressed into convulsions. Everything soon went black.

***

Samuel woke on the timber-thatched floor of a treehouse. Even though his eyes were open, he could barely see his

129

surroundings. But his instincts instantly remembered the layout of the woody stronghold. A pale red light seeped in through the windows along with a thick fog. A slight throbbing still bumped inside his head. As he stood on his wobbling knees, the sound of a mournful coo of a child echoed in through the window. Samuel froze. He looked around the inside of the tree fort, but did not see anyone.

"Hello?" he called. No one answered.

Still the woeful whimper of the child seeped into his ear. Samuel tread as softly as he could over the branch woven floor of the familiar treehouse and out onto the deck. The sound of branches cracking beneath his feet did not offer enough warning. With a thud, he hit the leafy ground face first. Woody shrapnel rained over him. As he spit dirt and dead leaves from his mouth, the crunch of the dirt between his teeth caused him to shudder. When Samuel finally lifted his head, he saw a young boy hunched over a short distance away. Lingering sobs echoed again from the boy.

Samuel got up once more on his quaking limbs, shaking off the remaining leaves and shards of bark. He gazed upward at the eerie sky. A blood-red moon, of imposing size, hung low in the wine-red sky. A miniscule cry drew his gaze back in the direction of the boy.

"Hello?" Samuel stepped toward the distressing sound. "Are you hurt?" He stopped at the boy's back and squatted down. In the scarlet light of the moon, he was able to make out the boy's shaggy blond hair. With his hand, he gently squeezed the boy's shoulder. "Do you need help?"

The boy slowly nodded, *yes.*

"Here." Samuel offered his hand. "Let me help you up." Samuel reached his arms around to assist the boy and his hands felt something else. The boy was carrying something large. Samuel walked around to the other side to face him. The boy held an enormous boulder. It was so big that Samuel did not see how it was possible that he held it on his own.

"I just wanted to play," the boy sniffled.

Samuel studied the boy further. His voice sounded eerily familiar.

Finally, the child looked him in the eye. "but she won't follow the rules."

Samuel gasped. His own twelve-year-old eyes glared back at him. On the ground, he saw what the boy had been huddled over. Raelle's teenage body lay lifeless, crushed on the forest floor.

"She has to be punished." The twelve-year-old version of Samuel raised the boulder above his head.

"No!" Samuel yelled. But it was too late. The adolescent Samuel smashed the boulder down on top of his sister and then disappeared.

Samuel immediately lifted the boulder from his sister and threw it into the woods. He scooped Raelle's crushed body from the forest floor and held her in his lap.

"No, please no." He cradled the young Raelle in his arms. "No, Sister, no!" Hot tears gushed from Samuel's eyes. He closed them tight and held his sister close. "Why?" he cried. "Why?" He looked down once again at the lifeless body in his arms, but it was no longer Raelle. Instead, Samuel now held his own broken childhood body. Suddenly, his youthful double opened its eyes. Its hand shot up, grasping Samuel's adult face tight with its hands.

"Help me!" the boy version cried. "Please!" Young Samuel began to cough. Blood projected from his mouth and dripped over his chin. "I don't want to die here," he pleaded.

Terror seethed through him as his childhood form suffered in his arms. Samuel froze in shock. His breaths drew closer and closer together.

All of the sudden, a shadow stood over him. "*You* can't save him." A woman's smooth voice slithered into his ear. "But *I* can."

Samuel looked up to see the silhouette of a woman. Her large headdress and wings loomed over both of them. She offered her hand.

"Who are you?" Samuel cried.

"I," the woman spoke with conviction, "am the one person who can save you. I am the one you can trust, my love."

Samuel did not blink. "Volshira?"

"Yes." Volshira helped him to stand. "It was a heavy debt you owed him, but I have paid your bail to Azmodil. Your life no longer belongs to him."

"Paid my debt?" Samuel still held the incapacitated boy close.

"Yes." Volshira coaxed. "Look." She caressed the face of the boy that Samuel held so tightly.

Samuel looked down. The boy he held no longer resembled his childhood self. Instead, a boy with brown shaggy hair lay motionless in his arms. After a number of fierce coughs, the boy's blue eyes shot open.

"Help!" the boy gasped and blood oozed from the corner of his mouth. "Please!"

Samuel did not recognize him.

"Give him to me." Volshira stretched out her arms. "He has paid your debt. Only I can ease his pain now." She stepped into the light of the red moon. For the first time, Samuel noticed that her fingernails looked more like talons than human nails. The left side of her enormous golden headpiece came down over her head and face like a mask, stopping just above her top lip. The intricate layers of gold fit her head perfectly. At the top, the layers came together to form rows of tall, sharp, spires ran down the center of her head. Large black feathers protruded from between the spikes. But on her right side, her face and hair were completely exposed. Her long crimson locks fell flawlessly around her gorgeous face and over her shoulder. Underneath, elaborate gold shoulder armor reflected the moon's rosy glow. Her ornate armor was decorated with runes and covered almost her entire body from neck to toe. But still, it complimented the flawless definition and curvature of her muscular physique. Only portions of her arms and mid-section were exposed, leaving her carved abdomen completely bare. Blowing in the hot breeze, a long, red, satin train flowed behind her. Her vibrant and lavish swords sat sheathed on either hip. The Rubiz gems on their hilts glowed.

Samuel squinted hard at the black feathery wings that adorned her back.

"Give the boy to me, Samuel." Volshira grasped again with her talons. "Let me ease his pain."

Samuel gazed into Volshira's exposed golden eye. It shimmered in the light of the moon. After she retracted her talons, Volshira gently grasped Samuel's trembling arm. Even though he was terrified, somehow her touch made him feel at ease.

"Give him to me," she whispered in Samuel's ear.

Volshira's voice seemed to hypnotize him and eased Samuel's grip into a slow surrender. His arms gave way, and he ceded the boy to Volshira's clutches.

The gut-wrenching sound of the boy's cries woke Samuel from his trance.

"Samuel!" the boy pleaded. "Help me! Please!"

"Who are you?" Samuel demanded.

"He is no one," Volshira hissed. "He is nothing but a memory."

Samuel panicked. He leapt for the boy, but it was too late. The wings on Volshira's back spanned out over him. Samuel looked on in awe as black-feathered wings flapped behind her. As Volshira took flight, the boy screamed and flailed in her arms.

"Tell Raelle!" the boy's voice trailed off. "Find her in the Verge! Tell her where I am!"

"Raelle?" Samuel's breaths grew hard and short. "You know where she is?" He ran after Volshira, trying not to lose sight of her in the blood-red sky above. Samuel paused only when he came upon a glowing path. Paved with hot red coals, the trail seemed to lead in the same direction as Volshira. Samuel gently pressed one foot to the smoldering road.

"Aagh!" Samuel's bare foot throbbed from the burn. He looked around to see if he could find another way. Nothing. The rest of the forest was a tangled mess of massive thorny branches woven together in a giant knot. Samuel took in as much breath as he could. Before stepping back out onto the burning road, he released it all. As fast as he could, he sprinted and stinted over the coals, trying not to let his feet touch the path for more than a second. The pain was almost unbearable, but he knew he had to get to the boy and discover the location of his sister. He would do whatever it took to get back to her.

After what felt like an endless uphill race, Samuel found himself standing in front of an enormous castle. Like the searing coals that led him there, the castle radiated a hot, fiery glow. Samuel stopped at the bottom of an enormous set of black, shiny stairs. At the very top, he could see Volshira's winged silhouette. She was no longer armored. Instead, she wore a stunning red dress. Its sheer material flowed in the hot breeze.

"I knew you could make it," she called down to him. "You are strong and tenacious, my love. You will make a great king."

"Where are we?" Samuel shouted as he ran up the steps to meet her. "What is this place? How did I get here?"

Volshira took Samuel's hand and helped him up the final step. "This is the Verge," Shira explained. "It is the place between the world of the living and of the dead."

"So am I dead?" Samuel asked.

"No." Volshira shook her head. "You are alive. Your physical body is still on Lerim. Your astral body is here."

Samuel and Volshira stopped at the massive double doors of the palace. "Did *you* bring me here?"

"No," Volshira clarified. "It was Azmodil who brought you here." She opened the doors with her black Opalz and entered.

Samuel followed closely behind. "Because I owed him my life? For not following through with turning Raelle?"

"Yes, but that debt has been paid. I took care of it."

"You gave him someone else's life? That boy, who was he? He knows my sister. Where is he now?" Samuel trailed Volshira through dark and narrow corridors. As they made their way through, Samuel swore that he could hear the faint cries of men, women, and children. But when he stopped to focus on them, they ceased.

"You don't need *him* to find your sister, Samuel. You need only *me*." Her voice hypnotized once more, easing his concern..

"You know where Raelle is? The boy said she was here, in the Verge."

"The *boy* was wrong. She is not here. She is alive on Lerim. And if you wish to be with her again, then you must do as I tell you."

"How do you know she's alive?"

"I can show you." Volshira stopped at the end of a hall at a blood-red door. She opened it to reveal a chamber bedroom decorated in extravagant gold furniture with red upholstery. An enormous circular bed made up in matching colors sat at the center of the room.

"Come." Volshira motioned him to the far corner of the room to a lavishly carved basin. Inside, black liquid filled it with a flat calm.

"What is this?"

"It's a fenazra, a window to another's world."

"And how does it work?"

"Like this." Volshira took Samuel's hand. With one of her talons, she pierced a tiny hole in his finger.

"What are you doing?" Samuel yanked his hand away.

"You are Raelle's blood relative. If we wish to see her, then we must pay the fenazra with her blood, or the blood of her blood."

Samuel swallowed hard. He had only just learned that his own father was a patron of the darkness. Lochran too had tricked him into using his own blood to "turn" his sister. Was Volshira an agent of his father? Was she too corrupted by evil? Samuel wanted nothing more than to trust her. When he was with her, he felt safe and secure. His feelings for her seemed to defy his logic. But still, his anger allowed his guard to remain intact.

"Go ahead." Volshira pulled Samuel's hand back toward the fenazra. "Squeeze some into the fenazra. You can trust me,

Samuel. How many times have I saved your life? You know how much I care for you."

Samuel released a long sigh. Volshira was right. She had protected him and helped him. But she had also taken him from his sister and left him to his father without warning. "You have been the one person I can count on. But look at you, Shira. What have you become? You are a loyal servant of my father. And—"

"No." Volshira stopped him. "I am loyal to you and you alone. Your father is responsible for the death of my family. He is responsible for a great many things that brought suffering and torment to my life. My gifts..." She stroked her black wings with her talons. "...Are my reward for serving Azmodil, not your father."

Samuel felt the frustration boiling up inside him. "If that's true, then why did you pledge your allegiance to my father *and* this Azmodil?"

Volshira retracted her talons and grasped Samuel's face. "I did what I had to do to survive long enough to take my vengeance." She let go. "Your father imprisoned me, tortured me, forced me to endure what no woman should have to endure. Azmodil came to me in a dream. He helped me to endure."

"The scars on your legs and back," Samuel muttered. He felt disgusted that his father had done such things, especially to her. In a way, it made him care for her more. He now felt the need to protect her. He hated that she felt she had no other choice but to submit to evil in order to survive. The thought killed him inside.

"Yes," Volshira replied with a fretful nod. "And Lochran will do the same or worse to *you* if you do not submit to his will. Son or not, he does not care."

"Yes, I know that, now." Samuel knew she was right. "But Azmodil is a demon, Shira. What did you have to give him in order to receive such *gifts*, as you call them?"

"That is between me and Azmodil. If it weren't for my relationship with him, you would be his prisoner right now. But I struck a deal with him, and now you're free. I made that sacrifice for you, Samuel. For *us*."

"I understand that. And I'm so incredibly grateful to you." Samuel's heart sank. Volshira had already sacrificed so much just to survive, and now even more to save *him*. He owed her his life. "I just don't know if I trust—

"I was going to kill you, you know." Volshira cleared her throat.

"What?" Samuel lifted his head.

"My plan was to earn Lochran's trust, and I did. He thought he had tortured me into submission. He then entrusted me with looking after you. My plan all along was to kill you once you arrived. I would earn your trust and murder you while you slept."

"And why didn't you?"

Volshira reached for him. "For the same reason I made a sacrifice to pay your debt. I feel weak admitting it, but the truth is, I've fallen for you, Samuel." She lovingly caressed his face. "You're nothing like your father. As I got to know you, I saw that you, like the rest of us, were just another victim. Another pawn in Lochran's game of power."

As much as the situation terrified him, Samuel cared deeply for Volshira. Finding out that she too was a victim of his father only strengthened his bond with her. His passion for her was undeniable.

Samuel pulled her in close. "You know I care for you, too." He kissed her deeply. "And I'm deeply sorry for what my father has done to you. But how can we make things right again? Where do we begin?"

"First, we will take back Abequa as king and queen." Volshira looked into Samuel's eyes with conviction. "We will take back Abequa as king and queen. Abequa is my home. It was taken by your father. I will do whatever I must to take it back."

"But how am I to help you? My father has me locked away alongside my mo—

"What is it?" Volshira stroked his somber face.

"My mother. He has me locked up with my mother."

"Your mother?" Volshira shook her head. "I thought she was killed."

"No… another lie." Samuel shifted his gaze toward the floor, ashamed to tell Volshira what his father had done to his own mother. "She is the woman in black, my father's companion. The one who cannot speak. He removed her tongue."

"I can't believe it." Volshira gently lifted Samuel's gaze and stared into his eyes with conviction. "Then this is a good thing. We can save her too."

"And Raelle?"

"Yes, and Raelle. Here…" Volshira took Samuel's hand and squeezed a few drops of blood from his punctured finger. The red droplets sent tiny ripples through the black liquid. "Now tell the fenazra who you wish to see."

Samuel swallowed. "Raelle Jowellia."

The vat of black fluid started to swirl. Lights and colors streaked through each and every twirl like a spinning cosmos. When it finally stopped, the colors came together to form an image. In the fenazra, Samuel saw a young woman with auburn hair curled up on a strange bed with two little dogs.

"Sasha." Samuel smiled. "She's still alive and with Raelle."

"Yes." Volshira grinned. "Is Sasha your pet?"

"She is," Samuel replied. As he looked closer at the image, he could see Raelle moving. The sound of sobs accompanied her movement.

"She's crying" Samuel's heart sank. He wanted so badly to comfort her. "Why is she crying?" He felt helpless.

"She's probably distraught over losing you again," Volshira replied. .

"Then I must return to her. She's—

"In time, my love. In time." Volshira cut him short. "First we must take back Abequa. It's the only way we'll be able to get to her. Only once we've run Lochran out, will it be safe enough to reunite with her." She locked eyes with Samuel. "You don't want to bring her into something like this now, do you? She could be hurt or killed. You already know Lochran wants her dead. And as far as I know, he believes that she is. So it would be best to keep her a secret for now."

138

Volshira's words seemed to weave a web of trust. More than anything else, Samuel needed and wanted his sister alive and safe. And for now, it sounded like she was.

"You're right," said Samuel. "I just miss her so much, but I'm glad to know that she's alive. I'll do whatever it takes to make sure she's safe."

"She's safe in Ellios for now, I assure you." Volshira let go of him.

"Thank you." Samuel smoothed his hand over her shoulder. "I would surely be lost without you."

Volshira curved her red lips. "I know."

"Shira?" Samuel kissed her. "Why do you wear this crown that covers part of your face? You have such a stunning face."

"I was injured." Volshira looked down. "I do not wish for you or anyone to see what has become of that side of my face."

"Who did this to you?"

"I was attacked by a wraith." She hesitantly fingered the gold-plated mask. "It got me with its claws."

"A wraith? Where? Was it one of my father's minions?"

"It's not important."

"Was it one of Azmodil's?" Samuel reached for the mask. "Please, let me see the cuts. Maybe I can help."

"No, please." Volshira brushed his hand away and walked over to the bed. "They aren't simply cuts." She sat down, turning away from Samuel's gaze. "Wraiths have a demonic poison in their claws. Believe me, you do not wish to see it. I'm a monster."

"Please." Samuel approached the bed and sat next to her. "You don't need to hide from me. No matter how horrid *you* think you look. *I* love you." Samuel caressed Volshira's exposed cheek. "I *want* to see. I love you for everything you are, even this." Samuel took the helm with both hands. With a gentle tug, he removed the elaborate head piece. He studied the left side of Volshira's face. It looked as if her skin had been melted. Even her hair looked as if it were seared and melted away. Her eyelid was melted shut and her ear had shriveled away to almost nothing.

"I'm hideous." Volshira cringed in shame.

"No." Samuel lifted her face toward his. "You are beautiful." He caressed her mutilated cheek and pressed his lips to hers. "You are my love, my savior, my heroine, my queen." He took her in his arms and their passion swiftly ignited. Samuel lost himself inside her.

***

Samuel woke to find himself drenched in sweat. He felt a cool, wet rag patting his forehead and face. When his vision returned, his eyes were met with his mother's worried gaze. When she saw that he was awake, her trembling transformed to a grin and she kissed Samuel on the forehead. He sat up on his dungeon cot and hugged her.

"It's going to be all right, Mother. We have a plan."

# CHAPTER 13
## LIBERATOR

The day of Chrishtan's rebirth ceremony was upon them, and Cohlen and Oleevar had left Raelle alone to her own devices all day in order to go prepare for the formality. Oleevar had specifically told her that she could not and should not go, but being alone and getting left out of the loop again was driving Raelle mad. From a tall cabinet near the lab door, Raelle took some of Oleevar's leather garb and changed into it. Although the shirt and vest were too large and the pants far too long, she didn't care. This was what she was going to wear to Chrishtan's false wake. And even though it was still quite warm outside, she took a light green cloak as well. She threw it around her neck, buttoned it, and flung its hood over her auburn hair before leaving the lab.

As quickly as she could, Raelle snuck through the palace and out one of the back doors. From there, she commandeered a hover vehicle and drove toward the lakeside section of the city where the precession was being held. Before she got too close, she parked her vehicle and walked the rest of the way. She did her best to blend in with the crowd as she made her way to the front, where she could see King Adreahn, Queen Lamoore, Cohlen, and Oleevar. They stood tall and somber on a marble podium. The king had just finished giving a speech before Oleevar began his. He appeared stoic and regal in his tunic of copper and deep green. His head hung low before slowly rising. His expression was poise and his eyes flooded with conviction as he addressed the crowd.

"Good and diverse citizens of Ellios. We are gathered here today to say goodbye to our most beloved general and friend, Chrishtan Vilgare. As many of you know, Chrishtan's life was never easy. Many of you know this because you too experienced some of the same tragedy that he did under the occupation of the same man, Lochran Jowellia."

Raelle looked all around her. Everywhere she turned, tears flowed from devastated eyes. These people knew Chrishtan. They loved him. Like theirs, Raelle's heart ached with grief. Her hands shook with disdain. And her eyes wept with devastated tears. It was her family who had killed Chrishtan. It was her family that had drove most of these people from their homes in Huronus and Abequa. And in turn, she felt responsible for their suffering, and of course Chrishtan's death. The painful guilt poked at her like a woodpecker on the crumbling bark of a decaying tree. Raelle fell apart. She looked down and attempted to collect herself as Oleevar's speech droned on.

"And as you also know," Oleevar continued. "Lochran had been hunting Chrishtan since he was a young boy, fleeing from the madness of hostile takeover. But Chrishtan never allowed this fact to take away from the very core of his shining personality or the purity of his soul. His life touched everyone around him either directly, or indirectly. Many of you, like me, were educated with him. Trained with him, fought with him. And not for a single moment did he ever let any of us down. Not for an instant did he ever put himself before anyone else. It was always everyone else before him. That is what gave Chrishtan purpose and happiness. Doing right by others. Making others smile. Bringing joy and laughter in any way he could in any situation, no matter the serious nature of what was occurring."

Oleevar paused for a moment to allow the audience to revel in their memories of their departed general. "Chrishtan was a light in all of our lives. And now, that light has gone out. A brilliant and magnificent flame put out by one of the most evil and sinister individuals this continent has ever seen. You know of whom I speak. And for years we have sat by and watched as our fellow human comrades have suffered and died under his reign. Are we so privileged to believe that he will stop at mankind? Be happy with only the nations of man? No…" Oleevar shook his head and raised his fist. "He will not be content until the entire world of Lerim is covered in darkness. And that includes elf kind. That includes us!" Oleevar thundered. "Six days ago, our great city was attacked by this evil doer. And after we fought them off, fair and square, he sent an assassin to kill our brother right under our noses.

We cannot let this stand, Ellios! Today, we celebrate the life of a brave and honorable man. We say goodbye to him and pray for a peaceful rebirth within the light of our Grand Architect. But tomorrow, tomorrow we put our feet down. Tomorrow, we no longer stand complacent. Tomorrow is the beginning of a new era. Tomorrow, we begin making plans to take back this continent. Are you with me, Ellios?"

The crowd roared with cheers that rang through the city and echoed out into the lands that surrounded it. It was then that Raelle decided she could no longer take it. The sights, the sounds, the emotions, the guilt. It was too much for her to handle in her fragile state. She kept her gaze downward as she trekked through the frenzied crowd. With every step she took, she seemed to bump into people right and left. Each and every knock felt like a punch to the face. She swore they were all looking at her saying, "This is all your fault, evil wench!" But Raelle knew it was only her anxiety. In reality, no one noticed her, or cared. They were too enthralled with their leader's eloquent speech.

Raelle quietly slipped out of the crowd and made her way back to the palace. All she wanted to do was lie down, close her eyes, and escape this nightmare. After finally making it back down into Oleevar's lab, she went straight to her bed and pressed her face into one of the pillows. She screamed as loud as she could, channeling into it all of her pain and rage. As she screamed, it felt as if the bed and room began to shake. In an instant, she had drained all her energy and her consciousness shut down.

***

Raelle opened her eyes to find herself back inside her nightmare. Like every other night since Chrishtan's murder, she stood on the shiny black steps of a smoldering hot castle. Ambiguous whispers echoed all around her. And just like the night before, the shadow of a winged creature flew in front of a red moon and toward the castle. In its talons was the struggling silhouette of a child. Droplets of blood fell from the child, through the crimson sky, and onto Raelle's face. The taste of liquid iron slithered from the top of her lip down into the crevice of her mouth. She wiped the warm blood from her face and chased the winged kidnapper inside the sweltering stronghold. Once inside, Raelle gazed up at the immense ceiling that seemed to meet with the rosy sky. Near the very top, the winged creature flew in circles, still clutching the flailing child.

Suddenly, the castle doors slammed shut, trapping her inside. Raelle ran back to the gigantic red doors and tried to press them open, but it was no use. "No!" she yelled and pounded on the hot metal. Suddenly, her hands melded with the doors. The excruciating heat seared into her palms. Finally, when she was able to tear her hands from the scalding door, her melted skin stuck to the hot iron like honey. She gritted her teeth in anguish. Seeing what was left of her hands made her feel sick, but there was no time to dwell on her agony. In an instant, a second set of doors burst open, releasing a crimson flood. It rushed into the room like a raging river. Raelle did her best to stay afloat as the whooshing waves crashed and flowed all around her. With each moment, its depths extended, raising Raelle up toward the ceiling. She did her best to cling to a large column in the center of the room.

As she got closer to the top, Raelle could see that the child in the creature's clutches was a young boy. He was seriously injured. And the winged beast was no beast at all. It was the striking woman who had drove a knife through Chrishtan's heart. Her black wings carried her in circles around the column that Raelle held on to with all of her might. As she reached the top, Raelle noticed that the column was actually a sharp spire. She watched in horror as Volshira dropped the boy over the immense spike. His screams echoed from the ceiling as the spire impaled him.

"No!" Raelle cried. Still struggling to tread the blood all around her, she swam toward the boy. The flood's level was now high enough to reach him. As she extended her hand, the remainder of the room quickly filled. Raelle dove under, paddling down to the impaled boy. With all of her strength, she pulled him from the spire. Drowning in a red sea, Raelle cradled him in her arms.

Somehow, his weight caused them to rapidly sink. As tiny bubbles fleeted toward the ceiling, the blood around them seemed to glow. Raelle could now see the boy's brown wavy hair and the intense color of his dead, blue eyes. They continued to sink and the glow faded away. It was dark once more.

Suddenly, a flash of light shined beneath them. It seemed to be coming from a cave. Inside it, the silhouette of what looked like a mermaid was waving them over. Raelle kicked her legs as fast as she could toward the light. She held the boy tight in her arms. With her last few kicks, she entered into the brilliant light of the cave. It seemed to swallow them as it pulled them in. Raelle could feel a strange force acting on her, but all she could see was the light. Suddenly, a hand reached out for her. Raelle did her best to try and grab it, but she was not yet close enough.

*Almost there...* She continued to reach.

***

Oleevar's voice woke Raelle from her distressing dream.

"Wake up, you two. We must leave. Now."

Raelle opened her eyes and found Cohlen lying next to her. *He must have come down to check on Chrishtan's return.* Oleevar's voice had not been enough to wake him. Raelle shifted on the bed and the dogs began to bark with excitement. Cohlen's eyes burst open.

"What?" Cohlen rubbed his face. "What's happened? Has Chrishtan returned?"

"No." Oleevar grimaced. "He hasn't. Which is why we must leave."

"The third day isn't over yet. Give it some more time," Cohlen retorted.

"On the contrary brother," Oleevar said patronizingly. "It is the afternoon of the fourth day."

Raelle swiftly stood. "What? But—

"I waited all night and all day." Oleevar hung his head. "I never left his side. But he did not return as Raelle did."

"Olee! Why didn't you wake us sooner?" Cohlen wailed.

145

"Something is seriously wrong." Raelle grasped Olee's shoulder. "I've have been having these horrible nightmares. I think the boy I'm seeing is Chrishtan. It's like I can still feel his pain."

"It must be something Volshira did!" Cohlen exclaimed. "I've been having them too!"

"I believe Cohlen is right." Oleevar crossed his arms and wrinkled his brow. "But there is only one way to find out."

Cohlen stood. "The Lady of the Realm."

"We leave at nightfall," directed Oleevar. "Raelle," Oleevar said with urgency. "If you wish to come with us, we cannot risk anyone recognizing you. You're going to need a new appearance."

Raelle's guilt overwhelmed her. She had no doubt her dream was of Chrishtan. Deep in her heart, she knew her family was to blame for not only Chrishtan's suffering and death, but the misery of many others. She would stop at nothing to make things right. And that meant bringing Chrishtan home.

"Whatever needs to be done." Raelle stood tall. "I'll do it."

Oleevar pressed his hands together. "Perfect. Cohlen, please fetch her the proper attire from the armory."

Cohlen left Oleevar's sanctuary, quietly shutting the door behind him.

Oleevar directed Raelle to sit down in his lab chair. He opened one of his many drawers and pulled out a pair of metal shears. "The majority of the humans who dwell in and around this city are refugees or part of the resistance force. If you are to accompany us out of the city, we need to make you look like one of the Rogue resistance fighters. Which means I'm going to have to shave one side of your head. This is how they all wear it. It is supposed to represent the parts of them that they've lost. People, homes, lives..."

"It only seems fitting," said Raelle. "Like them, I have lost a great deal. It is time I joined them."

"Of course." Oleevar began cutting the hair on the left side of her head. Raelle watched anxiously as chunks of her waist-length auburn hair fell to the floor. Once finished, Oleevar brought out a strange metal object. "It's a new type of razor tool that I designed myself." He grinned. "It's hand-held and easily maneuverable."

Raelle returned a nervous smile. The razor apparatus felt bizarre as Oleevar moved it back and forth over the curvature of her head. Short shards of hair fell onto her body and over the floor.

"Almost done," Oleevar reassured her.

Once finished, he brushed the pile of hair from her shoulders onto the floor. "Now, as far as your hair color goes, I can do black. I think I have a chemical that will work."

"You think?" Raelle swallowed a lump in her throat.

"Yes, I'm almost one hundred percent sure." Oleevar smirked. "Hmmm…" He strode over to one of his many cabinets filled with vials of strange liquids and jars of chemicals. "Ah, yes." He pulled a container from the shelf. "This should do it." He returned to Raelle and removed the lid. "This may burn a little. But it shouldn't damage your skin."

Raelle gripped the arms of her chair and pressed her eyes shut. "Just do it."

"Yes, Milady."

By the time Cohlen returned, Oleevar had finished Raelle's physical transformation. In his arms, Cohlen carried an ornate chest that he dropped at Raelle's feet.

Oleevar opened the chest and removed its contents. Raelle could not draw her gaze from the beautifully crafted armor top. The teal ensemble was elaborately layered and decorated, with soft gold trim complementing every edge of its gorgeous design.

Cohlen and Oleevar helped Raelle get suited up in the extravagant attire. Underneath the top suit of leather, a long, flowing ivory colored skirt blanketed Raelle's legs. A matching hood and cape hung over her shoulders and flowed over her back.

Oleevar shuffled over to the far wall and pulled down one of his many levers. A full size mirror descended from the dome of the room. "What do you think?" Oleevar looked at her with anticipation.

Raelle examined her reflection. She barely recognized the young woman looking back at her. The left side of her head was bare, and the right side was now black and hung only to her shoulder. The image empowered her. She did not mourn the forfeiture of the helpless and dissonant young woman she was used to seeing. She knew this physical transformation was only the beginning of her new identity. With a newfound strength and grace, Raelle added the last pieces of her disguise. An equally elaborate mask of the same teal leather fit perfectly over her nose, mouth, and chin. Finally, she raised the hood from her shoulders and pulled it over her head. From here on out, she would no longer be Raelle, the long-lost helpless princess of Huronus. Soon, she would complete her Rogue training and become the woman she knew she was always meant to be. Queen Jowellia, Rogue rebel and freedom fighter. Savior to her people, her family, and her friend, Chrishtan Vilgare. In that moment, she found the source of her strength, her motivation, her true self.

"Nothing and no one will stand in my way," she said to herself in the mirror. "It's up to me to save my people. I *will* overcome my pain. I have to. For my people, for my family, and for Chrishtan."

Cohlen appeared behind her in the mirror. His hands squeezed her leather shoulders. "And we will be with you every step of the way."

Raelle grasped one of Cohlen's hands. "And for that, I am blessed. I have faith that we will return hope and order to Mirilan."

"And we *will* bring Chrishtan home." Oleevar stood tall. "No matter what it takes."

***

The vast blanket of twilight helped to camouflage their journey through the streets of Ellios. As Raelle made her way toward the bronze gates of the glowing city, she felt uneasy leaving Winston and the dogs behind, but it was for their own good. This time, she rode on the back of a grey steed with copper-red hair. And on her shoulder, sat a new companion and pet, a large brown and white spotted owl. To everyone Raelle passed, she was no different than any other Rogue of the resistance. It was not unusual for them to travel in the company of an elf in animal form. Some elves even preferred their animal state. With Oleevar safely perched on her shoulder and Cohlen trotting beneath her, Raelle felt safe in the company of friends.

But one thing weighed heavily on her mind: Chrishtan. She prayed that his body would be secure in Oleevar's secret lab. Oleevar had transferred Chrishtan to a strange, unbelievably cold chamber within his workshop. He assured Raelle and Cohlen that the chemicals and elements inside the chamber would safely preserve Chrishtan's vessel until his return. Hopefully, the Lady of the Realm would have the formula for Chrishtan's homecoming. And this time, Raelle would be *his* liberator.

# CHAPTER 14
## SHARE THE LIGHT

The entrance to Jenladra's sacred forest was exactly as Raelle remembered. The enormous cliff towered over them and jutted out into an undulating sea. Raelle observed in awe as the new sun slowly made its way up and over the ocean's vast horizon. Oleevar and Cohlen joined her at the edge of the surf. They basked in the purple, pink, and orange hues of a brand new day. Raelle did her best to syphon hope from the incredible view, allowing it to empower her further. Like the sun, she too had risen again. And like the sun, she too wanted to rise above each and every dark night and thunderous storm, no matter how extreme. Today was the start of a new beginning. A girl reborn into a woman. Her purpose was finally becoming clear.

"Gentlemen." Raelle rested her hands on the shoulders of her elven companions. "I would like to thank you for everything you've done for me. Without you, I would be lost. You've led me back to my true path. And together, I have no doubt that we will return our fallen comrade to Lerim and stand tall against the darkness of our realm."

Oleevar rested his hand on Raelle's. "We have no other choice. We must do as we were meant. We can either allow evil to rip us apart, piece by harrowing piece, or we can stand tall in the face of our enemy. I personally prefer the latter. If you are going to do something, you may as well do it correctly or not at all."

Cohlen chuckled and shook his head. "Yes, Olee, and so we shall. With you by our side I'm sure we will be making very few mistakes."

Raelle glanced over at Cohlen and grinned. They tried to hold back, but the laughter came nonetheless.

"What is it?" Oleevar wrinkled his brow. "Have I missed something?"

Cohlen laughed and patted his big brother on the back. "No, no, you haven't, Olee."

Raelle smiled. The laughter energized her. She couldn't recall the last time she had really laughed or felt joy. She reveled in the moment until it came time to enter the forest.

When the three of them finally made their way to the cliff wall, they stood in silence for a time and admired its greatness.

"And you two are positive this is the way in?" Oleevar unintentionally spoke in his patronizing tone.

"Yes, Olee." Raelle smiled and shook her head.

Oleevar crossed his arms. "Well, I do not see a door, a gate, or entryway of any kind."

"That's because we have to make one," Cohlen replied.

"With what tools, dear brother?" Oleevar said sarcastically.

Cohlen sighed. "For being so intelligent, you really aren't that good at listening when other people talk. Your mind is always off somewhere else, coming up with your latest invention."

"Not true," argued Oleevar. "I listen when things are important or relevant."

Cohlen raised a brow. "To your own purposes, you mean?"

"Well, yes. I am incredibly efficient in filtering out only the most important information. If not to suit myself, then who?" Oleevar paused. "Is that wrong?"

Cohlen rolled his eyes and chuckled. "No, of course not."

"I'm so confused," muttered Oleevar.

"Now, boys," Raelle interrupted. "We don't have time for this. Olee, what Cohlen is trying to say is that Chrishtan already explained to all of us, in detail, how to gain entrance to the forest. Remember? The night of our return?"

Oleevar rubbed his chin. "Yes, I vaguely remember skimming over the details."

"Right." Raelle sighed. "So, what we learned is that we must paint our own door on the rock wall and enter there."

Cohlen cleared his throat. "Using our own blood."

Oleevar's eyes opened wide. "Why, that is just down right unreasonable. What sort of place is this? I thought you said the

Lady of the Realm—

"Like I said," Raelle replied, cutting him off, "we don't have time for explanations. The point is, one or all of us need to use our blood to enter."

Oleevar shook his head. "This is just sadistic."

"Are you going to help or not?" Cohlen began to lose patience.

"I'll do what I must," Oleevar retorted. "But I don't like it."

"Then for the love of the Architect, let's do it already!" Raelle directed.

"Yes, Milady." Oleevar nodded.

Using Raelle's daggers, each drew blood from their wrist. After they drained a sufficient amount into a canteen, they bandaged their wounds. Raelle used their blended blood to fashion a magic doorway, just as Chrishtan had done. Within minutes, the doorway presented itself on the cliff wall and the three Lyre-blood royalty safely entered. They followed a short corridor, lit with white fiery torches, to the bottom of a stairwell. At the top of the stairs, a beautiful vista of green grass and tiny flowers welcomed them. Cohlen led the way to the familiar light path and they followed it to Jenladra's chateau. Along the way, curious albino fairies poked and prodded, trying to gather as much information as they could before reporting to Jabrat.

Just as before, Jabrat greeted them near the palace entrance. Raelle found humor in the fact that Oleevar seemed to immediately hit it off with the equally serious and cerebral spirit guide. She and Cohlen shared a look and quietly laughed to themselves, silently mocking Oleevar and Jabrat's boring, rational conversation. Oleevar was so enthralled with their discussion that he did not seem to notice the incredible sights and sounds of the citadel's seascape architecture. Even though Raelle had seen it all before, she took it all in, as if it were the first time. This time, it felt different. *She* felt different, as if her eyes were open for the first time.

As they made their way through the elaborate marine

stronghold, Raelle wished that her mother, father, and brothers could share in the divine experience. She missed them fiercely and her home dearly. Even the sound of her mother's nagging would be a pleasant reminder of her life before. But those days were gone. It was up to Raelle to make the best of her arduous journey. To fight for her people, her companions, and her beliefs. This time, no one could shelter or protect her from the evil of the world. Eventually, she would have to protect herself, guide herself, and teach herself to be a beacon of hope for all those afflicted by her uncle.

Nearing the end of their sea-scape tour, Jabrat produced one last series of echoing clicks and signals to open the last clamshell door. Raelle took in a deep breath and slowly released. She knew that she would find Jenladra, and hopefully answers, on the other side of the door. But just as before, she feared that the answers would most likely enlist her in another sinister battle for life, love, and reparation. This time, she assured herself that she would be prepared to do whatever it took. She had to, for Huronus, for her family, for Chrishtan. They were all depending on her. But this time, she would not be alone. Raelle found solace in knowing that so many others would rally for her cause.

Jabrat stepped aside and motioned for Raelle, Cohlen, and Oleevar to enter Jenladra's chamber. Raelle was the first to go in. Inside, it was completely dark. Raelle's eyes took a moment to adjust. Once they did, she could just barely make out the ceiling that looked like a sky full of faded stars. In the back of the room, she could scarcely see the dim glow of Jenladra's bioluminescent skin.

"Welcome." Jenladra's voice sounded feeble and faint. "I have been expecting you. Though I wish it were under more pleasant circumstances."

Through the darkness, Raelle approached Jenladra's throne. "We've come for Olee and also –

"For Chrishtan," Jenladra interjected.

"Yes," replied Raelle, "for Chrishtan. Can you tell us—

"They have gained entrance to our world." Jenladra raised her hands and a dim glow flooded the giant Opalz stones around

153

the perimeter of the room. Raelle did her best not to gasp at Jenladra's current state. The silky violet hair that had once blanketed her head and body was now scarce. Her bright blue skin no longer exuded the vibrant glow of a full moon. Wrinkles and lines seemed to dim it further. The glowing green scales that decorated much of her arms, shoulders, and abdomen looked as if they were molting away.

"Their numbers are growing, and fast," Jenladra continued. "With each and every dark entity that enters this realm, a life of the light doth perish. And when that light goes out, so too does my life fade away with it."

"Chrishtan..." Raelle looked down.

"Yes, his life has been the greatest loss by far. His Lyre, his life, and his light was a powerful force. Without it, dark entities can more easily slip into our world."

Raelle approached the throne. "What do you mean?"

Jenladra released a lengthy sigh. "A multitude of smaller, less powerful entities have been entering Lerim for quite some time now, since Lochran took power. Despite this, I have remained with most of my energy. And if Chrishtan's life had simply been taken, then, yes, I would have been weakened. But, in three days' time, his light would re-enter the world. But as you all have seen, this is not the case."

"What's wrong with him?" Raelle asked.

"When Chrishtan was killed, whoever took his life traded it to a demon," Jenladra replied. "They sacrificed his life for another. Most likely to pay a debt, a very large debt. This inevitably grants Chrishtan's soul to the demon, and his body becomes its vessel into our world. Now, this is no ordinary demon. Its effect on me has been far too great. It must be one of the six princes."

"Volshira..." Raelle muttered under her breath.

"But, Milady," Oleevar chimed in. "Pardon me, I am Oleevar Jurlorne, prince of Samisius and king of Ellios."

"Yes?" Jenladra humored him with a slight scowl.

"Almost five days have already come to pass since

154

Chrishtan's murd—I mean passing. And no demon has come to possess him. Most certainly not one of the six princes."

"If Oleevar Jurlorne, prince of Samisius and king of Ellios, were to train a bit more in patience and regard, he would know that I am getting to that."

"My apologies, Milady." Oleevar bowed. "I am—

"Very intelligent." Jenladra grinned. "But have much to learn about listening."

"Yes, Milady." Oleevar's face flushed with discomfort. "Please, continue."

Jenladra got up from her throne. "On the sixth day, the demon will possess Chrishtan's body."

Raelle followed the Lady down the platform. "And how do we prevent this from happening?"

"You can't," Jenladra expounded. "It is too late. The possession *will* take place, and the demon, whichever it may be, *will* enter Lerim through Chrishtan's shell."

Raelle raised her voice. "So there's nothing we can do? I refuse to believe that! There has to be—

Jenladra turned and cradled Raelle's face in her blue hands. "But when the time comes, you *can* bring Chrishtan back and return the demon's vessel to its rightful owner."

Raelle gently grasped Jenladra's wrists. "Just tell me what I have to do, and I'll do it." Raelle had waited her entire life for this moment. The moment when her purpose would become clear. Surely, Jenladra would set her on that path.

"Very good." Jenladra smiled. "It will require a great deal of patience and instruction."

"Yes, Milady." answered Raelle.

"You are not yet strong enough, or wise enough, to find Chrishtan within the Void and defeat the demon. You must first train and learn to harness your Lyre if you are to succeed. You must also work as a team. Which means that, Cohlen, you too must complete your training before embarking on this challenging task. Now, because of your Opalz stones, your learning curve will be highly advanced and the time frame much shorter. But it will still take time and require a great amount of work and unwavering discipline. It could be months or even years before you are ready. Are you certain that you are prepared for this commitment?"

"I am ready." Raelle knelt with reverence. "As ready as I'll ever be."

"As am I." Cohlen stepped forward and knelt beside her.

Oleevar followed suit. "And I will do everything I can to guide them through."

"Thank you, Oleevar." Jenladra smiled wryly at the usually arrogant elf. "Of that I have no doubt." Jenladra motioned for them to rise. "Oleevar has done well in making sure to hide Raelle's true identity. From here on out, you are no longer Raelle Jowellia, heir to the throne of Huronus. It is far too dangerous. You must bring to life a new identity. The camouflage will provide you with another means of defense."

"Yes, Milady," Raelle said humbly.

"Young heirs to the dominions of Mirilan, I still have faith that you will bring hope and peace to our world. May you share in that belief."

"Yes, Jenladra." All three of them stood tall in front of her.

"One last thing." Jenladra addressed them with a serious glare. "The Opalz stone does not grant you immortality. You will not be reborn an infinite amount of times."

Raelle, Oleevar, and Cohlen exchanged concerned glances.

"Every time you are reborn, a piece of your soul will remain on the other side. Those bearing white Opalz leave their souls in the light. Those bearing black Opalz leave theirs within the Void. The entirety of your soul does not return with you. So each time you are reborn, the soul that you bring back is smaller."

Jenladra hesitated with severe eyes. "This also means that you are weaker. You and your Lyre will never be as strong as before your death. Eventually, the pieces you have left each time will remain, and you will have nothing more to bring back with you. If you are to be reborn again, it will be as a new entity. Inevitably, the you that exists now, will never be able to return. You will be dead, just like anyone else."

Oleevar raised his eyebrows. "And how many times can we do this before our soul is used up and can no longer return?"

"That is dependent upon the soul," Jenladra replied. "Each one of you is unique. And each rebirth is unique. The first time, you may only leave behind a small portion. The second time, a larger portion. In the past, I have seen some return over one hundred times and others only three. There is no way of knowing the precise number of times you can return. So do not use the Opalz gift as an excuse to be reckless."

Raelle, Oleevar, and Cohlen all looked at one another before nodding to Jenladra.

"Very well then." Jenladra glided over to her chest of gemstones. From the trunk, she chose a small Opalz stone. From a second chest, she seized a green cloak. In spite of her wilted appearance and stamina, Jenladra gracefully compressed the Opalz stone with Oleevar's Lyre ring and presented him with his gifts. "Like Cohlen, Raelle, and Chrishtan, you are now a guardian of the realm. May you uphold your duties as such and return light, life, and peace to Mirilan. You are now a bright light in a dark world. Become a beacon for others. All of you. Share your light with those who seek it and guide them to salvation."

Raelle, Oleevar, and Cohlen bowed and thanked their Lady of the Realm.

"We will." A tear escaped one of Raelle's green eyes. "We promise."

"Then it is time for you to leave me." Jenladra moved sluggishly toward the steps and returned to her throne. "There is not much time before Chrishtan's possession ensues."

"Yes, Milady." Oleevar bowed. "For now, he is securely locked away in my low-temperature preservation chamber. It should hold him until we get back."

Jenladra's gaze penetrated into all three of them. "By the grace of the Architect, I pray you are right."

\*\*\*

Raelle lay wide awake on her bed inside Oleevar's lab. Pip and Sasha were fast asleep on either side of her. Pip's fur felt soothing in her palm as she stroked it. Raelle turned her head toward the sound of Cohlen as he turned over on the fainting couch across the room. Like the dogs, he too was sleeping like a baby. In an attempt to force sleep to come, Raelle shifted her position and pressed her eyes shut.

Time slowly drudged on in the darkness, and still Raelle was unable to quiet her restless mind and body. She tossed and turned, hearing Jenladra's words in a loop inside her mind. *It is too late. The possession will take place, and the demon, whichever it may be, will enter Lerim through Chrishtan's shell.* Raelle's mind flashed back to Volshira. The warrior's demonic chanting echoed inside her head. Images of Chrishtan's dead body, soaked in his own blood, played relentlessly on. Intermittent flashes of Volshira's strong arms and legs pinning Raelle to the floor swirled around, accompanied by the vision of a boy impaled on a spire. Raelle opened her eyes. She clenched her teeth hard before throwing the covers from her body. She let out a long loud sigh and pressed her feet to the cool marble floor.

As quietly as she could, Raelle tip toed across the room to where Cohlen slept. From his neck, she removed a chain that held a small Chocaz stone. Cohlen stirred and Raelle froze. She immediately held her breath. When he did not wake, she maneuvered quietly to her destination. Raelle shuffled over to the entrance of a short hallway at the rear of Oleevar's lab that led her to a temperature-controlled chamber. The enclosure had two glass walls, making it easy to view what was inside. Raelle pressed her hands and face up against the glass, but was only able to make out the silhouette of Chrishtan's lifeless body. Jenladra's voice echoed once again inside her restless mind. *It is too late. The possession will take place...* Raelle longed for a way to stop it, but knew she was currently powerless against the enemy. She desperately needed to see Chrishtan one last time before he would become unrecognizable.

Using Cohlen's Chocaz gem, she unlocked the chamber door. She listened anxiously to the sound of gears clicking and bolts retracting inside the complex lock mechanism. Once it finished, Raelle quietly pressed open the heavy bronze door. A burst of cold air flowed out from the chamber causing the hairs on Raelle's skin to stand on end. She quickly stepped inside and shut the door. In the very back of the chilly chamber, Chrishtan's body lay motionless on the bottom most mantel. On the mantels above him, sat enormous jars of soil and plant samples, animal tissue, and glowing liquids alongside other unrecognizable items.

Shivers and goosebumps took over Raelle's body as she made her way to Chrishtan's shelf. She could see each of her breaths billow into the frigid air. With gentle ease, she knelt next to Chrishtan. Raelle lovingly caressed his face with her hand. Against the warmth of her palm, Chrishtan's skin felt ice cold. In the darkness, his shirtless physique looked white and his blue lips almost black. Nonetheless Raelle pressed her own warm, pink lips against them.

"You were a light in this world," Raelle managed through shuddering teeth. "You didn't deserve this. You are a pure soul. And I'm going to do everything in my power to make sure that your pure and good light returns to our world, to our people. They need you, Chrishtan." Raelle reached over and embraced Chrishtan's cold dead body. "I need you. I must understand why you didn't trust me. Surely, this is not goodbye. I need answers."

Warm tears trickled down her cold cheeks. Raelle ran her hand over Chrishtan's icy skin, but something didn't feel right. It felt as if his body were covered in scars. Raelle backed away and squinted hard to get a better look. She gasped and threw her hand over her mouth.

What she saw caused her head to shake. "No. What is this?"

Chrishtan's entire body was covered in strange brandings, foreign symbols that Raelle had never before seen. Suddenly, she felt a cold, hard hand clutch the back of her neck.

"As beautiful as that was, I'm afraid this *is* goodbye."

In an instant, Raelle felt herself being thrown across the room like a ragdoll. She crashed into one of the glass walls and onto the floor. Her body rattled with pain. Warm blood trickled from her forehead and down her face. With an aching skull, Raelle looked up. She watched in horror as Chrishtan's body re-animated. His stiff figure snapped and popped as he moved. Raelle cringed as he eerily leaned his head from one shoulder to the other, cracking his neck.

"There is no hope for you or your precious Chrishtan." The demon's voice cackled from Chrishtan's throat. "You should have known I would come for you, all of you. After all, those that steal from me never get away with it."

"Wh—who a-are you?" Raelle's voice trembled.

Chrishtan's new eyes swirled with a glowing fire. "I am the scorcher, the handler, the warden of stolen souls. With my five hands, I brand the living. I destroy their innocence. I corrupt their feeble minds. I defile their fragile souls. Surely you remember this."

Raelle's mind flashed back to the blackness. For the first time, repressed memories of Azmodil's twisted defilement flooded her consciousness. The pain of his burning hands as they desecrated her skin caused her to cry out in agony.

"Finally, you remember the time we spent together. How touching. Not to worry, I will never forget how I killed you this night. Your soul will rot within the confines of my Void for all of eternity, just like your darling Chrishtan!"

As the demon stepped toward her, Raelle concentrated on collecting every ounce of energy she could. She screamed in terror and released ear-wrenching soundwaves that blew the demon backward. He slammed into the shelves, sending them crashing to the floor. Bottles and jars burst apart from the intense sound waves, but the glass walls remained intact. Raelle crawled as fast as she could toward the chamber door. *What was that? What did I do?* She glanced behind her to see the demon unconscious on the floor. She pushed the door open just enough to slip through. Suddenly, a frigid hand seized her ankle.

"You couldn't possibly believe I'd let you get away that

easily," the demon growled and slowly pulled her back inside.

Another hand grasped Raelle's wrist from the outside.

It was Cohlen. "Give me your other hand, Raelle!" he yelled. Behind him, Pip and Sasha tugged as hard as they could on Cohlen's pants, trying to help.

While Cohlen and the dogs yanked, Raelle focused once more on her energy. She released a small blast of sound waves at Chrishtan's possessed shell. It did not blow him back like before, but offered just enough force to remove the demon's grasp. Cohlen yanked Raelle back into Oleevar's lab. The bronze door of the temperature chamber slammed shut, trapping Azmodil inside.

Suddenly, the lab door burst open and bright Diamoz lights illuminated the room. Raelle and Cohlen swiftly turned their heads to see Oleevar coming toward them where they lay on the floor.

"What's happened?" Oleevar called.

Raelle and Cohlen struggled to their feet.

"It's Chrishtan." Raelle wept, her bottom lip shuddering. "He's gone."

Oleevar rushed into the corridor where they stood. "What do you mean he's—

Oleevar's eyes doubled in size. His gaze was met with the demon on the other side of the glass. Oleevar trembled as he backed away. "Everybody get back." He motioned to Raelle and his brother. "I'm not sure if that glass can hold him." Oleevar looked at Raelle with surprise. "What on Lerim happened to your head?"

Cohlen was still trying to catch his breath. "I just pulled her out of there, Olee."

Oleevar's mouth gaped. "What?"

"It threw me against the wall." Raelle wiped her hand over her injured head. Her eyes did not blink as she stared at her shivering, blood stained hand.

"Raelle?" Oleevar's voice snapped her back to reality.

"And then, I screamed. It blew him back. I don't know how I did it, but I did. The jars all broke, but the walls held. I

161

think they can hold him, too."

"For now," Cohlen cut in. "Raelle, it's your Opalz ability."

Raelle swallowed hard and nodded with a gasping breath. "I think you're right."

"Listen, you two," Oleevar exclaimed. "That glass is very strong. But I'm not certain how much it can take, or how much time we have."

Chrishtan's demonic form tapped on the glass with jagged claws. A sinister grin exposed Azmodil's rows of small, serrated teeth and long canines. With his black eyes, he showed no emotion and his head twitched to the side. "She will be coming for me," Azmodil hissed through a foreboding vibrato. "You shall see."

"Who?" Oleevar demanded. "Who is coming for you?"

"There will be no stopping her," Azmodil snickered. "And *you* will all *die*."

# CHAPTER 15
## SCARS

Volshira rapped forcefully on Lochran's chamber door.

"Who is it?" Lochran's muffled voice came from the other side.

"Volshira, Milord."

The door slowly opened and Volshira entered. Lochran's chambers were dark, almost too dark to see. The dim orange glow of the candles on Lochran's desk was the only thing keeping her from bumping into furniture as she made her way toward him.

"I come bearing good news, Milord." Volshira stood fully armored in front of her master. Her elaborate helmet covered the entire left side of her head and face.

Lochran paused his quill and gazed up at her with vexed eyes.

Volshira swallowed hard. "I've just come from Samuel's cell. The transformation has begun. It's time to remove the hindrance."

"Very good." Lochran stood. "You may bring him to dinner this evening. And tomorrow morning, you will return with him to Abequa. There, you will do his bidding and await any further instructions from me."

"Yes, Milord." Volshira bowed. "Azmodil will be pleased. Samuel will make quite a fine vessel for him."

Lochran reached out and snatched Volshira's hair. He pulled hard, bringing her in dangerously close. "Do not speak of the loss of my son as if it were nothing. As if it were a choice that pleases me." he snarled. The scent of his foul breath wafted into Volshira's nose. "I did not *want* this. I wanted my son alive. I wanted my son by my side. But he gave me no other choice! He chose the wrong path, and for that he has paid the ultimate price. I mourn his loss each and every moment of each and every day."

"I'm sorry, Milord. I—

Lochran's other hand clutched Volshira's throat. "You are

not sorry. This is *your* fault!" Prominent blue veins on Lochran's neck and face protruded through his almost transparent skin. His appearance grew worse with each passing day. Volshira knew she was the only one with the ability to see what he truly was.

Lochran's claws dug into Volshira's neck. "You failed him. You failed me. It was your job to use your Opalz gift to manipulate his Lyre. To stir his rage and force him to see our vision. But you are not royalty and so your powers are weak, even with the supremacy of the black Opalz. You *disgust* me. And the *only* reason I have not killed you is because you redeemed yourself somewhat with Vilgare's assassination." He sneered. "Don't you ever forget that you are nothing but a *slave*."

Lochran loosened his grip and threw Volshira to the floor.

"Yes…" Volshira coughed. "Milord."

"Get out of my sight! And prepare our guest for dinner."

Volshira stood, holding her throbbing throat. "Yes, Milord," she uttered in a small, hoarse voice. As soon as she found her footing, Volshira left Lochran's chambers and closed the doors behind her. As she made her way down the hall, the pain in her neck slowly dissipated. She paused for a moment in a dark corner to collect herself. Focusing only on the rise and fall of her chest, she honed in on her Lyre. With her nerves calmed and her Lyre flowing steadily once more, she continued her journey. But instead of making her way to the dungeon as Lochran requested, she went directly to her own private chambers.

After she slipped inside, Volshira quietly closed the door and locked it. Just like her chamber within the Void, an enormous circular bed sat in the center. With experienced ease, Volshira removed her armor and hung it inside her massive armoire. She carefully removed her extravagant helm and set it on the bed. With assertive grace, she lay her naked body down next to it. In the shiny gold of her headdress, she saw the reflection of her hideous injury. The left side of her face had been eaten away. It was unrecognizable, courtesy of the young elf's demonic poison —a constant reminder of her sacrifice.

Suddenly, her reflection transformed and she was looking into the eyes of her ten-year-old self.

"What have you done?" the young girl asked. "Is this really what you want for Chrishtan?"

Volshira closed her eyes and tried to shake the girl's image away. When she opened them once more, the girl was still there. "Mother and father, what would they think? And Shurtan, would he be proud?"

The memory of the day her life changed forever struck Volshira like a sword through the gut.

***

Volshira's ten-year-old body trembled in the darkness of the closet where her mother had told her to hide. She held her knees close to her chest and tried not to make a sound. Suddenly, a vein of light cut through the darkness like the blade of a sword. Volshira gasped as an enormous hand with metal claws reached in and dragged her out by her hair. Volshira screamed and cried and tried to fight, but the hand was much stronger than she was. She thrashed and flailed and sobbed as the putrid-smelling monster carried her into the next room. As they entered, she eyed two Rogue sentries that held daggers to her mother and father's throats. A third sentry seemed to be in charge.

The Minotirr threw Volshira to the floor.

The sentry in charge squatted down and grasped her chin. He shifted her frightened face toward him. "Now who do we have here?" He examined her with a menacing grin.

"My daughter hasn't done anything!" her father cried. "Let her go!"

"Don't you lay a hand on her!" her mother demanded.

"Mother!" Volshira reached for her and tried to pull away from the Minotirr.

"I'm sorry little one." The sentry grabbed her before she could reach them. "Your parents have been very, very bad."

Volshira's teeth chattered violently. "Mother? Father?"

The sentry scoffed. "And you know what happens when

you're bad, don't you?"

"Don't listen to him, Volshira!" her father pleaded. "He's a bad man."

"My parents aren't bad!" Volshira scowled. "They haven't done anything!"

The sentry grabbed Volshira's mouth and squeezed a hand over it. "You had better watch your mouth, little girl. Or else you will meet the same fate."

"Get your hands off her!" her father shouted.

The sentry let go of Volshira and signaled his man. "Give him to the Minotirr."

"Yes, Sir." The other sentry threw her father into the Minotirr's arms. The revolting creature caught her father by the throat and lifted him off the floor. Volshira's mother screamed as she tried to escape her captor's arms and help her husband.

"No, please!" she pleaded to the sentry. "Volshira! Close your eyes!"

Volshira did not listen. In one vicious swipe, the Minotirr sliced her father from his abdomen to his throat. Blood splashed over the revolting beast and over the floor. It grinned as it licked the fresh gore from its lips. Pure terror infiltrated Volshira's mind and body. She knew in that moment that she would never, ever be the same.

Suddenly, the door opened and Volshira's teenage brother stepped inside. The gruesome scene caught him off guard.

"Shurtan, run!" Volshira's mother cried.

He tried to leave, but it was too late. One of the sentries grabbed him and threw him to the floor next to Volshira.

"Please," Volshira's mother begged, "please do not hurt my children. They haven't done anything. They're innocent. They know nothing of our involvement with the Inclusionists."

The main sentry approached Volshira's mother. "No need to worry," he sneered. "They will be well taken care of." He turned around and signaled his man. "Do it."

The sentry sliced her mother's throat and then let her drop. Volshira crawled across the floor to her. "Mother, no!" she cried out as she pressed her hand over her mother's throat, trying to stop the gush of blood. But it was too late. Behind her, her older brother Shurtan continued to fight against the two sentries that held him back.

"You're evil! All of you!" he shouted.

"I think we're done here." The main sentry walked toward the front door. "Take them to the transport. He'll make a fine addition to Lochran's army, and *she* will make a perfect pet for his Abequan palace."

The Minotirr's heavy metal boots shook the floor as he approached Volshira where she mourned her mother's bloody departure. She kicked and screamed as the monster pried her bloody hands away from her mother's throat. She clawed into his rotting flesh with her fingernails and screamed at the top of her lungs. The revolting creature wrapped his arm around her neck and applied pressure until everything went black.

When Volshira woke up, she found herself still covered in blood, inside a dungeon cell filled with at least fifteen other girls. Some of them looked younger and others older. But, like her, they were still little girls, and, like her, they all appeared to have suffered a tragedy. Blood, bruises, lacerations, and their dirty clothes were evidence of their comparable tales.

It felt like she had been rotting away in that dark, dirty, dungeon cell for days before a familiar voice woke her from her starvation coma.

"Shira, pssst." A hand tugged on her dirty sleeve. "Wake up."

Volshira opened her eyes to see someone she thought was her older brother. It sounded like him, it smelled like him, but his face had been badly beaten. His eyes were almost swollen shut and his nose did not resemble anything like a nose that she had ever seen.

"Wake up." He pulled on her sleeve once more. "I'm getting us out of here."

Volshira moved as quietly as she could so as not to wake the sleeping girls all around her. "What about them?" she whispered.

Shurtan held up a key. "I'll leave the cell unlocked. When they wake up, they can all escape. But you and me, we're going it alone for now. Come on Shira, you can do it."

Volshira crawled over more sleeping girls toward the cell door. A number of them woke to her stirring.

"Shira?" one them murmured. "What's happening?"

"My brother is taking me away from this place."

"Can we come?" another of them asked.

Volshira looked at her brother. She saw the reluctance in his eyes. But he finally answered, "All right, fine. Hurry up. But we must be very, very quiet."

As more girls stirred, more of them woke. By the time the original few had exited the cell, every girl was now making the escape along with them. As they made their way down the hall, Volshira eyed the dead guards that had gotten in her brother's way. He had stolen a dagger early on, and used it to kill them. Pretending he was a lost boy, he let them get close, then sent them to their end.

Volshira was unsure how, but somehow they had made it out of the Abequan dungeon, through the palace, and left the city unnoticed. Along the way, her brother had grabbed two swords and scabbards and promised Volshira that he would protect her, no matter what. She would never return to those dungeons again.

The next time Volshira woke, it was inside the warm, moist woods of the Roeesar Forest. It was the sound of trampling feet and screaming girls that had woken her. They had found them. And they had come to either kill them, or take them back to the dungeons.

It all happened in slow motion. The girls ran off in so many different directions. Volshira's brother shook her and told her to run. She froze as if she couldn't understand the words that were coming from his mouth. Just as a Rogue sentry grabbed him by the shirt and dragged him away, she finally got the message and darted off into the forest. Without any sense of direction, Volshira lost herself within the maze that was the Roeesar forest, hoping that by some miracle, her brother had made it out alive and would find her soon.

Volshira woke alone to the sound of two birds causing racket above her in the leafy green branches. She had fallen asleep against a tree trunk, but had no memory of doing it. Her stomach was grinding and her head was pounding. She had no idea how long she had been asleep, but her body thought she hadn't eaten in what felt like weeks and had begun eating itself. Her body also told her not to get up. It would be too costly and she had no energy left to spend. As she lay back against the tree once more, her eyes gradually closed and her consciousness slowly waned. Though she knew she was only dreaming, she felt a pair of gentle arms lift her from the forest floor and carry her off. Volshira knew that this would surely be her last dream and she reveled in its liberation.

Volshira had been wrong. It had not been her last dream. It had not been a dream at all. She woke to find herself inside an enormous room in an enormous bed. Green velvet blankets and a fire in the fireplace across the room were keeping her warm.

"Hello?" She slowly sat up and stretched her weary limbs. "Is anybody there?"

She heard someone stir, followed by the shadow of a young figure that entered her room.

"Hi." A young boy with messy brown hair stepped into the firelight. "I'm Chrishtan. What's your name?"

"I—I'm Volshira." She wiped the sleep from her eyes. "Where am I?"

"You're in Ellios. At the palace. It's brand new. They're still building it."

"How did I get here?" she probed as he stepped closer.

"A Samissian found you in the Roeesar Forest. The king and queen had you transported here to be with me. Since we are alike."

Volshira tilted her head. "Alike?"

"Yes." Chrishtan nodded and came to sit with her on the bed. "We are both Abequans, and we are both without family. This will be our new home and our new family."

169

"But what about my brother and the others?" Volshira asked. "Did you find them too? Are they here?" She didn't know why she was asking. She knew what had happened to him. They had killed him. She felt it. But deep inside her, she didn't want to believe it.

"They didn't find any others." Chrishtan looked at her and sighed. "But we can go look for them. I'll tell Oleevar and the king and queen. We'll put together search parties. Anyone who escapes Abequa will be brought here. Heck, anyone who escapes Lochran from anywhere can come here. Oleevar and I are going to help start our own academy. Where people like me and you can continue to train. And once we're strong enough, we can fight back. We can take back our nation and save everyone."

Chrishtan's sense of hope and purpose were infectious. Everything he said sounded wonderful. From that moment forward, they would work as a team to get back what was taken from them and in the meantime, provide shelter and education to those who needed it. Volshira never wanted him to leave her side, not ever.

"That sounds like a wonderful plan." She smiled for the first time in weeks. "I'll help in any way I can."

"Great." Chrishtan grinned. "Tomorrow, you can help by telling us where people are escaping from and how we can best get in to set people free."

"All right." Volshira repositioned under the covers to make more room for Chrishtan. "I'll try my best."

He hopped onto the bed and took her hand. "That's all you can do."

In an instant, flashes of the next fourteen years with Chrishtan played through Volshira's mind. Every class, every smile, every embrace, every kiss, every touch, every fight. Each and every important moment sped through her memory until finally she found herself back on her bed, naked, staring at the reflection of her melted face in the gold plating of her helmet.

Volshira closed her eyes tight and tried to erase her past from her mind. Using the tip of her finger, she caressed the golden

170

spires of her extravagant headpiece.

"It's your turn, Samuel," Volshira whispered. "It is time." With her other hand, Volshira grasped a small vial of blood that hung around her neck. She pressed its smooth, cool, surface to her lips. "I'm coming to set you free."

Volshira rolled over and left the red velvet sanctuary of her bed. She opened her armoire once more and removed a red dress. The top was made of gold mail and the bottom a sheer red silk. Volshira slipped her muscular yet curvaceous frame into the beautiful gown. Once dressed, she made her way to the back corner of the room to her fenazra. It was hidden underneath a red silk sheet. Volshira removed the cover and peered into the basin at the flat, calm black substance. Volshira's reflection peered back at her. She closed her eyes and tried to erase her own disturbing form from her mind. From her necklace, she opened the vial of blood and poured a solitary drop into its abyss.

"Samuel Jowellia." At Volshira's command, the fluid abyss swirled with a radiance of light and color. When it finally coalesced, an image appeared. Samuel lay patiently on his dungeon cot, waiting for their plan to commence. "Fendishta," Volshira instructed, and the fenazra gently erased the picture, leaving no trace of Samuel behind on its calm surface.

Volshira quickly covered it with the red shroud and returned to her bed. She rested her head on one of the large pillows behind her. She then closed her eyes and began to meditate. She focused on her Lyre, igniting the power within both her Rubiz and black Opalz stones. Volshira reached deep within herself, opening her connection with Samuel. At the same time, she allowed the dark energy of the black stone to connect her with the Void. She chanted to her demon within it. He answered her call, inviting her back to his abysmal realm. Just as she had so many times before, Volshira allowed the darkness to swallow her.

Volshira fell breathless through the Void for what seemed like forever. Just when she thought she might suffocate to death in the perpetual nothingness, she landed in a pool of red liquid. On the other end, she came up gasping for air. Inside a dark cave, she

R. J. JOJOLA

swam until she found her footing in the shallow end and walked out onto a slimy shore. Volshira then made her way out onto the trail of burning hot coals that led her to a dark, swirling wall. She walked directly through it and found herself back in her chambers with dry, clean, clothes. Now back inside Azmodil's realm, she reached over her shoulders to feel her gifts intact. The soft touch of her black feathers made her smile. She extended her wings to their full span.

"Samuel!" Volshira quickly remembered her purpose and dashed out from her room. She sprinted through the shadowy maze and foreboding corridors of Azmodil's palace. When she finally made her way through the colossal front doors and out onto the steps, Volshira spread her tremendous wings. She flew through the hazy red sky in search of a tiny treehouse near the forest. With the structure in her sights, she dove from the sky, landing softly among the dead leaves of the forest floor. She was met with the subtle sobbing of a young boy mourning the mutilation of his sister. Volshira did her best to ignore the morbid scene as she made her way up a wobbly stick ladder and into the treehouse. Inside, she found Samuel. She cradled his heavy frame in her arms.

"Samuel, my love." She patted his face and ran her fingers through his hair. "It's time to wake up." Her subtle gestures did not work. Still, Samuel lay incapacitated in her arms. Volshira closed her eyes and harnessed her Lyre. With a jolt, she surged it into him and his eyes sprang open.

Samuel gasped. It took a few moments for him to catch his breath. When he finally did, he took Volshira in his arms and embraced her tight.

"We can do this," he said. "I know we can."

"You are my true king." Volshira smiled and caressed his face.

"And you are my queen." His lips met with hers and their connection kindled.

"We don't have much time." Volshira paused. "Your father is expecting us very soon."

"Then we must hurry." Samuel kissed her once more

172

before they both stood.

"Come with me." Volshira took Samuel's hand and led him back down the treehouse ladder. "Grab my ankles."

Samuel did as Volshira requested. With a whoosh, her wings expanded, blowing leaves everywhere as she flapped vigorously and took off into the red sky. She felt Samuel's tight grasp around her ankles, but it did not hinder her ability to fly. She was strong, stronger than she'd ever been on Lerim.

They landed safely atop the massive black steps of Azmodil's castle.

"Come, this way." Volshira led Samuel through another maze of ominous corridors. They stopped only when they came upon a colossal door. Seeping with red and brown ooze, the entryway towered over them.

Samuel's eyes grew large. "What is this place?"

"Ssssh." Volshira put her finger over his lips. She closed her eyes and chanted in the old language.

*Corontis isk dispoz im sisti spironir.*
*Gesp desmont.*
*Waltim isk ire fragim.*
*Grom mit evasa.*

The loud echo of the door as it creaked open seemed to startle both of them. Volshira cautiously stepped inside, motioning for Samuel to follow. It was dark, too dark to see. Suddenly, the gigantic door slammed shut behind them. As they attempted to navigate through the blackness, their feet seemed to stick to the floor.

"Sssh, wait." Volshira grasped Samuel's arm. "Do you hear that?" She couldn't see Samuel, but she felt him pause.

"I hear it," he said. "It sounds like breathing."

Volshira continued to listen. It sounded as if it were getting closer. After a moment she could no longer hear it. "Aagh!" She cried as a hot steam seared the skin on the back of her neck.

"Shira!" Samuel cried.

"Welcome," a voice rumbled.

Volshira gasped at the glowing red eyes of her master.

"Azmodil," she whispered.

Samuel helped Volshira to her feet. As she stood, hot fire flooded the ceiling. Like fluid, it dripped down the mammoth columns exposed by its light. Surrounding them at their feet, flames glowed and flowed toward them. Azmodil's two-meter-tall, horned silhouette walked away as if nothing was wrong.

"Azmodil!" Volshira shrieked. It didn't take long for the inferno to reach them. Engulfed in an excruciating hell, Volshira and Samuel howled and contorted in agony.

"Please!" Volshira pleaded. And just as the blaze burned her and Samuel to bone, the firestorm that raged above, below, on and around them, transformed to blood. Red liquid dropped on them like the rain of a monsoon. Tiny flames still burned amidst the surface of the bloody river that now flowed through the grand hall, giving them enough light to see that their hair, flesh, and clothing were soaked in blood, but still fully intact. There were no burns to be seen.

A deep and devious cackle echoed from the back of the grand hall. Sitting upon his throne of boney spires was Azmodil's enormous silhouette. "Aah, my pets," he laughed. "How I do enjoy toying with your human sensibilities. Come to me. We have much work to do."

"Yes, Master." Volshira bowed. She and Samuel waded through the knee-high river of carnage to Azmodil's platform. As they did, the liquid gradually drained from the room, leaving behind strange vines that looked like throbbing veins. Once they reached the bottom step of Azmodil's pedestal, Volshira dropped to her knees and bowed in reverence. Samuel followed her lead.

"Rise," Azmodil hissed.

Volshira gaped at his grand stature. Even though he was sitting, Azmodil's tremendous size was terrifying. He had no skin and no muscle, just an enormous and strange skeletal frame. Unlike the skull of a human, Azmodil's mouth sat right in the center, where it almost met with his eye sockets. There was no nose cavity between them. From his ominous grin, sharp teeth protruded. And from the top of his head, tall, thick, horns harbored the slight curve

174

of a claw. The incredible and narrow length of his arms, legs and fingers reminded Volshira of spindly spider legs. Inside Azmodil's chest cavity, his rib cage glowed with his demonic fire. It shrank and grew as he spoke.

"You have done well, my pet. And for that, you shall be rewarded. Your gifts will now travel with you to Lerim."

"Thank you, Master." Volshira stood. "I have brought Samuel. He is ready." She looked over at Samuel, who swallowed hard.

Samuel took her hand. "I will do what I must to save my sister and the people of Mirilan." He turned back to Volshira. "I trust you."

Volshira smiled with her lips. "We can do this." She squeezed his hand. "But in order to fool your father, he must believe that Azmodil has taken your soul and is using your body as his vessel. Because of my sacrifice, Azmodil now has a new vessel, but you must still appear demonic to your father, and there is only one way to do that."

*＊＊

Samuel stood before Volshira and the daunting demon. He did his best to contain his fear by putting all of his trust in Volshira. Surely, if she truly loved him, she would not let any harm come to him. Samuel swallowed the enormous lump in his tight throat. "I am ready."

"Very good," Azmodil hissed with hot breath. "And so it shall be." The demon stood on his long boney legs and raised his equally lengthy arms. As he did, vines of red veins moved around Samuel. They wrapped around his legs and arms, stringing him up in midair. Samuel's heart began to race out of control. His breaths grew loud and fast.

Volshira must have seen the terror in Samuel's eyes. "It's going to be all right, my love."

Samuel pressed them shut and nodded to the sound of her voice. Now at Azmodil's eye level, the demon finally approached him. Azmodil slowly extended one of his long, boney fingers. It touched Samuel's lip. Suddenly, the finger transformed. It became a black, slimy, serpent-like creature. It hissed in Samuel's face, exposing its strange tongue. Its breath reeked of rancid death. Samuel quickly turned his head away from the eyeless serpent.

"Do not fight it." Azmodil's hot breath scorched Samuel's face.

When Samuel opened his eyes, the sickening serpent left Azmodil's hand. It slithered onto Samuel's shoulder. After wrapping itself around Samuel's neck, it slithered toward his lips. Samuel closed his eyes once more along with his mouth. He clenched his teeth hard and tried to lock his jaw. Throughout the cavernous hall, the sound of his own muffled groans echoed back into his ears.

"Don't fight it!" Volshira called. "This is the only way."

Samuel opened his eyes long enough to glare down at Volshira before taking a deep and anxious breath. As his mouth opened, the demonic serpent slipped inside. Samuel screamed in terror as it forced its way down his throat and into his body. His squeals only ended when consciousness escaped him.

***

Samuel woke with an intense gasp. His dungeon cell was dark and he was unable to sense his mother's presence.

"Mother?" he called, but she did not answer.

Suddenly, the light of a Diamoz stone seeped in through his barred window. Still, his mother and her black dress were nowhere to be seen.

"Samuel?" A woman's voice called amidst the sound of someone unlocking the cell.

The door opened and Volshira stepped in followed by one of the guardsmen. In the light of Volshira's lantern, Samuel was now fully aware of black veins that ran through his now virtually transparent skin. His transformation had already begun.

"Take him to the alteration chamber. Lock him down," Volshira commanded.

"Yes, Milady." The guard heeded as a second sentry entered.

Volshira flashed Samuel a cautious expression. Samuel nodded in acknowledgement of their plan. The guards threw him to the floor and chained his wrists and feet. Samuel put up as much of a fight as he could to seem convincing. They dragged him down the hall kicking and screaming. Once inside the alteration chamber, they shackled his wrists and ankles to a large stone slab.

Samuel struggled against the cold metal and rock.

Volshira grabbed a scalpel from a countertop that was littered with an array of surgical and torture devices. "If you do not lie still, I'm going to have to slit your throat, do you understand?"

Samuel continued to tug and squirm until Volshira pressed the scalpel to his throat. He felt a hot thick substance ooze from his neck. His blood was no longer human. It was now infected with a demonic venom. Samuel knew that the transformation would not be complete until his Lyre connection was reopened. That meant cutting him open and removing the hindrance from his arm. Samuel stopped wriggling and Volshira removed the scalpel from his neck.

"That's what I thought." She smirked.

The guards stood by as Volshira made an incision over the scar on his arm. Samuel did his best not to cringe at the pain, but when Volshira dug her fingers deep inside his forearm, the intense torment of his nerves sent an agonizing burning sensation throughout his entire body.

"Aaaggh!" Samuel's screams did not halt until the excavation had finished and Volshira plucked the compressed stone from his arm.

He attempted to sit up, but he instantly lost control of his body. His head crashed back down into the slab as he convulsed. His chains rattled violently against the slab as they cut into his skin. After losing his vision completely, Samuel could feel the demonic entity slithering around inside of him. Excruciating pain radiated throughout his entire body. With his Lyre now flowing free, the slimy serpent took over and completed the transformation.

Suddenly, the convulsing stopped and Samuel's head smashed back into the stone slab.

When his vision and energy finally returned, Samuel swiftly sat up and vomited over the side of the slab. What emptied from his gut resembled black tar. He looked across the room to see Volshira sitting in the corner. The Diamoz lamp in her lap nearly blinded him and incited an intense throb inside his head. As Volshira got up, he heard her lock the door. Samuel squinted hard and held his aching head.

"Sorry." Volshira turned down the brightness of the lamp. She set it down on the floor before rushing over to him. As she unlocked his shackles, Samuel's vision continued to focus in and out. He could barely make out the shape of her head.

"Samuel, are you there?" Volshira's hands grasped his face.

"Yes." The scratchy sound of his own voice startled him. "I—I'm here."

After gently cleaning Samuel's face with a wet cloth, Volshira pressed her lips to his. "We can do this." She held him close. "How are you feeling?"

Samuel squinted hard. His vision was still not back to normal.

"Here." Volshira returned to the lamp and doused its light almost completely. "How's that?"

Samuel rubbed his eyes before opening them once more. This time, he was finally able to focus. But he could no longer see in color. Samuel blinked hard a few more times. "My vision..." he muttered.

"Yes." Volshira smoothed her thumb over his lips. "It will be different. But you'll be able to see in the dark. Don't worry. You'll get used to it."

Samuel rubbed his eyes once more and tried to shake the new vision away. "I sure hope so," he strained through his sore throat. "Now what?"

"Now I've got to get you dressed. Your father is expecting us at dinner, which is very soon. We do not want to be late." Volshira handed him two vials, one of blue liquid and the other black. "Drink up. You're going to need all the energy you can get."

Samuel downed the vials. He felt better almost immediately.

From the table where she had set the lamp, Volshira grabbed an elaborate outfit. She helped Samuel dress, making sure to fasten all the buttons and buckles of his ornate tunic. The final piece was a crown. Samuel would once again be king of Abequa.

With Samuel fully dressed, Volshira rummaged through the drawers in the alteration chamber until she found a mirror. She handed it to him.

"You're a king once more." She grinned.

Samuel looked at the design of the mirror. For some reason it looked familiar. He held it up and studied the image. Suddenly, he gasped and let go of the mirror. The intense beating of his heart drowned out the sound of glass shattering all over the floor.

"What is it?" Volshira cried. "What's wrong?"

Samuel backed away and shook his head. "No, no, no..."

"Samuel?"

He breathed hard. "I've seen this before."

"Seen what?"

"This... me... *that* reflection. The mirror! All of it!" he wailed.

"What?" Volshira shook her head.

"In my nightmares. Almost every night for the past twelve years. The protruding veins, the blacked out eyes, the crown—

Volshira reached out to comfort him. "Calm down, my love. It was meant to be. This was all meant to happen. That must be why you dreamed of it."

Samuel growled and pounded his fist into the counter. "No! I don't know. Maybe—maybe I've chosen the wrong path, maybe I—

Volshira silenced him with her lips. "No..." Her kiss was deep. "You are doing what has to be done to save your kingdom, my kingdom, and your sister. Nothing good ever comes without sacrifice. We are sacrificing ourselves for the good of the people.

For the good of Mirilan. This *is* your chosen path, Samuel. This is right. I can feel it. Tell me you can feel it too. I love you."

Samuel clung to her. "I do. Of course I love you." He kissed her once more. "I want this to be right. I trust you. I trust us. It's just, all of this is terrifying. You can't tell me you're not afraid."

Volshira's golden eyes looked deep into his. "Of course I'm afraid. I'm absolutely frightened. But, I'm also used to it. I've been in a state of fear and survival for so long that it's all I know. It feels familiar to me."

"I know." He caressed her lips with his. "You've been through so much, and yet you're still so strong. You are the strongest woman I have ever known. The most beautiful woman I have ever known. I almost envy your steadfast diligence. You always do what needs to be done, no matter what the cost."

Volshira grinned. "You too can have that. Let me help you. You can conquer all of your fears. Together, we will surmount all of it. Just have faith in me, in us."

Samuel ran his fingers through her hair. He felt more connected to Volshira than ever. "You're right. I'm sorry. I just..."

"These are dark and confusing times." Volshira locked her eyes with his. "There are many grey areas. But if there is one thing I do know with absolute certainty, it is that you and I were meant to be together. We were meant to find one another. And we are both destined for greatness. Nothing worth having in this world is easy. Our path will be flooded with many obstacles and much opposition. But I believe that it's worth it if we wish to regain the people and things that have been taken from us."

Samuel held the curves of Volshira's solid body in his arms. "I would be lost without you."

"And I without you." Volshira stretched her black feathered wings. Samuel was so used to seeing them in the Void that he had not questioned their presence.

"I see Azmodil was good to his word. He let you bring them with you this time."

"Yes." Volshira bowed slightly.. "He is a gracious and

true master."

"And you are a gracious and true woman." Samuel engaged her in a lingering kiss. "Shall we to dinner?"

"Yes." Volshira smiled. "And may our plan continue to fall into place as it has thus far."

"If we stick together, I have no doubt that it will and that I will be with Raelle again soon."

Volshira brushed her hand over his cheek. "Soon enough."

Samuel took Volshira's hand and walked her to the door. They shared in one last kiss before heading to Lochran's private dining hall.

# CHAPTER 16
## MONSTER

Lochran paced the white marble floors of his bedroom chamber. A knock at the door paused his redundant voyage. With reluctance, he glanced one last time at his monstrous reflection. Braided rivers of blood meandered through the whites of his eyes, which were almost yellow. The bloody streams met at the center, flowing into the circular pool of his red irises. The skin around his eyes appeared pink and swollen. His middle-aged face no longer reflected his true age. Grotesque wrinkles lined his face, and gross protrusions bulged under his pale, almost violet skin, changing his facial structure into a demonic guise. With each sip of Lyre blood and use of his black Opalz gift, his appearance grew more and more gruesome.

*I've done what I've had to do. I will rectify what has been done to me, to my father, and to the true heirs of this realm. Such anarchy, such betrayal. My own mother, my wife, my sister… all of them. And now, my own son…* Lochran's red eyes welled with hot tears. He did his best to keep them at bay, but the painful memories broke through his mental dam, taking him back to the night it all began.

***

Lochran woke on the floor of his royal chambers. The back of his head throbbed. With a shaky hand, he reached around to feel for the injury. It was warm and wet. Lochran painstakingly eyed his shaking palm, now painted in the blood of the wound. As he stood on his wobbling legs, his vision gradually returned. He was surrounded by the shattered glass of the vase that had bludgeoned him.

"Patrilla?" Lochran called for his wife. "Patrilla!"

Lochran's head was still spinning from the blow. The last thing he remembered was their argument. It was her defiance that had forced him to pin her on the bed. "Patrilla?" He searched their chambers, but still there was no sign of her. Lochran raced from their bedroom into the nursery. "Samuel?" He rushed to his newborn son's cradle. The baby was gone.

"Patrilla!" His dizzy head made it hard to keep his footing. Panic rose in his chest. "No, no, no... Patrilla!"

With his Lyre, Lochran tried to gain as much strength as he could. With Rogue speed, he sprinted down the palace hall to his sister's room.

"Shellere!" he cried. There was no answer. He rushed through each room of her chambers. Her nursery too was empty. Just like Samuel, Raelle was missing. "Son of a—

Lochran's words transformed into a raging growl. He ran out of his sister's quarters and made his way down several flights of stairs to the back exit of the palace. As he entered the small room of the rear foyer, he found Patrilla and Shellere creeping back in. Both of them were clad in blue cloaks.

"Where is my son?" Lochran demanded.

Patrilla pulled back her hood. "He is safe."

"Tell me where he is, now!" Lochran barked.

"We can't do that, Brother." Shellere removed her hood and gripped her weapons.

"You can, and you will!" Lochran glared at his wife and sister. "You have no right to take my child from me!"

"Yet you had the right to murder my husband?" Shellere cried. "And our mother and father?"

"*He* was *not* my father. Our mother had our *real* father murdered so she could marry that scrub! And then what do you do? You marry a filthy, half-blood, too! I'll be damned if the throne goes to another tainted-blood scrub!"

"Patrilla told me everything!" Shellere's eyes filled with tears as she stepped toward him. "You possess not even the valor to own up to your own self-proclaimed racial cleanse. And to think, I believed your lies about the rebels and their assassination of mother and father. And then Dalan? I loved him, Lochran! He was my husband, my choice!"

"Mother brain washed you, Sister," Lochran asserted. "It is unnatural for us to procreate with those animals. You have forsaken the purest teachings of our people. And for that, you will be punished, unless you repent now. I am giving you one last chance, and one chance only to do so. You will tell me where my son is!"

"I'm sorry, Brother." Shellere drew her weapons. "But I cannot do that. You'll destroy the children. Patrilla told me what you plan to do, and we cannot let that happen."

"Patrilla?" Lochran glowered at his wife. "Is that true? You agree with this rubbish?"

Tears rolled down Patrilla's cheeks. "Yes. I'm sorry Lochran, but I cannot—

"No!" Lochran roared. He glared without pity at his crying wife. He had no time for her tears "I do not want to hear your excuses. You have both made your choice, and you will suffer greatly because of it. I will make sure of that!"

With both daggers out, Shellere leapt at her brother. She did not make it far before it hit her. Lochran raised his hands and black lightning shot out from his fingertips. It blasted his sister back against the wall.

Patrilla dove at his feet, tackling him onto the floor. "Lochran, no!" she cried. "Don't do this!"

"Get off me!" Lochran threw his wife across the room. Her head crashed into a nearby wall, rendering her unconscious.

Lochran stood and approached his barely conscious sister. His ability had left her body covered in burns. Lochran clenched his teeth and grabbed a hand full of his sister's auburn hair. With his other hand, he squeezed her charred chin. "Because you are my sister, I still love you, despite your shortcomings and plethora of treacherous offenses. So, I will let you live. But while you live, you will be my prisoner. And every day that passes by that you refuse to tell me where my son is, you will suffer."

Shellere glared up at him with wet and distressed eyes. Her body shook with pain. "How did you become such a monster?"

184

Lochran leaned in close to his sister's frightened face. He did his best to shut out the love he had once felt for her. She was now an Inclusionist and *they* had been responsible for his father's death. Shellere had betrayed him in more ways than one, and now she had to be punished. "I know that you filled my wife's head with your corrupt propaganda. You turned her against me. You stole my child. And for that, you will suffer. For as long as you are alive, you will never see your child again, or anyone else for that matter. And thanks to you, my beloved and naïve wife will never speak your sacrilege or any other word for as long as she lives. I will make sure of that. And when I find Samuel and Raelle—and I *will* find them—I will make sure that your dirty-blood daughter suffers just as much as you, if not more. You made your decision, Sister, and now you must *live* with the consequences." He threw Shellere's head into the wall, knocking her out cold.

***

Lochran roused from his vivid memory. Still he stood in front of the colossal mirror, observing his ghastly reflection. "Why?" he whispered. "Why did they have to do this?" Tears slithered from his swollen eyes. "They know not what they've done. The sacrifices I've made to rectify their indiscretions, their debaucheries." He wiped the wet feebleness from his face. "I will continue to do what I must in order to keep the Lyre pure. I will not allow the animals and ingrates to take from us again. They will no longer impede upon our birth right. I will avenge my father, no matter what it takes."

A barely audible knock sounded at his chamber door. With a swift sigh, Lochran quickly hid the mirror behind its blue velvet curtain.

"Come in." Lochran called. With confidence, he strolled out of his bedroom and into the sitting room.

Naruncia swiftly entered, her sheer blue maiden dress swirling about her. "Milord, dinner shall be served very soon. May I help you prepare?"

Lochran nodded to his servant.

185

Naruncia bowed and followed him back into his bedroom. He stood tall as Naruncia undressed him, admiring the alluring curvature of her figure and the revealing nature of her dress. With his hand, Lochran stroked her shoulder, down over her chest, and through the lowest regions of her waist. He knew that she could not see the truth of his hideous image. Only a mirror or a patron of the blackness could see the truth of his malevolent transformation. To the naked eye, he appeared as he always had, the spitting image of his son Samuel. Lochran's middle-aged lines and unique mouth were the only things that set them apart.

Lochran continued to pet Naruncia's frame. "If only you had not so easily surrendered your virtue to my son, I may have kept you for myself. But I do not breed with tainted concubines such as yourself." He squeezed her chin tight as he examined her faced. "Nor do I lay with the secondhand garbage of my son. But you are a fine specimen, indeed."

Naruncia attempted to hold back her discomfort as Lochran released, leaving behind the red imprint of his hand. The welt pleased him.

"Please, continue," Lochran instructed. "Tonight is a very special night. A sort of reunion. I must look my best."

"Yes, Milord." Naruncia said frailly. Once she had completely dressed him, Lochran eyed his new garb from head to toe. A self-satisfied smirk crept over his lips.

"Splendid job as always, Naruncia."

"Thank you, Milord." She bowed.

"Now get out of my sight," he said scornfully. "Your shameful and provocative nature is more than I can stand."

"I am sorry, Milord." Naruncia looked down as she exited.

With a pleasant air of confidence, Lochran made his way to his private dining hall. The guards outside the doors swiftly parted and allowed Lochran to enter. Inside, his wife, Patrilla and sister, Shellere sat in their usual places in their normal black attire. On one side, his veiled wife stood as soon as Lochran entered the room. On the opposite side, his sister did not stand to offer her reverence. Instead, she remained at her seat. Without her eyes, it was true that she could not see, but he knew she could still *hear* him come in. Lochran sat at the head of the table and violently seized his sister's hand. Even with the elaborate headdress over her eyes, her expressions reflected the pain of his ferocious grip. The spectacle gave him great pleasure as did the loud cracking of her frail fingers.

"You will learn some respect," he snarled. "We have a very special guest dining with us this evening. Therefore, you *will* behave or you *will* be punished."

Shellere said nothing.

"Do you hear me, Sister?" Lochran hissed, clutching her hand even tighter.

Still, she said nothing.

"The answer is, *Yes, Milord,*" Lochran jeered as Shellere turned her head toward him. He waited for her to answer. But to his dismay, her lips puckered and fired a wad of spit onto his cheek. Without hesitation, Lochran raised his hand high and brought it down like a paddle over his sister's face. Along with her body, her chair flipped over backward. Her headdress flew across the room, exposing her shriveled eyelids. Shellere pressed her hands against the floor and lifted her head in an attempt to get up. Blood-tinted saliva drooled from her mouth and she spat a shattered tooth onto the floor.

From the corner of his eye, Lochran saw Patrilla rise from her chair. With a palm to her chest, he pushed her onto the floor. "You will not help her!" he commanded. "My sister has chosen her own fate."

From the floor, Patrilla grasped Lochran's leg and tried to pull him away from Shellere. Lochran looked down at his wife's grimacing face as she pleaded without words. Tears streamed from her striking blue eyes. Lochran used his free leg to kick her off. A single blow was all it took.

Lochran made his way back to his sister where she struggled on the cold hard floor. He pressed his foot firmly into her back.

"Pathetic." He shook his head. "You still haven't learned your lesson. And do you see what you've done to my wife?" Lochran yanked Shellere's head up by her auburn bun and turned it toward Patrilla. "You bring out the worst in her. You have done this to her. And for that, you will both be punished." Lochran unraveled his sister's bun and held her hair tight in his grasp. He listened with pleasure as tiny gasps involuntarily left Shellere's throat. With his other hand, Lochran removed one of his daggers from its sheath. He slowly pressed the knife to the auburn fibers and began to saw through. He did not stop until every strand of his sister's hair had been severed. Once finished, her head hit the floor and Lochran removed his foot from her back. She did not try to get up.

"Monster..." Shellere uttered under her breath.

"Guards!" Lochran called. "Get these impudent creatures out of my sight! I am done with them. And clean up this mess. Our guest will be arriving soon."

The guards did as Lochran asked and began dragging both women out of the dining hall.

"Take them to the penance cell," Lochran directed.

The guard stammered. "But Milord, are you sure you—

"Now!" Lochran billowed.

"Yes, Milord."

Lochran sat back in his chair and awaited the arrival of his guest. The demon would appear as his son. But Lochran knew that it was only what was left of Samuel, a demonic shell, a mere vessel for the demon Azmodil. A sudden and unexpected wave of emotion fell over him. Lochran's entire body shuddered. Even he could not hide his pain over the loss of his first born. *It was not I who chose Samuel's fate. It was his choice, and his choice alone.* The rationalization only slightly eased his grief. *He gave me no other option. It had to be done.*

# CHAPTER 17
## A TOAST

Samuel took in a deep breath and slowly exhaled as he followed Volshira down the hall toward his father's private dining room. Volshira walked tall and proud as she glided along. Her new wings were tucked away above the long, red flowing material of her dress. Samuel admired the way her hips swayed and her hair flowed. He was drawn to her. Mesmerized by her. Enchanted with her. He constantly ached and longed for her. He wanted her. He needed her. The thought of losing her made him shiver with anguish. Without her, he would surely be nothing.

As soon as Lochran's guards saw Volshira, they too felt the need to obey her. Without prompting, they parted and allowed Volshira access to the door. She looked around to make sure the guards were not paying them attention.

"You can do this," she whispered. "I love you."

She gently bit the corner of Samuel's ear. Chills of pleasure radiated through his body. With her mouth, Volshira traveled across the bottom of Samuel's jaw line to his lips. She pressed hard and massaged his tongue with hers. Lyre gems glowed softly in both Samuel's ring and Volshira's necklace.

"You and me." Volshira's voice wove a silky seductive web. "Forever."

"Forever." Samuel's lips tingled as he spoke. His fear subsided. His confidence grew. And his determination flourished. "My father will not get away with what he has done."

Volshira caressed Samuel's cheek before turning to open the door. Using her Lyre, she unlocked it and gently pressed it open. "Milord." She stepped into the dining hall and bowed. "May I present to you, Azmodil. The second prince of the Void."

Samuel stood tall next to her. He did his best to remain cold and emotionless.

Lochran did not blink as they entered the room. Samuel's tan skin was now a transparent white, covered in grotesque protruding veins of black. And his big brown eyes had been swallowed by a black abyss. His fingernails had become claws and his teeth like knives.

Samuel thought he saw a flicker of sadness in his father's eyes. Lochran seemed to wince. But in an instant, his father's lament seemed to flee even faster than it had come.

"Welcome, Your Majesty." Lochran approached Samuel. He stared into his son's new eyes as he bowed.

Samuel did not answer back and confidently took a seat in Lochran's usual chair. Samuel examined the veneration in his father's eyes. Volshira took her place and stood next to Samuel and Lochran's eyes grew with intrigue at the sight of her new feathered appendages.

"Volshira, I see our master has rewarded you well."

"Yes, Milord." She stroked her black wings.

"Thank you for showing him in." Lochran sat at the opposite end of the table. "You may leave us now."

Samuel glared at Lochran through his shadowy eyes.

"My master wishes for me to stay and speak for him." Volshira sat down next to Samuel.

"Is that so?" Lochran furrowed his brow as though he could not believe that .

Samuel glared once more. He wanted nothing more than to jump across the table and teach his father a lesson. But he could not. He had to stick to their plan.

"Yes," Volshira replied confidently. "He finds it beneath him to speak with mortals."

"Then by all means." Lochran's expression shifted to slight aggravation. "Please stay."

"Thank you, Milord." Volshira tilted her head with a stern expression. "My master wishes to thank you for your loyalty and hospitality. Also, he assures me that you too will be rewarded after he has settled into his place as king of Abequa."

"Yes, Your Majesty," Lochran replied. "It is my pleasure. And as our cause progresses, each of the remaining princes of the Void shall enter and rule the grand provinces of Mirilan. Ire

190

Oblitora will have dominion over us all as he enters in our final days, insuring the purity of the Lyre."

Volshira lowered her head. "My master is very pleased."

Samuel could not believe what he was hearing. Most of his life, he had been told that his father had been victimized, that he wanted only to uphold the word of the Architect. *Lies, all of it. My father has become an agent of the Destroyer. I was nothing but a pawn in their game. All of them. My father and my captors. Not anymore. Now, I make the rules. I will set things right.*

"Very good. I am glad." Lochran lifted a hand and signaled one of his servants. "Please bring out our first course." He clapped and the servant exited the room.

Lochran lifted his elaborate chalice. "A toast is in order." He smiled. "To finally ridding Mirilan of Chrishtan Vilgare and his scrub companion, the false queen of Huronus, Raelle Jowellia. I now raise my glass in honor of the true and just ruler of our world, Ire Oblitora. May he and his princes restore order to our world."

Samuel did his best not to pound his fist on the table in anger. *He never cared about Raelle. He only wanted her out of the way. I was such a fool. I believed every word he said. I did everything he asked. It's my fault Raelle is in danger... I will come for you, Sister. I promise.*

"To restoring order!" Volshira toasted. She made a face at Samuel and he raised his glass.

As soon as they finished their toast, the servants brought in their first course.

Lochran smiled. "I had my chefs prepare something special for us tonight."

The servants set a solitary plate in front of Lochran, Volshira, and Samuel. In the center of each dish sat a heart the size of a fist.

"Swine heart." Volshira grinned. "How very considerate of you, Milord. Such a delicacy."

"Oh no, my dear." Lochran shook his head. "This is far superior." Lochran cut into the bloody organ. "I know what a demon craves. I know because I have tasted it. I may never go back. And once you've tasted it, neither will you, Shira."

She pursed her lips. "I trust your palate, Milord."

Lochran stabbed into the newly trimmed piece with his knife, opened his mouth, and began to chew. Blood dripped from the corners of his mouth as he savored the delicacy. He swallowed with pleasure and wiped his face with a blue silk napkin. "Nothing is more satisfying than the taste of fresh Lyre blood. It is the taste of perfection, power, and euphoria. It gives even more power to your Lyre than is already flowing through your veins." Lochran closed his eyes and leaned back. "I can already feel it."

Samuel did his best to hide the disgust rising like bile in his throat.

"You're killing pure-bloods?" Volshira questioned. "And harvesting their hearts?"

"Only the pure-blood traitors, my dear." Lochran opened his eyes and leaned forward. "And not *just* their hearts. We wouldn't want to be wasteful, now would we?"

Volshira's voiced wavered slightly. "No, um, of course not."

Lochran reached again for his knife. He opened his other hand and lay it on the table. "You see, Shira…" he opened his palm. "Drinking the blood of the Lyre has its benefits." With a startling jolt, Lochran stabbed the knife right through his hand. Fresh red blood seeped from the wound. "But wait." Lochran grinned. "Just watch."

Within seconds, the wound healed as if it had never been there.

Volshira's eyes grew wide. "Indeed, Milord. I never knew Lyre blood carried such benefits."

"It is a secret of Ire Oblitora." Lochran shifted his gaze to the voiceless Samuel. "Your Majesty, you have not yet touched your plate and it is only the first course. Are you displeased?"

Samuel leaned into Volshira. The thought of eating another person's heart made him sick to his stomach. Surely Volshira could sense his abhorrence.

She cleared her throat. "My Master asserts that he is very pleased. He only wished to observe your pleasure before partaking in his own. It thrills him to witness such things."

"Thank you, Your Majesty." Lochran clapped his hands and a servant entered. On a large serving tray, they carried three glass goblets containing thick, red liquid. The servant placed a goblet at each of their places.

Lochran picked up his new goblet and raised it to his nose. He swirled the liquid inside and sniffed it as though it was a fine wine.

As soon as the servant placed the goblet in front of Samuel, the metallic smell of blood wafted into his nose. His stomach turned and jumped into his throat. The longer it sat there, the more Samuel could smell. It was the aroma of the mage it belonged to. With reluctance, Samuel lifted the goblet to his lips and let the room-temperature blood enter his mouth. He held his breath and swallowed. Instantly, the essence of the dead mage's life presented itself. What the mage ate, what he drank, where he once lived. Samuel could taste his happiness and his pain. His love, and sorrow. A wave of emotion came over him, and Samuel did his best to contain the grief he felt for the departed mage and his family.

The sound of Lochran's voice snapped Samuel out of his Lyre trance. Lochran raised his goblet high. "My treat to you both. Tonight we shall dine on the power of those who would deny the true order of the Lyre."

***

After dinner, Samuel followed Lochran and Volshira to his new quarters. *Azmodil's quarters.* At the end of the hall opposite Lochran's chamber, they stopped just outside an enormous pair of double doors. Lochran opened them and stepped inside. Samuel and Volshira followed closely behind.

"These are your accommodations for the evening." Lochran bowed.

Samuel entered with a flat expression. He looked around and pretended to examine the area. For some reason, the room felt incredibly familiar. Images of his mother's face hovering over him flashed through his mind. Samuel pivoted around and nodded to Volshira.

"My master says that this will suffice," she affirmed.

Lochran bowed obsequiously to his master. "Very good. Please, rest well tonight, and tomorrow I will travel with you to Abequa."

Samuel shook his head slowly at Volshira.

"My master says there is no need for you to travel with us."

"Does he, now?" Lochran glowered petulantly. "And why is that?"

Samuel reached deep within himself. Inside, he could feel the demonic essence of Azmodil writhing through him. Within the Void, it had wriggled and squirmed its way inside him. Samuel channeled his Lyre and honed in on the quintessence of the demon.

"There is no need for an escort." Samuel's voice was layered and thick and sounded as if it echoed inside the depths of a deep, dark cave. "I also have no need for your questions or your insolence. It was *you* who called upon *me*. *You* who granted me entrance to your world. I trust that you will see fit to give me full reign over my own endeavors. If not, the consequences will be grave."

Lochran averted his gaze. "Of course, Your Majesty." He cleared his throat. "I apologize for my interference. I shall leave you then to your own devices."

Samuel watched intently as his father turned and made his way out of the room. Lochran shut the door abruptly behind him.

Samuel felt as if he had been holding his breath the whole time. With a large gust, he finally released it all.

"Are you all right, my love?" Volshira rushed to him and pressed her head against the rapid rise and fall of Samuel's chest.

"Yes." Samuel struggled in between breaths. "I'm fine, I just—

A sudden dizziness swept over him like a cyclone. Samuel's body contorted like a branch whipping in the wind, and

194

black bile ejected from his mouth. It spattered across the white marble floor.

Volshira backed away from the black gooey mess and made her way behind Samuel. With both hands she massaged his shoulders and led him over to the bed. "Channeling the demon, it's made you ill. Here, lie down." She helped him prop his head against a couple of pillows and stroked his face with her hand. "You need to rest."

Samuel did not have the strength to speak. He simply lay back, closed his eyes, and focused on Volshira's gentle touch as she removed his clothing. Her tender hands seemed to send steady warmth through his Lyre. She rubbed his aching muscles and caressed his tingling skin. With her soft lips, she left a trail of kisses from his belly button all the way to his mouth. Samuel fell deep into ecstasy as his desire for her flamed. Volshira was his miracle. She took away his pain. She warmed his cold body. She filled his emptiness. She loved him and he loved her. Samuel surrendered himself fully and completely to her love.

# CHAPTER 18
## BLOOD & TRUTH

Samuel woke to the feeble cries of an infant. He opened his eyes to a sliver of light cascaded over the bed. It was coming from a doorway across the room. Samuel sat upright to find that his head was no longer spinning and his stomach no longer churning. He looked to the pillow next to him, but Volshira was not there.

"Hello?" he called softly among the baby's coos. "Volshira? Are you in there?" Samuel pushed away his covers and slowly made his way toward the light. He gently slid the pocket door open the rest of the way. In the low light of Diamoz sconces, Samuel could see the shadow of a woman in a nursery. With a crying baby in her arms, she swayed back and forth in a rocking chair. The tune of her tender voice sang along with the whimpers of the fussing babe.

"There, there my love." The woman allowed the newborn to feed from her breast. "All better now."

"Hello?" Samuel stepped into the room. "Volshira, is that you?"

The woman did not answer or acknowledge Samuel in any way. Suddenly, he heard the pitter-patter of soft footsteps behind him. He turned around to see the shadow of yet another woman come through the chamber door and make her way toward the nursery. She grasped the hand of a small girl who toddled next to her. Neither of them seemed to notice him as they walked right past and into the nursery. The woman in the rocking chair looked up at the visitors and smiled. She tucked her breast back into her dress and greeted them.

"Hello?" Another voice startled him from behind. "Who's there?"

Samuel craned his neck to see a third young woman coming toward him. But unlike the other two, she seemed to be staring right at him.

"Hello?" She stepped closer. "Where am..." She froze. In the dimness of the Diamoz, her familiar green eyes halted on Samuel and brought a wet gloss to his gaze.

"Raelle?" Samuel waved his hand in front of her. "Can you, see me? Can you hear me?"

Raelle nodded slowly. "Yes," she whispered. "Where are we?"

Still, the other two women inside the nursery did not seem to notice them.

"We're in the Huronus palace." Samuel hugged his sister. "How did you get here?"

"I don't know." Raelle winced with confusion. "I woke up here."

"Raelle?" the woman with the baby spoke. Both Raelle and Samuel looked directly at her. "Would you like to see your baby cousin?"

"Wh-what?" Raelle began to step forward. Samuel pulled her back.

"Wait..." He held up his hand. It took a moment for Samuel to realize that the woman was not talking to the Raelle next to him. She was speaking to the little girl. Like Raelle, she too had auburn hair and green eyes. The little girl nodded, and let go of her handler's grasp. She quietly approached the woman with the baby. The woman looked up and smiled.

"That must be *my* mother..." Samuel whispered.

"*Your* mother?" Raelle squinted. "But we have the same mother, Samuel. That is not her."

"And that..." Samuel pointed at the little girl. "That must be you. And the baby, that's me."

"Samuel?" Raelle shook her head. "What are you talking about?"

"This chamber, it must have been my father and mother's. This must have been my nursery."

"I don't understand." Raelle's voice wavered.

"And that..." Samuel pointed to the other woman. "That must be *your* mother." he grinned. "You look just like her, Raelle."

"Samuel." Raelle raised her voice. "You're not making any sense."

"I'm sorry, Raelle." Samuel turned to his sister. There was so much he wanted to tell her. So many things he had to make right. But he had to wait until he knew she was real, when it truly counted "It's time you know the truth. And when I find you, I'll tell you, all of it."

Raelle swallowed hard and looked down. "This must be a dream."

Samuel lifted his sister's chin. "The best one I've had in a long time."

"This isn't *your* dream, Samuel." Raelle frowned. "It's mine."

Samuel smirked. "Why do you say that?"

"Because..." A tear trickled over Raelle's cheek. "You're dead. Is this the Verge? Are we in the Verge?"

"No... I don't think so." Samuel looked into his sister's somber eyes. "I'm not dead. I'm alive. I'm here, in Huronus."

Raelle's head continued to shake. "No, Samuel—

"I'm not dead. You know I'm not dead," Samuel interrupted. "You saved me, remember?"

"Saved you? No, I found you in the forest torn to pieces. You're dead. This has to be the Verge."

Samuel's head mirrored her shake. "No, Raelle. We may very well be in the Verge, but I'm not dead. I'm alive and I'm going to rescue you. I'm coming for you. Very soon, I promise."

"No, Samuel—

The lights vanished and darkness consumed him.

"Raelle?" Samuel called. No one answered. "Raelle? Are you there?" Still, he heard nothing.

Samuel felt a startling pair of hands digging into his shoulders. Two bright blue eyes glowed in front of him.

"Help me, Samuel!" a raspy voice pleaded.

He recognized her eyes. "Mother?"

"Help me, Son!"

"What's happened, Mother? Where are you?"

"Find me, Samuel!" she cried. "Help me!" She shook him violently.

"Mother!"

\*\*\*

Samuel shot up from his pillow. The bizarre dream had left his naked body and silk sheets drenched in sweat. "My mother, she's in trouble," he mumbled between rapid breaths. "I have to find her and take her with me."

Samuel brought a slight glimmer to the Diamoz lamp on the nightstand. To his left, Volshira lay fast asleep, unclothed beneath the sheets. Samuel moved closer to her. With his hand, he gently caressed her shoulder. Volshira stirred slightly, but did not wake. The left side of her face was now exposed. With a gentle ease, Samuel ran his fingers over the melted and mutilated flesh. Even her eyelid had been melted shut. It no longer resembled an eye at all. A mangled and melded mess of flesh was all that was left. Samuel knew that the grotesque sight of her injuries should have disturbed him, but it didn't. To him, she was still the most beautiful creature he had ever lain eyes upon. He pressed his lips to her muddled cheek and took in the intoxicating scent of her damaged skin.

"I will be back," Samuel whispered. "I'm going to find my mother so we can get her out of here."

Volshira did not wake. Samuel knew that she too was exhausted. She needed rest in order to recharge her Lyre. He kissed her shoulder. "Rest up, my love."

Samuel threw off the soaking wet sheets and found his way to an enormous walk-in closet. He slipped into a set of teal linen pants and left the room. He quietly shut the doors behind him.

The halls were silent. Not a sound could be heard except for the tiptoeing of his own feet. As swiftly as he could, Samuel made his way toward the secret door of the back stairwell, opened it, and followed the seven flights of stairs down to the dungeon level. At the bottom of the stairwell, there was no door to be found.

"What the?" Samuel released a long sigh. "This can't be right." He looked all around for an indication of an entry. "Nothing..." He sat down on the floor and began to meditate. He honed his Lyre and the energy of the room in search of a hidden entrance. After a few minutes, he could feel a separate energy radiating from the floor. Samuel opened his eyes and noticed that in the midst of the marble flooring, a microscopic gem sat in the center of the Huronus crest. Samuel pressed his hand against it and activated his Lyre. Instantly, the emblem turned and a large hatch opened. Samuel climbed inside and stepped down the ladder. Near the end, he dropped down into what looked like an altar room. In the center sat a large white marble platform with three tiers. Samuel slowly approached the base of the immaculate altar. Black Opalz stones lined the perimeter of each step. With a gentle hand, he eased his fingers across the decorative gems. In an instant, blood began to pour over the top tier of the altar and down over the steps like a waterfall. Samuel pulled his hand away. The blood disappeared.

Samuel backed away from the sacrificial podium and took a moment to study his surroundings. In the faint light of the sconces, he could make out large shelves that lined the walls of the room. Samuel brought more energy to the Diamoz. The new light exposed the contents of the shelves. Each one was lined with labeled jars. Samuel eased his way toward them. The closer he got, the more he could see what was inside. Some were filled with red liquid and others with organs or appendages. Samuel eyed the jar closest to him and carefully removed it from the shelf. He read its label out loud, "Bruelle." For some reason, he felt compelled to open it. With ease, Samuel twisted the lid until it came loose and placed it on the shelf where the jar had been. The scent of the jar's contents wafted into Samuel's nose. *Blood... human blood.* Samuel sensed that it did not contain Lyre. He swirled the jar around to get a better whiff. *Female... pregnant...* The swirling exposed something else hidden within the red fluid. Samuel moved underneath one of the lights to get a better look. With his fingers, he plucked the object from the container. It was long and thin, like a vine, but it was not vegetation—it was some type of human organ. He allowed his Lyre to connect with the tissue. He sensed that unlike the blood, the organ *did* contain a small amount of Lyre. Instantly, the sound of a baby screaming behind him rang out in Samuel's ears. He spun around in the direction of the horrible sound, but saw nothing. The crying abruptly ceased.

*What happened here?* Samuel swallowed his apprehension. He needed to know. *What is the truth, Father? Who are you? What are you?*

Samuel recalled the blood at dinner. When he had ingested it, it presented him with the memories of the person to whom it belonged. Samuel took in a deep breath and slowly released. With his finger, he stirred the crimson contents of the jar. He closed his eyes and moved his blood-soaked finger to his mouth and licked it clean.

Suddenly, Samuel felt his black Opalz stone ignite. At the same time, six Minotirr immediately appeared. They surrounded him against the perimeter of the circular room. Once again, the distressed screams of a newborn reverberated in his ears. This time, when he turned toward the altar, he saw his father. Lochran stood over the body of a pregnant woman. Her throat had been slit. Her blood pooled around her and cascaded over the steps below. Over her, Lochran held a newborn baby. With one fell swoop, he used his dagger to sever the umbilical cord.

"Father!" Samuel screamed. "What have you done?"

Lochran did not acknowledge his son.

Samuel ran toward the altar. With Rogue agility, he jumped directly to where his father stood. He fell right through him and rolled into a summersault. *It's only an apparition...*

Where Samuel landed, he found himself face to face with his mother. A Minotirr held her as she struggled and sobbed. Her blue eyes were filled with tears of terror. Standing next to her was another woman in black. Her face seemed familiar, but was mostly covered by a black headdress that went down over her eyes. She too struggled in the arms of a Minotirr. "Brother! What have you done?" she cried. "What have you become?"

Lochran slid his feet across the floor to where both women mourned. "Now you know how I have suffered. Now you can feel the pain that I felt when you took them from me. Each and every day, for the rest of your pitiful lives, you will relive the traumas that you have brought upon yourselves and this kingdom."

The masked woman shook her head, "You're a monster."

Lochran smirked. "Yes, I suppose you're right. I have become a bit monstrous, but I couldn't have done it without you and the people who murdered *my* father. So I suppose I have you all to thank."

The masked woman stood. "You have no one but yourself to blame..."

The apparition faded away. There were no more screams and there was no more blood. The only thing left was the truth. "He's a monster." Samuel shook his head and fell to his knees. "And now, I too am a monster. You did this, Father. *You* did this to me." Tears welled in Samuel's eyes. He shut them tight and let them stream down his face. "I trusted you. I believed you. I wanted to be with you, Father. I loved you. All I wanted was to know you. I gave up everything..." Samuel tried to regain his composure. He slowly stood and wiped the tears from his face. "But I *will* get it back. My mother. My sister. My place in Huronus. Your reign of terror will come to an end. I will make sure of that."

Once composed, Samuel stealthily made his way toward the altar room's main exit. With his Lyre, he sensed the presence of Rogue guards on the outside. In a split second, Samuel opened the door. The guards instantly turned around at the sound of the door slamming behind them. There was no one there. Samuel reappeared at their backs. In one fell swoop, he lifted the guards' daggers and sliced their throats. As quietly as he could, he dragged the hefty weight of their lifeless bodies back into the altar room and shut the door. He swiftly removed the armor, tunic, mask, and hood of one of the sentinels. He changed into the guard's leather uniform. Before exiting the chamber, Samuel took a few more minutes to collect himself and to connect with his Lyre. He had to be prepared for whatever obstacle would come his way. Nothing would stop him from freeing his mother.

After pulling the hood over his head and fastening the Rogue mask, Samuel quietly exited the chamber. At the end of the long hallway was a set of double doors. Samuel made his way toward them. At the center of the hall, something caught his eye. Samuel paused and admired the enormous gold-framed painting of a forest. The trees had leaves of red; underneath, smiling children chased their parents. Samuel felt drawn to it and moved closer. He looked high up into the oil-painted branches to see tiny owls perched among them. He ran his fingers over the bumpy canvas. The blue gem of his Lyre ring began to glow. It seemed to ignite something within the painting. Samuel now saw the owls' eyes were glowing red. The children's teeth had grown sharp and were now dripping with glowing red blood. Their parents were covered in it. *They're tearing them apart!* Samuel gasped and stepped back. The light of his ring went out and so did the glowing red gore of the painting. The scene looked deceptively cheerful once again.

Samuel shook his head and grimaced. "Nothing around here is what it seems." He gazed down the hall to his exit and took in a deep breath. "I'm coming, Mother." He stood up straight and headed toward the double doors. Close enough to open them, he paused and pressed his ear to their smooth surface. Once again, he used his Lyre to sense what or who was waiting on the other side. *More Guards. Nothing I can't handle.* With his head down and his hood low, Samuel nonchalantly exited into the hall

"Where do you think you're going?" One of the guards stepped in front of him.

Samuel cleared his throat and used a voice that was different from his own. "Nature calls. Ate some bad meat at dinner, I think."

The guard laughed. "You were eating the leftovers again, weren't you?" he shook his head and smirked. "That ought to teach you."

"Yeah, I suppose I'm learning my lesson the hard way." Samuel kept walking.

"You need coverage?" asked the guard.

"No." Samuel paused. "I'll be back."

The guard bellowed. "You'd better be!"

Samuel casually continued down the cellblocks. With his black eyes toward the floor, he did his best to remember the location of his and his mother's compartment. At the end of the final passageway, the hall came to a T. Samuel turned right toward the familiar prison. To his surprise, there were no guards posted outside. Samuel approached the cell and peered through the barred window. He did not see anyone inside. Samuel opened the door and quietly stepped inside. Still, no one.

*What have you done with her?* Samuel's heart began to race. He needed to find her before it was too late. *Hopefully one of the guards will know where she is.* Samuel left his mother's empty cell and locked the door. He did his best to stay calm as he strode toward the dungeon's main entry. Standing on either side were two more guards.

"Aye," Samuel called.

"What do you want?" one of the guards demanded.

Samuel stopped just in front of them, his hood pulled down over his eyes. "I went to my post at the King's companion quarters, and there's no one there."

"Oy!" The guard shook his head. "Didn't anyone tell you? They're in penance tonight."

"Penance?" Samuel disguised his voice.

"Yeah." The guard nodded. "In the penance room."

"Penance room?"

"You must be a new recruit." The guard turned to his partner with a shrug. "I'm really getting sick and tired of them bringing in these young cadets without any training."

"Aye. It's downright unnerving." The other guard grimaced.

Samuel stepped back. "I apologize."

"No need." The first guard said. "Not your fault."

"So, uh, where is this penance room?" Samuel inquired.

"It's in the restricted area. You have to have a special clearance. Which I'm assuming you don't because you're new."

"No, I suppose I don't." Samuel replied. "So who does?"

"It requires a special stone, kid," the sentry answered. "We don't have those. The king is very specific about who receives one."

"I see," said Samuel. "So where is this restricted area? You know, so I don't make the mistake of going somewhere I shouldn't."

"Well," the guard said, shrugging, "you really can't. It's on the level below this. There are no main entries. Only the king and his selected sentinels know where to enter."

"Understood." Samuel threw his hands in the air. "So I guess this means I have the night off?"

The guard chuckled. "I guess it does. Lucky break, cadet. But, uh, I would go double check with the captain first. He's in in his office down the hall. Back that way."

"Thanks. I'll do that." Samuel saluted the guard and headed back the way he came instead of toward the captain's office as instructed. *The altar room is the only empty room with guards posted. That must be part of the restricted area. Or at least lead to it somehow.*

"That was quick!" called the altar room guard.

"Indeed," Samuel replied. "It wasn't as bad as I had anticipated."

"Good to hear." The guard unlocked one of the doors and stepped aside. "Now get back to work."

Samuel pushed open the door and entered the passageway. He heard the sentry lock it on the other side. With his Lyre sharp, Samuel sped down the lengthy corridor. He did his best to sense any hint of energy from a secret entry. Once again, he felt drawn to the solitary painting in the passageway. Just as before, the deceitful piece seemed to stir his Lyre. Samuel pressed his hands against the textured canvas. This time, he made a conscious effort to connect with his black Opalz. Surely this stone would be the special clearance that the guard had mentioned. Samuel closed his eyes and the energy of his black stone sent a burning rage flowing through him.

"This has to be it," Samuel said through clenched teeth. His body shook with involuntary rage. He did his best to push down his fury. If he could not remain calm and collected, he would surely blow his cover. He focused on the memory of his mother. The day he had woken in their cell, it was to her brilliant blue eyes watching over him. It was her arms that had held him. She gave him the truth that day. She was alive. And she still loved him.

"I'm coming for you, Mother." Samuel looked up at the painting and noticed something he hadn't before, the dark silhouette of a woman in the bottom corner. Around her neck was a chain that housed an empty amulet. Samuel brushed his fingers over it and they fell inside the hollow talisman. With his other hand, he reached for the black Opalz around his neck. He unlatched the chain and lifted the gem to the painting. He gently placed it inside the empty talisman. The red blood in the painting glowed with an almost blinding light. Samuel heard something shift inside the wall. Within seconds, the painting moved back and lowered down into the floor, leaving an open doorway that exposed another wall. Samuel stepped in to see that he could go either right or left. The sound of the wall closing from behind startled him. After taking a deep breath and letting it out, Samuel decided to go right. He stealthily crept around the other side to find a large hole. From where he stood, it looked as if it opened up into a large, cavernous room. He drew on his Lyre to sense the energy of the surrounding area. The smell of death wafted into his nose. The sound of terrified screams echoed into his ears. And the essence of agony radiated against his Lyre.

*No one nearby.*

Samuel stepped through the hole and out onto the top of an open stairwell. All around him, the enormous walls of the cavern were slick with moisture. The red flames of sconces along the stairwell gave Samuel just enough light to tread safely down the seemingly endless steps to the bottom of the cave. With each step, the screaming grew more intense and the smell of blood and rotting flesh more potent.

"What in the name of the Architect is this place?"

At the end of the stairs, Samuel was met with a rusting pair of tall iron doors. The smell of the rust was overpowered by the pungent odor of death and decay. It was coming from behind him. From beside the door, Samuel grabbed a torch from its bracket. He turned around and brought light to the malodorous location. What he saw made his stomach jump into his throat. He did his best not to vomit at the sight of a deep pit filled with black ooze. Floating amidst the viscous fluid were human bones.

Suddenly, enormous bubbles gurgled within the ooze and exposed a human skull. Samuel gasped and jumped back. After regaining his composure, he stepped closer as the skull slowly sank back down into the putrid goo. He moved the torch closer to the grotesque pool and noticed that it was not black. It was a dark and gory hue of red and brown.

Samuel's breaths grew rapid and his body quaked. "Why?" was all that he could think. With his stomach churning, he turned back toward the iron doors and re-mounted his torch. The gruesome sight had replaced his fury with fear. But fear would serve neither him nor his mother. He needed to remain poised and resilient. But what he sensed lay beyond the iron doors made it a difficult task. Samuel took a deep breath before reaching for the handle and opening the giant door.

He stepped inside gingerly and was met with another large cavern. Two guards stood on either side of the entryway. They did not speak or acknowledge his presence. Within the cave, the sound of horrified and tormented screams infiltrated Samuel's ears. It sounded as if they were right there next to him. The petrifying and inhuman sound of predatory shrieks and growls sounded off within them.

As he ascended the steps to the bottom of the room, Samuel looked up and around. Unlike the cave he had come from, this one had many levels. Hundreds of steps led to each one almost to the very top of the cave. At the bottom, Samuel stood at the edge of a gigantic pit. But the pit was not empty. What he saw took his breath away. An enormous mass of armed wraith forces occupied the quarry. In their midst, were droves of demonic monstrosities. It was unlike any army he had ever seen. Its ranks were filled with turned Rogues of the Lyre; no doubt tortured and twisted by his father. The screams Samuel had been hearing were that of his father's atrocities. And within them, the tormented human slaves from which the monsters fed.

*If this is the army my father intends to release on the rest of Mirilan, we don't stand a chance. I must warn Volshira. But first, I've got to find my mother.*

Samuel jumped at the sound of a raspy and unfamiliar voice behind him.

"Looking for something?" It was a Jassokian priest, dressed in elaborate, deep purple robes with gold trim. A golden mask covered his face. It had no eye holes or a nose and his tall, pointy elven ears protruded from its sides.

Samuel stared at the priest's purple lips and tongue as he spoke through the mask.

"Sir?" the priest asked once more. "Looking for something?"

"Yes, uh…" Samuel choked down his fear. "Master Jowellia requests that his companion be returned to him."

The faceless priest eerily tilted his head to one side. "But they have not yet finished paying their penance."

Samuel cleared his throat and summoned his most confident voice. "I do not care. These are the master's orders. Do you wish for me to make him wait? Tell him that you—

"No." The priest shook his head. "Of course not. I… um… We can fetch them straight away."

"Thank you." Samuel followed the priest through the only door on the bottom level. Once inside, he found himself in a new cellblock. Echoes of desperate voices filled the halls. As they walked down the passageway, each cell contained a wild-eyed Lyre-blood Rogue covered in filth and driven mad by torture. Some of them had lost limbs, others their eyes, ears, or fingers. But all of them had lost their minds. Their incoherent mumbling filled the cellblock. At the end of the corridor, the priest stopped and opened another rusty red door.

Inside, the room was dark. But with his demonic eyes, Samuel could still see. Suddenly, a fire ignited on the priest's palm. With it, he lit some of the torches along the walls. The dim light of the fires exposed more of what Samuel had so dreaded to see. Two women hung almost naked, strung up by their arms to a tall, white slab of marble. Droplets of blood slithered down their slabs like raindrops on a glass window. The top of each woman's right foot had been sliced open. The blood from their feet and their backs slowly collected in ornate gold basins at the bottom. They were half full.

Samuel held back his shriek at the state of his mother. He did his best not to look at her. Instead he eyed the woman to her right. Her face looked badly beaten and her hair had been chopped into disarray.

"Some assistance, please?" the priest rasped from his throat.

"Yes, um, of course." Samuel rushed to his mother. It took everything in him to keep his composure as he assisted the priest in removing his mother from her bindings. Once loose, he cradled her unconscious body in his arms.

"This way."

The priest led him to a marble slab similar to the one in the altar room. Rows of similar slabs lined the wall that was ornamented with instruments of torture. After laying his mother on the cold stone, Samuel helped the priest remove the second woman from her shackles. As he carried her away, he noticed that the woman's eyes had been removed long ago, and her lids sewn shut. He placed her gently on the platform next to his mother's. With the light of the torch above her, her face looked so familiar. It reminded him of Raelle. Samuel realized then that this was not his first time seeing the woman's face. First, in his dream of the nursery, and again in the appalling altar room apparition.

The priest's voice cut in. "It will take me a few moments to wake them."

"Do you not think it vital to close their wounds and clean them first?" Samuel demanded.

"Yes, Sir. Of course, Sir." The priest made his way to the water pump. He quickly filled a bucket and grabbed a rag. The water sloshed from side to side, spilling onto the floor as the priest lugged it over.

"It will be much more time efficient if I assist." Samuel took a second rag. "I don't want to keep our master waiting."

"Of course." The priest bowed.

Samuel went to his mother's side. He carefully cleaned and bandaged her feet where they had been sliced. Then, he gently turned her on her side to clean her back. It was covered in lacerations where she had been flogged. His jaw clenched at the sight of her brutal wounds. Samuel clamped his fists tight in an attempt to push down his rage, but it was no use.

"Is this your work?" Samuel's vengeful glare penetrated into the priest.

"Indeed, it is," hissed the faceless priest.

Without hesitation, Samuel leapt over the slab. In an instant, he crushed the priest's throat in his hand. His death was swift. Samuel ripped off the tormentor's mask to see what lay underneath. His entire face had been burned so badly that his eyes and nose looked as if he was wearing a mask of melted skin.

Samuel dragged the priest's body out the door and through the cellblock. He stormed through the iron doors at the end and into the main level of the cave. Samuel dropped the priest and pulled both of his daggers from their sheaths. With flawless precision, he threw them directly at the two guards at the top of the steps. The blades pierced through their throats and the guards fell dead where they stood. Samuel continued on with the priest, dragging him like a ragdoll over the floor. Once close enough, Samuel tossed the nameless executioner into the pit along with the two dead sentries. He their bodies hit the ground accompanied by the screeches of wraiths and demonic creatures as they tore them apart.

Samuel returned to the penance room to wake his mother and aunt. He clothed them with Jassokian priests' cloaks he had found hanging on the wall. Then, from one of the many shelves, he collected two small vials of Torpaz blood. Samuel carefully poured them into the women's mouths. It took several moments for them to rouse.

Samuel waited anxiously for his mother's eyes to open. When she finally sat up, her face contorted with fear. Samuel removed his sentry hood and mask.

"Mother, please don't be frightened." He embraced her. "It's me."

Patrilla was too weak to reciprocate her son's embrace. She buried her face in his chest and wept. Samuel held her close and stroked her long black hair. "I'm going to get you out of here."

"Samuel?" His aunt sat up. "Is that you?"

"It is," Samuel coaxed. "I'm here to set you both free."

"We are so sorry," his aunt whimpered. "It never should have come to this."

"But it has," Samuel sighed. "And now we will make it right again. I promise."

Samuel's mother touched his face and stared at him with distressful eyes.

"I know, I look different." Samuel tried to ease her concern. "But this is what I had to do to stay alive. This is what I had to do to get you out of here."

Patrilla sobbed at his sickly and demonic appearance.

"I don't regret it, Mother. I did what I had to, to save you. To give the people of Mirilan a chance."

"What have you done, Samuel?" His blind aunt stood on trembling legs. "What's happened?"

"I'll explain it all later. After we are safely inside Abequa and away from this place."

"Abequa?" his aunt asked.

"Yes." Samuel helped his mother off her slab. "But there is no time to talk now. We must get you out of here and depart before sunrise."

His aunt nodded her disheveled head in agreement.

After reattaching his mask and pulling up his hood, Samuel led them out of the cave. When they exited into the hallway, Samuel made sure that the painting went back to its original and secure position. He then took them down the hall to the altar room. As they entered, Samuel saw that it was no longer empty and they were no longer alone.

"I suppose this is your mess?" Volshira put one hand on her hip and pointed at the two dead guards on the floor.

Samuel expressed a sigh of relief. "Yes. It is. I'm sorry I—

"Are there any other messes I should know about?" Volshira shook her head. "I see you've stolen these two. Which means more dead men, I assume."

"Yes," replied Samuel. "They're coming with us to Abequa."

Volshira stepped forward. "And when were you going to let *me* in on this little plan of yours?"

"Um." Samuel's eyes shifted back and forth. "Right now?"

"Splendid." Volshira rolled her eyes and smirked. "So you make messes, and I get to clean them up?"

"I'm sorry." Samuel hoped and prayed Volshira would understand. There was no way he was leaving his mother behind. His entire reason for sacrificing himself had been to save both her and his sister. "I can't leave without her."

"I see." Volshira bit her lip. She looked back and forth at the two women, both still weak from torture. "And how do you plan to get them out of here unnoticed? I'm fairly certain Lochran is going to notice when his two companions, that he eats breakfast and dinner with every day, are no longer here."

"I didn't know what else to do, Shira!" Samuel's voice cracked. "Now are you going to help me or not?"

"I suppose I really don't have any other choice," Volshira said, flustered.

"Thank you." Samuel approached her, removed his mask and kissed her on the cheek. "I don't know what I'd do without you."

Volshira grinned. "That is definitely true."

"I recognize that voice," his aunt said fretfully. "You work for Lochran. You are a ruthless and downright *evil* woman." She turned to her nephew. "Samuel, what business do you have with her? She's done things that—

Volshira glared at Samuel's aunt. "I guess that means you'd like to stay here with Lochran?"

Samuel took his aunt's hand. "Volshira is on our side," he said in a soothing voice. "She has made many sacrifices to help us. You can trust her. Like you, she too was Lochran's prisoner. Please, give her a chance. I would be dead without her. She's going to help get Raelle back."

"Raelle?" his aunt's voice grew shrill. "I thought her dead. Lochran said—

"Lochran lied!" Samuel interrupted.

"Fancy that," Volshira chuckled. She paused for a minute. "But there's no time for discussion. Samuel is right. Raelle is alive. And if we want to get her back, we need to get out of here. We don't have a lot of time before sunrise." Volshira shifted her stance. "Now, I'm going to go work this out. I'll frame someone else for the deaths. I'll report that they stole the two of you as well. By the time Lochran wakes up and receives the message from the idiot I give it to, we'll be long gone. We just need to find these two some disguises."

"I'll figure it out," Samuel chimed in. He kissed Volshira. "Thank you, again."

"Raelle is alive." His aunt pursed her lips. "My daughter is alive."

Samuel's mother smiled and embraced her sister-in-law.

Samuel grinned. "We're going to get her back. I promise."

# CHAPTER 19
## READY

Raelle weaved and dodged in and out through the maze of enormous pillars. As dark clouds sprinkled her in fresh snow, she stabbed, then disappeared, appeared elsewhere and stabbed them again. The only evidence of her invisible journey were the bodies scattered on the ground and her footprints in the snow. Carefully and stealthily she approached her final foe. He stood in the center of the snowy labyrinth, waiting for her to strike. He would be a great challenge. Like her, he was still a young and spry Rogue. His knowledge and skills of the Lyre far outranked hers. His lean, muscular stature gave him an edge. And his intimate relationship with his daggers made him precise and deadly.

With intense force, Raelle launched herself to the top of his platform. Sensing her presence, he spun around and stabbed his dagger toward her chest. Raelle parried and spun around, landing a kick to his chest. The force of the blow sent her adversary flying. As he landed on his feet in the snow, Raelle leapt down from the platform. In midair, she disappeared and reappeared on the ground, flanking her formidable foe. But before she could strike, he disappeared. Taking a play from her book, he attacked at her rear. Raelle whirled around and parried one of the blows, but one of his legs pulled her feet out from under her. Raelle rolled into a summersault, leaving behind tracks of her armor on the snow covered ground. Her opponent disappeared and reappeared where her summersault ended. But Raelle was already gone. She had stinted two meters behind him.

Her enemy ran at her with inhuman speed. He launched himself into the air and landed at her feet. Raelle disappeared and reappeared, blocking his dagger strikes. Raelle focused as deeply as she could with her Lyre. She studied his moves until she noticed a pattern that exposed his weakness. Raelle closed her eyes, called on her Lyre, and struck twice. When she opened her eyes once more, her enemy lay on the ground in defeat.

Raelle smiled and stood over his body. Her foe opened his dark green eyes and grinned with all of his teeth. Raelle offered him her hand and helped her trainer up off the ground. He pulled off his hood and shook the snow out of it. Raelle chuckled as she helped him brush the remaining snow from his short beard and woven strips of dirty blonde hair that covered the top of his head. The rest of his braided dreads were pulled back in a long ponytail, held together by rows of leather bindings. Like many of the other Rogue resistance fighters, the sides of his head were completely shaved and tattooed with the symbolic story of his journey thus far. With his free arm, he waved his hand and made a circular motion in the air.

"Thanks for your help, everyone!" he hollered. "You're dismissed. Great job!"

All at once, the Lyre-blood students scattered throughout the garden maze rose to their feet, brushed the snow from their armor, and left the training course.

"So." Raelle shrugged with a smile. "Did I pass?"

Her trainer looked down with a stern face.

"Tonz?" Raelle lifted his head.

Tonz did his best to hold back his smile. "Yes. Of course you did!" His grin took over and he hugged Raelle. "But you seemed distracted. Your stinting was a little off today. Is everything all right?"

Raelle removed her mask and hood and snuggled her head in his chest. She took a moment to take in his familiar scent. With a deep sigh, she looked up at his smiling face. "I couldn't have done any of this without you." Raelle took in a hefty breath and let it go. "And it's also impossible to hide anything from you."

"Both true," Tonz laughed.

Raelle socked him in the shoulder. "I'm being serious." She shook her head. "With everything I've been through, this could have been a disaster. I was so scared. I had no idea what to do or where to begin. But when I met you, your positivity, your support, your friendship, and your genuine passion to teach made it not so scary anymore. Three months ago when I started my training, I had no idea how far I'd come in such a short time. I have you to thank for that."

"Well." Tonz swept some of the remaining snow from her shoulder. "You've got to give yourself some credit. Your royal blood and that Opalz stone helped a bit."

Raelle raised an eyebrow and smirked. "Gee, thanks."

"But in all seriousness," Tonz said, his smile fading. His dark green eyes looked deep into hers. "You are the hardest working student I've ever had. And granted, I've only been doing this for five years, but I know you are the hardest working student I'll ever have. You truly want it. I can feel it. I can sense it. Your drive is unmatched. And your heart is... Well, it's in it, Raelle. So what's bothering you?"

"This dream I had," Raelle said, perplexed. "I just can't get it out of my head."

"Is it one of your night terrors?" Tonz asked. "A recurring one?"

"No." Raelle shook her head. "This is much different than any of my other dreams."

"How so?"

"It's not a nightmare," Raelle explained. "It's a good dream. But it also doesn't make any sense."

Tonz dropped his brow. "All right..."

"I'm running through this beautiful palace I've never seen before. And for some reason, I stop at these two doors. I open them, and when I go inside, I find my brother, Samuel. He's watching these two women in a nursery. One of them has a baby and the other a little girl. The girl is called Raelle, like me. Then, Samuel tries to explain to me how he's not dead and how that little girl is me. He says that woman is *my* mother. And the woman with the baby is *his* mother..." Raelle shook her head. "It just doesn't make any sense."

"Maybe it's because you felt so alienated from him before he was killed," suggested Tonz. "Maybe it's just your mind making you feel like you didn't know him the way you thought. Our minds have a tricky way of working through things."

"But it just felt so real." Raelle crossed her arms. "His touch. His voice. His smell. Everything. I thought maybe we were actually in the Verge, but he said he wasn't dead. I don't know..."

"I don't know, Raelle," said Tonz. "I wish I had the answer. I hate to see you like this."

"I know." Raelle bit her lip. "I'm sorry. I don't want to let this affect me. I don't want to let my people down. *Our* people, who have suffered because of *my* family. You lost your father, and you and your mother escaped Huronus to come here. You are of noble blood. You didn't have to do that, but you did. And now, you're teaching others like yourself how to best fight for their freedom. I don't want to let *you* down, Tonz. But I'm still so afraid."

Tonz lifted Raelle's chin. She had never seen him look so solemn.

"Look at me, Raelle. I don't ever want you to worry about letting people down. Do you hear me?"

Raelle nodded.

Tonz brushed Raelle's black hair away from her face. "Spending almost every single day over the past three months with you has been one of the greatest experiences of my life. And let me be very clear. There was *never* a moment, not *ever* that I thought you would let me or anyone else down. In fact, you have done quite the opposite. You've given me hope. You've given me friendship. You've given me..."

"What is it?" asked Raelle.

Tonz grasped Raelle's face and pressed his lips to hers. Raelle didn't know why, but she didn't try to fight it. His touch was gentle and his kiss comforting. Over the past three months, Tonz had truly become her best friend. Raelle was overcome with emotion. Tears rolled into Raelle's confused eyes.

"What is it? What's wrong?" Tonz held her tight.

"I'm just feeling very overwhelmed." Raelle held her breath to keep from crying. "I've worked so hard to get here. And now that I am, I know what's next and I'm terrified. I'm so scared. And these feelings I'm having, they're even more confusing. I don't want to hurt you, Tonz. I don't want to hurt anyone."

Tonz caressed Raelle's somber face. "It's all right. Just slow down. Take a deep breath and talk to me. This is what we do. We talk. We support one another. I'm sorry if I crossed the line. I don't want to put more pressure on you than there already is. I don't want to push you away."

"No, please," Raelle said with a sigh. "This is not your fault. You're not pushing me away. It's my fault. I didn't anticipate this. And I'm sorry."

"I didn't anticipate it either," Tonz said with adoring eyes. "But it happened. We've spent almost every waking moment together. We know each other inside and out. Our habits, our mannerisms. Our likes, dislikes. I know what makes you laugh, what makes you mad. I know who you really are and I love it. I love that I know all of that and almost no one else does. I see how special you are. And I feel lucky for all of it."

Raelle looked down and mumbled under her breath. "I just. I—I can't do this to him. I just can't."

"Do what? To who?"

Raelle looked into Tonz's evergreen eyes. "Chrishtan."

"Chrishtan?" Tonz frowned. "Is that what this is about?"

"Yes, you see he—"

"I understand," Tonz cut in. "You're not ready to move on. It's difficult to lose someone you love. And that's all right. I'm not going anywhere. And when you are ready, just know that I am. I miss him too. He was a dear friend of mine. We grew up together. Went to the academy together. We started the mission troops together. And when I decided I wanted to train our best and brightest, Chrishtan was there for me every step of the way. His loss is a loss for everyone."

Raelle averted his reminiscent gaze. "Chrishtan isn't dead, Tonz."

"What?"

"He's not dead. He's here, in Ellios."

"What? Where?" Tonz took a step back. "They faked his death too? Why?"

218

"Our deaths weren't fake."

"Our?"

"My death wasn't fake, Tonz. I died that day. The day the Huronians came for Chrishtan."

"But, Oleevar said it was fake. He said you were only in hiding. He said—

"I don't give a damn what Olee said. I'm telling you the truth."

"I don't understand." Tonz shook his head. "What do you mean, you died?"

"I was shot and killed. I assume you were there. You must have seen it happen."

"Yes, I did see it happen. You ran out after Chrishtan. He was about to kill the Elite Echo, but then you stopped him. That's when you were shot. Oleevar told me you survived."

"Well, Oleevar lied. I died. Then, I—wait... I did what?"

"You ran out screaming for Chrishtan to stop. He was about to kill the Elite Echo and then you stopped him. You stopped Chrishtan with your ability, which happens to be the exact same ability as the Echo. You were trying to revive him when you were shot."

"I—I don't remember that." Raelle felt a lump in her throat. "I was trying to revive who?"

"The Echo. We all thought you'd gone mad. You attacked Chrishtan."

"Why would I do that?"

"I don't know. Do you really not remember any of it?"

"No. The last thing I remember was going to bed the night before. And the next time I woke, I was in the palace mortuary lying on a sarcophagus. That was three days after the attack. When I died, it seems it muddled my memories somehow." Raelle's face tightened with bewilderment. "And obviously Oleevar left some things out." *I knew he was keeping things from me...*

"How is that possible?" Tonz asked. "How could you come back to life?"

"Olee did not want us to share this, because he thinks that

219

people will be scared by it or even try to steal it."

"Share what?" Tonz's face twisted with confusion. "I don't follow."

"You know that my ability comes from the power of the Opalz stone."

"Yes."

"Well, that's not the only ability it provides," explained Raelle. "It also allows us to go into the Verge. The space between the living world and the world of the deceased."

"Okay…"

"But it also gives us the ability to return to the living world once we have been killed. After three days, our spirit returns to our living bodies. But each time we do, a piece of our soul remains within the Verge. So there is a limit to it."

"Three days huh?" Tonz mumbled. "Just like our rebirth ceremony…"

"Precisely," said Raelle. "In the beginning times, it was more literal. All Lyre-bloods possessed the power of the Opalz stone, and returned in three days."

"I'm going to take your word for it because I trust you. And I can see how knowledge of this gift could cause problems." Tonz sighed. "Especially in the human realm. Some people would do anything to get their hands on a stone."

"Then you understand why you must not tell anyone what I've just told you."

Tonz closed his eyes and nodded. "I do. So what about Chrishtan? Where is he? What has he been doing?"

Raelle could see the hurt in Tonz's eyes. She knew how much he cared for her, that he might even be in love with her. But his respect for her was unwavering. Now that he knew Chrishtan was still alive, he would most likely never mention his feelings for her again, despite their potency.

"He's been possessed," Raelle explained. "His body has become a vessel for the demon Azmodil. We're keeping him in a cell in the basement of the palace."

"A demon?" Tonz's eyes grew wide. "But how?"

Raelle shifted her gaze to the snow. "Volshira...".

"Volshira? But she died. She—wait... is she like you? Does she have one of these stones?"

"I'm not sure if she ever really died. But I do know that she has a stone. I saw it when she killed—

Raelle felt as if her breath had been pilfered from her lungs. The recollection of Volshira making love to Chrishtan and then stabbing him sickened her.

Tonz reached out and pulled her into his arms. "Are you all right?"

Raelle reached for her Lyre and did her best to push the memory from her mind. "Yes." She tried to mask her anguish as she looked into Tonz's concerned eyes. "I'm fine."

Tonz held her close. "We don't have to talk about this if it's too difficult. I'm sorry."

"No." Raelle shook her head. "It's fine. I'm fine. I have to be strong if I'm going to bring Chrishtan back."

"So what did she do? Volshira..."

"She murdered him. And she cast some kind of spell on him. A dark spell, of the Void. She wants to be his queen. And if she can't have him, no one can."

Tonz shook his head with a distraught expression. "I have to say, I'm a bit shocked. I mean, yes, Volshira has always been very domineering and forceful, maybe even a little manipulative, but killing Chrishtan? I don't know, I mean I warned him about her when I noticed how volatile their relationship was getting early on. But he just said that anger was her way of dealing with things. He was in love with her. It was a strange and strained kind of love, but it was real."

"He never told me about her." Raelle shifted her gaze to the snow. "I may have never known about her had I not seen her k—kill... him."

"I'm so sorry, Raelle." Tonz formed a deep frown. His genuine sympathy for her was more than apparent. "I'm sure you two would've gotten to that conversation eventually. You couldn't have had much time for small talk, I'm assuming."

"No." Raelle rubbed her chin. Tonz always had a way of explaining the practical reasons for things. "I suppose not."

"So what about this demon?"

"Well, now that my Lyre is strong and my skills are proficient, we go into the Void and find him. Then we bring Chrishtan home."

"Find him? What do you—

Tonz opened his eyes wide and looked to the sky. High above them, battalions of Ellosian air raiders flew overhead in bird form carrying Chocaz energy grenades.

Raelle whipped around at the sound of someone yelling behind her. Both she and Tonz rushed toward the Rogue resistance trainee.

"It's the Abequans!" the young Rogue hollered. "Get your gear! We're going to need all the help we can get."

"How many?" asked Tonz.

"At least five thousand strong." The Rogue tried to catch his breath. "But they're not just soldiers, Tonz."

Raelle saw the intense fear in the Rogue's eyes.

"Th—there are monsters. Things I've never seen. Things of nightmares. I think they've awakened the Destroyer."

Raelle looked at Tonz. "We have to hurry. I'm sure Volshira is with them. She knows how to take down the force field! And I'm sure she'll have someone on the inside."

"You're right," Tonz agreed. "Let's go."

Raelle, Tonz, and their messenger ran at Rogue speed to the palace. They rushed to the royal armory where they found Cohlen.

"Cohlen!" Raelle ran to him. "What's going on?"

"She's back. Volshira is back."

"How do you know? Did you see her?"

"I didn't need to see her. I know it's her. No one else would attempt an attack on Ellios like this. Especially in the name of Abequa. She's here for her king. I'm sure of it."

"For Chrishtan?"

"Yes. Remember the first night of his turning? He said

222

*she* would be coming for him. And honestly, I didn't know what he meant until now."

"You may be right," said Raelle. "Do you think he's safe where he is?"

"I hope so," Cohlen replied. "No one knows about the secret lab, so I don't see how she could find him."

"I hope you're right." Raelle rushed to her armoire. Tonz helped her remove her training gear and change into royal armor.

Raelle turned to Cohlen. "Where is Oleevar?"

"He's out there, among them. He's looking for her."

"What is he going to do?"

"Well, you know Oleevar and his genius ideas." Cohlen forced an uneasy laugh. "He's going to find Volshira and stop her with his new ability."

"She'll never let him close enough."

"He says he has it all figured out."

Raelle shook her head. "Of course he does."

"But the mechanized soldiers are ready to go," Cohlen added. "They're going to try and flank from the rear exit, from the lakes."

Raelle could feel her heart thumping. "Have you seen them yet? Volshira's forces?"

"No." Cohlen grew pale with terror. "But I heard."

Raelle ran to Cohlen and threw her arms around him. "You've got control of it. Please don't worry. This is what you've been training for. Your wraith form is *you,* Cohlen. You are not one of *them.* Do you hear me? You are no demon." She knew he needed more reassurance.

An insecure grin flashed across Cohlen's face. "I know."

Raelle smiled and squeezed Cohlen's arms. "Good." She hugged him once more. "Now let's get out there and help Oleevar."

They rushed out from the armory and leapt down the snowy palace steps. Cohlen hopped onto a gold-plated speeder and Raelle and Tonz followed behind him on foot. Their Rogue speed made it easy to keep up. Once they reached the main gate, they hurried up the steps in order to get a better view of what they were up against. As they stood among the ranged fighters a top the Ellios wall, they peered out past the city's domed force field. Elven soldiers in their mechanized suits and armor did their best to push the enemy back as their avian counterparts dropped Chocaz energy bombs overhead.

"What in the name of all that is good and light is..." Tonz's voice drifted off.

What they saw left Raelle speechless as well. She was bombarded with terror. She stared out over the horde of Abequan soldiers. They rode on foreboding behemoths she had never before seen. And in the midst of their daunting ranks, grotesque demonic creatures snarled and seethed alongside them. The scent of their decaying flesh and the indescribable nature of their revolting forms forced Raelle to take a step back. She was overcome with dizziness. She squatted down to remedy her symptoms. Flashbacks of the revolting Minotirr as it chased her through the Didumos wilderness overwhelmed her. Vivid images of her parents' brutal murder danced in and out of the haunting playback. Raelle was unable to move. She tried to fight it, but the memories left her incapacitated.

As she crouched, she felt the gentle touch of a familiar hand and the soothing sound of a familiar voice. "Listen to your breaths, Raelle. Listen as they blend with the cool winds of your serene valley. The sound of your young brothers' laughter. The smell of breakfast coming through the chimney. The warmth of the sun on your face..."

Raelle did as Tonz instructed. She went to that place. It was her place of focus and concentration, her sanctuary of serenity. After a few moments, Raelle opened her eyes to see her best friend squatting down in front of her. All she could see of Tonz were his dark green eyes. The rest of his face was covered by a mask and his hair hidden by a hood. His eyes smiled at her through his Rogue guise.

"Thank you." Raelle began to feel better.

Tonz brushed his hand over Raelle's shoulder. "You're getting better. Every time you do it, the time it takes to recover becomes less and less. Are you sure you're ready to go out there? I know we would all understand if—

"No!" Raelle snapped. "No…" She took a deep breath. "Our people need me *now*, not later. I can't hide away in fear. I can't let what happened to me keep me in this prison. I have to face reality and the world. I'm ready."

Tonz helped Raelle to her feet. "I know you are."

"Look!" Cohlen pointed over the wall. "It's Oleevar."

Raelle left the refuge of Tonz's embrace and peered out over the wall and through the force field. She focused her Lyre on her sense of sight. Suddenly, she could see much further. And the silhouette of someone running in their direction became a detailed image of Oleevar.

"He must not have been able to find Shira." Cohlen raced back down the steps.

Raelle and Tonz followed closely behind as he opened the gates and rushed out to meet his brother.

"Oleevar!" Cohlen called.

Oleevar ran right past him.

"What's going on?" Cohlen shouted. "Where are you going?"

Oleevar stopped and glared at Raelle, then back at Cohlen. It took him a moment to respond. "I—um—They're trying to take down the grid. And if they do, they will get inside the palace."

"What?" Tonz asked. "How?"

Oleevar ignored him "What about Chrishtan?"

"*What* about him?" asked Raelle.

"What if they get to him?" Oleevar heaved out the words between breaths. "That's what Volshira came for. I'm sure of it."

Raelle tossed her hand in the air. "We can't let that happen! What do you suggest? You're the one with all the big ideas."

"I think we should move him." Oleevar seemed to lack his usual precocious confidence. "Get him out of the city. Take him into the wilderness until this is over."

"Are you serious?" Raelle's eyes widened in disbelief.

225

"We'll have to wake him to do that. Right now his sedated state is the only thing keeping him from breaking out of there and trying to kill all of us."

"We don't have any other choice, Raelle." Oleevar's tone was sharp. "Just trust me on this. It's the only way to ensure his security."

Raelle sensed that something was off. Oleevar didn't seem like himself. Even the way he spoke seemed different. His diction lacked its usual patronizing complexity. *Maybe it's this unexpected attack. It's got him spooked. Or he really is hiding something from me...*

Cohlen looked at his brother. "You're absolutely sure about this?"

"Yes, I am," Oleevar answered impatiently.

Tonz turned to Raelle. "I have to go help my troops. They'll be looking for me."

Raelle felt sick to her stomach at the thought of Tonz going out to confront the putrid army of creatures from the Void. She couldn't stand the thought of losing him too. But she knew it was his duty and his honor to serve with his mission troops. She felt torn. She too wanted to join her Rogue forces against the enemy. After all, it was what she had been training for. But it was not the only thing. Her training would also allow her the skills and prowess to find Chrishtan within the Void and bring him back to Lerim, so that together, they could bring light back to their world. But things had changed since his departure. Raelle had changed.

Raelle's mind took her back to the night of Chrishtan's death. He had kissed Volshira the same way he had kissed her. He had held Volshira the same way he had held her. *If he loved me, why would he lie with her?* The thought shook her. *Oleevar said she had manipulated him... cursed him. But I—*

"Raelle?" Tonz gently shook her.

"Yes, I... um..." Raelle tried to shake away the heartbreaking memory.

"I'm going out to the troops now," Tonz reiterated.

"Yes, I understand." She swallowed the lump in her

throat. "Please, be careful I don't know what I—

"I'm a soldier, Raelle," said Tonz, "and soldiers die. It's a promise I made to my people."

Raelle loved the way Tonz always explained things, so simple. So straight forward. He always made sense. It was hard to argue with him. She admired him for that and also for his unwavering sense of honor. "I'm sorry," said Raelle. "I'm being selfish. I can't do that anymore. They are *my* people. *Our* people."

Raelle could see Tonz's eyes wrinkle as he smiled under his mask. "That's right."

"Maybe you should join him," Oleevar suggested.

Cohlen shook his head. "What? No."

"Maybe she should go with him," Oleevar continued in a harsh tone. "After all, it was *her* people who got us into this mess. So it seems only fitting that she should go fight with them."

Raelle was speechless. Oleevar's words cut her deep. But in her heart, she knew there was truth to them.

"Olee?" Cohlen shot him a quizzical look. "Raelle is not to blame. What's gotten into you?"

"Nothing." Oleevar turned to his brother. "I'm just saying. We can take care of Chrishtan and she can go fight with *her* people."

Tonz stood tall by her side. "I think Raelle is perfectly capable of making up her own mind without you berating her."

"Is that why *you're* defending her?" Oleevar snapped.

Tonz pulled down his mask and stepped to Oleevar. "What is your problem?"

"I don't have a problem," Oleevar retorted. "I'm solving problems. Now take your mate and go."

"My *mate*?" Tonz's face was only a centimeter from Oleevar's. "She is my comrade and yours."

Cohlen pulled on his brother's arm. "What's going on with you? We're in the middle of an attack and you're picking fights?"

"Sorry." Oleevar backed away from Tonz. "Let's go get Chrishtan."

Raelle took a deep breath. "Oleevar is right. This *is* my family's mess. I need to clean it up."

"Raelle, you don't have t—

"No, Cohlen," Raelle protested. "I don't need you to protect me. I don't need Tonz to protect me, or Chrishtan. I don't need any of you to protect me. I'm tired of being the victim. I'm tired of hiding away. It's like Tonz said. This is my decision. And I choose to go be with our people. I choose to fight. I know the two of you will keep Chrishtan safe."

Oleevar motioned to his brother. "Let's go!"

Cohlen's face flooded with disappointment.

"I'm sorry." Raelle shrugged. "It's my duty."

As Cohlen hopped onto his speeder with Oleevar, Raelle felt a twinge of regret. She watched as they faded into the distance, torn between her duty to her people and her worry that the two brothers would be unable to control Azmodil. After all, Chrishtan's life was hanging in the balance. But so were the lives of her people.

Tonz pulled his mask back on. "You sure you're ready?"

"As ready as I'll ever be."

"That's my Rogue."

# CHAPTER 20
## THE ENEMY

Snow fell as Raelle and Tonz dashed to meet their comrades. Raelle focused her Lyre to enhance her senses. She was now able to see through the winter storm that swirled around them. As she followed Tonz into battle with the mission troops, her Lyre raged through her with an intensity she had never before experienced. Tonz led her to the head of the brigade and into a ghastly mess of Abequan warriors littered with demonic creatures. As soon as she made it to the front, Tonz signaled her. With all of the energy Raelle could muster, she recoiled and released her power. Magnificent waves of pilfering sound radiated from her vocal chords onto the battlefield. Hundreds of enemies in her path dropped to the ground.

As soon as the sound exited her lungs, feebleness took hold. Her Lyre was spent. Raelle fell to the ground alongside her enemies on the icy snow. Tonz rushed to her, propping her up in his lap. From his pocket, he pulled out a vial of Torpaz blood and poured the warm fluid into Raelle's mouth. As her body absorbed the gem's energy, Raelle could feel her Lyre return. It did not take long for her to recover.

Tonz helped her to her feet. "You've got this." He handed her a few vials. "Keep these on you for recovery until your body becomes more accustomed to your gift."

Raelle took the vials and reveled in the sound of the rebel troops as they cheered and rallied behind her. The sound boosted Raelle's confidence. She felt unstoppable. Raelle's stealth, strength, and stamina were unmatched as she and Tonz fought their way through lesser mobs of repulsive creatures. Trails of rotting flesh and putrefying fluids stained the snow where monstrosities had fallen. Raelle and Tonz's armor dripped with the same decaying carnage as they sliced, stabbed, and maimed their way through the mobs. They left nothing but a trail of mutilated atrocities behind them. Raelle gained more and more power with every strike of her blade and parry of her feet.

They continued the slaughter as they made their way into the brush. Suddenly, Raelle lost her footing. Something in the immense brush held her by the ankle. It pulled her to the ground. Raelle gasped at the freakish hand that held her. It belonged to one of the most disturbing entities she had ever seen. Low to the ground, the humanoid creature's narrow arms and legs stretched out far beyond its body like an insect. Its shoulders looked as if they had been bent and twisted. Attached to its emaciated human chest and back was the abdomen of an arachnid. It spun its head around and showed its mangled human face to Raelle. It hissed and sniffed her before opening its foul-smelling mouth to expose its long, red, tube-like tongue. She grabbed the creature's neck with both hands and struggled to force its disturbing face away from hers. Raelle moaned in fear as its tubular tongue extended out toward her like a long, skinny arm

Raelle turned her face away and saw another soldier lying in the snow next to her in the same predicament. The soldier panicked and the humanoid arachnid stuck its rigid tongue through the soldier's eye. The soldier screamed in terror as the monster sucked up the contents of his cranium using its tongue like a straw.

Freeing up one of her hands, Raelle grabbed one of her draggers and sliced through her captor's tongue. Pink soupy ooze spilled onto Raelle's face. The creature's scream burned in her ears. She jumped up and tackled the beast back into the snowy brush. The creature tumbled onto its back, its belly exposed. Raelle sliced it open from the bottom of its abdomen to the top of its throat. Its slimy pink contents of the creature spilled out over the white snow.

Raelle stinted toward the next enemy. All around her, Rogue fighters fell to the ground, pulled under by the slinking, spider-like horrors. Surely their troops would not survive if this continued. Raelle closed her eyes, charged her Lyre and recoiled. Not wishing to kill her comrades, she harnessed just enough energy to stun them. Her company's screams promptly ceased.

"Help us wake them," Tonz said, rushing over to the closest of his troops.

Raelle followed him and the troops' medics to the stunned soldiers. After killing the stunned monsters that lay atop each fighter, they opened the soldiers' mouths and fed them the Torpaz blood. Within moments, they woke ready to return to the fight.

As they sprinted toward the main front of Abequan warriors and demonic creatures, thousands of elven combatants rose up in mechanized suits from the lakes that surrounded them. They shot their energized weapons, sending pieces of the grotesque demon army into the air. Elves with mechanized extensions and enhancements followed through calculated gaps in the Ellios force field that closed behind them. Elves in avian form dropped their Chocaz explosives across the snowy field, now spoiled with muck and mire. Monsters of diverse shapes and sizes, rancid smells, and disturbing comportments lay mutilated across the battlefield.

Raelle and Tonz were almost to the outskirts of the battle when Raelle stopped dead in her tracks. An imprint in the snow caught her eye.

"Raelle!" Tonz stopped and hollered back at her. "What's wrong?"

Raelle squatted down and flipped over the familiar frame of the elf that lay lifeless in the snow. Her troops continued to run past.

"Oleevar?" Raelle studied the elf's familiar face. "Oleevar!" She shook his limp frame.

Among the passing troop's shadows, one paused and hovered over her. "Olee?" Tonz crouched down and pulled off his own mask to get a better look. "I thought he was going to get Chrishtan? What is he doing out here?"

"I don't know." Raelle checked Oleevar's hand, a sense of urgency rising in her. "Is he dead? Someone's taken his ring."

Tonz used his Lyre to check Oleevar for signs of life. "Look here, he's been stabbed." Tonz turned Oleevar on his side to expose the wound and the crimson snow. "It was a short sword, but it went all the way through." Tonz opened the pouch on his utility belt. "Here, we need to wrap his wound to prevent further blood loss. I sense a very faint heartbeat." Tonz grabbed Raelle's hand and pressed it to Oleevar's body. "Here, sense it. Just like in your training. Sense the life force. Feel for the energy. Listen for the heartbeat."

While Tonz wrapped Oleevar's wound, Raelle called upon her Lyre, magnified her senses and honed in on Oleevar's aura. She could still feel his life force. It was weak, but present. Raelle listened closely for the beating of his heart. Every once in a while a faint thump could be heard.

"I feel it. I can hear it." She grinned at Tonz. "He's still with us."

Tonz laid Oleevar on his back. "Now." Tonz grasped both of Raelle's hands and laid them on either side of Oleevar's upper chest. "Transfer some of your life and Lyre to him. Just like we practiced. You can do it."

Raelle closed her eyes once more and collected all of her energy in the same way she harnessed her Opalz gift. Once composed, she focused hard and sent the energy through her hands. Her arms went numb as the vitality surged into her friend's chest and jolted his body.

Oleevar coughed with a harsh, raspy sound.

Raelle expelled a sigh of relief. "Oh, thank the Architect."

"I knew you could do it," Tonz said with a grin. "Let's wake him up and find out what happened." Tonz removed a vial of Emeralz blood from his pouch and poured it through Oleevar's lips.

After a few moments, the elf's eyelids fluttered open. He squinted hard as his eyes shifted back and forth. Raelle and Tonz helped him to gradually sit up. "Where is she?" Oleevar seemed to panic.

"Who?" Raelle asked.

"She's going to take Chrishtan." Oleevar's tone matched his frightened expression. "Sh—she stole my ability."

"Who did?" Tonz questioned.

"Shira," Oleevar said weakly. "She has a black Opalz stone. It's given her the ability to manipulate others' Lyre. And if she touches you, she can tap into *your* Opalz ability. She stole mine."

Tonz looked at Raelle with big, confused eyes. "What is it?"

"The Opalz stone has given Oleevar the ability to transform," she replied.

Tonz shook his head. "But all elves have ability to shift. That's what they are, they're shifters."

"No," Raelle explained. "Oleevar can take on the form of *anyone* he touches. Not just animals." Raelle looked into Oleevar's golden brown eyes. "You were trying to transform into *her*, weren't you?"

"Yes," Oleevar said wincing in pain. "In her image, I could send her army back to Abequa. I flew out here in the form of an owl and landed on her shoulder. Somehow she knew it was me. She seized me and syphoned my Lyre. Then she threw me to the ground. She completely depleted my Lyre, and I transformed back. That's when she stabbed me and left me for dead. Before taking on my figure, she took my ring, and tossed it into the snow. I think this is how she was able to influence Chrishtan. She was literally manipulating his Lyre, his energy, his reality."

"So the person we let into Ellios was her?" Raelle stood.

"What?" Oleevar scrambled to his feet "Oh, no. Where is she?"

Raelle began to panic. "We thought she was you! She took Cohlen to go move Chrishtan's body."

"She's going to take him!" Raelle had never seen such fear in Oleevar's eyes. "We need to get to him before she does!"

Suddenly, a look of horror came over Tonz's face.

"What is it?" Raelle turned around to see what Tonz was gaping at.

"She's shut down the force field!" Tonz yelled. "She's going to get Chrishtan next!"

"We must go now!" Oleevar stumbled toward the main gate. Raelle could tell he was in pain and his wound continued to soak through Tonz's wrap.

"Tonz!" Raelle called. "We're going to need all the help we can get to stop her. Come on!"

They sprinted toward Oleevar. Tonz threw the struggling elf over his shoulder.

"Put me down!" Oleevar demanded.

"Not a chance!" exclaimed Tonz. "You're slowing us down."

Oleevar released a long sigh of defeat, and they continued on toward the gates. Along the way, the glimmer of something in the snow caught Raelle's eye. It was Oleevar's ring. She swiftly picked it up and put it in one of her pouches. As the three of them approached the gates, the guards opened them straightaway.

"Oleevar," Raelle called as Tonz put the elf back on his feet. "Here!" She tossed Oleevar his ring.

"Thank you." Oleevar caught it and slipped it on. He hopped onto a speeder and the three of them took off toward the citadel. Once they reached the base of the grand fortress steps, Oleevar dismounted his vehicle and they sprinted up the steps to the palace doors. They raced inside and down the hall to Oleevar's underground workshop. They flew down the stairs and Oleevar opened the final door into the lab. Inside, they found Cohlen unconscious on the floor. The door to Chrishtan's cold cell hung wide open.

"We're too late," Raelle cried.

"Maybe not." Oleevar hurried to his brother. "She might still be on the palace grounds. We know she only just shut down the grid. You two go stop her! I'm going to wake Cohlen and come after. And remember, do not let her touch you!"

Raelle and Tonz rushed from the lab and up the stairs.

The snow fell much harder as they left the castle and dashed across the white palace grounds toward the silo that housed the power grid. Half way to their destination, Raelle noticed two winged creatures hovering above them. She could barely make them out through the intense snowfall, but *they* seemed to notice her. The winged figures dove down from the sky straight for Raelle and Tonz. They landed just meters ahead and blocked their path.

"Looking for something?" A woman tucked her black feathery wings against her back.

Raelle stepped closer and glared at Volshira. Next to her, Chrishtan stood tall and confident. But Raelle knew it was not really him. His pale, veiny skin covered in demonic branding, black eyes, and sharp claws gave the demon away. Raelle swallowed hard as she eyed the enormous set of black leathery wings on his back.

Raelle looked back to Volshira. "Why are you doing this?"

"Don't play dumb with me, girl." Volshira stepped forward. "That little innocent act isn't going to work on me. You know exactly why I'm doing this. You and your family brought this on yourselves and have forced the rest of us to clean up *your* mess. I had no other choice."

"You always have a choice, Shira," said Tonz.

"Oh please," Volshira laughed. "I've heard enough of Tonzelle Lorestia's idealistic propaganda over the past fifteen years to last me a lifetime."

Raelle stepped to her. "We're not letting you take him."

The demon chuckled. "It would bring me great joy to see you try and stop us." His voice was strangely deep, scratchy, and layered. It sent shivers through Raelle's body.

"Shira!" Raelle shouted. "If you truly love Chrishtan, you will not let this demon have him. I know you still care for him. You can't do this."

"You're right." Volshira winced and tilted her head. "I do care for him, deeply. We were going to have a life together. We were going to take back Abequa and make things right again. But you ruined all of that. This is the only way to ensure the security of my nation. No warrior prince is going to wed a Rogue. Especially a Rogue whose family turned this continent upside-down. Lochran was right about one thing, though, the throne is no place for a dirty-blood scrub. Samuel *is* the rightful and pure-blood heir to your kingdom, not you."

Raelle recoiled from Volshira's claim. "What are you talking about? You know nothing of my brother. He and I shared the same blood." Raelle took another step toward her enemy. "How dare you speak his name. Because of people like you, he was murdered!"

Volshira shook her head. "Tsk, tsk, tsk, little girl." She smirked. "Sounds to me like someone has been keeping things from you. Samuel *is not* your brother. And he *is* alive. Although, not quite as you remember him." She leered as if in victory.

Raelle's fear and disgust heightened as the demon licked Chrishtan's blue lips and dragged its purple tongue across his razor-sharp teeth. "Samuel's soul belongs to me, and soon, so will yours. And this time, your precious Chrishtan won't be able to save you."

"You're lying!" Raelle shouted, her body taut with tension.

"If you haven't learned by now, these are dark times." Volshira teased in a satirical tone. "Not everyone is what they seem. I bet you thought *your* parents raised you, too."

Suddenly, the missing memories of her last encounter with her brother flashed through Raelle's jumbled mind. Visions of Chrishtan and Samuel's duel forced her heart into a vicious drum roll that shook her tightened chest. She recalled every vivid detail. She felt every ounce of rage against Chrishtan that sparked her Opalz ability. Her grief flowed through her like a steady river as she cradled her brother in the grass. Warm tears of joy cascaded from her eyes as Chrishtan returned her brother to life. Finally, she cringed at the intense pain as the broad-headed arrow sliced through her armor and into her heart. *My brother is alive...*

Raelle gasped and choked the memory back down into her soul like an un-masticated chunk of red meat. Her breaths thrashed in and out of her like the crashing waves of a hurricane. *They lied to me. Why would they lie to me?*

"Volshira, stop it!" Tonz bellowed. "That's enough!"

"Raelle!" She heard someone calling her name and quickly turned around to see Cohlen and Oleevar running in their direction.

"Stay away from her!" Oleevar hollered as he came upon

them. "Don't let her touch you!"

"Are you all right?" Cohlen asked, rushing to Raelle's side.

Volshira cleared her throat. "You've arrived just in time. I was just telling Raelle how her life is a lie." She scoffed with a menacing grin. "Oh, and also that her brother is still alive. Isn't that right, Olee?"

Oleevar swallowed hard. "I, uh—I mean he—

"No need to worry, Raelle." Volshira's short swords clanged as they left their scabbards. "It'll all be over soon."

Volshira lunged at Raelle. Raelle swiftly stinted, disappearing and reappearing amidst the curtain of snowflakes behind the warrior. Using both her short swords, Volshira blocked Raelle's attacks from the back and Tonz's from the front. Raelle could feel Volshira's strength with every parry of her sword. As the Huronian Rogues and Abequan warrior danced across the snow, Raelle could hear her two elven companions doing battle with the demon. Oleevar had taken on the form of a white leopard and Cohlen a white bear. Their ivory fur made it difficult to see them among the thick screen of snowfall.

As Raelle and Tonz continued their attack, Raelle could tell that Volshira was growing weak. She slipped a foot through the warrior's legs and sent her tumbling into the snow.

Volshira smiled as she hit the ground. "Thank you."

*Oh no! I let her touch me.* As Volshira stood, Raelle turned and ran. "Tonz! Run!"

Tonz looked at Raelle and back at Volshira. Instead of sprinting away, he leapt toward Volshira. As the warrior recoiled to use Raelle's gift, Tonz landed a potent boot to Volshira's chest and sent her flying backward. The kick seemed to diminish the intensity of the blast of sound, but nevertheless, Tonz took all of it.

Raelle dashed back to her comrade. She dropped to her knees and checked Tonz for any sign of life. Fresh red blood dripped from his nose and ears. As she pressed her hands against his chest, a faint stirring in the snow stole Raelle's attention. A few meters across the intense snowfall, Volshira was regaining consciousness. Her hands moved toward a slot in her armor and opened it. From the compartment, Volshira removed two vials, one black and one red.

Raelle disappeared from where she hovered over Tonz and reappeared over Volshira. She kicked the vials from Volshira's hand and crushed them with her boot. Their black and red contents stained the snow's glimmering surface.

"I'm afraid I can't let you do that." Raelle rested her boot on Volshira's injured chest. "Didn't anyone ever teach you not to mess with others peoples' abilities, or family members?"

Volshira struggled to speak. "That's funny coming from *you.*" She coughed.

"Give me one reason why I shouldn't kill you." Raelle moved her boot to Volshira's throat.

Volshira barely managed her answer. "I can't." The warrior's normally arrogant expression transformed and a look of regret swiftly took its place. Tears quickly welled in Volshira's, golden eyes. "Do it. If you don't kill me now, she'll never stop."

"She'll?" Raelle asked. "Who?"

"Lilazz ," Volshira's voice scratched through her crumpled throat. "She's in me."

"Lilazz?" Raelle wrinkled her brow. "I don't—

All of the sudden, an enormous shadow swooped over her. Raelle felt the demon's claws dig into her armor and lift her off the ground. Down below, she saw Cohlen and Oleevar in white tiger and bear form running in her direction. The demon dropped Raelle from the sky. Her legs buckled as soon as she hit the ground. From there, the demon swooped down and picked up Volshira. In an instant, Chrishtan and Volshira disappeared high into the dense clouds of the blizzard.

By the time Cohlen reached Raelle, he had returned to his elven form. His worried face hovered over her.

"Are you hurt?"

"My legs." Raelle winced. "I think they're broken." Cohlen helped her to stand, but she immediately collapsed in pain. As the shock of the injury set in, Raelle found it difficult to focus.

Cohlen squatted down and picked Raelle up from the ground. He carried Raelle from where she crashed to where Oleevar was attempting to revive Tonz. Out of nowhere, a flash of blue light lit up the clouds above them.

"The force field." Cohlen smiled. "It's back up."

In the distance, a figure ran toward them. It stopped as soon as it reached Oleevar and Tonz.

"It's Zeell." Cohlen quickened his pace. It didn't take long for them to reach their companions.

"We were able to fend them off for now, Master Cohlen," Zeell reported. "The Abequans have retreated."

"Let's get these two to the healing paddock." Oleevar directed Zeell to help him to pick up Tonz's unconscious body.

"Is he going to make it?" Raelle asked from Cohlen's arms.

"I think so," answered Oleevar. "But we must hurry. He's not got much time."

The intense shock of Raelle's injuries were starting to make her feel as if she were outside her body. Her eyes grew heavy and her mind blurry.

"Hang in there, Raelle…" Cohlen's voice faded out and everything went black.

# CHAPTER 21
## REVELATION & LIBERATION

Raelle woke to find herself in Chrishtan's room, tucked into his bed. The light of the late afternoon seeped in through the slightly parted curtains. Raelle watched the snowflakes as they lightly descended over the palace grounds. The faint throbbing in her legs immediately reminded her of her recent skirmish. She lifted the green silk covers and saw that her legs were now tightly wrapped in splints.

"You've got to be kidding me." Raelle sighed and shook her head. The sound of her voice woke the dogs from their slumber in front of the fireplace. Pip and Sasha ran over and jumped onto the bed to greet their mistress. Raelle giggled as the dogs' tongues consoled her.

"You two always know how to make me feel better."

A sudden clicking sound sent the dogs leaping to the floor and rushing to the chamber door. They barked viciously until the intruder revealed himself.

"You're awake." Oleevar strolled into the room, his head held high. "And right on schedule."

"Schedule?" Raelle groaned.

"Yes, I've been experimenting with the dosage of your Chocaz elixir." The elf stood next to her and smiled as if nothing were wrong. "I believe that it will ensure a speedy recovery for your legs. It's time for me to check them." He reached for the blankets.

"Don't you touch me!" Raelle slapped his hand away.

Oleevar raised both hands and stepped back. "What's gotten into you?"

"Oh, I don't know." Raelle scowled. Even though it appeared that Oleevar had forgotten about her brother, *Raelle* had not. "Maybe your lies?"

"Raelle, I—

"No, Olee!" Raelle used her arms to shift her body and sit up. She wished she could push Oleevar out of the room—out of her life, maybe—instead of being stuck in bed. "I don't want to hear your shite!"

"I beg your pardon?" Oleevar frowned, seemingly clueless. "You've spent far too much time with those rugged Rogue fighters. You know—

"Spare me your belittling banter," Raelle snapped. "You don't get to tell me *anything*, Oleevar! Do you hear me? Nothing! You lied to me about my brother. You lied to me about Chrishtan! I'm out of here. I'll go to the Lady of the Realm on my own." Raelle threw the blankets off her legs and pushed herself toward the edge of the bed. "I don't need you, or your family, and I most definitely don't need your falsehoods!"

"Oh, Raelle, please." Oleevar crossed his arms and rolled his eyes. "Spare me the human melodrama. I made a decision that I thought was best for both you and the group."

Raelle gritted her teeth. She wanted so badly to rip the splints from her legs, jump out of bed, and punch Oleevar in the face. "You know, I'm getting sick and tired of you and everyone else making all of my decisions for me. That was not your call to make, Olee, and you know it!"

Oleevar nonchalantly shook his head. "I know nothing of the sort. I did what was best. And now that I see your true Rogue nature setting in, I'm glad I made that decision."

"Screw you, Olee." Raelle grimaced. Her legs ached beneath their bindings. "You know, sometimes you're a real pretentious arse!"

"Do you think that bothers me? You're not saying anything I haven't heard from Cohlen." Oleevar shrugged. "I do not use my emotions to act or make decisions. The exponential success and progress of Ellios is due to *my* concise decision making. Neither your words or anyone else's faze me in the slightest."

Raelle scowled. "So I'm assuming an apology is far outside the realm of possibility?"

"That is correct," Oleevar said. "I am not sorry for what I did. It was the best decision I could have made at the time. The only thing I am sorry about is the fact that *you* are unable to see that."

"You know what, Oleevar!" Raelle clenched her fists and pushed out a long loud groan. "I swear to the Architect, when I get out of this bed I'm—

"Well, there is no way you're getting out of that bed in that condition. It's only been a couple of days." Oleevar explained in his usual patronizing tone. "Broken bones don't heal overnight, you know. But with my Chocaz elixir, it will be a much shorter duration for repairs."

"I've been asleep for *two days*?" Raelle's eyes bulged out of her head. "We're wasting time. I've completed my training with Tonz and now I'm..." Her heart sank. "Tonz, where is he? Is he all right? Did he make it? I—

Oleevar interrupted with a wave of his hand. "Tonzelle is recovering down the hall. Like you, he's going to need time and lots of rest."

"Is he awake?" Raelle asked. "I need to see him." She made it to the edge of the bed and threw her completely straight and splinted legs over the side.

"Not right now." Oleevar grasped her shoulders and pushed her back onto the bed. "You're probably going to need another week before you're fully recovered. Then, once you're in good health and able to walk on your own, you can see him. We have a difficult task ahead of us in the Verge."

Memories and questions overwhelmed Raelle's mind. She couldn't think straight. Oleevar's uninvited touch lit a searing flame of rage within her. She threw his hands away as her mind zigged and zagged from one thing to another.

"Raelle, please!" Oleevar stepped back. "I'm only—

"He came to me in a dream, you know." She cut him off. "He tried to tell me. He said he was coming for me."

"Who?" Oleevar asked.

"My brother," Raelle replied crossly. "A few months ago when I first began training. I thought it was only a dream because it didn't make sense. But now, I think it might." She heaved out an irritated sigh. "It's been weighing on my mind for so long. This whole time, I've felt like something was missing. I felt like I was losing my mind. But I wasn't. *You* were lying to me."

"For the last time! It was for your own good," Oleevar said. His voice was filled with exasperation. "We were just trying to keep you safe."

"Once again, you were making my decisions for me!"

"*I* wanted to tell you, Raelle." Cohlen rushed into the room and planted himself at Raelle's side. "But Oleevar had a point. We just—

Raelle was overcome with anger. She felt like she was back in the valley arguing with her mother. "I don't give a damn! It wasn't your decision to make." She went back to clenching her teeth. She wanted desperately to bolt from the room, like she would have back in the valley to escape her mother's ranting. But her body wouldn't let her. Her heavy, stiff legs had her trapped in the Ellios palace with two brothers she no longer trusted. Tears of frustration sprang to her eyes "You two had better tell me everything you know, right now. Volshira also said those weren't my parents who raised me. I want the whole story. I want the pieces you kept from me."

"I know nothing about your parents," Oleevar protested, his hands up in defense. Something about his tone of voice made Raelle believe him. "I only know what happened the day you were killed."

Raelle looked him straight in the eye. "I'm listening."

Oleevar began to pace. "Well, after you were shot, Samuel handed you over to Chrishtan and he carried you back inside the palace walls. We rushed you to the healing paddock. We did everything we could to save you, but it was no use. We—

"And my brother?" Raelle's voice was thick with tears. "Did my brother not come with me?"

"No." Cohlen took Raelle's hand. "He took out half of his own army with his scream. That's when the battle ensued. We lost sight of him. I assume Volshira took him back to Abequa with her since she says that's where he is now."

243

"So he came *with* Lochran's army?" asked Raelle. A cold realization poured over her. Samuel hadn't been taken prisoner at all. He'd abandoned her. *Because he isn't really my brother?... like Volshira said.*

"Yes," Cohlen answered sullenly. "As Lochran's general."

Tears slipped from Raelle's eyes. "So he wasn't coming here for me?"

"Not that *we* know of," Oleevar replied. "He came to kill Chrishtan."

Raelle's heart broke into a million pieces. Her trust and faith in everyone she had ever cared about was completely shattered. Resentment shot through her like an electric shock. *All along, Samuel knew and yet he said nothing. He left me there. He told me he would be back, but he never returned. Instead, he made himself a general? Am I cursed? Can I trust no one? Am I never meant to have control over my own life? My parents, my brother, Chrishtan, Cohlen, Oleevar... All of them kept things from me.* Raelle buried her face in her hands. *I feel so alone.*

Cohlen gently squeezed her hand. "I'm so sorry Raelle, I—

"No!" Raelle forcefully yanked her hand from his grasp. "I don't want to hear it. Just leave me alone!"

"Please, be rational," Oleevar pleaded.

"Get out!" Raelle pointed at the door. "Both of you! I want to be alone."

Oleevar was the first to retreat. "I just don't understand these human overreactions," he mumbled under his breath. "Especially Rogues... so hot headed..."

"Now!" Raelle yelled.

"I'm sorry, Raelle." Cohlen paused at the door before leaving. His face held an expression that mixed sorrow and concern. "Truly I am."

Raelle ignored him, her eyes fixed on the window and the snow coming down outside. Tears cascaded down her face as memories of the past few months bombarded her mind. The Lantern Forest. Jenladra. Turning. Being Trapped inside the Void.

Chrishtan. The Minotirr. Samuel's death. Her parent's murder. *And now they may not have been my parents at all?* All of it blurred together like swirls of paint. *From the beginning, I knew I shouldn't have trusted anyone. But I let Chrishtan in. I told him everything. I gave him everything. He knew how vulnerable I was. He knew I needed him. The entire time, he never mentioned her.*

A knock came at the door.

"Go away!" Raelle called through her sniffling.

"Raelle?" the door opened a crack.

"I said, leave me alone!"

The door eased open and Raelle saw Tonz standing in the entryway. "Raelle, are you all right?"

"Tonz?" Raelle expelled a sigh of relief. "You're all right."

"Not completely. I'm still a bit dizzy and I'm having a hard time hearing certain frequencies."

"I'm sorry."

Tonz sat down on the bed. "Not your fault. Not directly anyway." He teased, trying to make her feel better. But it was not working.

"What are you doing here?" Raelle asked. "Shouldn't you be resting?"

"When I woke up, I sensed something was wrong. So I came looking for you."

"Tonz?" Raelle looked into his evergreen eyes. "Have you ever omitted any information or kept anything from me?"

Tonz formed a clueless expression. "Such as?"

"Such as, *anything*. Something you didn't want me to know. Something you kept from me to try to protect me?"

"No, I don't think so," Tonz answered earnestly. "I try to provide you with the greatest amount of information I can in order for you to learn and make the best decisions. I'm an instructor. That's what I do. I like to have all variables accounted for." He reached for Raelle's hand that sat perched on her thigh. "Why? Did something happen? Have I done something?"

Raelle saw the devastation in his glossy green eyes. The thought of hurting her was clearly something Tonz abhorred.

"No." She shook her head. "You didn't do anything... that I know of."

"All right." Tonz took a moment to wipe the tears from Raelle's face. "So tell me what's going on."

Raelle averted her gaze. She hated that he had come upon her in such a vulnerable state. In a way, it embarrassed her. In Tonz's eyes, she wanted to appear strong at all times. Raelle did not want him treating her like the others —a helpless wreck in need of rescuing. She cared deeply about his opinion of her.

"Raelle, look at me." Tonz gently turned her cheek. "You think I haven't had days like these? You think I'm tough all the time? I'm not. Not even close. There are days when I feel like a complete failure. Days when I want to shut myself in my room and never come out. Days when I feel like everything I've done is for nothing. But it is *those days* and those *hard times* that make me stronger. I learn from them. *I'm* not here to judge you. I'm your friend. I'm here to help and support you. I hope you know that."

The utter sincerity Raelle saw in Tonz's eyes and heard in his voice made her melt. He was right. He was not strong because he pretended things were fine when they weren't, he was strong because he acknowledged and learned from the tough times. They made him better. And it was what made him such a phenomenal teacher, fierce friend, and desirable companion.

"I *do* know that," said Raelle. "And I want *you* to know, that I feel lucky to have you as a friend. Because right now, my entire world is crashing down around me. I feel so alone." Raelle buried her face in her hands.

"You're not alone," said Tonz. "*I'm* here for you. Olee and Cohlen, they're—

"Part of the problem." Raelle cut in. She welcomed the feel of Tonz's caress on her back. It was the only thing that drew her attention away from the pain. And at the same time, made her feel more connected to him.

"Raelle, what happened?"

She breathed in deep and then slowly released. "Oh nothing... just Oleevar and Cohlen, keeping secrets from me. Oh, and the Elite Echo is *my brother!*"

"What Volshira told you…" Tonz groaned with concern.

"Or, Samuel may have never been my brother at all," Raelle continued in her sardonic, fast-paced rant. "My parents, they may never have been my parents. I have no idea! The man I thought I loved made love to another woman, whom I never even knew about, and then she murdered him right in front of my eyes. And now she's trying to kill me! Everyone I have ever known has lied to me. My whole entire life! It's one big messy web of lies! "

"Whoa! Slow down." Tonz looked both dumbfounded and vexed. "That is a lot to process. And it's not something you should do alone. And definitely not on an empty stomach." He did his best to try and lighten the mood. "How about, you let me take you to our favorite pub, and we work through it over a nice big meal and a few pints of ale?"

Raelle took in another deep breath before answering. "I suppose," she said with a sigh. "I am pretty hungry." Raelle's eyes locked with his. "Thank you."

"For what?" Tonz leaned into her.

Raelle felt their connection like never before. Tonz had done something no one else had. He made her feel at home. "For calming me down. For genuinely accepting me. For being a true friend. For not letting me give up on myself."

"It's my duty." Tonz smiled. "And my honor."

Raelle cracked a smile. "As with everything else." She chuckled. "You have successfully tamed the beast that is my anger. For now…"

"I get that." Tonz smiled back at her. "And if I were you, I would be angry too. I would be beyond angry. Betrayal is not an easy poison to swallow. It hurts the whole way down."

"That it does." Raelle loved how easily Tonz understood things. The depth of his insight. The truth of his analyses. The wisdom of his maturity. It made her feel safe and understood.

"Shall we on to the pub then?" Tonz planted his feet on the floor.

"Well yeah, but uh… I'm going to need a little help,"

Raelle said as she lifted her covers and fiddled with the splints on her legs. Tonz was not aware of her injuries, as he had been unconscious when they occurred. "Will you help me take these off? I can't go anywhere with these things on."

Tonz grimaced. "What happened?"

"I broke my legs, ok?" explained Raelle. "I'm not too happy about it. But I'm not going to let it stop me either."

"You are something else." Tonz laughed. "But whatever you say." He reached for the splint closest to him and began unharnessing it.

"Thank you." Raelle said warmly.

Once Tonz finished removing the splints he methodically poked and prodded Raelle's legs.

"Ouch!" She recoiled. "They still hurt to the touch. They're really sore."

"Well." Tonz continued his examination. "The good news is, they're no longer broken. But they're not yet fully healed. What did Oleevar tell you?"

"It doesn't matter what he says. I can make my own decisions."

Tonz nodded and smirked. "Yes, ma'am." He left the bed and reached for Raelle. She scooted to the edge and let him help her up.

"Aagh." Raelle winced as she attempted to stand. "They still hurt." An intense ache surged through her lower limbs.

"Here." Tonz smiled and lifted her off her feet. "I can carry you to the speeder."

Raelle laughed. "Don't be ridiculous." She forced Tonz to set her back on the floor. "I'm sore but I can walk... I think." Raelle hobbled across the cool marble to the chamber door. Every sluggish step sent a somewhat bearable jolt of agony through her legs.

Raelle heard Tonz chuckling behind her. "At this rate, we'll make it to the tavern by tomorrow morning." Tonz snickered as he walked up behind her. In an instant, he picked her up and threw her over his shoulder.

"I said, I can do it!" Raelle tried not to laugh as she pleaded. "I'm not an invalid. I'm a fighter."

"Yeah, yeah," Tonz laughed. "Not today, you're not."

The entire way out of the castle and down to the speeder, Raelle laughed as she struggled in Tonz's arms. "Thanks." She tried to force a serious face as he set her on the vehicle seat.

"You're very welcome." Tonz grinned and threw his leg over the speeder. Raelle wrapped both arms around his waist and held on tight. With a Chocaz stone, Tonz energized the speeder and took off toward the bright lights of Ellios City.

***

By the time Raelle and Tonz decided to head back to the palace, they had finished two meals and at least three times as many drinks at the Emeralz tavern. Raelle always reveled in her outings with Tonz. They were the only times in her life that she felt truly free and somewhat normal. With him, she was useful, capable, strong, and independent. He treated her as an equal rather than a sheltered child or fragile flower. He listened when she talked. He gave his honest opinion regardless of whether he thought it would hurt her feelings. He was her best friend and a priceless mentor. With him, she felt like she belonged. After all, he was her kind. He was Rogue.

"I told you she could out-drink you!" One of the Rogue fighters called Tonz out as she slammed her pint glass onto the tavern counter.

"She did, didn't she?" Tonz said to Raelle. "Well then we shall crown her the new champion, for now." He laughed as he bowed out gracefully. All around them, the rest of the Rogue fighters cheered Raelle's victory over the reigning pint champ, Tonzelle Lorestia.

"Aaaw it's ok, Tonz." Raelle drunkenly leaned in and patted Tonz's face. "I had an edge. That stuff Oleevar gave me raised my tolerance for spirits!" she hopped down from her stool, forgetting that her legs were no longer in working condition. She stumbled for a moment over her own feet and Tonz caught her. A

249

loud belch escaped her and Raelle immediately covered her mouth. Everyone around her cheered once more. Raelle laughed uncontrollably in Tonz's arms. In her distracted and intoxicated state, her worries were now far from her mind. She was living in the moment, and at this moment, all she could see was the comforting forms of Tonz's face and the gleam of his confident green eyes.

"I think it's time I get this one home," Tonz announced to their friends. "Until next time!"

Raelle continued in her giddy laughter as their friends raised their glasses and bid them good night. She didn't stop until Tonz set her gently on the speeder.

"I beat you!" Raelle pointed at him with an enormous grin. "I finally beat you at something!"

"Yes you sure did." Tonz straddled the seat in front of her. "But it's like you said. Oleevar's elixir gave you an edge." He craned his head to smile at her. "I challenge you to a re-match. Next time. Fair and square."

Raelle wrapped her arms around his sturdy frame. "I accept sir!" She held on tight as they took off toward the palace. Once they arrived, Tonz helped Raelle off the speeder and carried her inside the palace despite her verbal protest. Instead of taking her back to Chrishtan's room on the royal floor, he carried her to his quarters at the top level of the citadel.

"I feel like an idiot," Raelle twittered over Tonz's shoulder.

Tonz unlocked his door and carried Raelle inside. "Well, I'm not going to lie and say you don't look like one too." He winked as he set her on the sofa in his sitting room.

"Gee, thanks." Raelle chuckled. "Now what?"

"Oh, you're not done for the night?" Tonz smiled.

"I don't want to rest right now. I've been sleeping for two days. I'm wide awake."

Tonz laughed. "And I'm sure all those chugs of Tiznic didn't help either."

Raelle made a loud hiccup and covered her mouth. "You're probably right." She grinned.

"You want another drink?" Tonz poured a gold-colored liquid from a decanter into a green tumbler.

"Sure, why not." Raelle shrugged.

"You really can hold your own with fighters now." Tonz poured a second glass and sat down on the sofa with Raelle. "So, are you feeling any better?"

"I don't know." Raelle took a sip of her drink. "I'm not sure how I'm supposed to feel. My entire life has been a lie. I don't know what to believe anymore. People in my family have done horrible things. I don't want to end up like them. I feel lost." She sighed. "This woman you see sitting here now, she's nothing like the girl from the valley. Hell, I don't even feel like the same person I was when you first started training me. I don't know who I am anymore."

Tonz moved closer to her. "There is nothing wrong with that. That's what life is. You learn, you grow, you change. Besides, *I* know exactly who you are."

Raelle took another drink. "You do?"

"Yes." Tonz grinned and tucked Raelle's black hair behind her ear. His touch was kind and consoling. "You are Raelle Jowellia, rightful heir to the kingdom of Huronus. You are an intelligent, dedicated, passionate, sensitive, and strong woman who has been through hell and come out stronger on the other side. Since the day I met you, it has been an honor knowing you. And when the day comes that we return to Huronus and take back our kingdom, I couldn't serve a more righteous queen."

Tonz's touch felt safe and warm. Raelle looked down and tried not to stare into his striking green eyes. "I wouldn't know the first thing about being queen."

"You'll learn." Tonz rubbed her thigh. "Just like you learned how to be an amazing fighter."

No one had ever touched Raelle in such a way. Not even Chrishtan. It scared her, but at the same time excited her. She was unsure which feeling was the right one. *Should I be afraid? Or should I be... whatever this is...* Raelle gently grasped the hand that rubbed her leg. "I just feel so ill-equipped for everything. Being sheltered and lied to my entire life, there are so many things I haven't experienced. Things that I know nothing about."

"Like what?" Tonz asked.

"Like everything." Raelle quickly took another sip of her spirit. "I barely know how to act around other people. I don't know the rules. I don't know the way things are done. You've all experienced things that I never have. It's pathetic. And now I'm supposed to save the continent. It's terrifying. And on top of that, I don't know who to trust anymore. But *you*, Tonz you're different."

"I'm not different, I'm just more transparent. My duty was and always has been to help you get stronger, not to protect you. It's my job to teach you realities, not shelter you from them."

"I don't know." Raelle struggled to get her thoughts straight. "Interacting with everyone and deciding who and what is best for me is not easy."

"I understand Raelle, and you're right. I can see how all of this is overwhelming. You feel like you don't speak *our* language, because you were so sheltered, but *we* speak the *same language,* we don't need words. Can't you feel it?" He moved Raelle's hand to his heart. "The guiding force. The trust. It's here."

Raelle recalled doing the same thing to Chrishtan. In that moment, Chrishtan had finally trusted her, and she him. Was it wrong that she now felt something similar with Tonz? *No...* she told herself. She wanted more than anything to live in the moment. To let her feelings guide her. For most of her life, everyone else had controlled her fate. *This* was real. *This* was now. *This* was the life she had missed out on.

"*This* is how *we* interact." Tonz caressed her cheek and looked deep in her eyes. "There are no rules."

"You make me feel alive, Tonz." Raelle mirrored his gaze. She could feel his passion radiating into her. "I can't explain it. You've given me something no one else has. You've given me independence. Your unwavering confidence has given *me* confidence. You've liberated me."

"No Raelle, *you've* liberated *you.*"

Like magnets, their lips were drawn to together. Tonz

held Raelle close as he combed his fingers through her hair and massaged her tongue with his. It was like nothing Raelle had ever felt. She had shared a genuine and deep connection with Chrishtan, but this was different. She couldn't tell whether it was Tonz or the Tiznic, but she lost control. She surrendered her apprehension and a wave of passion and desire crashed over her.

As Raelle lost herself in Tonz's kiss and touch, he carefully picked her up. Raelle's ache only magnified as he carried her into his bedroom and gently laid her on the bed. With playful hands, they took turns unbuckling the plethora of fasteners on one another's light leather garb. Raelle was first to remove Tonz's belt and scabbards. Tonz followed suit and threw hers onto the floor. Their game of kisses and buckles continued until they were both completely bare. Hovering over Raelle, Tonz looked deep in her eyes. He softly caressed her cheek with his hand before treating her lips to a long, passionate kiss. In the same way he had taught her to fight, he was patient, generous, and confident. She followed his lead and he guided her each and every step of the way. Raelle closed her eyes and let go. At last, she had truly been set free.

***

Once again, the blood swallowed Raelle like a raging river. With the impaled boy in her arms, she swam toward the light of the cryptic cave. Inside, the shadow of what looked like a mermaid waved her in. Raelle paddled as fast as she could until at last, the light pulled her in. It was the first time she had not woken after entering. This time, the dream played on. Once the blinding light dissipated, Raelle could finally see. She realized she was now at the bottom of the sea. Floating in front of her was a beautiful mermaid with long flowing red hair and light green skin. The scales that covered the mermaid's hands and wrists shimmered in the light that shined from above.

"Give him to me." The mermaid reached out her arms. "I help."

The seductive tone of the mermaid's voice seemed to grant Raelle's trust. She handed the small boy with blue eyes and brown shaggy hair over to the stunning creature.

The mermaid pressed her pink lips to the boy's. Raelle watched in awe as his fatal injury gradually closed. Once fully healed, the mermaid let go and allowed the boy's body to float freely. Shimmers of light gleamed all around him and he began to transform. His body twirled slowly in the water until he disappeared. Left in his wake was a school of brightly colored, glowing fish. The small school swam toward Raelle and engulfed her in their gentle typhoon. They whooshed and swooshed and covered her with their gentle kisses as they carried her to the surface.

As soon as her head exited the water, Raelle gasped for air. Somehow, her feet were planted firmly on the sandy bottom of a shallow pool. Immediately, she recognized the spring. She had once used it to bathe the blood, sweat, and tears from her weary body. Raelle waded to the edge and stepped out of the Emeralz meadow spring. All around her, she gazed into the sparkling night sky. Directly above her, the energy of a colorful nebula ebbed and flowed like a soft sea. Off in the distance, a large celestial body seemed to steal her attention. Raelle ran toward the edge of the spring to get a better look. At the top of the edge of the waterfall, she noticed that it did not cascade down into the mouth of a canal as it had before. Below it, there was no land, no river, and no ocean view. Instead, it cascaded into the vast abyss of space. This was no meadow of Lerim. It was the island of a dream that floated through the galaxy. And from where Raelle stood, she now recognized the celestial body as her home world of Lerim. She was overcome with the desire to reach out and touch it. When she did, her hand sent ripples through the star-studded sky like a rock into a pond.

"I thought you'd never come." A voice eased through the atmosphere and into her ears. Raelle turned around in the direction whence it came. Leaning against the trunk of a familiar tree was the shadow of a sturdy man. Raelle squinted at the figure and made her way through the grass toward it.

"Chrishtan?" As her eyes adjusted, she recognized his striking face.

With quiet feet, Chrishtan left the shelter of the tree and met Raelle half way. Once close enough, he reached out with both hands. He pulled her gently in and pressed his lips to hers. In an instant, Raelle lost all reservations. His embrace felt like home, his kiss like rapture, and his energy the essence of love. With every passionate kiss and moment that passed, he melted away the frozen pieces of Raelle's heart. Any doubt of his love for her dissolved into the infinite chasm of space and time.

"I love you." Chrishtan held her close.

Raelle rested her head in his chest. She listened closely to the soothing beats of his heart. "What is this place? Is this a dream? You feel so real."

"So do you." Chrishtan swept his hand over her shoulder and down her arm. "It's not a dream, Raelle. It's the Verge. I've been waiting for you."

Raelle looked down. " But, Jenladra said—

"Said what?"

"That your soul is trapped in the Void. That Azmodil has it. I've seen it. On Lerim, he has control of your body."

"Wait." Chrishtan's expression shifted to confusion. "What are you talking about?"

"I've seen it with my own two eyes on Lerim," Raelle explained. "Jenladra said it would—

"How? You're dead. We're both dead. How could you have seen me on Lerim? When did you speak to Jenladra?"

"I'm not dead, Chrishtan."

"But I saw you. I felt you. You were—

"I came back."

"Came back?"

Suddenly, the island began to shake. The immense cracking of the ground severed beneath them.

"Raelle!" Chrishtan reached out for her, but it was too late. The ground opened up and split the space island in two. Raelle was swallowed into an endless chasm. She fell through the blackness of the rift for what felt like forever. As she plummeted, the descent and its soul crushing journey were all too familiar. *Not tonight, Azmodil. When I do return to your Void, it will be on my own terms. And I will not leave until you are destroyed.*

# CHAPTER 22
## FOR ALL

Raelle woke with a gasping breath. She sat up with a jolt against Tonz's headboard. She brought a dim glow to the Diamoz fixture next to her. Once her eyes adjusted, she looked over at Tonz. He lay fast asleep beneath the cerulean blue covers of his bed, unaware that Raelle had bolted awake from another dream of the Verge.

It had been almost a week since she first entered his quarters. She refused to see Oleevar and Cohlen until she was completely healed and ready to embark on their expedition. It was Tonz who helped her get well. Tonz who kept her company. And Tonz who listened and lifted her spirits. But starting today, she would have to truly embody everything he had taught her. Today, Raelle would journey to the Lantern Forest and she knew that what lay ahead would be the true test of her training.

Raelle took in a deep breath and let it all out before pressing her feet to the fluffy blue rug beneath them. She did her best not to wake the dogs who lay fast asleep on top of its soft fibers, but they soon opened their eyes and began stretching. They wagged their tails back and forth as they followed Raelle to the window. She parted the curtains to let in the morning sun. Over the white glimmer of the palace grounds and snow-covered lands, the sun seemed even more luminescent. It shone like an ethereal spotlight over Tonz's peaceful slumber. Raelle did not wake him before heading downstairs for breakfast. Tonz had already done so much for her. The least she could do now that she was healed was to bring him breakfast. After all, it would be their last morning together. In less than an hour, she would leave for the Lantern Forest and return with Chrishtan. The thought riddled her mind with confusion. But she did her best to turn it off and keep her focus only on her mission. Mirilan was depending on her. They needed Chrishtan back.

***

Raelle stood with poise in front of the mirror. She concentrated on maintaining deep, meditating breaths as Tonz dressed her in her Rogue armor. While he tugged and buckled, Raelle focused upon her mission ahead. *We will bring Chrishtan and Samuel back from the Void. Then I'll get my answers. Hopefully...* Raelle released a long, drawn-out sigh.

"You doing all right?" Tonz asked.

"Yes." Raelle pursed her lips. "I'm fine. I just..."

Tonz fastened the final buckle on her boot. "What is it?" He stood.

"Nothing." Raelle shook her head. "Nothing. I don't know. I mean, I know I can do this. I have no doubt in my skills. Your training was flawless."

"Then what is it?" He pressed with a reassuring grin.

The honesty in Tonz's stunning green eyes told Raelle how much he cared. She would surely miss the comfort of his gaze and the warmth of his smile; the way his tattoos decorated the strong shape of his face and his dirty-blonde dreadlock hung like a majestic tail over his back. It was then that she realized how much leaving him behind bothered her. But it did not matter. Her journey was her own. Raelle struggled to find her words.

"After I release my brother from the Void... I just, I don't...Things will never be the same between us. Not after what he did."

Tonz pulled Raelle's hood over her head and looked her in the eye. "You're right. Things won't ever be the same. *You'll* never be the same. *He'll* never be the same. But Raelle, *nothing* will ever be the same. We all change. The world changes. And we need it to change, for the better. I'm sure if you allow your brother to explain, there will surely have been a method to his madness. I find it difficult to believe any scenario where your brother would purposefully hurt you. No one, after getting to know you, would ever *choose* to hurt you."

Raelle wanted nothing more than for Tonz to be right, but she had learned not to get her hopes up a long time ago. "You say that, but you don't know for sure. Just because you believe something, doesn't make it true."

"You're right." Tonz took her in his arms. "But one thing I *do* know is that you are special. And anyone who doesn't see that or takes advantage of that, is not worth your time or energy."

"Easier said than done." Raelle stepped back. She tried to find strength in her own reflection. "But I'm going to try my damnedest not to let it get me down."

Tonz's gaze did not falter. "Nothing in this world is easy. You of all people should know that."

"I know," said Raelle. But knowing the way things *were* did not make them any easier to deal with. The weight of all the things that hung on her mind was pulling her back down. "And then Chrishtan. What am I going to...?" Raelle's words faded into a lengthy breath.

"You don't need to worry about that right now." Tonz grasped her shoulders and turned her back toward him. "When the time comes, we'll work it out then. No one is asking you to make those kinds of decisions right now. And whatever you decide, I'll respect it. This is mainly my fault. I shouldn't have..."

"No." Raelle held Tonz's face and locked her green eyes with his. "Don't you say that, Tonzelle Lorestia. *You* didn't do anything. *We* did what we did, and *I* do not regret it. Life is about experiences, right? That is one of the first experiences in my life where I felt truly free to choose. And I wouldn't take it back for anything."

Tonz's expression shifted to one of genuine distress. "So, it's not because you care for me?"

"Yes." Raelle pressed her lips to his. "Of course I do, very much."

Tonz looked intensely into her eyes. "I love you, Raelle."

Last night's dream of Chrishtan flashed through her mind. Raelle swallowed hard. "I—I... I—

"Raelle?" She heard Cohlen's voice in the doorway. "Are you prepared to leave?"

Raelle and Tonz immediately let go of one another.

"Yes." Raelle turned toward Cohlen. "I, uh—

"She's all set." Tonz hurried out the door, leaving Raelle and Cohlen behind.

"Is everything all right?" Cohlen asked with a look of genuine concern.

"Yes," Raelle replied. "Everything is fine. As fine as it can be anyway."

"Raelle." Cohlen took her hand. "I really am sorry. I never wanted—

"I don't want to talk about it." Raelle moved toward the door. "We have people depending on us. We can't afford to waste any more time."

"Y—you're right. I just..."

"Let's go."

Avoiding further excuses from Cohlen, Raelle sprinted past him with Rogue speed toward the stables, where Oleevar waited atop his packed horse. On one side of him stood Raelle's horse Winston, and on the other was Cohlen's red mare. They too were fitted with full packs and canteens.

"Raelle!" Oleevar waved. "Very nice to see you again. I see Tonz gave you the Chocaz elixir as I instructed. You've healed very ni—

"Once again, I don't need to hear it, Olee." Raelle mounted Winston.

Oleevar's face twisted in shock and disgust. "Excuse me?"

"Spare me your explanation of how amazing you and your creations are. Everyone already knows," Raelle snapped. "We have a mission to complete. Our brothers need us."

Oleevar wrinkled his brow. "There is no need for such—

"We're done talking," said Raelle. She already had enough weighing on her mind, the last thing she needed was to incite an argument with the most pretentious elf she had ever met.

"Whatever you say," Oleevar said as he looked away.

They both watched in silence as Cohlen trekked through the snow in their direction. As soon as he arrived, he climbed aboard his packed mare and grinned. "Let's go get our brother."

"I'm sure you mean *brothers,*" Raelle reminded him. "Unless we're going back to *that* again."

"Damn it, Raelle." Cohlen shook his head. "I've already tried explaining this to you multiple times. I—I mean *we...*" Cohlen looked at his brother. "*We* made a mistake. We never should have kept anything from you. Please, can you forgive us?"

Raelle nudged Winston forward. "I'll think about it. Let's see how this goes, first." In truth, she did believe him, but she was still angry about the situation and not quite ready to let it go just yet.

"Whatever you say," said Cohlen

Oleevar shook his head. "Humans," he mumbled and followed behind his brother.

The three rode through the palace grounds and out into the city. Elves dressed in fluffy winter dresses and coats, furry hats, and animal hide gloves made their way through snow cleared walkways and venues. Each one of them bowed as Raelle, Oleevar, and Cohlen passed by. The trio reciprocated each citizen with a solute and continued on to the city's main gate. From atop the lookout, Zeell rushed down to greet them before opening the gates.

"Milords and Lady." He bowed. "Is it time to bring home Master Vilgare?"

"Indeed, my friend," replied Oleevar.

"I bid you safe travels." Zeell retracted the gate. "And may the Architect be with you."

"And so with you." Cohlen nodded.

"Thank you, Zeell." Raelle said as she rode out into the whipping wind of the frigid winter morning. Like the sand of a desert, the brisk breeze carried snow particles across the frozen landscape and pelted them in the face. Raelle winced at the feel of her skin being burned by the coarse snow particles. With a shivering hand, she reached for her mask and pulled it up over her nose and mouth. "I sure hope this storm doesn't get too much worse."

Raelle watched as both Oleevar and Cohlen closed their eyes and focused their Lyre. After a moment, they opened them once more to observe their surroundings. Using their Emeralz abilities, they honed in on the natural elements that surrounded them.

Oleevar opened looked out over the land. "The sudden energy and warm temperatures provided by the morning sun is the cause of this sharp wind. Within a couple of hours, the rest of the environment will heat up and balance out. The wind will slowly die down. But I sense a storm moving in from the west. We had better reach the Lantern Forest before it hits."

"Then let's pick up the pace," Raelle suggested. She squeezed Winston with her legs, sending him into a slow gallop. Oleevar and Cohlen dashed along by her side toward the sanctuary of the Lantern Forest.

*** 

As the enormous cliff of the *light* entrance jutted into view, Raelle pulled on Winston's reins to pause their journey. Cohlen and Oleevar did not notice Raelle's recess and continued toward the entrance. Raelle turned Winston around to face the trail they had left behind in the snow. Raelle closed her eyes and honed her senses.

"Do you feel that, boy?" She patted Winston. "I keep feeling as if we're being followed." Raelle channeled her sense of vision to look deeper into the snowy, tree-scattered abyss of the rolling Emeralz Hills. The long tendrils of the trees that she had once used as shelter were no longer encased in blueish green leaves, but rather a thick blanket of ice and snow. For a moment, Raelle thought she saw someone standing within the icy abode of a nearby copse. But in a flash, it disappeared. She channeled her Lyre once more to gauge the aura of the imaginary figure. When she sensed there was no hostile energy, she bumped Winston a few times with her foot and they raced off after Cohlen and Oleevar.

Raelle reached her companions just as they were dismounting their steeds.

"Where did you go?" Cohlen asked.

"Thought I saw something," Raelle answered.

"What in the name of..." Oleevar stepped toward the cliff wall. "Come you two." He motioned. "Look at this."

Raelle climbed off Winston and into the knee-deep snow. She raised her legs high as she traipsed toward Oleevar. As he ran his gloved hand over the rock wall, Raelle could now see that it was crumbling and breaking apart with every swipe. "What's happening?"

"The enchantments..." sighed Oleevar. "They're breaking down." The more Oleevar touched the wall, the more it crumbled away. "Once it has completely broken down, anyone will be able to get in here."

"So what do we do?" Raelle asked.

"We don't waste any more time." Cohlen used his teeth to remove his glove and pulled a knife from a strap beneath his leather greaves. He carefully dragged the blade over his palm until blood trickled into the snow. With his wet, red hand, he drew a door large enough for the three of them to squeeze through. Each one of them tied their horses to a nearby tree and proceeded through Cohlen's jagged archway. Unlike before, the wall did not seal behind them as new. Instead it merely patched itself up, leaving holes and crumbling rubble behind them.

"We'd better hurry." Raelle raced up the steps. At the top, what she saw took her breath away.

"What in the name of the Architect?" Cohlen froze next to her.

Their mouths gaped at the disheartening scene. The beautiful trees that had once been decorated in gentle gray bark and soft violet leaves were now naked and black. Branches crumbled away and the winter wind whipped the deceased foliage into the snowy abyss. What lay in the snow beneath them brought tears to Raelle's eyes. Children of many different sizes, ages, and colors of skin lay scattered, frozen in the snow.

"Hurry!" Raelle rushed to the closest child, a young girl with violet skin and white hair. "We must help them!" Tears rushed down Raelle's face.

Cohlen ran to her side and tried to revive a young boy not

263

far away. "Oleevar!" he called. "Help us!"

Oleevar did not move. "It's all in vain."

"What?" Cohlen glared.

"What you're doing?" Oleevar raised his voice. "They're already gone. You can't save them now."

"You don't know that!" Raelle continued to pump Lyre into the child's frozen chest.

"Raelle!" Oleevar grabbed her by the shoulder. "You can't save them! We're wasting time."

Raelle looked into Oleevar's concerned eyes. She knew he was right. She let her head fall onto the child's ribcage. Deep sobs echoed from Raelle's throat and fortified her tears. "Who are they?"

"I'm not exactly sure." Oleevar furrowed his brow. "They're ancient. Elves of this pigment have not been seen since Jenladra and Hazale's reign."

"We're too late." Raelle shook her head as she cried. "I'm always too late. I was too late to save Browden. Too late to save Chrishtan. Too late on my training. Everything! I wasted my whole life in a valley when I should have been here!" Raelle's rage kindled her Lyre. She felt its energy course through her like a thousand bolts of hot lightning.

"Raelle." Cohlen took her hands. "Don't let the anger take you. Don't let the grief win. Focus on your Lyre. Remember your training with Tonz."

*Stages        of        grief...        shock,        denial...pain, guilt...anger...sadness, reflection... acceptance... hope...*

"Accept it?" Raelle sniffled. "I have! I've accepted it! And I've tried to find hope. But every time it seems that things are starting to look up, something else happens and I'm right back where I was before. I'm sad. And I'm angry, at everyone and everything. I don't want to be, but I am. Because of me, these children are dead. How are we to find hope when we are constantly surrounded by tragedy?"

"There is hope," Cohlen said, with kindness in his voice. He reached down to Raelle and helped her stand. "It's there, I know it. We can't give up. We can't let our anger and the evil of the world get the best of us. If we do, then Lochran wins. The Destroyer wins. I know you've been through a lot. And it seems like it never ends and really it hasn't, not yet. But it will. We can't give up now. Chrishtan never gave up, on any of us. Don't give up on him, Raelle. Don't give up on your brother. There is good in him, I know it. Don't give up on us, please."

Oleevar crossed his arms. "Not to mention, this is incredibly unproductive."

"Can it, Olee," Cohlen snapped. "Now is not the time."

"That's precisely what I'm saying." Oleevar shrugged.

Cohlen scowled. "Just be quiet, all right?"

"There is no point in dwelling on these things that have already happened. We only have time for the future." Oleevar shook his head and walked away. "And right now, you are wasting that time."

Raelle knew Oleevar had a point. His way of seeing the world was more straight forward and concrete than hers. And his way of dealing with grief was to make progress and solve problems. It came off cold, but also made sense. There was no time for grieving. Raelle closed her eyes and took a moment to mediate. Once she felt ready, Raelle and Cohlen followed Oleevar through the frozen and decaying Lantern Forest. The path to the Lady of the Realm was littered with crushed lanterns that had once hung in the trees. When they finally came upon the seascape citadel, Jabrat was not there to greet them as he usually was.

"How are we going to get in?" Cohlen asked.

Oleevar rubbed his chin. "That is a very good question."

"Well, you guys are elves, right?" asked Raelle.

"Yes," Oleevar replied. "And your point?"

"Don't you have the ability to mimic animal calls? You know animal languages?"

"Yes," replied Cohlen.

"So what's the dolphinia's call for *open*?"

"Indeed." Oleevar smiled. "I was just about to think of that."

Raelle rolled her eyes. "Just open the door, Olee."

Oleevar closed his eyes and connected to his Lyre. Within seconds, he opened his mouth and let loose a barrage of clicking noises, just as Jabrat had typically done. The ice around the clamshell drawbridge cracked and came down over the frozen lake in front of them. They walked across it and into the palace. Inside, the once-flowing rivers around the edges of each and every corridor were almost completely dried up. What was left of them was frozen solid.

Raelle shook her head. "I thought this place was supposed to be an endless summer."

"According to legend, it is," Oleevar explained. "But the enchantments are all breaking down."

"That means there is a great deal of evil in the world." Raelle frowned. "Remember what Jenladra told us the last time we were here. The more evil entities and energy that enter our world, she loses more of her power."

"We all saw that demon army Volshira brought with her to Ellios," Cohlen added. "And with Azmodil taking Chrishtan's place, there must be more dark energy than light."

"Azmodil claims to have Samuel as well," Raelle said, with a dismal expression. "Another light extinguished."

They journeyed down the spiral stair case and opened the door to Jenladra's quarters at the bottom of the lake. They stepped inside and were met with complete darkness. Oleevar used his Lyre to ignite any Diamoz stones in the vicinity. A few stones in Jenladra's numerous chests around the room provided enough light for them to see. Near the bottom of Jenladra's empty throne something caught Raelle's eye. It looked like the silhouette of someone sitting on the floor. It held something or someone in its arms.

"Hello?" Raelle stepped toward the shadow.

"Here." Oleevar handed Raelle a Diamoz stone.

As Raelle approached the silhouette with her light, she saw a very old woman with wrinkly blue skin and molting grey hair. "Jenladra?"

266

Jenladra lifted her head. "Raelle," she sighed. "He's dying." A tear slipped from Jenladra's glowing green eyes and slithered down her face. In her arms, she held a man. His skin was far more wrinkled than hers, his body even more frail. His breaths rattled slowly in and out.

"Who is that?" Raelle questioned.

"My love," Jenladra said through her tears. "My precious Jorland."

"Your human lover?" Oleevar stepped forward with a look of intrigue. "How has he lived this long?"

Jenladra swallowed her tears. "You knew him as Jabrat."

"Jabrat?" Raelle shook her head. "But he was not human."

"At one time he was. He was my love, Jorland," said Jenladra. "But as punishment for our indiscretion that led Hazale to the Destroyer, Jorland was transformed and made to live as Jabrat, spirit guide of the Lantern Forest. Here, we would live together forever. But he would not remember our love. He would not remember his human life. Each day, I would be reminded of what I had done and the evil it unleashed. I would live with my love, but I would not ever have his love again."

Raelle sat down next to her. "And now that the enchantments are breaking down, he's returned to human form?"

"Yes," Jenladra answered solemnly. "And he is dying. I am dying. The light is dying. The Opalz stones are the only thing keeping me alive. Jorland does not have the blood of the Lyre. He is only human."

"The children in the snow..." Raelle thought out loud. "Are they—

"They are the *faithful.*" Jenladra said gravely.

"*The* faithful?" Oleevar questioned.

"Yes," Jenladra replied with wet eyes. "They are my children."

"What are *the faithful?*" asked Raelle.

"According to legend..." Oleevar began. "They are the direct offspring of Jenladra and Hazale. They were not part of the human-mermaid hybrid slave army that Hazale created. And they

267

did not leave with the slave army exodus of our descendants. Each bred faction of the army settled a different region. But Jenladra and Hazale's pure offspring chose to stay with their parents. Half of them banished with Jenladra, and the other half to Hazale's side of the forest."

"This is true." Jenladra hung her head. "And like Jorland, my children too were punished. Those that stayed with me became the pixies of the light path. And those that went with Hazale became the Red Owls. They too had no recollection of me, or their father. They did not know of their lives before banishment. For eternity, I would see the faces of my children and I would know who they were. But they... they would never know their parents. They would only know the Lady and the Demon of the Lantern Forest."

"It's going to be all right." Raelle put her arm around the once beautiful Jenladra. She could feel the sorrow in each of the woman's shaking sobs. "Maybe they still have a chance. We're here now and we're going into the Verge to find Chrishtan and my brother. That will bring some light back into the world."

Jenladra leaned toward her. Her hand gently held Raelle's face. "I know you will." She smiled wistfully. "All faith and hope is in your hands." Jenladra looked directly into Raelle's eyes. "There is another."

"Another?" asked Raelle. "What do you mean?"

"Another child," said Jenladra

"Who?"

Jenladra looked down at Jorland. "*Our* child. *Our* hope." Her glowing green eyes shifted back to Raelle and gazed deep into her soul. "He needs you, Raelle."

Somehow Raelle knew precisely of whom Jenladra spoke. She could see his face in her mind. "Chrishtan..." Raelle whispered.

Jenladra nodded, *yes*.

"But how?" Raelle asked.

"He is my last living descendent. He is the last and only offspring of me and my love, Jorland. The last descendent of our one and only child, Abequelar."

"Abequelar?" Oleevar asked with disbelief. "The founder of Abequa was your and Jorland's love child?"

"Yes," said Jenladra.

"And Chrishtan is your great, great, great, great... grandson?" Oleevar's eyes grew wide. "That is insane."

"I saw him," Raelle sighed. "I saw Chrishtan last night. I spoke to him."

"You did?" Jenladra asked with a new glimmer of hope. "How?"

"In the Verge."

"In the Verge?" Jenladra closed her eyes. "Yes." She smiled.

"What is it?" Raelle asked. "How was I able to see him?"

Jenladra called to Oleevar

"Yes, Milady."

"Do you remember the night you gave your love?"

"What? Um. I'm not sure I..."

"For a piece of light?" Jenladra reminded him. "You were a boy then and so was Chrishtan."

"Are you speaking of that foolish night swim Chrishtan and I took over fifteen years ago?"

"Indeed."

"Yes, I remember. Why do you ask?"

"That night," Jenladra continued. "You gave *love* in exchange for light. But to a mermaid, *love* means something much deeper than the feeling or the act."

Oleevar crossed his arms. "And what does that mean?"

"It means you gave them a piece of your soul," Jenladra replied. "And to them it will belong until your dying day."

"Are you saying that we are betrothed to mermaids? And that she owns a piece of my soul?"

"Yes," said Jenladra. "I suppose you may think of it like that."

Oleevar threw his hands in the air. "Well, that's just wonderful." His sarcastic tone made Jenladra smirk.

She cleared her throat. "I suppose that is something you will have to work out at another time. For now, it is a good thing. Raelle, Balee must have allowed you access to Chrishtan inside the Verge. I'm sure she knows that he is in trouble. I have no doubt she can feel it to. But mermaid law prevents her from interfering in human lives. She may have called you."

Raelle shook her head. "Great, another one of Chrishtan's lovers that he failed to mention to me."

Oleevar snorted with dismissal. "I would hardly call her his lover. It lasted for all of about sixty seconds. We were young and foolish. We had no idea what we were doing."

"I see." Raelle winced before looking back at Jenladra. "Balee was there. She brought me to him."

"Good." Jenladra curved her purple lips. "That means that no matter what happens, Azmodil will never fully control Chrishtan. Chrishtan may even have moments when he is lucid. But we still have to get the rest of him out of the Void. Each moment he is in there, that part of his soul is damaged."

"We will get him back." Raelle saw the urgency and fear in Jenladra's eyes. Chrishtan was more important than any of them could have ever known. "I promise."

"I have the utmost faith that you will." Jenladra looked at Cohlen and Oleevar. "But before you go, I need your help."

"What is it?" Cohlen asked. "Anything you need."

"I won't make it through the time it takes you to find them without hibernation. Will you help me get Jorland and myself into the hibernation chamber?"

"Yes, of course," answered Raelle. "Where is it?"

Jenladra closed her eyes and raised her hands. Suddenly, a giant spherical tube rose from the floor. Cohlen bent down and took Jorland from Jenladra's arms. Raelle helped Jenladra to her feet and they slowly walked to the giant chamber.

"But won't we need you?" Oleevar asked as Jenladra stepped inside. "Won't we need your help with entering the Verge?"

"You never needed my help." Jenladra smiled. "You've

had the means to do so the moment you possessed the Opalz. I was only here to guide you and watch over you. I am no good to you now in this state."

"I see," said Oleevar. "So we won't need your guidance?"

"No," Jenladra clarified. "Chrishtan gave Cohlen everything you will need to enter the Verge."

"He did?" Cohlen asked.

"Yes." Jenladra grinned. "You have his memories, do you not?"

"Yes."

"Then that is all you will need. Remember how Chrishtan entered the Verge. Then, you will, too."

"Yes, Milady."

"Give him to me." Jenladra reached out and Cohlen placed Jorland in her arms. "Once you've closed the door, use your Lyre to activate the Opalz stone you see at the top. Once you do, this chamber will fill with Opalz and Chocaz blood from the compartment above me. Don't panic. I will not drown. The combination of the blood of these stones will keep us alive."

"What a beautiful technology." Oleevar's eyes nearly popped out of his head.

Jenladra cleared her throat. "I'm glad you approve, Oleevar." She closed her eyes. "I am ready."

"Yes, Milady." Raelle shut the door and made sure it was secure. Jenladra nodded once more and Raelle summoned her Lyre to call upon the Opalz stone at the top. Almost instantly, Opalz and Chocaz blood poured in from a crystal tank above the chamber. Once completely full, Jenladra lost consciousness. "I think she's in hibernation now."

"Allow me to check." Oleevar pressed his hands against the transparent chamber. "This isn't glass at all," he murmured. "This is rishitite. I can't sense a thing."

"What's rishitite?" Raelle asked.

"It's a virtually indestructible mineral found only at the deepest depths of the oceans. I suppose it would make sense that Jenladra would possess such a mineral. She is from the sea, after all."

"Yes." Raelle rolled her eyes. "Thank you for stating the obvious."

"Precisely." Oleevar grinned.

"All right, you two." Cohlen moved toward Jenladra's throne and sat down at the base of the bottom step. "It's time."

"Lead the way, Cohlen." Raelle sat down in the sand next to him. She crossed her legs in meditative fashion. On the other side of Cohlen, Oleevar did the same.

"Are we ready?" Cohlen asked as he took both Raelle and Oleevar's hands in his.

"Ready." They responded.

All three of them closed their eyes and channeled their Lyre. At the same time, they focused their energies on the Verge.

"Took you long enough."

A familiar voice prompted Raelle to open her eyes. Standing in front of her in the midst of a bright white abyss was Browden. An enormous smile came over Raelle's face and she hugged him tight.

"Welcome back." His goofy grin greeted her.

"Good to be back."

"Cohlen." Browden turned to the younger elf. "Fantastic to see you again."

"You, too." The two embraced warmly.

"And who is this?" Browden approached Oleevar. The elf immediately stood tall to illustrate his superiority.

"I am Oleevar Jurlorne, ruler of the elven throne of Ellios."

Browden leaned into Cohlen's ear. "Wow, this guy's really something, isn't he?"

Cohlen grinned and chuckled. "Browden, *this* is my brother. He and Chrishtan grew up together. They're like brothers."

"And who might you be?" questioned Oleevar.

"Well, I'm Browden, of course!"

"Of course?" Oleevar shrugged. "How was I to know?"

"Well, for starters," Raelle interjected, "Chrishtan told you all about him and the Verge when he returned home."

"Ah, yes." Oleevar raised a finger. "Now that you mention it, yes, he did. Sorry."

Raelle and Cohlen shook their heads.

"Are you all prepared for our journey?" Browden asked.

"Yes," Raelle replied. "I believe so."

"You had better *know* because this is not going to be pleasant," Browden scoffed. "I can already tell."

Raelle shook her head with a crooked grin. "You have a feeling, do you?"

"Yes, as a matter of fact I do," Browden answered pompously. "How did you guys get into this mess anyway?"

"It's sort of a long story," Raelle explained. "Maybe some other time?"

"Right." Browden smirked. "Then let's get on with it."

Oleevar bowed his head. "I couldn't agree more."

"Hands, everyone." Browden held his hands out, and the five of them grasped onto one another. Once again, they closed their eyes and channeled their Lyre. They focused their energies on Chrishtan. Memories of their closest moments with Chrishtan flashed through their minds, revealing both shared and private moments. For the first time, Raelle got a glimpse into Chrishtan's life before he met her. She felt closer to him than she ever had. She reveled in each memory until the uncanny hoot of an owl startled her.

Raelle opened her eyes to find herself lying on the ground at the base of an incredibly large pine. She gazed up past the enormous trees that surrounded her and into an obscure red sky. She used the light of the blood-colored moon to study her surroundings. She recognized a familiar treehouse built within the branches of the massive tree above her. The sound of a child's whimper shifted her attention back to the trunk. Raelle gripped her scabbards and walked around the bulky base to find a young boy. His head hung low as he sobbed. In his hands, he held an enormous rock. Raelle silently gasped at what lay at the boy's feet.

Another young boy lay bludgeoned. His entire body, including his face, had been crushed.

Raelle carefully stepped toward the crying boy. "I'm here to help you." She inched closer.

"I didn't mean to do it." The boy sobbed. "They made me do it." The boy finally lifted his head and glared at Raelle. "I swear it."

The boy's face caused Raelle's stomach to leap into her throat. She did her best to swallow it. "Samuel." Raelle offered him her hand. "I'm here to help you."

"You can't help him!" Suddenly, a teenage girl stepped out from the bushes. In one swift motion, she sliced Samuel's throat and pushed him to the ground. "You can't save any of us!" she cried. "Not even yourself!" Raelle gasped. The girl was her. "No!" Raelle leapt toward her teenage self, but it was too late. The young Raelle swiftly sliced the blade through her own gullet. Raelle collapsed to the ground. She mourned the loss of herself and her two brothers who lay dead before her.

Suddenly, their bodies began to melt. They slowly transformed into piles of black ooze. As the ooze spread, it disintegrated the ground along with it. Raelle crawled away as quickly as she could, but the forest floor gave way beneath her. She fell into a hole filled with bones and human debris. From above, the black, acidic ooze dripped onto her face and body. She screamed in agony as it ate away her skin.

"Raelle!" A voice called out to her. "Raelle, it's not real!"

Raelle writhed in pain. She had never felt such agony.

"Raelle, come back to us!"

She recognized the voice. *Browden.*

"Focus your Lyre, Raelle. Go to that place. Remember your training." Cohlen's shouts trickled in, sounding like they were from very far away.

Raelle did as he instructed. She found her peaceful place in the valley. The warmth of the sun. The gentle touch of the wind. The soothing smell of the flowers. And the comforting sound of the song birds. Raelle opened her eyes once more to find herself laying on the forest floor, surrounded by three young men.

"She's back!" Browden greeted her with an enormous grin. "Sorry, forgot to mention that imagination thing. Don't believe everything you see here. It's most likely in your head. The Void will play upon your fears."

Raelle let Browden and Cohlen help her up. "Gee, thanks for the belated warning."

"Sorry." Browden shrugged. "You know how I can be a bit forgetful."

Raelle rubbed her hand through his scruffy hair and laughed. "Indeed, I do."

Browden pointed at Oleevar and Cohlen. "I found these two in a clearing running in circles from something called Kyre." He chuckled.

"I do not find that humorous in any way, shape, or form." Oleevar scowled.

"Sorry." Browden cleared his throat. "Shall we proceed?"

"Yes," replied Cohlen. "Which way do we go?"

"Well, that would involve looking for clues." Browden rubbed his forehead. "It looks like Raelle and I are controlling the current setting. Surely the two of you have never been in this forest."

"No." Oleevar shook his head.

"If these are our woods..." Raelle looked around to gauge direction. "Then this is the way back out into the valley. We'll be able to see everything from there. Come on, this way." Her elven companions trailed her in a steady run behind Browden.

Raelle did not stop until she hit the highest point of the valley. At the top of a hill stood a small cottage. Raelle could not bring herself to enter. She knew the tragedy that lay inside. Instead, she leapt from the ground directly up onto the roof of the humble wooden structure.

"See anything?" Oleevar called from the porch.

Raelle magnified each and every one of her senses. When she opened her eyes, her vision was much sharper. With each squint and focus, she could see further away.

"Over there." Raelle pointed toward the mountains to the west. "In the mountain pass. There's a structure there."

"And is it something that has always been there?" questioned Oleevar.

"No." Raelle nimbly jumped from the roof onto the grass. "If it were, I wouldn't have mentioned it." She glared at the condescending elf. "I've never seen it before. There was no one else settled in our valley, and there definitely weren't any structures like that one."

"Like that one?" Cohlen asked. "What is it?"

"It looks like some kind of castle," said Raelle. "I think I've seen it before."

Cohlen jumped off the porch and met Raelle. "Where?"

"In my nightmares." The vision of Chrishtan's young body as it fell onto the spire played inside her head. Raelle shook it from her head. "Chrishtan is in there. I know it."

"Then by all means." Oleevar motioned them forward. "Let's go retrieve him."

Raelle took off in a sprint toward their destination. As she reached the edge of the valley at the outskirts of the forest, she noticed that it looked nothing like the forest of *her* valley. It was much denser, and the leaves of the strange-looking trees were deep red and purple rather than green. Purple vines seemed to slither across the ground like snakes.

"Oh, dear Architect." Oleevar's voice sounded off behind her.

Raelle turned around to see a look of despair on his face. "You know this place?"

"We sure do." Cohlen walked up beside his brother.

"The Red Lantern Forest," Browden added. "This is definitely the elves' doing." He rubbed his head. "Not this again."

"*I* did not do this." Oleevar's face contorted with disdain.

"I'm not saying you've done it on purpose," Browden argued. "But you are to blame."

"It doesn't matter." Cohlen cut in and turned to Browden. "It is what it is. Yes, you're right. This is our part of the nightmare.

But, it could be worse, right?"

Browden shook his head and chuckled. "I suppose it could always get worse."

"Brow." Raelle grasped his shoulder. "Please don't say that. We *can* do this."

"I know we can," Browden replied. "But this obstacle is going to lengthen our journey. It may take days to reach the palace. Not to mention, it offers many more places for enemies to hide. Real enemies."

"What do you mean?" asked Oleevar. "I thought the only obstacle was our imagination."

"Well." Browden bit his lip. "Yes, there is that as well. But this time I know they'll be expecting us. Which means that other entities may have been brought here to guard the palace, which I'm assuming is Azmodil's."

"Entities?" Raelle asked. "What kind of entities?"

"Um, well." Browden's eyes darted back and forth, as if he did not wish to say. "The kind that exist in both the living world and the shadow world."

Raelle suddenly felt a twinge of fear radiate through her entire body. "Minotirr…"

"I'm afraid so, yes," Browden said in a matter of fact tone. "And also—"

"Also?" Raelle's fear cut him off. "There's more?"

"Uh, well," Browden continued, "there is a possibility that—"

Raelle snapped again. "A possibility?"

"Raelle, please," Browden begged. "Let me finish."

"I'm sorry." She grimaced.

"Rogues…" Browden laughed and shook his head. "All right, so there is a possibility that whatever creatures of the Void they have brought to life on Lerim could be here as well. Those creatures transformed from previously living beings on Lerim are genuinely *alive*, just like you. They *can* genuinely hurt you."

Oleevar probed. "Are you talking about the ones we encountered in Volshira's army?"

"Yes," said Browden. "They created those creatures out of living people. They tortured them, mutilated them, cursed them and distorted their souls. Those people become the monsters you encountered in Volshira's army."

The thought of being tortured into oblivion sent a surge of pain through Raelle. *So many have suffered... their souls twisted...* She did her best to refocus and quiet her fears before delving further. *You can't help them now. All you can do is move forward in the hopes of putting an end to it all.*

"But if they're on Lerim, then they're not here," said Raelle

"*You're* here," Browden retorted.

"Yes?"

"They bring them here the same way you came," Browden revealed. "They create a portal using massive black Opalz stones."

Raelle released a deep sigh. "Great. So there could be a whole army of them in there?"

"It is possible," Browden grasped his chin. "Like I said."

"We can do this." Cohlen squeezed Raelle's shoulder. "We can."

Raelle grasped Cohlen's hand. "Together."

"Together." Browden took her other hand.

"Together." Oleevar joined them and they focused their energy as one.

They closed their eyes and drew on every ounce of Lyre they could. Raelle had never before felt such strength. *We will find them. We will bring them home. We will begin to right our world of wrongs. Bring light to the darkness. Replace death with life. Lies with truth. And despair with hope. For Lerim. For us. For all.*

# CHAPTER 23
## LILAZZ

The darkness of the forest made it almost impossible to see. The dense foliage made it virtually impossible to move. And Raelle's fear of wandering into the unknown made it somewhat difficult to focus. If it weren't for Oleevar's Diamoz crystals and Browden acting as their guide, Raelle knew that they would surely be lost forever. She squinted hard and lifted her light crystal high. "This place is horrible."

"Tell me about it," retorted Oleevar. "This is my second visit."

Raelle shook her head. "I don't know how you and Chrishtan survived."

Oleevar shrugged. "I'm not quite sure how we did it either."

"You had help," Browden expounded. "Just like you do now."

"Help?" Oleevar didn't seem to know what Browden was referring to.

"Ssssh, wait." Browden motioned for them to stop. "Do you sense that?" He walked to the rear of their single-file line.

Oleevar, Cohlen, and Raelle froze. What Raelle saw when she turned around seemed to pilfer the words from her throat. She pointed at the disturbing creature that slunk across the ground toward Browden.

Browden turned around to the faceless entity that oozed toward them like a pile of black slime. From its gooey form, it conjured a revolting head and mouth followed by a long arm with ominously extended fingers. Raelle shrank even more at the disturbing sounds it made as it slurped toward them.

"Run!" Browden screamed.

The revolting entity dug its elongated fingers into Browden's flesh. Blood trickled from his injury and down his leg.

He cried out as the creature opened its grotesque mouth and began to swallow him whole.

Raelle jumped forward and reached for him. She grasped Browden's forearm and pulled with all of her strength. With each tug, the entity seemed to swallow faster. Raelle freed up one of her hands and grabbed her dagger. She swiftly struck into the demon's makeshift arm. The dagger sliced right through, but the arm instantly repaired itself.

"Go, Raelle!" Browden cried. "It's no use. Leave me!"

"No! I can't do that!" Tears welled in Raelle's eyes as she tightened her grip. "I won't lose you again!"

"You *can,* Raelle." Browden placed a hand on Raelle's cheek. "And you *will...* for Chrishtan and Samuel."

The entity continued to swallow her surrogate brother and conjured a second arm to reach for Raelle. With haste, she jumped back to avoid its grasp. "Help!" Raelle shrieked as she watched Browden in horror. Her mind raced as she tried to think of a solution. She quickly recoiled and released just enough of her ability to stun. Browden immediately went limp. Raelle gasped and fell to her knees. The stun had no effect on the creature. With one final gulp, Browden was gone and Raelle's Lyre weakened.

"Raelle!" Cohlen shouted behind her. She felt him grab her arm and he dragged her away from the entity that drew ever closer. "Come on!" Cohlen helped her up and they ran toward Oleevar.

"We've got to recharge her Lyre." Oleevar reached into his bag as they ran. "Here!" He handed her a vial of Torpaz blood.

Raelle pulled out the cork and drank. Within minutes, she had regained all of her strength. They did not stop until they could no longer see, hear, or sense the horrifying monster that had taken Raelle's beloved brother. In the middle of a large clearing, they attempted to rest. Once Cohlen seemed to have caught his breath, a look of terror came over him.

"What is it?" Raelle asked. She then looked toward Oleevar, who harbored a similar expression. The elves' eyes darted around the clearing as if they were watching something. "Oleevar?"

Raelle waved a hand in front of his face. "What is it?" Raelle looked around and saw nothing.

Oleevar pressed his eyes shut. "It's not real. It's not real." He opened them once more just to close them again. "Not real. Not real. Not real…"

"Olee!" Cohlen screamed and fell to the ground. "Don't let them take me again! Olee, please!"

Oleevar grabbed his brother. "I'm here!" Oleevar began to swat and sway his arms in the air as if fighting off a swarm of flies. "I've got you, Cohlen!"

"Olee!" Raelle pulled him off Cohlen. "Look at me!" She tugged on his chin and forced his gaze upon her. "Wake up! It's not real!"

"You can't see them?" Oleevar asked, bewildered.

Raelle shook her head. "No."

"Cohlen!" Oleevar returned to his brother. "It's not real, Brother. Focus! Meditate!"

"I can't. They're eating me!" He cried out in pain.

"I'll get him." Raelle crouched down and pressed her hands to Cohlen's chest. She channeled her own calm energy into him. She showed him her serene valley. After a few moments, his struggle ended and he opened his blue eyes.

"Thank you." Cohlen's trembling slowly dissipated. "Thank you." He took Raelle in his arms and hugged her tight.

"We're a team." Raelle grinned. "That's what we do. Help one another. Plus, I kind of owe you from back there." She instantly remembered what they had been running from. Browden was gone and she could not save him. She tried, but she had failed. Tears began to slip from her eyes. "I couldn't save him." She covered her face with her hands. "I couldn't save him. I'm too late. I'm always too late."

"We were all too late," said Cohlen. "I'm so sorry. I don't know what that thing was, but I don't know if there was any stopping it."

"Really you two." Oleevar shook his head. "There was nothing we could have done. And there is no time or need for feeling sorry for ourselves."

"Olee, knock it off." Cohlen scorned. "Just give us a minute. She just lost her brother, for Architect's sake. That was Chrishtan's brother too, you know."

"Yes, I realize that." Oleevar crossed his arms, his eyes darting back and forth with a sense of urgency. "But if we do not get a move on, we may never see Chrishtan again either. That we *can* prevent. That thing that took Browden, there is nothing we could have done. We're lucky it didn't take Raelle as well. The Morbas is a lethal and unstoppable spirit. They are also very rare."

"Morbas?" Cohlen asked. "What the hell is it? And how do you know?"

Oleevar began to pace. "While you two were training, I did a bit of training of my own. Well, research anyway. I wanted to know what kind of obstacles we may face before coming here. The Morbas is conjured from suffering. It feeds off pain of trauma, grief, sorrow, distress, and the like. I'm sure with us channeling both Chrishtan and Samuel, who both seem to have suffered a great deal, in addition to all of the things you, me, Raelle, and Browden have been through, *we* conjured it. And I am certain it is still out there looking for us. Which means we need to keep moving, no matter what."

"So what happens to Brow?" Cohlen probed. "He's already dead?"

"I'm not exactly sure." Oleevar pursed his lips and looked down. "I believe it feeds from his soul... which he still has."

Raelle lifted her head and glared at Oleevar with wet eyes. "So how do we destroy it?"

"We don't," said Oleevar. "It can't be destroyed. It was created from us. I suppose we'd have to destroy ourselves. But I really don't know."

Cohlen shook his head. "Well, we can't destroy ourselves. So I suppose we just keep moving." He helped Raelle to her feet.

She wiped the tears from her face and took a deep breath. "I'm sorry. Channeling the boys is making me incredibly emotional. Losing Browden has really set me over the edge. I don't want to lose Chrishtan because I can't keep it together. I can feel his pain, my brother's pain, and my own grief on top of that."

"You're human," Oleevar asserted. "It's going to be more difficult for you to contain them. But you must do your best to try."

"I can do this." Raelle reassured herself.

"Good." Oleevar looked around as if searching for something. "Now, let's see if we can get some type of energy signature to follow. It will most likely lead us out of here and to Chrishtan."

The three companions held hands and rechanneled their Lyre. They focused hard on Chrishtan and his location for the slightest indication as to which direction they should go. Without their fourth companion and guide, it turned out to be a far more challenging task than before.

\*\*\*

The dead silence of the forest was beginning to get to all of them, and their inability to navigate through forest maze had drained some of their confidence. Purple vines with minds of their own slithered and slunk through the heinous jungle and wrapped their prickly climbers around feet, ankles, and arms. Each time, the group hacked and sliced away at their floral hijackers. Sinister voices arbitrarily whispered the groups' life shortcomings, mistakes, fears, and flaws through the never-ending copses of mangled and contorted trees. To Raelle, it felt as if they had been lost inside the Red Lantern Forest for days. But in reality, there was no way of knowing.

"Oleevar," Cohlen called. "There must be a better way. How did you find your way out before?"

"The same way I am now." Oleevar paused and turned to face his brother. "I'm trying to sense any outside energy."

"And where did it lead you before?" Raelle asked.

283

A rare look of confusion crept onto Oleevar's face. "I don't know." He shook his head. "I just remember sensing an energy. I traveled toward it until I found a bright light. I couldn't see anything. A hand reached out for me. It drew me in. Then, the next thing I remember is waking up in my bed in Samisius. My parents said they found me with Chrishtan at the front gate. We were both unconscious atop my horse."

"Jenladra..." Raelle whispered.

"What?" Oleevar did not seem to catch on.

"She must have found you," Raelle suggested. "Browden said someone was watching out for you."

Oleevar shook his head. "Then why didn't she prevent Cohlen from being taken?"

"Maybe she couldn't sense you until afterward," Raelle guessed. "Or maybe she sensed Cohlen was in trouble during or after the fact. Maybe that's how she found you."

"I don't know about that," said Oleevar doubtfully. "Then why wouldn't she take us to her citadel and give us our Opalz?"

"Maybe she thought you weren't ready," Raelle replied.

"Well, she won't be helping us to get out of here, that's for certain," Oleevar sighed. "Right now she's safe and sound inside a rishitite chamber."

"We need to figure something out," Cohlen groaned. "Because right now it feels like we're going in circles."

"I agree," Raelle said.

"Wait." Oleevar lifted his nose. "Do you smell that?"

Cohlen followed suit and tried to pick up the scent. "Wait, yes. I do smell it." His face shifted to a look of disgust. "What in the name of Lerim is that?"

Raelle closed her eyes and enhanced her sense of smell. The putrid aroma that wafted in hit her like a slap to the face. "I know that smell." Raelle's hands made their way to her blades. "It's the smell of the dead and the mutilated. The cursed and the evil. Browden said they might be here. And I think they are."

Raelle, Cohlen, and Oleevar crept toward the rancid smell of rotting flesh and demonic ichor. The closer they got, the less dense the forest became. Finally, they could see a way out. As quietly as possible, they crouched down behind a large bush of blood-red flowers and sharp thorns. A sense of horror crept over Raelle as she looked out at the view. Right outside the forest, hundreds of demonic atrocities awaited them along a narrow cliff road. On either side of the path were endless gulches of guaranteed oblivion. Raelle felt a sharp pain radiate through her body when she realized what flew overhead.

"Oh, dear Architect." Raelle pointed into the sky. "Minotirr."

Oleevar moved forward to get a better look. "Yes, at least five of them that I can see."

"What are we going to do?" asked Cohlen, his breathing suddenly rapid.

"What we were trained to do," Oleevar proclaimed. "What we were bred to do. We fight."

"Oleevar's right." Raelle turned to the red-headed elf. "It's in our blood. It's in our heritage. Hazale created us to fight. And Jenladra bestowed these gifts upon us to fight the darkness."

"You see this Minotirr here?" Oleevar directed their attention to the low flyer closest to them.

"Yes." Raelle and Cohlen nodded.

"I'm going to take on his form." Oleevar pulled the cross bow from his back and fit it with a large and unique arrow. From his pack, he removed a long, thin rope.

Raelle knew that they could conjure anything they could imagine here in the Verge. If Oleevar could create something in his mind, he could create it in the Verge.

"Is that rope made of metal?" she asked.

"Yes." Oleevar grinned. "It's a new technology I've been working on. I've discovered the way to weave metal into light yarn-like fibers, without losing its strength. We shall see if it stands up to this test." Oleevar latched one end of the thin metal rope to an attachment at the back of the arrow. Then, he wrapped the other end around a tree and latched it. "Once I've got the arrow in him, it will immediately open up into giant barbs inside him. This will allow us to pull him into the forest. But we must be careful that the other Minotirr don't see this."

"All right," Raelle chimed in. "So you need us to create a diversion?"

"Precisely." Oleevar grinned. "Raelle, you can stint throughout the outskirts of the group. Disappear and re-appear, taking a few down here and there as you go. But do not cause a serious ruckus." Oleevar turned to his brother. "Cohlen, there are other wraiths in there. Not many, but enough for you to join them. Just try to blend in until I take form."

"Got it," said Cohlen.

"Then, once I've taken form, Raelle I want you to release the most intense sound wave you can in the middle of the horde. Try to take out as many of those revolting creatures as you can. I will give you a few vials to recharge. Then Cohlen and I will hold the rest, just in case you're unable to administer them yourself. Meanwhile, Cohlen and I will focus on taking down the remaining Minotirr. And if you succeed in completely clearing the path, then please feel free to join us.

"Yes, of course." Raelle felt a surge of fear burn through her. "I'm not going to lie, I'm feeling a bit nervous."

"As am I." Cohlen's eyes opened wide. "As am I."

"We all are." Oleevar squeezed the armor on Raelle's shoulder. "But we have a plan, and we have our Opalz gifts. Use your nervous energy and transform it into strength and confidence."

Raelle took Oleevar's advice. She closed her eyes and harnessed her Lyre. She focused on Tonz. She channeled his energy, her memories of him, and everything he had taught her. He was the very definition of confidence. After a few moments, she felt ready.

"Let's do this." Oleevar raised the crossbow and set himself up to aim for the Minotirr. He signaled for Raelle and Cohlen to exit the woods. They paused at the very edge. Raelle watched intently as Cohlen transformed. The sounds of his body as it shifted and cracked made her shiver. When he was ready, he nodded at her and she disappeared, stinting out into the horde. Raelle re-appeared within them and sliced the legs of multiple monstrosities. And before they knew what had happened, she disappeared and reappeared in a different location to cut more of them down. The ear-wrenching howls of the injured creatures quickly drew the attention of the Minotirr.

As she slowed down time, popping in and out of the horde, Raelle eyed the Minotirr Oleevar had his sights on. Just as the other Minotirr gave their attention to the screams of the flock, Oleevar shot his prey from the sky. Raelle disappeared from the injured part of the demonic crowd and reappeared elsewhere within it. As soon as she saw Oleevar fly out from the trees in Minotirr form, she charged, recoiled, and emitted an incredible scream. As she did, she spun three hundred and sixty degrees. The horrifying creatures around her either fell from the cliff road to their doom or burst into bloody shrapnel.

After clearing the way for Cohlen, Raelle drank her vial. She watched as he ran and jumped into the air. With his claws out, Cohlen leapt onto the back of an airborne Minotirr. He screeched and slashed at the monster, forcing it to land at the edge of the forest. Raelle made sure Cohlen had the situation under control before leaping into the next mob of repulsive creatures. High above her, Oleevar battled two Minotirr. Although he looked just like them and flew just like them, Oleevar had something they did not—a bow in hand and the superior skills to use it. With precision and elite ability, Oleevar impaled his grotesque enemies with arrow after arrow. Each one of them found its way between gaps in the Minotirr's armor and penetrated into their rotting insides.

The sight sent a glimmer of hope tingling through Raelle's spirit, and she used it to charge her ability even further. She raced toward the horde in front of her and disappeared. When she reappeared once more, she found herself in their midst. Once again, she charged and released. Her enemies did not stand a chance. Her hope would not let them.

As Raelle drank a vial, in the distance, she saw Cohlen running toward her at an incomprehensible speed. She could hear him calling to her, but was unable to make out his words. Suddenly, an intense force pilfered the air from her lungs. The Minotirr clutched her arms tight and dragged her across the ground before ascending into the rosy red sky. Panic ensued when Raelle realized what the Minotirr intended to do. Her entire life played before her as her heart leapt. Over the abysmal gorge, the Minotirr released its grip, and Raelle plummeted down toward the infinite chasm. She closed her eyes and let the darkness take her as it had many times before.

Raelle's eyes bolted open at the sensation of something beneath her. She stared into the eyes of the creature that held close. "Olee?" It nodded, *yes.* Raelle smirked. "I owe you one." Oleevar landed them both safely on the carnage-covered palace road. After setting Raelle on her feet, he returned to his usual form.

"Yet another successful strategy developed by yours truly." He bowed.

"Oh, get over yourself," Raelle teased. "We each had our own moments of improvisation that helped as well."

Cohlen ran up behind them and returned to elven form.

"That is likely." Oleevar embraced his brother and patted him on the back. "Having a well-trained team does help immensely."

"I'm sorry," Raelle interrupted, laughing. "But did he just give us credit for something?" She winked at Cohlen.

"I believe he did, Raelle. I believe he did."

"Well, don't get used to it." Oleevar smiled. "The probability of it happening again is rather low."

"Yeah, yeah." Raelle shook her head. "Now let's get inside that palace and get our people out."

"You, uh, you might want to clean the guts and such off your face before you see him." Cohlen laughed.

"Oh, uh." Raelle wiped her face with her hand and looked over her armor. "Gross! I'm covered in it. Oh boy, do I smell ripe."

"Indeed." Oleevar wrinkled his nose ."We all do. But I must say, you are rather drenched in it." He opened one of the pouches on his pants and pulled out a rag. "Here, you can at least get your face with this."

Raelle took off her mask and lowered her hood to wipe the revolting ichor away. She tried as best she could to get some of her armor as well, but the cloth became far too drenched to make a difference.

"That's going to have to be good enough." Raelle threw the gore-soaked rag on the ground.

Finally, the three of them made their way to the palace.

"I know this place." Oleevar studied the structure. "It's the Abequan palace."

"These doors are enormous," Raelle commented. "And these statues…"

"Yes, the Abequans like everything *big*, like them. Except the statues at the real Abequan castle are not of Azmodil."

"I figured as much," said Raelle.

Oleevar leaned in to touch the doors.

"Don't!" Raelle grabbed him and pulled him back.

"Why?" Oleevar glowered. "What's wrong?"

"In my dream, those doors were incredibly hot." For a moment, Raelle's hands burned with the scorching memory of the nightmare. "They seared the skin right off my hands."

Oleevar moved as close as he could to the doors without touching them. "You're right." He backed away. "I can feel the heat from here."

"So how do we get in?" asked Raelle.

"That I do not know." Oleevar continued to study the stronghold. "There should be somewhere to insert a stone and activate it, but I don't see one."

Cohlen interrupted. "We don't have time to figure this out. There are a bunch of windows right there. Olee, you can just transform again and break through one of them. Then, once you're inside, you can find a way to let us in."

"I must say, dear brother." Oleevar tilted his head and smiled. "I'm rather impressed."

"Just do it, all right?" Cohlen retorted.

Oleevar said nothing and morphed back into the hideous Minotirr. He spread his leathery wings and flew up to the first window. From his pocket, he removed a small tool and broke the glass. After sweeping the shards away, he climbed through and disappeared into the palace. After several moments, Raelle heard a loud clunk and what sounded like giant gears turning. In front of her, the doors slowly opened to reveal Oleevar in elven form, waiting for them on the other side. Once inside, Raelle was met by a large familiar room. Its floors were lit by a perimeter of fire. And in the center stood the enormous spire. Her mind imposed an image of Volshira impaling Chrishtan's young body overhead. Raelle shook the playback from her mind and tried to refocus.

"I wonder what sort of obstacles are waiting for us in here." She looked around.

"We can never be too sure." Cohlen swallowed. "Except to expect the unexpected."

"Not my favorite thing." Oleevar clarified. "I prefer to be highly prepared."

"I hate to break it to you," said Raelle. "But there is no preparation, no rules, no guidelines, or even a shred of decency in this realm."

"Yes, I caught on to that very early on," Oleevar replied. "Which is why I prefer to get this over with so that we don't have to come back."

"That sounds ideal," Raelle snickered sarcastically. "But highly unlikely considering the way things have been going. This probably won't be our last visit."

"Ssssh." Cohlen raised his hand. "Do you hear that?"

Raelle paused and focused her Lyre on the mysterious noise. After a moment, the sound of children groaning echoed into her ears.

"Yes." Raelle listened once more. "I can hear it. It sounds like children."

Oleevar pointed to a large archway that led into a long corridor. "It's coming from that direction."

"I agree," said Cohlen "Let's go."

Raelle rested her hands on her daggers and followed her elven companions into the hallway. On the walls, depictions of warriors in combat with demons had been carved into the stone. The disturbing pictures oozed with thick, coagulated blood and demonic ichor where the demons tore the warriors apart. The putrid smell made Raelle gag. She quickly reattached her mask and pulled it over her nose and mouth.

As they made their way down the extensive and gruesome corridor, the children's groaning grew louder. Amongst their moans, Raelle could hear whispers accompanied by the heavy beating of a low drum. They warned not to go any further. They advised the three to turn back. They assured them that they would regret it. Raelle did her best to ignore it, but the rapid thumping of her heart could not. The three continued to the end of the hall where they were met with a single giant door. Like the carving in the hall, blood and gore seeped from its edges. Slimy vines that looked like veins throbbed over the door's exterior.

Cohlen crossed his arms. "So how do we open this one? I don't see a handle, or a lever, a key hole, or a gem slot."

"Patience." Oleevar sat down on the floor.

"Patience?" Raelle raised a brow.

"Yes," Oleevar said with a hint of authority. "We will meditate and focus on the answer. Then, hopefully it will come to at least one of us."

"If you say so." Cohlen joined his brother on the floor.

Raelle followed suit and closed her eyes. She focused on her breathing and channeled her Lyre. The meditation calmed her nerves and whisked her into a state of peace. She was not sure how long she had been meditating before Samuel's voice seeped into her mind. It carried a vision with it.

*What is this place?* Samuel turned to Volshira. They

stood in front of the very same door.

*Sssssh.* Volshira put her finger over Samuel's lips and closed her eyes.

Raelle listened closely as Volshira chanted in a language she had heard several times before, but still did not understand.

*Corontis isk dispoz im sisti spironir.*

*Gesp desmont.*

*Waltim isk ire fragim.*

*Grom mit evasa.*

The vision ended and Raelle was awakened by the sound of her own voice. She was now chanting the same words that Volshira had spoken. Oleevar and Cohlen simply stared at her.

"What are you—

The sound of the door opening severed Cohlen's words.

"She did it." Oleevar looked delighted with Raelle's success.

"How?" Cohlen asked.

"I'm not sure." Raelle rose to her feet. "It must be my connection with Samuel. I had a vision. He and Volshira were here. She knew how to open the door."

Cohlen rolled his eyes. "Of course she did," he whispered. "You know, from the moment I laid eyes on that woman, I knew she was trouble."

"We get it Cohlen," Oleevar said, vexed. "You were right." The elf locked eyes with his brother. "Is that what you want to hear? I was wrong, all right?"

"Sssh! Not now you two," Raelle snapped. "You can bicker later."

"Of course, "said Oleevar.

"Sorry." Cohlen looked through the open doorway. "It's pitch black in there. Who knows what's hiding inside."

"That's what these are for." Oleevar lit his Diamoz stone.

"Right." Cohlen drew one his from his pocket and illuminated it.

Raelle did the same. "I'm going to go in first. If something is in there, I can stint back out here."

Oleevar removed his bow from his back and knocked an arrow. "I'll be ready to pick off anything I see from here."

"Same here." Cohlen prepared his bow. "And if you need more help than that, we'll shift and get you out of there."

"All right." Raelle lifted her Diamoz light above her head in one hand and grasped a dagger with the other. After taking in a deep breath and releasing, she stepped into the dark room. The limited light of her crystal exposed a grand hall full of pillars. They extended up to the extraordinarily tall ceilings. Raelle paused and focused on the sound of the moaning children. Moving in the direction of the whimpering, she stealthily stinted from pillar to pillar. As she moved, she noticed her boots sticking to the floor. It was covered in gooey vines like the ones on the door. They throbbed and pulsated like the artery in Raelle's neck. Now aware of them, she did her best not to trample them. As she moved, foreboding whispers transformed into a harsh chant of the unknown language. The deep beating of a drum assisted their invocation rhythm.

Raelle did her best not to let them frighten her, but nothing could stop the chills that ran through her entire body. She focused on her destination. She could sense that she was almost there. The children were close. The last leg of her journey through the grand hall led her to the base of an enormous platform. Raelle raced up the massive steps. What she found at the top halted her journey like a stone wall. In front of her, two young boys and a young girl hung by their arms from spire-shaped pillars. Raelle instantly recognized the boys that hung in the rear. Samuel was on the left, and Chrishtan on the right. Their bodies were bound and pierced by the same throbbing vines that crawled across the room. Where the vines had punctured and entered their small frames, blood dripped steadily into a pool of black liquid that surrounded each of them.

"Oleevar! Cohlen!" Raelle called out. "I found them. I need help!"

In the distance, Diamoz lights bobbed up and down as the elves raced toward her. Raelle waited anxiously as they sprinted up the steps.

"Oh, my Architect," Cohlen panted. "What kind of evil is this?" He shined his light over the disturbing display.

Raelle panicked and raced toward the girl, who was closest. "Help me get them down!" she cried.

"Raelle, wait!" Oleevar's voice echoed. "Don't step in the—

It was too late, her foot sank into the black liquid. It drowned her in darkness. Raelle struggled to swim to the top, but it was no use. Her mind carried her back to that day. The day she had tried to take her own life. Back in the valley spring, she sunk lower and lower until her toes touched the sandy bottom. With her feet, she propelled against the sediment and pushed herself toward the surface. But something grabbed her leg. Raelle looked down to see the lake weeds wrapped around her ankles. They pulled her back down and tied the rest of her to the floor. The last of Raelle's breath fleeted in bubbles to the surface. She couldn't fight the reflex, her mouth opened and took in the water that surrounded her. Everything went dark.

Raelle opened her eyes to the sound of rapid breathing next to her. In the darkness, she could see nothing, but she could tell she was inside a small room. The hasty breaths continued next to her. Suddenly, a door opened and light poured in. Raelle saw that she was sitting in a closet. The breaths she heard were coming from a scared little girl with crimson hair.

Raelle leaned toward the girl. "Are you all ri—

A hand with metal claws reached in and dragged the little girl out by her hair. The girl screamed and cried and tried to fight, but the hand was much stronger than she was. Raelle chased after her and leapt toward the Minotirr. She went right through him. He did not seem to notice her as he dragged the flailing and sobbing girl into the next room. Raelle followed. As she entered, the Rogue sentries inside did not seem to notice her either. Two of them held daggers to a man and woman's throat. The other seemed to be in charge.

The Minotirr threw the little girl to the floor.

294

"Volshira!" Her mother cried out.

Raelle could do nothing but watch as the Minotirr and the sentries murdered Volshira's parents. She watched on in terror as the young Volshira lay in a pool of blood, mourning the death of her mother, until the sentry dragged her away. She kicked and screamed and pleaded, but there was nothing Raelle could do.

*This is Volshira's nightmare. Volshira's memory. Volshira's horrific past. And it's all because of my family.* A heavy wave of guilt crushed Raelle. Suddenly, a loud cracking noise paused her heavy grief. She looked around as fissures cracked through the ceiling and the floor. The ground suddenly caved beneath her, and Raelle fell into the nothingness. She closed her eyes and let it take her. It was what she deserved. She and her family.

The feeling of someone tugging on her arms woke Raelle from her abysmal journey. She felt her body being dragged over a slimy surface. When she finally came to a halt, a violent cough spewed black liquid from her lungs.

"Raelle?" Cohlen asked, his voice filled with fear. "Are you all right?" She felt him wipe away the goop from her face and eyes. "Can you hear me?"

Raelle nodded and opened her eyes. "I don't deserve to live." She shook her head.

"What happened?" Oleevar asked.

"I saw her life," Raelle said distraughtly. "I saw her suffering."

"I told you not to step in—

"Quiet, Olee." Cohlen silenced him.

"I see now why she hates me so much." Raelle felt ill after witnessing the horror of such a young girl. "This girl, it's Volshira."

"Already knew that." Olee stood and folded his arms.

Raelle snapped. "Well, I didn't! All right?"

"It's all right," Cohlen comforted Raelle. "We're going to rescue her, too."

"Sssssoooo paathetiiiic." Voices taunted all around them.

295

Raelle watched in horror as the pulsing vines broke off and slithered toward them. Each one of them hissed through a mouth full of razor-sharp teeth. At once, they charged past Raelle, Olee, and Cohlen and into the black pool below Volshira. Raelle watched as the faceless creatures slithered together in the fluid and transformed into the curvaceous figure of a woman. Her skin was deathly white and her body nearly naked except for red armor that barely covered her breasts and lower region. An enormous headdress came down over her forehead and eyes. It stood tall over her long locks of hair that were not hair at all, but faceless serpent creatures.

Raelle, Oleevar, and Cohlen immediately backed away.

"What is that?" Raelle asked.

"I don't know," Oleevar's mouth and eyes opened wide. "But something tells me that it's not good."

"Ssssooo pathetiiiiic." The words hissed from the demon's tongue.

"Who are you?" Cohlen demanded.

"I am Lilazz," the demon answered. "Mistress of the Destroyer and his six princes."

Cohlen stood. "You can't hurt us here."

"Yes," she cackled. "You are correct, my little elven pet."

"Then why show yourself?" Raelle demanded. "You're vulnerable."

"Oh, jusssst for a little bit of fuuuun." Lilazz sneered as she floated across the black fluid in their direction. She pointed at them with a long, thin finger that ended in equally lengthy claws. "And to let you know that Volshira belongs to me. And now, sssoooo do yooou." Her slimy serpent hair slithered from her head, down her body and raced toward them.

"They can't hurt us," Cohlen shouted as he grasped Raelle's hand. "She can't hurt—

The slimy herd of creatures smothered and choked them. One slithered into Cohlen's mouth and down his throat. He cried out in pain. The malevolent serpents hissed and bit as they tied Raelle, Cohlen, and Oleevar down. Raelle focused her Lyre and tried to wake from the gruesome illusion. She reached for tranquility and her happy valley. Outside, she could still hear the horrified screams of her companions. *This isn't real. It's in my head. This isn't real. It's in my head. Wake up, Raelle. Wake up. The summer breeze. The moist blades of grass. The cool spring water. The smell of mother's cooking coming through the chimney. I am at peace. I am safe. I am home.* Raelle drifted off to her valley. She now lay in her bottom bunk in the sanctuary of her own bed. The cozy comfort of her familiar cottage made her eyes feel heavy. She needed to rest. Raelle was overcome with drowsiness and drifted off to sleep.

***

Raelle's eyes fluttered open at the smooth stroke of a gentle hand across her cheek. They revealed to her the blurry image of someone leaning over her. She pressed her eyes closed and opened them once more in an attempt to focus. It did not help. As she closed them again, Raelle's lips were met with a familiar and tender caress. She reached up and smoothed her hand across a scruffy face.

"Chrishtan?" she murmured between kisses.

He smirked. "Who else would it be?"

Finally, Raelle could see his facetious grin. She grasped his face with both hands. "Did it work? Did we get you out?" Raelle swiftly sat up. "Where are we? Are we back..." Raelle realized that she was still inside her peaceful valley bedroom.

"Back where?" Chrishtan's eyes squinted with confusion. "You mean the Verge?"

"Where are Oleevar and Cohlen?" Raelle jumped out of her bed and nearly hit her head on the top bunk. "Are they here? Are they all right?"

"Raelle." Chrishtan hopped up and gripped her shoulders. "Calm down. What's happening? Have they come to speak with us?"

"No." Raelle groaned and grabbed two fists of her auburn hair. "We were trying to get you out of the Void." She threw

Chrishtan's hands from her shoulders and began to pace. She could feel the panic taking over. "This is a disaster." Her voice trembled. "We lost Browden. He's gone and I—

"Browden?" Chrishtan spun her around to face him. "Raelle, please. Calm down and tell me what is going on. This isn't like you."

"You don't even know me, Chrishtan." Raelle pushed him away. "And *I* don't even know you."

"Raelle?" Chrishtan's breaths became rapid. "What are you saying? Of course we know one another. We've been through—

"No, Chrishtan!" Raelle shouted. "This is not the time. I need to find Oleevar and Cohlen."

"You're not making any sense." He grabbed her arm. "Please, tell me what's going on."

"Let go of me!" Raelle tried her best to tear her arm from his grasp. "Please!"

"No!" Chrishtan pulled her in close and held her in his arms. "Let me help you. I love you."

Raelle's fear and frustration forced her to struggle inside his firm embrace. "How could you?" She pounded violently on his chest. "How could you..." Her tears drowned away her angry rant and she broke into sobs. "I can't do this anymore." She rested her face in his chest. "I can't... I just can't..."

Chrishtan held her close and soothed his fingers over her auburn hair. "Sssssh," he whispered. "It's going to be all right. I'm here."

Raelle felt his lips leave a kiss atop her head. "I thought I could do this without you," she sputtered through her tears. "But we're nothing without you. We're trying so hard to bring you home... I just... so many lies..."

"What lies?" Chrishtan gently stroked her back. "Please help me to understand."

"I hate this." Raelle lifted her head and wiped her tear-stained face. "I don't know anything anymore. Everything I thought I knew. Everything I thought I was. Everything I felt. I don't know…"

Chrishtan looked deep into her eyes. She felt herself nearly hypnotized by his intense blue irises. "No matter what, I love—

"No!" Raelle shook her head. "No. You don't get to do that." She tried to pull away, but his embrace was far too strong. "I hate it. Damn, I hate it!"

"Hate what, Raelle?"

"You! This! I hate how I love you. I hate how you do this to me. I hate *you*! I'm so angry with *you*. But damn it, I still love *you*. I have all these things I need to say to you. All these things burning inside of me that I loathe you for." She squeezed his arms and tried to shake him. "But the moment you touch me. The moment I see your face. It's like none of those other things matter."

"Okay…" Chrishtan's face contorted. "I know I'm not the brightest star in the sky, but I still don't follow. Have I done something? Is this about me and your brother? I had no idea that was him. I swear it, I—

"No." Raelle looked away. "It's not about him. In fact, I would say you and he are two peas in a pod."

"Now I definitely don't follow."

"You've even shared the same woman."

"Raelle?" Chrishtan turned her head. "What are you talking about?"

"Volshira, damn it!" Raelle clenched her teeth hard. "I'm talking about Volshira."

Chrishtan took a deep breath. "I—I'm—I don't—

Raelle saw the sudden regret in his eyes. "I saw you two together." She tried to hold back the tears welling in her eyes. "I saw you and her. I saw you…" She couldn't bring herself to say it. The hurt was far too great.

Chrishtan's eyes darted back and forth. "You saw us when?"

"The night…" Raelle's bottom lip did a frantic dance that kept her words from coming. "The night you…" The morbid memory slashed through her wounded heart. "The night she killed you. I saw you in your room. I saw you through the keyhole. From the hallway I saw you…" Still she could not say it. "Why did you never mention her? You kept it from me. You hid it from me!"

Chrishtan hugged her tight. "I'm so sorry. I'm so, so, so sorry, Raelle. I can't even imagine what you must have felt. I didn't tell you because I wanted to be done with my painful past and she was a part of that. And you're right, I should have told you, but I didn't. I didn't because I am an absolute idiot. But you must know, I do not love her. I'm not in love with her. I thought I was, at one time in my life, but that was before I met you. That was before I truly knew what it felt like to be in love. I know now what that is. It's a feeling. It's an energy, its everything. It's you, Raelle. From the moment I met you, I was drawn to you. I knew you were special. And that night, I thought she *was* you. I saw *you*, not her. I felt *you*, not her. Until it was too late. I don't know how or why, but that is what happened." His look of misunderstanding returned. "And I still don't understand how you saw it. You were dead. I had lost you forever. My heart and my body ached with your loss. You must know this."

Chrishtan's words seemed to partially patch the gash in her damaged heart. The love in his eyes. The genuine tone in his voice. The loving touch of his hands. The enticing forms of his face. They obliterated the anger that trundled through her like an avalanche.

"I do. I know." She caressed his face with her hand. "I've always known. I just… I needed to feel the anger. I needed it to get me through. To help mold me into what I've had to become. I needed it to survive. To train. It made me stronger."

"To train?"

"Yes. I've been training in Ellios."

"But you're—

Raelle clutched his face. "I'm not dead, Chrishtan. And neither are you. Not for good."

"What? What do you mean?"

"The Opalz stone." Raelle pursed her lips. "It's a

resurrection stone. I'm alive, Chrishtan. And I've been training in Rogue arts for the past three months."

"But... how— then..." Chrishtan tripped over his words. "How long have I been dead? When will I resurrect? How do I—

"That's what I've been training so hard for," explained Raelle. "To come and get you. Because of what Volshira did to you. You can't resurrect."

"What? What has she done to me?" Chrishtan swallowed hard. "I knew something wasn't right. Since I've been here, I've suffered bouts of intense fear and pain. I get flashes of myself as a child. Flashes of death and pain. I thought it was just from what Hazale took from me."

"No, it isn't." Raelle looked down. The memory of Volshira chanting over Chrishtan's dead body stabbed into her mind. "Volshira surrendered your soul to Azmodil, the demon you rescued me from. He now walks on Lerim." It was hard for Raelle to look him in the eye. It pained her to tell him. "In your body." She looked back up into Chrishtan's terrified eyes. "And she may have done the same with my brother. I'm so sorry, Chrishtan."

"No." Chrishtan's eyes welled and a single tear escaped them. "I'm sorry. I should have known something was wrong. I thought it was you, but it couldn't have been. I should have—

Raelle pressed a finger to his lips. "There is nothing you could have done. She has a black Opalz stone. And with it, the ability to manipulate others' Lyre. She can even take another's ability. This is how she got to you."

"So, if my soul is being held hostage by Azmodil, within the Void, then how am I here? How am I also in the Verge?"

"Apparently..."Raelle was still trying to wrap her mind around what Jenladra had explained to Oleevar about the mermaids. "That is yet another thing, besides Volshira, that you forgot to mention to me."

"Are you serious?" Chrishtan threw his hands up and shrugged. "I swear, I honestly did not have any other lovers."

"Her name was Balee," said Raelle. "And she was a mermaid."

301

"That?" Chrishtan shook his head in disbelief. "I was ten years old, and *she* kissed *me*. I swear."

"Nonetheless, you gave her a piece of your soul with that kiss. And apparently it belongs to her... forever."

"You must be joking."

"I'm afraid not." Raelle crossed her arms. She did not feel sorry for him. "But on a more positive note, she cares enough for you to let me come see you so that we can get you out of here. So, I'm letting it slide."

"Well, aren't you a reasonable woman," Chrishtan said and pulled Raelle back into his arms.

"There is one other thing." Raelle took a deep breath. "I am almost positive that Volshira has allowed a demon to rule her. Someone called Lilazz."

"Lilazz?" A look of dread took over Chrishtan's grin. "She is the mother of demons. She seduces men and..." Raelle could feel his heart begin to race. "Oh, my Architect."

Raelle's eyes widened. "What is it?"

"She is trying to create more princes of the Void." Chrishtan yanked on his hair. Raelle had never seen him so visibly distraught. "Oh, no, no, no. Raelle, we have to stop her."

Raelle tossed her hands in the air. "That's precisely what we're trying to do."

"It may be too late." Chrishtan started to hyperventilate. "Oh no. No, no, no..."

Raelle tried to pull him back to her. "Chrishtan, please. Calm down. Talk to me. I—

"Have you seen her? Volshira?" Chrishtan cut her short. "Did she look preg—

A shock of intense and debilitating pain hit Raelle like a boulder from the sky. She collapsed to her bedroom floor.

Chrishtan knelt down and cradled her in his arms. "What's wrong? What's happened?"

"I don't know. I can't breathe." Raelle tried to move, but she felt as if something was chaining her down. "Aaaagh!" a sharp pain ripped through both her hands.

"Oh, my Architect!" Chrishtan's grim expression grew more severe and his eyes much larger. "Your hands, look at them."

Raelle couldn't believe what she saw. Like a small sink hole, the skin of her palm caved in and blood surfaced like a weak geyser. "It feels like someone is stabbing through them. "Aaagh!" The pain struck again, only this time through her feet. Like her hands, they too now harbored small bloody wells. "Chrishtan, help!" Raelle screamed before everything went black.

# CHAPTER 24
# HELL

It was the intense pain roaring throughout her entire body that woke her. Still very groggy, Raelle tried to adjust into a more comfortable position. She realized then that she could not move her arms. They were stretched out to her sides and locked into their current position. They throbbed with pain. Raelle's blurred vision made it difficult to see where she was. With hazy eyes, she looked down and ascertained that she was in the upright position. Her feet were somehow strung together where they perched on a tiny platform below. It was the only thing that kept her body from dangling. As Raelle's vision gradually returned, a massive headache moved in along with it. She squinted and pressed her eyes shut in an attempt to find some relief, but to no avail. As her cognition and other senses slowly returned, she began to shiver. The room was cold and the surface of the stone slab she was chained to felt like ice against her scantily clad body.

Raelle squinted around the cave-like room lit by fiery torches. Directly across from her, three more people were in the same predicament. Two women hung on either side of a young man. Their heads slumped over in a way that Raelle could not see their faces. The woman closest to her had raggedy auburn hair that looked as if someone had at one time carelessly sliced it with a blade. Next to her, the young man looked dead. His skin was so pale that it looked almost purple and the veins that ran through it almost black. Next to him hung a woman with long black hair.

Raelle shifted her aching neck to see Cohlen and Oleevar strung up on either side of her. *What is this awful place?* She struggled to release herself from the metal cuffs that restrained her wrists. The pain was unbearable. It was then that she noticed that the cuffs were not the only things holding her against the slab. The same type of slimy vines from Azmodil's keep had wrapped themselves around her and dug holes through her hands and feet. Once more, Raelle looked across the room at the others. They two had been penetrated by the same evil creepers. Blood slowly dripped from their open impalements and trickled into a basin below.

A shock of terror and panic surged through Raelle's aching body. She tried to scream and cry for help, but her throat was much too dry to generate a proper noise. She writhed in an attempt to pull herself free from the torturous nightmare, but each and every time she moved, the vines crawled further into her like a hellish splinter.

"Try not to move," Oleevar moaned. "It only makes it worse."

Raelle's tender neck muscles would not allow her to look directly at him. "Where are we?" She shut her eyes and shivered. "What is this hell?"

"I'm not sure," Oleevar wheezed. "Someone's dungeon?"

"On Lerim?"

"Surely it is." Oleevar shivered. "They can't hurt us in the Void."

Raelle's cold body continued to quake. "H—how is that p—p—possible? We were in the Citadel of the—

The creaking of a large iron door interrupted her queries.

"Quiet," Oleevar whispered. "Put your head down." He panicked. "Pretend you're unconscious."

Raelle did as Oleevar instructed. Along with the sound of the door slamming shut, she heard Volshira's voice along with one other echo into the cavernous room.

"Are they ready yet?"

"I highly doubt it, Madam," A scratchy male voice replied. "They've only been in penance for a short while."

Volshira moved toward them. Her steps sounded like hissing snakes as the train of her dress dragged across the floor. "Isn't there some way we can speed up the process?" Her shadow loomed over Raelle.

"I'm afraid not," the man's voice rasped. "If we do it too quickly, then they will simply die."

"This one here." Her shadow pointed to Raelle. "It's my

drink of choice for the nativity rite. I need the Huronians ready in one hour's time," Volshira demanded. "The king and I will settle for nothing less. Do you understand me?"

"Yes, Milady," the man answered. "Of course. And how are our little ones doing?"

"Very well, Master Virtoss, very well." Volshira's shadow rubbed her abdomen. "And within a few months' time, they will be with us all."

"I assure you that I am looking forward to that day." Master Virtoss bowed. "They will be the first of their kind for centuries. This is a grand and holy achievement."

"Indeed." Volshira spun around and made her way back toward the door. "Would you please tell Master Fendriss to meet me in my chambers. I'd like to go over the plans for the ceremony one more time."

"I shall do that." Master Virtoss followed her to the door.

"Oh, and one more thing." Volshira paused in the doorway. "I almost forgot. Did you remember to take their rings?"

"Yes, Milady." The elf patted his side pocket.

"I expect you to dispose of them properly and bring the stones to me when you are finished. They are melded with Opalz and are of great value to me."

"As you wish." Master Virtoss bowed and Volshira closed the door.

Raelle's mind began to race. *Volshira is pregnant? No... no, this can't be...* She heard Master Virtoss move across the room. Without giving herself away, Raelle gradually lifted her head to get a look at him. He was a pale elf with exceptionally tall, pointy ears. The only color to his skin was the reflection of the torches that danced over his completely bald head. Beneath the elaborate purple robes covering his feet, Master Virtoss moved eerily across the room. After snatching something from a red marble table, he headed back to Raelle. She swiftly hung her head and listened to the elf's footsteps as he moved closer. Within a few seconds, she saw his naked feet directly below her.

Master Virtoss lifted Raelle's face and head to examine

them. She opened her eyes just enough to see him through the tiny gaps in her eyelashes. Over his face, the elf wore a gold mask that had neither a nose or holes for his eyes. Raelle shivered as he pressed his fingers against her neck.

Next he squatted down to her feet. Raelle watched anxiously from above as he pulled a scalpel from his pocket. "This should do it." He swiftly made two incisions at the top of Raelle's feet where they met her ankles. She did her best not to cringe as the sharp pain shot through her like a whip. Blood began to trickle out from the new wounds and into the basin below.

Suddenly, out of nowhere, two hands with arms garbed in white leather armor grabbed the elf's head. They snapped his neck, and Master Virtoss landed face first in the basin of Raelle's blood. Raelle froze. She was much too afraid to move. She silently gasped as the hands reached next for her. They lifted her heavy head and Raelle was now face to face with a hooded Rogue. He swiftly pulled down his mask and Raelle began to cry.

"It's okay." Tonz did his best not to weep along with her. "I'm going to get you out of here, all right?"

Raelle nodded through her tears. "I—I—I can't breathe. It's like I'm, being c—crushed!"

"What is this stuff?" Tonz examined the vines. He reached to pull one of them out of Raelle's hand.

"Tonz, wait!" Oleevar's scratched from his throat. "Don't pull them out. It will only drive them in deeper and cause her to bleed more. You must cut them. Leave the head of the vine inside her and hope that it will eventually die."

"Got it." Tonz pulled one of his daggers from its sheath. He carefully cut through each of the vines where they entered Raelle's skin. He then reached into one his pockets and retrieved a metal pick. As soon as he picked the locks that confined Raelle's wrists, he opened them and she fell like a corpse into his arms.

Now free, Raelle felt the air rush back into her lungs. Although it hurt like hell, she reveled in each new breath.

"Thank you." She looked into Tonz's troubled eyes.

He wiped the hair from her face and then poured two

small vials of blue liquid into her mouth. "I know it's going to take more than that to get you back to normal, but you should be okay for now."

Raelle could not control her shivering as he helped her to stand. She felt as if she were frozen solid.

"Here." Tonz rushed to the other side of the room and stole an elaborate purple cloak from where it hung on the wall. "Put this on." He helped Raelle slip into the long bell sleeves and wrapped the robe snugly around her.

"Thank you." Raelle's teeth chattered as she tied it closed. "W—w—what is th—hat thiiing." Raelle pointed at the strange, faceless elf.

"He's a dark Jassokian priest." Tonz kicked him over and removed his mask. "He's pledged his life to the Destroyer."

Raelle gasped at the elf's face. He had no eyes and his nose had also been removed.

"As interesting as that is." Oleevar struggled to breathe. "Could someone please get Cohlen and I down, *now*, and discuss that *later*."

"Yes, of course, sorry." Tonz turned to cut Oleevar's parasitic vines.

Raelle took Tonz's second dagger and started on Cohlen.

"Raelle..." Cohlen's murmur was barely audible.

"Stay still, Cohlen. I'm going to get you down from here."

Cohlen nodded in slow motion. Once Raelle finished cutting his vines, Tonz tossed her his pick and she unlocked Cohlen's wrists. They carefully helped the two elves to the floor.

"Oh, please tell me you brought Emeralz blood as well" Oleevar managed through his gasping throat.

"You must be ill." Tonz grinned. "Do you know who you're talking to?"

Oleevar struggled between labored breaths. "Just give it to me, you smartass."

Tonz smirked and handed Oleevar two vials of Emeralz blood and then two more to Raelle.

"Cohlen?" Raelle patted the elf's face. "Can you open

your mouth for me?"

Cohlen did as Raelle asked. As quickly as she could, she poured the contents over his tongue. Like his nods, he swallowed them sluggishly, and Raelle helped him to sit up.

"Where are we?" Cohlen's voice was even hoarser than his brother's.

"We're in Abequa, below the palace dungeon," Tonz answered as he helped Cohlen to his feet. "I don't know what they're doing down here, but it's truly wicked, whatever it is."

"How did you find us?" Oleevar stood on wobbly legs. "How did you know we were in Abequa? Even I don't know how we got here."

Tonz looked down. "I may have followed you to the Lantern Forest."

"What?" Raelle shook her head. "Why?"

"I wanted to keep an eye on you," he clarified. "Make sure everything went smoothly."

Raelle folded her arms. "You were trying to protect me, weren't you?"

"Call it whatever you want." Tonz stood tall and put his hands on his hips. "I just wanted to make sure *all of you* were safe. And it's a good thing I did. Or else you'd still be hanging there."

Oleevar walked across the room and stole two more robes. "How did we get here?"

"After you three entered the Lantern Forest, Gralend and I posted up outside the enchanted wall," said Tonz.

"You brought Gralend with you?" Raelle brooded.

"Yes, I brought someone else along just in case you three needed me and I needed to send someone back with a message to Ellios."

"All right..." Raelle rubbed her forehead.

"We waited five days for the three of you to exit the forest before the Abequan soldiers arrived. It wasn't a large group, but enough that we wouldn't have been able to take them on our own. They had a Jassokian priest with them. They must have used him to break down the enchantments the rest of the way because somehow they entered into the Realm of the Lady. When they came back out shortly after, they had the three of you. Each one of you were in some sort of sleep state. Since we couldn't take them on our own, I followed them and you back to Abequa. I sent Gralen back to Ellios with your horses and a message to our troops. If we do not return before the sun goes down, then they are to launch an attack on Abequa to retrieve us. The Samissians will most likely come along with them since Cohlen and Oleevar are being held captive."

"No," Oleevar protested. "The Samissians don't like to fight. I won't have them come here just for me and Cohlen."

"You're their heirs, their sons." Tonz shook his head and rested a hand on Oleevar's shoulder. "They *will* come for you."

"So then we must leave this place and in a hurry." Oleevar began to pace. "What was your plan to get us out of here?"

"Well, in truth, I hadn't really thought about that yet." Tonz cleared his throat. "I was hoping you could help with that."

"Oh, you must be joking," Oleevar sighed. "Senseless Rogues, always acting before thinking."

They all spun around at the peculiar sound of a low and gruff voice. "I can get you out," the voice spoke between heavily strained breaths.

"Who said that?" Raelle felt dread crawl over her.

"It's coming from him." Cohlen pointed at the young man Raelle thought to be dead.

"Help me get him down." Raelle began cutting the young man's vines. Overhead, Tonz swiftly set free his wrists.

"Help me set him down." Raelle motioned to Tonz. "He's quite heavy." Suddenly, a familiar and haunting image flashed through Raelle's mind, followed by the familiar feeling of her brother's cold, dead weight.

"Flip him over."

The sound of Tonz's voice brought Raelle back to the cavernous dungeon and she helped turn the prisoner over onto his back. As soon as she saw his face, Raelle could not shift her gaze away. Her mind continued to flash from the past, back to the present over and over again.

Tonz poured two viles of Torpaz blood into the young man's mouth.

"S—S—Samuel?" Raelle ran her hand along the edge of the young man's scruffy face. "Samuel, is that you?"

The young man opened his eyes and Raelle gasped. They were not her brother's big brown eyes. Instead, they were completely black. No brown, no white, no humanity.

The young man reached for Tonz's arm and Tonz assisted him upward. As the young man sat up, he coughed violently, projecting a black mucus from his lungs. Once he was finished, he reached for Raelle. Raelle's first instinct was to recoil, but her heart told her not to.

The young man's hand felt cold as ice against her warm skin. "Raelle?" His purple lips quaked and black tears trickled from his emotionless eyes. "You look... different."

"My hair... my hair is different, but it's me."

"I'm so sorry..." The young man wept. "I left you... I..."

"Samuel! It is you." Tears cascaded over Raelle's somber face.

"Yes," he wept.

Raelle leaned in and embraced her malformed brother. "What have they done to you?" She felt comfort in his familiar frame.

He could barely speak. "I'm dying, Raelle."

"No." Raelle relinquished her embrace and took her brother's cold hands. "No, we won't let that happen."

"It *will* happen." Samuel squeezed Raelle's hand. "I'm infected with a demonic poison. I drank it willingly. Therefore, when I die, my soul will belong to Azmodil for all eternity."

"No." Raelle did her best to swallow her tears. "We won't let that happen. We'll go back into the Void and we'll free your soul. We already know where to find it. We just have to get back there."

Samuel hung his heavy head. He was visibly scared. "I'm not sure how much longer I have."

"Well, I can tell you one thing I know for sure," Oleevar interrupted. "None of us has much time before that nativity ceremony Volshira is preparing for. They'll be back for us very soon. And frankly, I don't want any part of that. I want to get the hell out of here and get home."

"I can help you do that." Samuel struggled to his feet and Raelle assisted him. "If we can get our hands on some disguises, I can lead us out." He paused before discharging a hefty sigh. "But we must bring these two women with us."

"And *why* must we do that?" asked Oleevar.

Straight away, Tonz began cutting the auburn-haired woman's vines. "We don't have time for explanations, Olee. If that is what Samuel requires, then that is what we will give him."

"Here." Raelle tossed Tonz's second blade to Oleevar. "Help Samuel get the other woman down."

"It's as if I'm talking to a wall when I'm with you Rogues," Oleevar murmured under his breath and started to cut. "I don't know why I even bother."

"Just be quiet and get her down." Cohlen assisted his brother. "Not everything has to be Olee-approved."

Raelle picked the auburn-haired woman's locks and she fell into Tonz's arms.

"Here, Raelle." Tonz placed the woman on the floor. "Let me rest her head in your lap."

Raelle sat atop the cold stone with her legs crossed and Tonz eased the woman's head back into her lap. A splinter of pain slithered through Raelle's extremities at the sight of the woman's shriveled eye sockets. She gently wiped the disorderly hair from the woman's face and noticed that it was precisely the same color that hers used to be. And in spite of the woman's age and grim appearance, Raelle thought she was beautiful.

"They'll both need Torpaz blood." Samuel instructed as he helped Oleevar and Cohlen with the black-haired woman.

"I'm afraid I've only got one more vial of Torpaz." Tonz opened his pouch and fumbled his fingers inside. "Damn it."

"They'll have to split it." Raelle lifted the vial from

312

Tonz's hand.

"Raelle's right." Tonz turned to Samuel. "It'll be enough to begin the healing process, but it may not be enough to revive them."

"Well…" Oleevar shook his head while he poured the other half of the vial into the black haired woman's mouth. "We're going to need quite a spectacular plan to smuggle two unconscious prisoners out of the palace."

"I think I have a plan." Samuel affectionately brushed the black woman's hair from her face.

Oleevar pursed his lips as he raised his eyebrows. "You *think*?"

"Yes," Samuel replied firmly. "I *think*."

"Well, I'm afraid you must be *certain*," Oleevar retorted as he shifted to his feet. "If we wish to get out of here unscathed, anyway."

Samuel's face twisted with irritation. "Where did you find this fellow?"

Raelle mimicked her brother's expression. "It's a long story."

"What's your plan, Samuel?" asked Tonz

"Since we have these two." Samuel pointed to Cohlen and Oleevar. "They can pose as Jassokian Priests."

"My name is Oleevar," he corrected. "And *this* is my brother, Cohlen."

"Right." Samuel seemed to blow him off. "Then Tonz and I will pose as Abequan guards carrying the women out. As if we're taking them to the nativity rite." He turned to Raelle with an uneasy air. "And, Raelle, we'll caddy you out along with them."

"Great idea. Raelle will make for a perfect decoy," Tonz added as he affectionately squeezed Raelle's arm. "They're expecting her body for the ceremony. I know that for certain."

"So, you four get to parade around in disguises while I play dead?" Raelle forced a crooked smile and shrugged. "Sounds easy enough to me."

Tonz picked up Master Virtoss's mask and tossed it to

313

Oleevar. "You'll have to wear this too. It's more likely people would recognize your face."

"Or…" Raelle tapped her foot. "Olee could just use his Opalz gift to shift into the priest."

Oleevar studied the mask without eye holes. "First of all, it will be impossible for me to shift without my Opalz ring. Not to mention, I'm pretty sure that I can't shift into a being that has no energy. I need to have at one time absorbed their energy in order to shift into their form. Seeing as he is dead, he has none."

"Duly noted." Tonz looked around the room. "But we definitely need to find those rings."

"I think I know where they are." Raelle squatted down over Master Virtoss and reached inside his pockets. "They're here."

"Oh, thank the Architect." Oleevar raced toward her. Raelle planted both his and Cohlen's rings into his palm.

Raelle slipped hers back onto her finger. Being reconnected with her power made her feel a little safer, and the presence of Samuel and Tonz even more so.

"They're not going to be safe there." Samuel walked over to the red marble table. "If we do get caught, the first thing they'll do is take them again. Shira has already taken both of mine. And without your Opalz stone, you won't be able to use your gifts."

"Then what do you suggest?" Oleevar asked as he fiddled with his ring.

"You may find this a bit extreme." Samuel chose a scalpel from the table. "But you need to make your stones a bit more permanent." He pointed the scalpel at the two comatose women. "Just as Lochran permanently crippled *them*."

Oleevar eyed the scalpel suspiciously. "I'm afraid I don't understand."

"Come." Samuel made his way over to where the two women lay on the floor. "I'll show you."

Raelle, Tonz, Olee, and Cohlen followed Samuel over to the women.

"Do you see this scar?" Samuel ran his finger along a short scar on the black-haired woman's arm. "There's a stone implanted inside her that keeps her from using her Lyre. The energy of this stone has essentially exterminated most of the Lyre from her blood."

"That's awful." Raelle was overcome with woe for the woman. "What kind of stone is it?"

"I'm not exactly sure." Samuel ran his thumb over the scar. "I just know that it feels like torture. I had one myself once."

He showed Raelle his own scar. "But mine has since been removed. And now, I'm going to remove theirs."

Oleevar cleared his throat. "This is all well and good, but are you suggesting we embed our own stones into *our* arms?"

"Yes," Samuel said as he sliced a deep opening over the woman's scar. "That's the only way your stones will be safe and with you at all times. Like I said, it seems a bit extreme, but these are dark times, and dark times call for extreme measures. There is no limit to what our enemy will do, and so we should not limit ourselves either. I've experienced it all firsthand. Do not underestimate Lochran or Volshira."

Raelle saw a look of deep regret come over Samuel's tormented face.

"Samuel." Raelle took his hand. "Are you all right?"

"Yeah." He nodded and forced a smile through wet eyes. "I'll be all right."

Raelle grasped her brother's hand. "We'll talk later."

"I see your point," Oleevar chimed in, seemingly unaware of Raelle and Samuel's moment. "And I agree with Samuel. If we were to be parted with our stones, then we would be rendered completely defenseless as we were when Tonz found us. We can't allow that to happen again. Our unique abilities may be our only saving grace if we're caught."

"Then we'll do it." The sight of Samuel digging his finger into the woman's arm caused Raelle's stomach to do a minor flip. She cringed as he removed the black stone.

Using the bottom of Raelle's robe, Samuel wiped the blood from the gem.

"Here." Oleevar put out his hand. "Allow me to take a

look at that."

Samuel dropped the gem into Oleevar's palm.

"But it can't be." Oleevar examined the gem. "How could—

"What is it, Olee?" Cohlen peered over his brother's shoulder to get a look.

"It's Chocaz." Oleevar shook his head in denial. "It's Chocaz melded with black Opalz. But Chocaz can only be found in *our* kingdom of Ellios. We keep it very guarded along with our technology."

"Lochran has admitted to me that he has stolen some of your technology." Samuel returned to the group with a needle and thread. With a shaky hand, he carefully sewed the woman's incision shut. "He uses it to power a carriage of his. It has no horses and hovers over the road."

"That son of a behemoth!" Oleevar threw the stone across the room. "Lochran will pay for that!"

Raelle was taken aback by his irate and aggressive reaction. It was not like Oleevar to respond with anger and profanity, or any real emotion, for that matter.

"I'll get this one." Tonz plucked the scalpel from the floor and moved over to the auburn-haired woman. As soon as he removed the stone, Raelle stitched the opening closed.

"Try not to handle the stone for too long." Samuel instructed as he picked up the black-haired woman from the floor and carried her to a gurney on wheels. It was large enough for two people. "It can take effect within minutes."

Tonz dropped the stone and kicked it across the room before collecting the auburn-haired woman and carrying her to the same gurney. With a gentle ease, he laid her next to the black-haired beauty. "Here, Raelle." Tonz fetched a second gurney and a scalpel from the table of torturous tools. "Hop up here."

"We should implant them underneath our arms where they meet the armpit," Oleevar advised. "The stitches will be well hidden there."

"Good idea." Raelle lay back on the rolling table and slid

her left arm from her sleeve.

"Hold it up above your head." Tonz gently tugged on her sleeve. "As high as you can."

Raelle closed her eyes and tried not to focus on what was about to happen. She did her best to meditate and drifted off back to her peaceful valley.

"Raelle... you can wake up now. We're all finished." The sound of Tonz's voice roused her from her meditation. "You dozed off there for a bit."

"Sorry." Raelle slipped her arm back into her robe and wrapped it around her chilled body. "I just feel so drained."

"It's to be expected. You've been through a great deal." Tonz was now dressed in gold warrior armor. In his arm, he held a matching gold-plated helmet topped with a fan of red feathers. "How do I look?" He grinned, trying to lighten the mood in an otherwise horrifying escape.

"It does hang off you a bit," Raelle joked. His smile had a way of making her feel more at ease, if only for just a moment.

"Very funny." Tonz smirked. "It is true that Rogues have a leaner physique. Makes us much faster and more agile. And loads more attractive if you ask me."

Samuel approached Raelle and Tonz wearing the same warrior armor. "I couldn't agree more." He patted Tonz's shoulder.

"Does it also make you Rogues vainer and more reckless too?" Oleevar said with snark in his voice.

Samuel winced. "What is his prob—

The remark seemed to send him into a coughing fit. Samuel's body violently contorted as more black mucus discharged from his mouth and onto the floor. The sound of clanking metal startled them as the helmet Samuel had been holding hit the stone floor.

With haste, Raelle jumped down from her gurney and rushed to comfort him. "Samuel!" She used her bell sleeves to wipe the demonic bile from his bewildered face. "Are you sure you can go through with this? Please, let us—

"No." Samuel cringed through rapid breaths. "I can do

317

this. I have to do this. You wouldn't be in this predicament if it weren't for me." He finally managed to steady his breathing. "I owe you at least this much, Raelle."

In the back of Raelle's mind, she agreed. He owed her a great deal more than this. He owed her an explanation. Something to ease the distrust and cynicism that had become her mechanism for survival. And although she was angry with him, she wanted more than anything for him to live. She wanted to give him a chance to reconcile with her and with the life they had been given.

"It's going to be all right," Raelle said as she cleaned the last bit of spew from Samuel's lip. "We're going to get you out of here. And we're going to cure you. Just hang in there."

"We had better get a move on before Samuel's condition worsens." Tonz grasped Raelle's hand and leaned into her ear. "I don't have any more Torpaz blood to get us by if something should happen. Who knows how much longer he has."

Raelle did her best to swallow her worry. "Is everyone ready?" She shrank from the thought of having to remove her robe and expose her body to the cold once more.

"We can use these to cover them." Samuel unfolded a sheet of black silk that he found on the bottom shelf of the gurney. "I know it won't be enough to keep you warm, but it's our only option."

"It's fine." Raelle did her best to think warm thoughts as she opened her robe and slipped out of it. Sharp chills returned to her as she mounted the gurney once more and lay back against its cold marble. As soon as she shifted into the center, her brother used the sheet to cover her from head to toe. Raelle closed her eyes and decided to use her time underneath the silky shroud to recharge her diminishing Lyre and pray that they would make it safely out of the torturous hell.

\*\*\*

Samuel did his best to walk tall and steady alongside Tonz as they trekked through the moist and cavernous halls that had been carved out below the Abequan dungeon. Every so often, Samuel would check on his elven companions garbed in Jassokian priest attire. Oleevar and Cohlen both walked with their heads down as they rolled the marble gurneys along.

Samuel took a moment to revel in the fact that his sister was alive underneath the sheet below. Finally, he would get his chance to rescue her. Not only that, he would be the one to reunite her with her true mother, just as he had been with his. Together, the four of them would take back Huronus. Together, they would right the wrong his father had succumbed to. Together, they would restore order to their land. But first, they needed to escape Volshira's clutches.

"Through these doors at the end of the hall." Samuel pointed to a pair of large, rusty iron egresses. "They'll lead us out into the main cavern. Then from there, we'll take the ramp up three levels to the dungeon."

"And then?" Tonz asked.

"We stop by the gem chamber. I'm going to need a harness ring." Samuel lifted his hand and studied his naked ring finger. "From there, we'll roll them up and out through the judgment hall ramp. It leads to the outside where prisoners are transported to the coliseum for punishment. We can take one of their transports and leave the city."

"Sounds like a plan." Tonz shifted his shoulders and cracked his neck underneath the heavy Abequan armor. "I don't know how they get around in this stuff. It's so stifling."

Samuel paused and opened the iron doors. They proceeded through the entryway and out into an open cavern. Much like the one in Huronus, the ramps of the circular cave wrapped around to different levels that looked out over a large pit below. Inside the numerous levels of the pit, legions of demonic creatures screeched and howled, waiting for their release.

"In the name of the Architect." Tonz gazed down into the demonic breeding ground. "There are more? Where do they all come from?"

"Many of them were human once." Samuel stared down into the pit. "Until they were starved, tortured, and made to eat and drink corrupted blood of the Lyre."

"Corrupted?" Oleevar questioned. "How does Lyre blood become corrupt?"

"That's what they were doing to us in the penance chamber," Samuel explained. "Those tendrils weren't vines. They're called grimfozza. They're a demonic and parasitic organism that grows from the blood of dark Jassokian priests and demons. Once they enter your body, they leech demonic toxins into it while at the same time feeding from the life force of your blood."

"They were trying to corrupt Raelle's blood?" Tonz eyes looked grim.

"Yes," said Samuel. "While at the same time draining her clean blood at the bottom in order to drink it."

"Drink it?" Oleevar gasped. "Why on Lerim would anyone do such a thing?"

"Because drinking the Lyre blood of another not only grants the drinker unimaginable healing powers, but magnifies their current abilities as well."

"That sounds like dark magic to me." Oleevar shook his head. "I imagine there must be repercussions for this."

"There are, over time." As they wheeled the gurneys up to the second level, Samuel recalled his father's gross and withering appearance. "But to some, it's worth it."

Once at the third level, Samuel led them through a vast and wide cell block. On either side, men and women pleaded inside their cells. Samuel could not bear to look at their filthy malformed figures as they screamed, cried, mumbled, and moaned. Some of them missing limbs, eyes, noses, fingers, or tongues.

"We had no idea any of this was going on." Oleevar's voice shook with regret. "Or else we would have stepped in long ago. If my parents had only known..." Oleevar seemed to lose his words in deep remorse.

At the end of the hall, they were met with a solid red marble wall crawling with grimfozza. "Don't let it reach out and touch you, and do your best not to touch it." Samuel directed before closing his eyes and focusing on the words Volshira had

320

used to open many a dark door.

Slowly, marble wall lowered, allowing Samuel and his small procession to move through. Once on the other side, the wall closed behind them. They were now inside the Abequan dungeon where Lyre-Blood criminals awaited trial behind gold-plated metal doors with a single miniature window.

Samuel and Tonz's boots clanged against the polished red marble floors as they made their way toward the gem chamber. Outside, two guards were posted. Samuel paused and motioned for the others to stop along with him.

"You think you can take them?" Samuel whispered through his sentry helm.

Tonz's green eyes met Samuel's and he nodded, *yes.*

Tonz stinted toward his targets. As quickly as Tonz had disappeared, he reappeared at the throats of the two guards. And before they knew what had happened, the sentries crashed to the floor. Fresh blood gushed from their throats where Tonz had used two short swords to slice them clean open.

Samuel motioned Oleevar and Cohlen in Tonz's direction. As they made their way forward, Tonz lifted a Rubiz ring from one of the dead guards and used it to unlock the gem chamber door. He opened it and disappeared inside. When he returned, Tonz tossed Samuel a white gold ring fit with a Torpaz stone.

"Thanks." Samuel caught the ring in midair and did his best to pull the snug band over his swollen purple knuckle.

"That was far too easy," said Tonz. "They really ought to think about improving the security around here." He shut the gem door.

"Thank you for the suggestion." The familiar and sinister tone of Volshira's voice made Samuel's heart from his chest. He froze dead in his tracks, unable to turn around to address her. He was unsure whether they had been caught or if their disguises still held true. But one thing he did know for certain: Volshira would recognize his black eyes and pale skin.

"I apologize, your majesty." Tonz spoke with a heavy Abequan accent, as most guards did. "It seems that these guards have been neglecting their duty and someone broke into the gem chamber. We are on our way from the Penance Chamber."

"Turn around," Volshira commanded. "All of you!"

Samuel didn't know whether to do as Volshira asked, or to reach for one of his blades. His gut told him to err on the side of caution, he was not yet sure if she was alone.

Samuel's party waited for him to make a move before complying. Once Samuel turned around, they followed suit. Each of them kept their heads angled toward the floor. In the shiny red marble, Samuel saw Volshira's reflection moving toward him. She strode tall and confident, garbed in a sheer red gown and her usual head piece. But Volshira was not alone. With her was a large warrior. Like Samuel, his skin was so pale that it looked almost purple. He was dressed in sleeveless royal attire that exposed his enormous arms covered in strange marks and branding. Dark messy hair hung in the warriors face, making it difficult to see who exactly he was.

Volshira approached Oleevar. "Funny…" She looked him up and down. "I've just come from the penance hall and all six of my sacrifices have been removed." Volshira lifted Oleevar's chin and eyed his mask. "…when I explicitly asked for *only* the Huronians this evening." Volshira clenched her fist. "Imbecile!" With a single blow, Volshira knocked Oleevar unconscious, and he crashed to the floor.

Suddenly, a horrible and demonic shriek burst from Cohlen's throat. He warped into wraith form and lunged at Volshira, knocking her to the floor. Volshira grabbed his wrists to keep his claws from cutting into her. Within seconds, she too transformed. She had stolen his ability.

Before Samuel could jump around the gurneys, Raelle had awakened. Barely clad, she hopped off of her rolling platform and grabbed one of Tonz short swords. But before she could get to Volshira, the demonic warrior raised a hand in the air and squeezed. Without touching Raelle, he lifted her off the floor and started to choke her.

Tonz rushed to help Raelle. But he too was thwarted by

the warrior's distant clutch. Instantly, Samuel's mind flashed back to the day he had faced Chrishtan. It was how he had defeated Samuel. *Chrishtan? But how? It was him Volshira was trying to get to this whole time! Did she ever love me?*

Back to the present, Samuel leapt stomach-first onto Raelle's gurney and rolled swiftly toward the warrior. He crashed into Chrishtan, swiping his legs out from under him. The blow was enough to release Tonz and Raelle, but it did not incapacitate the demon. Chrishtan stood and drew an enormous sword from his back. The hallway had only just enough room for him to swing it fully.

Samuel seized both of his short swords and engaged his enemy in battle. He swung and dodged as best he could, but his energy was almost entirely drained and his Lyre almost completely corrupted. It was then that he felt it. Chrishtan's sword had entered him. Samuel wailed in pain as the demonic warrior recklessly removed the blade from his gut. Along with the agony that now riddled his entire body, Samuel felt his legs buckle. That last thing he felt was the cold hard marble pummeling his face. The last thing he saw was the reflection of Tonz and Raelle fighting the demonic Vilgare. And the last thing he heard was the sound of his throat, gurgling and choking on his own demonic blood. Hell had finally come for him.

# CHAPTER 25
## ULTIMATE SECRETS & SACRIFICE

Volshira regarded herself in the mirror as she rubbed the small bump of her barely pregnant belly. She rejoiced in the two little miracles that were inside. As her glance shifted to her face, she felt disgusted by the reflection that gazed back at her. She cringed as she ran her fingers over the melted scars that had taken over the left side of her face and head. In the mirror, a pale and shirtless Chrishtan eased up behind her. He stroked his hands over her arms, across her shoulders, and down around her naked breasts. From there, his fingertips traveled to her mangled face.

"You are still beautiful," he whispered in her ear. "And now, you are queen." With his purple lips, he caressed her neck and nibbled her ear. A chill shivered through her. Chrishtan's affection had been returned to Volshira exactly as she remembered it. He touched her just as he had before, kissed her just as he had before, and made love to her just as before. But that was not the only cause for chills. Unlike before, Chrishtan's lips were now dark and almost icy. His skin was now pale and cold and covered in the scars of demonic branding. These times, the times when Azmodil allowed Chrishtan to come forth with only the memory of their love, were what Volshira lived for. The rest of her time was spent in the clutches of Lilazz and the company of Azmodil. Her body now belonged to the succubus, but Volshira told herself that it was worth the price of revenge. And tonight at the nativity rite, she would finally have that revenge. But first, she would let Chrishtan have her, all of her.

After they finished making love, she helped him to dress in his royal raiment. Unlike Volshira, he had the ability to make his leathery wings meld back into his body. And whenever he needed them, his back would transform in a painful and morbid fashion. As she helped him with the buttons on his elaborate coat, Chrishtan ran his hands over her naked belly. Azmodil had not yet taken Chrishtan back to the Void. Volshira was grateful for it and reveled in each moment of Chrishtan's false reality and transient memory state.

"Our child is such a gift." His eyes gleamed as he kissed her. "I know they will make a strong and just king or queen one day."

"Indeed." Volshira grasped the black Opalz amulet of his necklace and pulled him close. With her thumb, she brushed over his bottom lip. "And they will have the most extraordinary and loving father."

Chrishtan leaned in and bit down hard on Volshira's ear. "Father of demons," he hissed. Azmodil had returned. "Don't you forget, my little pet," the demon sneered. "Those are *my* children, not *his*. They are *not* human. It would do you well *not* to forget that." He glared into her gold eyes with his as black as coal. "He is right about one thing though." The demon's voice was low and coarse. "You are a treasure to look at. And the feel of you is even more pleasurable." He snidely ran his thumb over her naked chest.

Volshira swallowed her dread and looked the demon in the eye. "I am whatever you need me to be." She placed his crown on top of his head and bowed.

"Then you shall have your vengeance," Azmodil growled.

A knock came at the door. "Who's there?" Volshira inquired.

"It's Trishlan, your majesty," a young woman spoke through the door.

"Yes, come in," Volshira instructed and four maidens entered the royal quarters. With them, they brought light warrior armor and an elaborate red gown, as well as an extravagant crown. It had been custom made just for her.

As the maidens began dressing Volshira's bottom half in light, gold-plated armor, the demon exited the bedroom chamber and poured a dark red drink from a decanter inside the sitting room. Volshira knew that to be Samuel's blood. The fresh red liquid sitting in the vessel next to it was Raelle's. It would be Volshira's drink of choice for the rite.

Volshira stood tall and poised as her maidens latched her

armor and then fitted her with an armored corset. It was decorated beautifully with small Opalz stones and larger Rubiz gems. Below that, a long, flowing, burgundy gown was attached to the corset and covered her leg armor. On her forearms were buckled extravagantly decorated bracers as well as a matching neck piece. And as a final elegant touch, the maidens crowned their queen. The crown was very tall and very wide, with a magnificent and ornate gold design that fanned out over Volshira's head. Its gold was laden with more black and red gemstones. On the left side, the design continued over her forehead all the way down to the very top of her lip. Its gorgeous design hid her scars beautifully. Finally, she felt like a real queen. The genuine queen of Abequa, born of noble blood.

As soon as her maidens finished, Volshira opened her armoire and retrieved both her short swords. She carefully slid them into their sheaths underneath her detachable gown. On her way out to the sitting room, she stopped to admire her new and elegant reflection. *For Abequa...* She then continued to the sitting room where the demon stood to greet her. He downed what was left of Samuel's life blood and set the glass on an end table.

"You look like a queen," the demon rasped.

"Thank you." Volshira bowed. "Shall we to the rite?"

Azmodil took her arm. "We shall."

Volshira sat on her throne next to her demon king. In spite of the cold winter weather and light drizzle of snow, the coliseum was completely full. Steps below each seated row burned with coal and fuel to keep the crowd warm. But Volshira knew that it was not the warmth that filled the stands. What Abequans truly desired above all was to see a true and rightful Abequan back on the throne. The Huronian occupation was now over. And they were told that Samuel had returned to Huronus to help his father rule and that Chrishtan had returned to make right what his family had wronged. Today would be that day. Even more thrilling was the idea of a new and pure Abequan heir. Finally, Volshira had returned peace and order to her people. The cost of reconciliation was incredibly high, but seeing her people come together was worth it.

To her right, Azmodil occupied Chrishtan's shell and throne. His face was covered by the hood of his heavy red cloak. They both sat patiently, awaiting the arrival of their anticipated guest, the king of Huronus. After all, Volshira had a glorious surprise for him. She gazed out over the top of the coliseum at a distant sun as it sank over the white horizon. Its light shone through the wispy snowflakes that occasionally floated down like sheer prisms. To Volshira, it was one of the most incredible sights she had ever seen. To her, it was a sign. It was the symbol of things to come.

Volshira adjusted the burgundy cloak that rested on her shoulders. Between that and the warmth of the fire beneath her, she was more than comfortable. She felt secure and even relieved. She had guards posted all around her, her best men and women. They were loyal and highly trained warriors. There was no way her enemy would make it out alive. And if he did, she would hunt him down and kill him herself. But first, she wanted to make him suffer. She would let him know that *he* had been outdone. She would show him how *his* sacrifices have been in vain and her pain worth every single agonizing second.

The sound of light footsteps along with the smell of fresh leather armor floated into Volshira's heightened Lyre senses. Instantly, her guards stood at attention. She too stood as Huronian Rogue sentries made their way up the ramp to her royal balcony. In their midst was the Huronian king, Lochran Jowellia. On his arm was a young woman Volshira had never before seen. Her skin was the color of sand and her lips the color of eggplant. Her white hair and silver eyes reflected the light of the descending sun like the blade of a new knife. The elaborate golden designs of her deep purple dress along with the intricate tattoos on her face told Volshira one thing— this woman was Jassokian royalty. She had three purple Amythyz stones implanted into her face to prove it. One between her eyes, and two more on either side of her prominent cheek bones.

The Rogue sentinels parted and made way for Lochran and his new companion. As soon as they stepped onto the balcony,

Volshira moved to greet them. Usually, a king would receive a queen with a dainty shake and kiss of the hand, but Lochran had always treated Volshira as if she were beneath him. Instead, he presented only a miniscule bow and presented the striking Jassokian elf.

"Volshira, this is Karaleste." He motioned for the elf to remove her hood. "My fiancée."

The elf bowed, exposing the intricacies of her hairstyle at the crown of her head. The rest of her hair hung freely over her dainty shoulders.

*Fiancée? I knew that Jassokia was cooperating with the Huronians, but not to this extent. This woman is heir to the Jassokian throne...* Volshira took another moment to study the young elf. Her expressions, mannerisms and energy told Volshira that she was nervous. Maybe even terrified. *She is not here on her own accord...*

"Is our master Azmodil not in the mood for greetings?" Lochran took his seat in the throne next to Volshira's, one throne away from the demon. Karaleste elegantly sat down on his other side.

"I'm afraid he is feeling rather pompous this evening." Volshira glanced over at her hooded king. "He does not wish to present himself until the rite has begun."

"I see." Lochran removed his own blue hood. "I could not be more pleased to hear of your pregnancy. These children will be the first of their kind in over a thousand years."

"Indeed." Volshira rested a hand over her barely pregnant belly. "And Abequa shall welcome them with open arms."

"Soon enough." Lochran contemplated his bride to be. "We too shall bless this world with a child of equal, if not more substantial, holy magnitude."

*That poor girl.* Volshira swallowed her urge to pull the elf away from her devious captor and slit his throat. But she knew she could not defeat him without first touching him. Lochran knew that Volshira had the ability to manipulate Lyre, but her talent for stealing others' gifts was something she had kept to herself.

Volshira gave Lochran's arm a friendly squeeze. "May you and your bride be blessed by his holy Destroyer."

Lochran mustered a crooked grin of approval. "Why thank you, Shira. Surely I wish the same for you."

Volshira heard the insincerity in his patronizing tone. In her mind, she was pulling him out of his seat and beating him to a bloody mess. An act of pure passion and angst. She would need no weapon or skill. But back in reality, Volshira simply smiled and left her throne.

"It is time to address the people." She stood tall as her eyes darted around the crowd. Most of them were hooded and cloaked in capes of burgundy and gold, but some wore champagne white. It was not a usual Abequan color, but things had changed since Chrishtan's parents were killed and Abequa annexed. The color scheme looked both heavenly and honorable. They embodied purity, power, and blood.

"Good and true people of Abequa," Volshira spoke with a commanding yet compassionate voice. In the background, the sun said its final goodbyes, casting an unusual red hue over the snow-covered land. "Today is a day to remember. Today we take back what is and has always been ours. Today, we honor our Abequan heritage and welcome it back with open and tired arms. For years have we knelt to the tyranny of unjust and false rulers. For almost two decades have we searched for peace and order. For almost two decades have we not prayed for a righteous ruler to return and restore our culture, our practices, and our honorable way of life?" She paused and allowed the crowd to exchange their feelings amongst themselves. Behind her, she could hear Lochran mumbling his displeasure with her choice of words. It made her grin. "Today, my fellow Abequans, most righteous and pure, our prayers are answered. But first, to show our immense gratitude and thanks, we shall make an offering. Yes, it is true that this kind of offering has not been made for almost a thousand years, but today we must call upon the old ways that made Abequa great in the beginning. We must return to our roots. Then and only then, can I present to you the answer to your prayers."

329

The crowd went wild with cheers and clapping. They begged and pleaded for the ancient sacrifice. Volshira made a motion with her hand and a circular crest at the center of the coliseum slid open. In its place an enormous platform slowly rose high into the air. Around its perimeter, Raelle, Samuel, Tonz, Cohlen, Oleevar, and the two women were each chained to their own tall and sharp metal spire.

"Behold!" Volshira commanded. "The ultimate sacrifice!" She listened intently as the crowd jeered. "They took your lands. They took your cities. They stole your children and they decimated your culture!" Volshira's baleful smile took over her face as the crowd went wild. "I give to you Abequa, and to you, oh Architect most divine, *the Huronians* responsible for these atrocities, in addition to those that aided and abetted them!"

Volshira heard Lochran come up behind her. "Have you lost your pretty little mind?" he hissed in her ear. "This is treason!" He reached for her throat, but she was too quick. She squeezed his wrist as hard as she could.

"Look closer." Volshira used her other hand to direct his face outward into the coliseum. "I am only taking from you what you took from me, and many others of this great nation." She puckered her lips with a pompous smirk. "Your entire family and bloodline... This is where it meets its end." She whispered.

"Is that..." Lochran's words drifted off in his realization.

"Yes." Volshira smiled. "Your wife, your child, your sister, and your niece."

"It was you!" He glared at Volshira. "*You* turned my son against me!"

"That was the original plan." Volshira shrugged. "But I didn't have to. You did that yourself. And I assure you, he was never possessed by any demon. Every decision he made was his own. He loathed you even more than I."

"If that is Samuel out there..." Lochran shifted his gaze to the hooded figure in the king's throne. "Then who is—

Volshira shot a bolt of Lochran's own black lighting into him. He released his painful grip and fell to the floor. As Lochran writhed beneath her, Volshira returned to the balcony's edge. Her commanding voice sliced through the crowd. "In return for this holy sacrifice, *we* have been given a gift." The demon in Chrishtan's shell approached the balcony railing and removed his hood. "The gift of our true heir, Chrishtan Vilgare! He has returned to us after all these years of lies and persecution by our false Huronian leader. It was not Chrishtan and his mentor who murdered the king Sonee and Queen Jeanahn Vilgare. It was the Huronians! They took our kingdom, and today we are taking it back!"

The entire coliseum vibrated with stomping feet and elated voices.

"Why you ungrateful little wench!" Lochran painfully rose to his feet and pulled out his dagger. Volshira swiftly disarmed him and kicked Lochran back into his chair. All the while, Karaleste looked on, trembling in fear. Lochran tried to return to his feet, but Volshira struck him once more with the black lightning. "You will watch your whole family die, and your bloodline along with it. You will endure every moment of it in the same way we have all endured *you*."

Out of her peripheral vision, Volshira saw the sun dip below the horizon and with it, the ground began to shake. Suddenly, horrified screams could be heard throughout the coliseum. All around her, Volshira watched as balls of green gas exploded and filled up the stands.

"You fool!" Lochran struggled in his chair. "You've got two elves out there on that sacrificial stand!"

Volshira tried to keep her wits among the chaos that erupted all around her.

"They've come for *them*!" Lochran hollered. "The Samissians have come for them!"

Volshira felt taken aback by Lochran's eyes filled with genuine fear and outrage. "I didn't—

"You know nothing, little girl." Lochran formed a look of disgust. "The Samissians are incredibly powerful. I never dragged them into this for a reason! They mind their business, and we mind ours. Now you've destroyed that. And your so-called *beloved kingdom* along with it!"

Throughout the coliseum, deadly screams sounded off within the giant gas plume and arrows whizzed by in every direction. Volshira knew it would not be long before the Ellosian air raids began.

The grotesque sound of cracking, gurgling, and boisterous pain drew Volshira's attention away from the anarchy of the coliseum. It was Lochran. His body began to contort and bend in unnatural ways. Volshira watched in horror as Lochran transformed into one of the most disturbing and powerful creatures she had ever lain eyes upon. His face was no longer a face, his ears were no longer ears, and his body was no longer his body. He had become something that even the worst nightmare could never imagine.

"You thought you could deceive me?" the heinous creature that had once been Lochran cackled. "I am beyond suffering. I am beyond pain. I am beyond the trivial grief of your wretched and emotional species." He spread his enormous fleshy wings. "Silly little girl." His jagged claws clutched Volshira's throat. "I am the destroyer of things. I am the crusher of dreams. I am the demolisher of sanity and the father of vengeance." The devious emotion of his slimy black mouth made up for his lack of eyes as he hissed. "You and Lochran are one in the same. I created him, and *he* created *you*. Born out of the vengeance of loss." He tilted his head in an unnatural way as he lifted her by the neck. Her feet dangled over the floor as he brought her in disturbingly close to his freakishly empty face. She gagged even more on his repugnant breath. "You have made the perfect concubine for my son, Azmodil, and body for my slave Lilazz." The grotesque monstrosity squeezed even harder as it glared at her without eyes. "You cannot defeat me. I am Ire Oblitora!" the Destroyer thundered and released her.

Volshira floundered around on the balcony like a fresh catch gasping and flopping for breath. But her recovery was abruptly ended by the painfully firm and ferocious grip of

Azmodil's hands in her hair. Volshira heard him chuckle before dragging her toward the exit ramp. She tried to scream as she backpedaled against his pull, but her throat had not yet recovered. As Azmodil hauled her off, Volshira could not draw her eyes away from Ire Oblitora. The monster spread his wings of sheer flesh and narrow bone. He scooped up his horrified bride-to-be in one arm. Karaleste kicked and screamed, but it was no use. Lochran flapped his wings and disappeared with the terrified Jassokian princess into the gas-filled anarchy of the stadium.

Still in Azmodil's clutches, Volshira began to panic at the thought of what he intended to do to her. Her mind raced with thoughts of the demon's betrayal. Azmodil had tricked her. He had never been on her side. He had always been on the side of his father, Ire Oblitora. He had used her to rid him of all the remaining heirs, Samuel, Raelle, Oleevar, Cohlen, and, of course, Chrishtan. She practically served them up on a silver platter. The demon used her suffering as a weapon against her and she hated herself for it. She chose by her own free will to let the demon Lilazz bestow her with the power of seduction. It was her own desire to mate with the demon Azmodil in order to gain the power she needed to take her kingdom back. And now, she knew exactly where Lochran was headed in his new form—to the Void hole beneath the coliseum. Once there, he would awaken and release every single miscreation within the depths of the pit. *Abequa will surely be destroyed.* But still, Volshira clung to hope. She found comfort in the things she had kept to herself. The secrets she had kept inside of her. If she survived this day, surely *they* would bring both hope and light.

Half way down the ramp, the demon abruptly stopped and let go of Volshira's hair. Finally free of his grip, she flipped over to her feet and ripped the bottom of her gown away. In one swift motion, she pulled both her swords from their sheaths and flipped them like a lassoing rope upright in her hands. She jumped toward Chrishtan's demonic shell and was met with his one enormous sword. It clanged loudly against hers, pushing her back with brute force. In that moment, Volshira realized why he had let go of her. She gazed at his Opalz necklace that was no longer black, but a transparent milky white, speckled with an array of other colors. His lips were no longer purple, but the same fleshy color they had always been. And his skin had returned to its healthy tan that no longer bared the brandings of a demon. Volshira's golden eyes studied his familiar blues that were now filled with anger and hatred toward her.

"Look what you've done, Volshira!" Chrishtan cried, his face warped with intense devastation and rage. "Look at it!"

Volshira stepped backward and dropped her swords. With a heavy heart and a storm of tears, she fell to the floor along with them. Azmodil and Lilazz had somehow lifted from her, and the grief of the things she had done drowned her in a deep flood of sorrow. *I was never worthy of his love, or his kingdom...*

# CHAPTER 26
## TOGETHER AGAIN

As Chrishtan stood over Volshira, his fury allowed him to swallow his pity for her.

"I'm so... sorry..." Volshira wept on her knees.

Chrishtan closed his eyes. He erased her crying face and sniveling voice from his mind. From where he stood, Chrishtan leapt over the balcony and onto the coliseum steps. As the green gas began to dissipate, his eyes darted around looking for his comrades in the clash chaos of Abequan warriors and Samissian elves, both in and out of animal form. He knew that if the Samissians were in Abequa, surely one or both of his elven brethren must be too.

*What on Lerim would possess Samissians to leave their forest and attack Abequa?* Chrishtan could only think of one thing. *They came for someone or something. Samissians don't take lightly to the destruction of their people or culture. Have they come for me? No... An attack of this magnitude would only be for one of their own.*

Arrows flew and swords rang out. Off in the distance overhead, the Ellios avian forces headed straight for the coliseum. Chrishtan knew that once the elves had retrieved what or whom they had come for, they would more than likely gas the coliseum once more and retreat, locking their enemy inside to be obliterated by energy bombs. Chrishtan could not allow this to happen. These were *his* people. He had to find Oleevar or King Adreahn and beg them to call it off. Whatever Volshira had taken from them was not worth the mass slaying of his citizens.

With a deep breath, Chrishtan closed his eyes and honed his Lyre. His energy flowed through him like the warmth of a summer sun. He felt amazing. Chrishtan darted through the elves in white cloaks and the warriors in red in search of someone, anyone, who held a high enough rank to put a stop to the aerial assault. As he approached the center of the coliseum, he saw a group of elves fighting off warriors at the base of a tall podium. Each elf blocked the blow of a sword with their wooden staffs. At either end of each ornately carved staff, was a large and sharp end much like the tip of an enormous spear. As they held off their Abequan foe, a few elves scaled the podium along thick vine ropes that they had brought with them. In that moment, Chrishtan's jaw dropped and his heart sank. He saw exactly what the elves were attempting to retrieve. Oleevar, and Cohlen hung beside Raelle's brother, and a female Rogue with black hair. They were chained against tall spires, barely clad in the dead of winter. Around the other side, there were others, but Chrishtan could not see who they were.

Chrishtan raced toward the podium and engaged his Lyre. He focused all of his energy into his legs and leapt from his current location directly to the top of the podium. He landed in front of the black-haired Rogue. He could not see her face, but he could tell by her hair cut that she was an Ellios Rogue and resistance fighter of the mission troops.

"Chrishtan?" The woman raised her head and gazed at him with green eyes.

"Raelle?" Chrishtan could recognize her striking eyes and beautiful face anywhere. "Hang on!"

He raised the enormous sword from his back and swung through the first set of shackles and then the other. Raelle fell from the spire into Chrishtan's arms. He removed the heavy red cloak around his neck and wrapped her in it. She continued to shake viciously as her face transformed into a mask of pain. Her hands and feet were impaled with a strange entity and her feet and knees had been sliced open. They still dripped slowly with cold, coagulating blood.

"M-m-y b-b-brother." She managed through gasping breaths.

On the other side of the podium, the elves who had made it to the top had already begun rescuing Oleevar and Cohlen from their spires.

"I'll get him too." Chrishtan set Raelle down safely in the

center of all the spires and made his way back to the outside. Wearing fewer clothes than Raelle, Samuel hung against his spire unconscious. Chrishtan put his head to the Rogues chest. *He's not breathing.* Chrishtan pressed his hands into Samuel's chest. He charged his Lyre and sent a wave of it into Samuel.

Samuel awoke with a ferocious gasp and a look of terror.

"It's all right," Chrishtan assured him. "It's really me. It's not Azmodil. I swear it."

Samuel swallowed and did a slow blink of relief. "I was dead." Samuel hyperventilated. "I died. I—I—

"Calm down, it's going to be all right." Chrishtan grabbed his sword from his back. "Just hold still." Once again, his bulky blade severed the chains.

Samuel landed on his feet and attempted to slow his breathing. "Did you get my sister?" he asked. "Is she alive? Is she all right?" He rubbed his own arms as he shivered.

"Yes," replied Chrishtan.

"There are three more." Samuel led Chrishtan to the next spire.

Chrishtan regretfully eyed the next prisoner. "Tonz!" He barely recognized his injured and freezing friend. He had been badly beaten.

"Aye, brother." Tonz winced in frozen pain. "Get me down from here."

Chrishtan said nothing and swung through Tonz's manacles. Upon landing, Tonz was barely able to find his footing. "Did you get Raelle?"

"Yes," Chrishtan assured him.

"Over here." Samuel motioned toward the two women who remained shackled. "Them too."

"Who are they?" Chrishtan hacked through their chains and Samuel and Tonz caught them. As Chrishtan led them back between the spires into the center of the podium, he heard Oleevar on the outside.

"Let go of me!" the elf commanded. "We must release my friends and call off that air strike!"

Suddenly, the ground shook and the entire stadium along with it. Each one of them lost their footing as the podium reverberated. Tonz and Samuel were barely able to keep the unknown women in their arms. Using the spire he had leaned Raelle against, Chrishtan caught his footing. Beneath him, Raelle trembled with her eyes closed. He crouched down to pick her up. "It's all right," he coaxed. "I've got you."

Raelle's eyes opened with a look of scorn. "I'm perfectly capable of walking." She pried herself from his arms and planted both feet on the floor.

"I'm sorry, I..." Chrishtan was taken aback by Raelle's subtle protest.

"I recharged my Lyre while you got the others down." She wrapped herself tightly in the cloak he had given her. "Is it really you, Chrishtan? How did you—

Once again, the ground trembled violently. This time the evidence of the tremors sent cracks splitting through the marble floor of the coliseum. It felt as if their podium might collapse at any moment.

"We've got to get out of here!" Samuel hollered with the unconscious woman in his arms.

"Samuel?" Raelle's eyes bulged with relief at the sight of her brother. "You're alive?"

The ground shook once more.

Chrishtan turned to Samuel. "What is that?"

"No time for explanations." Samuel began making his way back through one of the gaps between the spires. "We must get out of here now!"

Chrishtan saw that Raelle did not question her brother's instructions and so neither did he. One by one, they squeezed between the spires behind Samuel and made their way to the outside edge. Standing next to one of the spires, they found Oleevar and Cohlen. They were still trying to convince their people to call off the air strike and let the Abequan people live.

"Do not call off that air strike!" Samuel interrupted the elves' heated conversation. "And get everyone out of here!"

Oleevar looked past Samuel with wide eyes. "Chrishtan? How did you—

"No time for reunions." Samuel snapped as the ground quaked even more than before. "Get every single person out of here, straightaway!"

The Samissian sergeant that Oleevar had been arguing with seemed to at least understand the gravity of *this* situation and grasped the large animal horn that was slung to his shoulder. He lifted it to his lips and blew into it. A loud and unique pattern of notes reverberated through it and echoed out into the coliseum.

Chrishtan's mind began to race. He needed to warn *his* people as well. He knew that not all the Abequans would flee the coliseum to go after the elves. "Give me that." Chrishtan snatched the horn from the sergeant and blew into it. The harsh notes of the Abequan retreat signal were much different than that of the elves, and took Abequan lungs to execute.

As soon as Chrishtan saw the Abequans heed his message, he too began his retreat. "Come on, let's go." Chrishtan jumped from the top of the podium directly to the coliseum floor. Behind him, Samuel, Raelle, and Tonz did the same, while Oleevar and Cohlen used the elven vines to rappel down. As they did, the ground shook and rumbled beneath them. Chrishtan eyed minor fissures as they cracked and grew along the thick marble floors. Once Oleevar and Cohlen's feet hit the ground, Tonz and Samuel took a moment to throw the lifeless women they carried over their shoulders before they all took off in a dead run toward the open coliseum gates.

"What's happening?" Chrishtan shouted as he ran beside Samuel.

"This coliseum is over a Void hole," Samuel explained between breaths.

"What's a Void hole?" Chrishtan struggled to keep up with Samuel's Rogue speed.

"Something you have to see to believe," answered Samuel.

Just then, the biggest tremor of all caused them to lose

339

their footing. The sound that followed felt like a blow to the head as the ground opened up and split the coliseum in two. All at once, crowds of elves and warriors were swallowed into the giant fissure. All around them, the walls of the colossal coliseum began to crumble. Giant chunks of stone and marble cracked and tumbled down toward the fleeing flood of people.

Chrishtan and his comrades had almost reached the open gate when they heard it. The jarring screeches of beasts from the Void warbled along with the drumming of the quake. As they crawled out of the enormous hole, the earth gave way to them. More fractures spread across the ground, splitting apart and swallowing more people into the demonic pit. Out of the corner of his eye, Chrishtan saw a fissure headed their way. It cracked right beneath their feet. In an instant, each one of them honed their Lyre and prepared to make the leap. They landed just outside the coliseum gates where they now stood over a crumbling makeshift bluff. The cries of those who did not make it echoed through the coliseum as they fell helplessly into the demonic mine alongside atrocious monstrosities that scaled the pit and crawled out. As the monsters made their way toward his group, Chrishtan hacked and slashed through them, spilling their rotting innards over the floor. As he fought, he kicked their decapitated heads back into the pit. All around him, other Abequan sentries were doing the same.

"Go!" Chrishtan hollered at Tonz as he held off the repulsive horde. "Get them to safety! I'll be behind you."

"Yes, Sir." Tonz began leading the group through the chaos, away from the demonic sycophants.

Raelle was the last to follow. She paused for a moment and looked at Chrishtan with regretful eyes. He thought she might say something, but her lips did not move. Weaponless and covered only by a red cloak, Raelle took off into the fleeing crowd after her companions.

Suddenly, out of the corner of his eye, Chrishtan saw the shadow of a winged creature flying overhead. In the light of the full moon that peeked out from the clouds, he saw that the shadow belonged to one of the most horrifying freaks he had ever seen.

And it was headed toward the people he cared for most in this world.

"Holy Architect!" He kicked his final kill into the Void hole and took off in the devil's direction. As he ran, another shadow flew overhead. He gazed up at Volshira's silhouette as she glided over the panicked crowd after the colossal demon.

"Damn it!" Chrishtan had no idea what her intentions were, but he did not want to be too late in finding out. His friends were without armor or weaponry and they were headed right for them. Chrishtan was their only defense.

At the same time Chrishtan caught view of his comrades, so did the monster. As the faceless demon dove down at them, Chrishtan focused every ounce of Lyre he could and used it to leap from where he was directly to their location. In midair, he caught the enormous atrocity's arm with his massive sword. The demon roared like a savage as its arm fell to the ground. The limb imprinted its shape into the snow and littered it with black blood. With its remaining arm, the demon grabbed Chrishtan's armor and tossed him like a rag doll into a snowbank. Noticing that Chrishtan was his only immediate threat, the wounded devil swooped down to finish the job. As it did, Chrishtan watched in horror as its arm bone regrew and then resealed itself with naked muscle tissue.

Chrishtan channeled his Lyre for his defense. Just as the demon flew within jump-strike distance, another winged figure flew in at full speed and tackled the horror to the ground. *Volshira...* The sound of her swords rang out as they left their scabbards. She sliced, stabbed, and dodged with both of them. The demon was very large and so very slow, allowing Volshira to escape every blow of its disturbingly long clawed fingers.

"This ends here, Lochran!" Volshira demanded as she threw off her stifling crown. "I won't let you have them!"

*Lochran?* Chrishtan dug himself out of the snowbank. *It can't be.* Back out in the open, Chrishtan saw his friends continuing in their retreat a short distance away. He felt a small amount of relief that he had allowed them enough time to gain some distance.

Once they rejoined with the Samissians, they would be safe. Chrishtan felt a chill reverberate through his spine as the light of the moon suddenly disappeared. He could see almost nothing. As he gazed up, what flew overhead eased his fear. *The Avian Strikers.* They had finally arrived to obliterate the coliseum and the horde of nightmarish creatures along with it. As the light of the moon returned, most of the Abequan people had already turned to flee back within the city walls and the Samissians were nearly out of sight. But one battle still raged on in front of him. Volshira and Lochran.

As he jumped from the snowbank to flank his monstrous enemy, the ground shook once more. The sound of energy bombs as they annihilated the coliseum boomed out over the snow-covered land. As Chrishtan came down behind the gigantic demon, he stabbed into its back with his massive sword. The freakish beast gave a monstrous roar as Chrishtan's feet used its back muscles as leverage and pulled the blade back out. In the very same moment, Volshira sliced open the demon's throat with her dual blades. From the new wound, black blood slowly oozed out of the monster's thick neck. Chrishtan and Volshira's gems glowed a radiant red as they simultaneously back-flipped off of the demon. Chrishtan thought surely they had defeated him, until Lochran's tissue healed itself just as before.

"You cannot kill me!" Lochran cackled through his demonic form. "I am Ire Oblitora!" The demon stretched his arms out to the side. In one of the demon's hands, he now held the elaborate Opalz neckpiece that Volshira had been wearing. The fastener was completely broken. *He must have torn it from her.*

Both Chrishtan and Volshira prepared for Lochran's next blow, but it was not what they had expected. In a split second, black lightning bolted from the demon's boney fingers. It breached their armor and Chrishtan seized violently. Inside, his body felt as if it were on fire. His muscles went into spasm, and his Lyre slowly burned away. The tormenting pain made him want to die. He welcomed it. He begged for it, but the brutal torture continued. *Help please.* He cried out inside his mind to a fictitious entity.

342

*Help... help... me!*

Just when he thought he would surely explode, the pain stopped. Chrishtan's body went limp and he collapsed face-first in the snow. His ears rang with intense pain and bled along with his nose. With what little strength he had, Chrishtan turned his head to the side. Lying motionless in the snow a few meters away was Volshira. Her helm glimmered in the moon light a distance from her body. Over the trampled snow, the shadows of two winged nemeses in aeronautic battle danced around them. Whoever the second creature was had saved Chrishtan's life.

Although his head and body still throbbed with intense pain and his ears still rang, Chrishtan closed his eyes and attempted to recharge his Lyre. After a few minutes, the buzzing in his ears began to subside, the pain began to dissipate, and a small amount of strength had returned. It was enough for Chrishtan to try and get to his feet. As he pressed his hands into the snow and used his arms to lift the rest of him, Chrishtan realized that he could not feel his legs. They were completely paralyzed. Using his forearms, he dragged himself across the snow over to Volshira. Unlike him, she had landed on her back. As he approached, Chrishtan was taken aback by the unfamiliar and grotesque scarring that covered the left side of her face and scalp. He then rested his head on her chest to listen for a heartbeat. It sounded faint among the gurgling of her lungs. Outside, Volshira struggled to breath.

"Volshira." He used one of his hands to shake her. "Volshira, wake up."

She did not respond and continued in her labored breaths. Chrishtan then noticed that the armor she wore was a corset. He turned her over and unbuckled the back. He heard an immediate difference in Volshira's breathing, but still her lungs sounded broken and her heart barely thumped.

Chrishtan pressed his hands against the top of her chest and sent a jolt of Lyre into her. Volshira began to cough. Blood sprayed out from her mouth and over her chest. She then grasped Chrishtan's armor and brought his face in close.

"My babies!" She managed to rasp through labored

343

breaths. "Are they alive?"

"Your *babies*?" Chrishtan looked at her face, then at her belly, then back to her face. "You're pregnant?"

"Y—y—yes." Volshira coughed and Chrishtan felt the warm blood on his face. "W—w—with twins."

Chrishtan swallowed hard. "Are they demon?"

Volshira shook her head, *No...*

Chrishtan's eyes grew large. "Who is the father?"

"S—Samuel..." She gurgled and blood dripped out of her mouth and over her lip. "And... y—you..."

"How?" Chrishtan gently shook her. "How can that be? For how long?"

"Th—three... m—moon... cycles..." Her shaky hand caressed his face. "The night I returned to you..."

"That *was* real." Chrishtan recalled what he thought had been a dream. Volshira really had come to his room the night before he found her at breakfast.

As she nodded *yes*, Volshira choked and coughed up more blood. "I've kept them a secret. I told the demon the babies were his." Tears welled in her gold eyes and ran down the side of her face. "He would have killed them. Please, they are my only hope left for this world. My secret light," she murmured through her blood-soaked mouth. "I can't feel my body. Tell me if they're all right."

Chrishtan's hand shook with apprehension as he slid his hand underneath her armor and over her belly. It did not feel like the flat abdomen he had known. Instead it was slightly distended and came to a minor curve. He closed his eyes and harnessed his Lyre. He tried to connect with the being inside. If it was his baby, he would be able to feel the connection. As he focused, he sensed two life forms. They were incredibly weak. Suddenly, the vision of his own birth flashed before his eyes. In that moment, he knew for certain. He felt his Lyre become one with the being inside her. *It is mine... but its dying... both of them are... and Volshira...*

"Are they all right?" Volshira could barely speak.

Chrishtan could feel her life force slipping away along

344

with the babies'. Inside, he wanted to cry. He wanted to bawl. He wanted to curse the Architect. But instead, he lied. "They're fine." He did not want Volshira to suffer in death. Believing that she and her babies would make it was his final gift to her.

Suddenly, a flash of light lit the sky above him. And then another, and another. Chrishtan looked up to see the other winged figure shooting rays of pure white light from its hands. They hit the demon like a boulder to the stomach. Chrishtan could tell it had injured the beast, and it sent Lochran fleeing into the night. Finally, they would be rid of the monster... for now. With a sigh of relief, Chrishtan looked back down at Volshira. The light had gone from her eyes and she was no longer breathing.

"No, damn it!" The tears cascaded down Chrishtan's face. "No, no, no!" He pressed his hands firmly to her chest and tried to reignite her life force. Even though he knew that there was none left, he persisted until the sound of flapping wings overhead set a pair of feet on the ground in front of him. They were dressed in pearly white boots decorated with ornate golden designs. As Chrishtan shifted his mournful gaze upward, he saw that they belonged to a young man with matching white warrior armor.

"I'm so sorry, Brother," The young man removed his helmet and tucked away the white feathery wings on his back. "I'm so sorry."

"Browden?" From the ground where he lay paralyzed and drained of all energy, Chrishtan gazed up into the eyes of his long-lost younger brother. Chrishtan's head felt light and his vision blurry. "Is this... real?" He let his heavy skull fall onto Volshira's cold, blood-stained chest. As his consciousness faded away, Chrishtan felt the slow struggling throbs of his own heart and the jarring vibration of hooves in the distance.

# CHAPTER 27
## YOU ARE THE LIGHT

Horror and despair cascaded over Browden as he allowed the Morbas to swallow him into what he knew would be the worst kind of hell. Browden closed his eyes as he came to terms with his dark and horrifying fate. He had no other choice. They had conjured the Morbas from their own suffering, and it had to take someone. There was no getting around that. Browden's mortal existence had already met its demise. The others still had lives left to live and a world to save. He loved them and Lerim needed them. It was only fitting that he sacrifice himself.

Once inside the belly of the beast, the fear, the pain, and the anguish only intensified. It was the culmination of each and every one of their past traumas and the sufferings of the world. What he felt could not be put into words. The hurt was indescribable, his terror inconceivable, and the depth of his hopelessness interminable. Browden was experiencing it all, living it all, tortured by it all. It was the devious hell of human nature, and he was reliving all of it. Every evil and sadistic deed anyone had ever done, he felt it, saw it, abhorred it. Inside the black chasm of suffering and nothingness, he felt his soul disintegrate. His light faded to black and the fullness of his heart became an empty space. He forgot who he was. Who he had been. And who he had loved. Hell chewed him up and swallowed him like a predator eating its prey alive.

Browden had been trapped inside the ceaseless hell for what seemed like an eternity when he felt it. Something other than the empty, sickening, abyss of pure hell. It was a hint of something familiar. *Remember...* a voice echoed inside his head among the torturous squeals and screams that had become his reality. It was the voice of a woman. And for a moment, he swore he could feel the warmth of her hand on his face. If only for a split second, he saw her face. Her light blue skin and green eyes soothed his pain for a segment of a second. Then, she showed him. Fractional flashes of all of them. Their smiles, their laughs, their tears, their love. *Samuel, Raelle, Chrishtan...*

Browden focused his Lyre. He did his best to meditate, if only for moments at a time for what seemed like a second eternity until he could finally control what he saw, felt, experienced, and remembered. The words he had always used to bring his people back from *their* nightmares helped him ease the intensity of his own. *Remember what Jenladra told you. You can only be imprisoned by your own fears. The demons that reside there will play upon those fears in order to make you more vulnerable. Do not believe everything you see.* What he was seeing, feeling, and experiencing, he knew did not belong to him. It belonged to evil and he refused to bear the burden any longer. He would search out the Morbas, and give it all back.

With his mind, Browden conjured just enough light to finally be able to see. Though it was dim and a disturbing hue of blood red, the glow exposed the other depraved spirits around him. Like him, they had once been trapped by the Morbas, but they had failed to find a way out. Their bodies were contorted, broken, and distorted. Their faces looked barely human. And their depraved groans were of a grotesque tenor he had never before encountered. The last thing he wanted to do was swim through a sea of these twisted spirits, but he knew that he had no other choice. Among them, he would find the Morbas. And once he did, he would destroy it.

As Browden waded through the shallow ocean of warped bodies and souls, he searched for any sign of something different, off-kilter, or even familiar. A sound, a sight, a smell, a feeling that would lead him in the right direction. He wasn't sure how long he had been searching for the sadistic entity before something caught his eye, but it felt like weeks or even months. Among the horrid and disturbing sounds of suffering souls, Browden could make out the faint weeping of the only thing that sounded human. They were the unmistakable sobs of a child.

Crouched in the midst of a daunting throng of distorted souls, was a small boy with messy hair. Next to him, sat a large jagged blade with a hilt of sharp, metal, thorns. As Browden made his way toward the boy, the long, mangled fingers of the surrounding horde tugged, scratched, and pulled on his extremities. He shrank back in pain as their sharp, grisly claws sliced through his flesh. Hot blood seeped from his wounds and dripped onto the indescribable surface on which he walked. *They can't hurt me. They can't hurt me. It's not real...* Browden closed his eyes, focused his Lyre, and calmed his fears. When he opened them again, the pain had subsided, the wounds had closed, and the horde had scattered. The only one left was a young boy with untidy hair. He was curled up in a ball, softly weeping. Browden bent over and gently grasped the boy's shoulder. At the feel of his touch, the boy's head and eyes twitched upward in a way that did not look human. The boy's familiar appearance forced Browden to gasp as his own ten-year-old face glared up at him with swollen eyes. They were wet with tears that continued to slither down over his fluffy, freckled, cheeks.

"Please," the boy whimpered, "I want to go home."

Browden stood frozen, unsure what to make of the disturbing anomaly.

"Take me with you." The boy twitched his head to one side and reached out one of his arms. "Please." The boy's hand trembled. "Help me. I want to go home. Can you take me with you?"

Flooded with dissonant emotions, Browden looked at the boy, then down at the mangled blade, and back at the boy once more.

"I want to go home," the boy's voice wavered through a river of tears. "Please, help me." The boy dropped his arms and pressed his hands against the floor. As he moved, he seemed to twitch and jerk rather than move in one fluid motion. His head tilted unnaturally from one side to the other as he dragged his limp legs across the floor.

With his twin's back now exposed, Browden could finally see the twisted and bloody injury that had severed his spine. He knew then that this had to be the Morbas. It had become his own personal suffering. *His* pain. *His* death. Just as the Morbas reached out to grab his leg, Browden lept over and lifted the sword from the floor. With both hands grasped firmly around the sharp and painful spikes of the hilt, Browden raised the enormous blade high and jabbed hard into the boy's back. As the boy's horrifying shrieks shook the ground, blood poured from wounds on Browden's punctured hands. Below him, the Morbas began to rot away like a dead body in the woods. When the shrieks and tremors finally ceased, it felt like a bomb had gone off at Browden's feet. It blew him back with intense force into what felt like the trunk of a large tree. The painful blow rendered him unconscious.

When Browden woke, he found himself leaning up against the base of an enormous tree with black bark and blood-red leaves. He looked down and inspected his hands that had been bloody and throbbing before the blast. Now, they appeared as good as new. As Browden hopped to his feet and dusted himself off, his memory of their mission returned. Raelle, Oleevar, and Cohlen had to have already made it to Azmodil's palace. Browden hoped that he would not be far behind. Picking up the trail of their familiar Lyre energy, he sprinted through the forest and made his way out. Once in the open, he eyed the rock bridge that led all the way to Azmodil's palace. The trail was littered with the ruined bodies and revolting ichor of demonic creatures that had gotten in his comrades' way.

As Browden journeyed toward the palace, he did his best not to step in the slimy and pungent mess. Once he arrived at the base of the stronghold's steps, he continued to follow his companions' Lyre trail inside and through the castle. It led him to a vast room filled with rows, upon rows of columns. Browden cautiously traced his groups' movement through them until he was met with the grand stairs of an enormous platform. What he saw displayed at the top, sickened him. Two young boys and a young girl were chained to spires. Their hands and feet were pierced and bound by parasitic vines. Browden froze at the bottom of the steps. *If Raelle, Olee, and Cohlen got here before I did, then why are Chrishtan and Samuel still here?*

Browden closed his eyes and honed his Lyre to see if he

could sense their location, but it led him right back to where he stood. *It's as though they made it here, and then they disappeared. Something must have happened.*

As Browden vigilantly scaled the remaining stairs, a sinister female voice slithered into his ears. "You are either very brave or very stupid to come here alone and unprotected, Spirit."

The low, layered tone of another followed it. "Indeed," it laughed.

As Browden glanced over the last step, he saw two enormous thrones on either side of the confined children. Sitting within them were the demons Azmodil and Lilazz. Like him, they too were not living creatures, but spirits. And in the spirit world, other spirits *could* do Browden harm. Without his living companions, he was defenseless. The burn of panic shook Browden's body and he slowly began to retreat down the steps, but it was too late. One of Lilazz's many serpent tendrils cracked out from her head like a whip and snagged Browden's ankle. As his feet flew up from beneath him, the back of his skull smashed into the stone steps of the podium. Although Browden was not technically alive, the pain that surged through him made him feel as though he definitely was. And the blood that poured from his wound reminded him how vulnerable he truly was in this wretched place.

As Lilazz dragged him up the remaining stairs, Browden closed his eyes and prayed to the light. But he did not pray for himself, he prayed for the lives of those that he loved. For those who still suffered. For the souls of Samuel, Chrishtan, the young girl, and all others that were trapped here within the confines of Azmodil's hell. Browden bid goodbye to those whom he would never see again. And to his soul that would now be destroyed and transformed. His fate had been sealed and his soul would become a twisted slave to the bidding of evil spirits. But Browden continued to pray nonetheless. In answer to his prayers, a voice echoed into his mind. *Your pure heart and sacrifices shall not go unheeded. You exude the light, you are the light, and thus shall you be so.*

Suddenly, a horrendous pain stabbed through either side of Browden's back. He felt his skin tear open at the shoulder blades

350

along with the pressure of something that now hung off of him. Whatever it was, it was now a part of him. And once the pain subsided, Browden could sense his new appendages the same way he could sense his legs, arms, and fingers. He vigorously began to flap his new wings until the force of his resistance was too much for the serpent's snare to hold. Lilazz sent out more tendrils toward him, but it was too late. Browden flapped as hard as he could and flew off toward the highest point of the towering ceiling. Like a bird of prey, he darted in and out through the maze of columns and headed back toward the children. He focused his Lyre and tried to conjure what he needed. If the light had blessed him with wings, surely he could will it to provide him with a weapon. After a moment, he felt something heavy in his hands. It was a sword, much like the one he had used to defeat the Morbas. Only the hilt was smooth and fit his grip just right.

Weapon in hand, Browden swooped down and sliced through Lilazz's serpent locks as she attempted to recoil them. Her shriek shook the enormous hall of columns, sending fragments of its structure crashing to the shiny black floor. As Browden landed in front of the gorgeous succubus, he saw Azmodil from the corner of his eye. The massive demon was leaving his twisted throne and headed right for him. At the same time, Lilazz tried to run, but Browden quickly swung his gigantic sword.

Browden's incredible Lyre senses told him that Azmodil was getting close. With his other hand, Browden harnessed the light. He felt its power within him. As his blade severed Lilazz's body, cutting her clean in half, his other hand released a ray of light that blew Azmodil backward. The demon crashed into a nearby wall as Lilazz's screams shook the room once more. Her ear wrenching squeals did not stop until the two halves of her body hit the shiny black floor.

With Lilazz defeated, Browden sprinted back toward Azmodil, who was once more headed in his direction. The enormous demon who dripped with black ooze over his skeletal frame had set himself aflame.

"I will burn you until there is nothing left of your pathetic soul!" The demon roared as he set something else into motion. The grand hall began to tremble and blood came flooding in. As it did, slimy, parasitic vines began to grow over every wall and column.

Browden lept from the top of the podium and his wings caught him midair. The demon willed the vines to lash out at Browden as he weaved in and out of the columns. Each time the vines would come for him, Browden would slash through them with his sword. As the blood rose higher, Browden had to fly closer to the ceiling. He knew he had to destroy the demon before he drowned in demonic ichor. Browden took as much time as he could to charge his Lyre. He would need it for the discharge. As soon as he felt the power burning through him, he blasted Azmodil once more with a light beam. As he swooped down toward the injured demon, Browden gripped his sword tight with both hands. In an instant, he brought it up to strike Azmodil, but something caught his leg. The vines pulled him away from the demon. At the same time, Azmodil grabbed him by the throat. Browden's mind raced. He had two choices. Either cut the arm of the demon, or cut the vines.

Browden sliced through the vines, and the demon added a second hand to his death grip. Pain surged through him as Azmodil dangled him over the raging river of gore. Browden channeled his Lyre and prayed it would not be too long before it charged. He closed his eyes and filled his consciousness with memories of the people he loved. Raelle, Chrishtan, and Samuel appeared before him. But the final face, was one he did not recognize. It was a young woman. Her violet hair flowed in an ethereal wind as her turquois eyes penetrated his. She reached out her hand and grasped his. Her earth-colored skin felt like silk against his. *We need you.* Her voice soothed from her full lips. *You are the light...*

It felt like an explosion. The light blinded him as it blew Azmodil to pieces. Browden hit the steps hard. After the blazing radiance of his blast faded away, he felt completely drained. He had used every ounce of his Lyre and spirit for the light bomb. All around him, pieces of the demon's shattered frame floated in the blood pool that was now draining from the hall. With what little energy he could muster, Browden flapped his wings and flew to the top of the spires where each child hung. With his sword, he hacked through their chains and vines, releasing them from their vile imprisonment. As soon as they were free, Browden lowered them onto the platform. He could feel himself fading, but knew he needed to use what little Lyre he had left to awaken their souls. Browden did what he had to do. And when he was through, his body grew limp and his head fell to the floor next to them.

# CHAPTER 28
## SALVAGE

After barely escaping the sacrificial spires of the Abequan coliseum, Raelle watched from a distance as it crumbled to nothing. Horrifying squeals of the demonic horde echoed over the land as Ellosian air raiders finished them off. At first, Raelle felt relief, but it was swiftly overshadowed by concern. *What about Chrishtan? Was it really him? Truly? Are we just going to leave him there?* It had been Chrishtan that had saved her and the others. He had returned to them, somehow. But Raelle had no idea how. *We must go back for him....*

As soon as they all disappeared into the outskirts of the Roeesar forest and were far enough away from the Abequan chaos, the Samissians paused to take care of the wounded. This included Raelle, Samuel, Tonz, Oleevar, Cohlen, and the two women from the dungeon. The Samissians treated their wounds and fed them Lyre blood and food. But with the limited amount of supplies, they did not have proper remedies to awaken the comatose women. The elven healer had explained that they had been through too much trauma, both physically and mentally. They would need more treatment once they arrived at Samisius. For now, their bodies and minds were protecting themselves in a comatose state.

As soon as they were clothed by Samissian leather armor and felt somewhat restored, Oleevar announced to his people that they were going back for Chrishtan and that any Samissian who was able and willing could accompany them. After the Samissians gave them five horses and five men, the group raced out of the forest and made its way back toward the Abequan wreckage. As they galloped on horseback at a grueling pace, Raelle grasped both of the large hunting knives the Samissians had given her to defend herself. They were no daggers, but they would work well enough.

"Look!" Oleevar pointed far into the distance.

Raelle searched over the snow covered hills to see what Oleevar was pointing at. A short distance outside the coliseum wreckage, two winged adversaries maneuvered through the sky, engaged in battle. Suddenly, bright flashes of light surged from one of them. The skies lit up all around them and one of them retreated into the night. As Raelle and the group raced toward the commotion, the other winged figure landed gently on the ground. Almost there, Raelle could now see that the figure stood over two bodies in the snow. Raelle had a sinking feeling that she knew who one of those bodies was. *Chrishtan.*

"We must hurry!" Raelle jumped from her horse and summersaulted into the snow. Using what little energy she had accrued in the woods, she made the rest of her journey at Rogue speed. In less than a minute, she arrived at the scene to find a man in white warrior armor with white feathery wings squatted over one of the bodies. As soon as she was close enough, she recognized the body as Chrishtan.

"Get away from him!" Raelle drew her large knives as she rushed the mysterious winged figure. He did not heed her warning, and instead removed Chrishtan's chest plate. "I said get away!" Raelle knew that her energy and strength was a fraction of what it needed to be, but she tried her best to channel as much as she could and prepared to stint. She immediately disappeared and reappeared at her enemy's flank. From behind, she put both knives to the front of his throat. "Get up," Raelle commanded and the winged man slowly stood.

"Any sudden moves and I'll slit your throat!" she warned.

The winged warrior slowly put his hands up. "I guess this war has made you feisty, Sister."

A hint familiarity in his voice vibrated into Raelle's ear. "Who are you?" She spun him around. With one glance, the stranger's face disarmed her and she threw her arms around him. "Dear Architect." Tears filled Raelle's cold eyes. "Browden, is it really you? How can this be?"

"Yes." He held her close. "It's me. But I need to help Chrishtan. He's dying."

Raelle looked down at Chrishtan, who lay on his back in the snow. His hair looked as if it had been singed and many of his veins were almost popping out of his skin. Lying next to him was Volshira. Her mouth, chin, and chest were spattered with blood. And she too looked seared.

"What happened to them?" Raelle asked.

"Ire Oblitora." Browden returned to what he had been doing before Raelle's assault. He pressed his hands into Chrishtan's chest and surged energy into him. Raelle watched in dismay as Chrishtan's entire body jolted and seized. When Browden was finished, he took a moment to listen and feel for any sign of life.

Raelle squatted down next to him. "Is he alive?" she sniffled.

"Yes." Browden looked up at her with his big brown eyes. "He's alive, but only just."

Raelle heard the others approach and turned around to see them dismount their horses.

"Raelle!" Samuel ran up behind her. "What's happ— He froze in his tracks.

"Brother..." Browden stood with a grin that he could not contain.

"Do I?" Samuel shook his head and opened his eyes wide. "Do I, know you?" He continued to study the young warrior in all white. When he finally blinked again, he stepped closer to Browden. "But it can't be..." he murmured with his mouth agape.

Raelle felt Tonz's hands on her shoulders as she backed away to give her brothers more space for their reunion. Oleevar, Cohlen, and the rest of their search party did the same.

"Who is that?" Tonz whispered in Raelle's ear.

Raelle grasped one of Tonz's hands. "The most wonderful person you'll ever meet." She watched as her brothers lovingly embraced. Tears flowed freely from both mens' eyes. "It's a miracle."

Like an earthquake, the ground quaked beneath them as the remaining ramparts of the coliseum collapsed into the Void hole a short distance away. The sound of horrified screams coming from the remaining Abequans and demons that were still left inside sent chills down Raelle's spine. *Chrishtan's people.* Her heart sank.

She knew that once he woke again, he would be devastated. Guilt slowly crept into her at the thought of her uncle and her family being responsible for such atrocities. Inside the city, Raelle could hear the chaos continuing. Although the demonic minions had not reached it, the sadistic nature of the people that lived there had. Raelle imagined that without a ruler and command of order, the city was going wild. Hopefully, Chrishtan would be able to return to them and restore order to his people. Hopefully, it would be sooner rather than later. But there was no way of getting him to the safety of his castle now. The anarchy was far too treacherous to risk it. The nearest and safest province was Samisius.

"We've got to get everyone out of here," Tonz announced. "It's not safe."

"I agree," Oleevar said with approval filling his voice. "We'd better go now."

"Have we got some way to transport Chrishtan?" Raelle asked.

"Yes," Oleevar replied. "I brought supplies to fashion a stretcher."

Relief rushed over Raelle. The elf might have been annoying at times, but Raelle was truly grateful for his tendency to prepare for every circumstance.

"Good." Raelle looked over at her brothers. "I'll round them up while you construct it."

She gently stepped through the snow to where her brothers were now leaned over Volshira. "Sorry, boys," She interrupted. "It's not safe here. We're constructing a stretcher to transport Chrishtan. As soon as it's ready, we must leave."

When Samuel looked up at her, his eyes glistened with fresh tears. "We must take Volshira with us, too," Samuel managed to say through his weeping. "It wasn't her fault what she did." The devastation on her brother's face told Raelle that she could not say no. Regardless of her feelings about the menacing woman, Volshira had suffered too and obviously meant something to Samuel. There was no time to argue.

Raelle sighed. "I'll tell them to make an extra stretcher."

"Thank you," Samuel said, his voice thick and teary.

Once the stretchers were constructed, Tonz and Oleevar attached them to the horses. Raelle and Cohlen helped them gently lower their injured comrades inside each one. With their cargo safely wrapped into their stretchers, they all remounted their horses. They turned back toward the forest and headed north until a strange voice with an eccentric accent began whispering through the wind. Raelle thought she was hearing voices inside her own head. But when she looked around, she could tell that the others heard it too.

"*Please, you cannot go. Not yet...*" a feminine voice pleaded in a warm tone. In the air around them, a strange purple smoke undulated and flowed.

Oleevar immediately stopped his horse and everyone else followed suit. "Show yourself!" he demanded. "What do you want? What are you doing in these lands?" It seemed that he knew what or whom he was speaking to.

Suddenly, the wispy purple smoke that surrounded them gathered in one location. It swayed and shifted like candle smoke until it finally transformed. In the light of the moon, a beautiful elven woman with long white hair, dark skin, and silver eyes stood before them in a beautiful gown and cloak. Her face was decorated with purple gems and ornate tattoos that almost matched the intricacy of her gown.

"Please." The striking young elf interlaced her fingers and pressed her knuckles to her chin, a gesture of prayer and desperation. "You must take me with you."

"Who are you?" Tonz demanded.

"*She* is Jassokian royalty," said Oleevar. "Aren't you?"

"Yes," the elf agreed with a long, solitary nod. "I am Karaleste."

*Karaleste?* Raelle thought. *That name sounds familiar.* Her mind flashed back to when she and Chrishtan were in Jenladra's palace. The lady's words echoed inside her mind. *In time, it will be the two of you who will guide others, such as Oleevar, Karaleste, and Lanadia to this path. And they will hopefully travel alongside you. Together, inside the Verge, you will all become a penetrating beam of light in the black Void of evil...*

"What are you doing here?" Oleevar questioned the Jassokian princess. "Where are your people?"

"My father," Karaleste's body sagged with sorrow. "He promised me to Lochran. He brought me here for the ceremony. When the Samissians attacked, I managed to escape." She pressed her hands together again. "Please. I know what my people have done. And I know it isn't right. I know I may be one of the only Jassokians who does. They're blinded by Lochran's lies and false promises. But *I* am not."

"And?" Oleevar snidely replied.

"Shut it, Oleevar," Raelle directed. "Let her speak."

"And I can help you," Karaleste continued. "I can help you to defeat him. And I am the only one here now who can close that Void hole."

"Close it?" Raelle tilted her head. "What do you mean?"

"If the Void hole is not closed," Karaleste explained. "Then it will slowly continue to grow. Day by day, it will continue to eat away and everything around it. It will replace the light with the dark. And the people of Abequa will be replaced by minions from the Void."

Raelle looked at Oleevar. "We've got to close it!"

"She's right," said Browden. "If we can close it now, then we can restore Abequa much quicker."

"You knew about this?" Raelle glared at Browden. *He may be more like his older brother than I thought...*

"Yes, but I knew that none of us could close it," Browden replied. "I was working out a plan in my head for our return. In theory, it would take quite some time for any irreversible damage to occur."

"Right..." Raelle rolled her eyes and shook her head. "These boys are always trying to figure everything out themselves instead of talking about it."

Karaleste smiled. "So you will take me with you?"

Raelle put out her hand for the princess. "I suppose, if

that's the cost of you closing that hole."

"I promise you won't regret it." Karaleste took Raelle's hand and she helped her onto her horse.

"Tonz, please escort our men back to Samisius with Chrishtan and Shira," Oleevar ordered. "Raelle, Karaleste, Cohlen, Samuel, and myself will stay and close the hole. We are the heirs of this great continent and so it is up to us to ensure its security."

For once, Raelle agreed with something arrogant Oleevar was saying.

"Yes, Sir." Tonz saluted. "Of course, Sir. Anything you need."

"I'll go with Chrishtan." Browden's worried gaze shifted to the incapacitated warrior. "He's my brother."

"We understand." Raelle knew that if anyone would make sure Chrishtan made it safely, it would be Browden. The thought brought a wave of emotion crashing over her. The bittersweet farewell reminded her once again how much she cared for Chrishtan. She did her best to keep her emotions at bay. "We'll see you back in Samisius." Raelle shifted her horse in the direction of the Void hole.

"Let's go close that hole." The sound of Cohlen's enthusiastic voice brought a slight grin to Raelle's lips.

"Glad to hear your voice again, Cohlen." She knew he was still struggling with adjusting to life as an adult. And in doing so, he sometimes lost his voice. He had said almost nothing since they woke up in the Abequan torture chamber. In those times, the small child within him took the reins, quiet and afraid.

"To the hole!" Oleevar led the group in a gallop toward the annihilated coliseum.

Karaleste clung to Raelle as they made their way through the brisk air of the night. As they got closer to the coliseum, Raelle could feel the negative aura of the Void battling against what little Lyre she had left. Visions of every tragic moment of her life played through her head as they galloped closer. She pressed her eyes shut as hard as she could and tried to throw the images out of her skull, but it was no use. The darkness had a hold on her. Until she felt it—the warmth of someone's hand on hers. Raelle opened her eyes to see Samuel riding right up beside her. It was his hand that held hers. She looked over at him and without a single word, his expression told her he loved her and that he was not going anywhere, no matter what. It was the expression of hope. He had faith and he was sharing it with her. Raelle sensed the power of the light within their bond. It brought her great relief. *If Samuel's support alone can wash away the effects of the Void hole, then what kind of power will we have once we're all together? All fighting for the same thing, all the heirs together as one.* Together was how they would tear through evil. Together was how they would bring light back into the world. Together was how they would bring clarity to a world of chaos. The thought washed away her fear and gave birth to confidence. *We can do this. We will do this. All of us. Together.*

# Chapter 29
## No More Pretending

The sound of concerned whispers woke Christian from his deep slumber. He tried as hard as he could to open his eyes, but they were far too heavy. He could only open them just enough to see what he thought were two people standing in the corner of the room. But it was too blurry to be certain. He assured himself that it was their fretful whispers he was hearing. *A man and a woman*. He could just barely make out their figures. Suddenly, their whispers came to a halt and the man kissed the woman. It lasted for a long moment until she pushed him away. Chrishtan's consciousness began to fade back out. But before he was completely lost to his slumber once more, he swore he could hear Raelle's voice and it drew him back.

"No, Tonz. Not here. Not now..."

"I'm sorry," Tonz whispered. "You're right... It's just, I still love you, Raelle. And there is nothing you can do to change that...." his voice trailed off.

*Tonz is kissing Raelle? He loves her? Does she love him?* Chrishtan tried as hard as he could to fight the drowsiness, but it swallowed him like quicksand.

***

The next time Chrishtan woke, it was to the gentle clasp of someone's hand over his. His eyes fluttered open to the blurry image of a dimly lit room. A figure dressed in all white, sat on the side of the bed. Chrishtan squinted and try to regain his vision as the figure helped him to sit up.

"Take your time, Brother." Browden's voice eased into Chrishtan's ears. "I'm here."

Now propped up against his pillow, Chrishtan's vision steadily returned. And when it did, he saw his grown brother Browden. He was dressed in a white linen shirt and pants.

Chrishtan looked around. "Are we in the Verge?"

"No," Browden replied. "We're on Lerim. In the Samissian palace."

Chrishtan studied his brother's appearance once more. Besides his white linen attire, a matching set of white feathered wings perched on his back.

Chrishtan's eyes grew wide. "How can this be? And where did you get those?" He pointed to Browden's new feathery extensions.

"I made a sacrifice. And I defeated my past." An angled smile formed across Browden's plump lips. "And for that, I have been given a gift. I'm here to help you. All of you."

"Sacrifice?" Chrishtan wrinkled his face. "What do you mean?"

"After you were killed, Raelle, Oleevar, and Cohlen went into the Void to find your trapped soul and release you along with Raelle's brother."

"Yes." Chrishtan said regretfully. "Raelle came to me in the Verge. She told me they were coming for me."

"And so they did." Browden moved closer. "I accompanied them within the Verge and into the Void. But along our dark journey, we were attacked by a Morbas. It is an entity conjured from suffering. It feeds off things such as pain of trauma, grief, sorrow, and distress of those it encounters. Since I was already dead, I knew I was the only one who would have any chance of overcoming it. So, I sacrificed myself to the demon. It fed on my soul as I wandered through an endless maze of torture and suffering. But then, I made myself see truth. I willed the light to help me see. The thought of you, Raelle, and Samuel helped me to see." He looked into Chrishtan's eyes. "That's how I found it. I found that Morbas, and I defeated it. Then, I went looking for you. I killed the demons that kept you, just as you did Hazale, and I freed your souls."

Chrishtan looked down. He hated that his little brother had suffered such atrocities in order to rescue himself and the others. It should have been the other way around. Chrishtan should have been the one to protect everyone. *I let my guard down. I let my pain get the best of me, again. I put myself in a situation that nearly destroyed the people who care for me. If only I had been stronger...* "The things the people I love have had to go through in order to protect me..." His eyes grew hot with tears. "I don't deserve—

"No." Browden squeezed Chrishtan's hand. "Don't say things like that. *We* are the ones who love you, and only *we* can decide what you deserve."

Chrishtan shook his heavy head. "It is my duty to protect the people. My place to make sure the people I love are safe. I've let you all down. Time after time, I continue to miss things and the people I love end up hurt or killed. I am a poison to those around me."

Browden grasped his brother's hand. "How can you say that? None of this was your fault. The horrible things that have happened are in no way your doing. We were born into this chaos. We did not choose it. *It* chose us."

"No brother. I *chose* to push Volshira away. I knew it would hurt her. I knew how unstable she was, I did, deep in my heart. Yet, I did it anyway. In doing so, I got her captured and tortured because she was trying to prove how much she loved me by protecting me. And now, Volshira has lost her life, her soul, an our—

Chrishtan choked on the sorrow of his dead child.

"No Chrishtan," Browden said with a sorrowful vibrato. "You are not responsible for *her* decisions. She alone chose her own fate. And although she had the best of intentions, she allowed her fears and her anger to get the best of her. I will be damned if I let you do the same." He looked at Chrishtan with wet eyes. "You can't blame yourself for what happened. The loss of your friend and your child is a deep and sorrowful defeat. When innocent lives are damaged or lost because of the denial, selfishness, and pain of their elders, that is the most depraved tragedy of all." Browden leaned in and wrapped his arms around Chrishtan's shoulders. "I'm so sorry," he wept. "I am so, so sorry."

Chrishtan held his brother close as they both continued to

cry. "That's what happened to *you*... It's why you lost your life."

"That's what's happened to all of us," Browden sniffled. "We are all paying for the debts of our elders. But we cannot do that to the next generation. We have to learn from past mistakes. We have to start over, not try to fix something that is way too broken. Which means we face the truth head on. Many more will suffer and even more sacrifices will be made, but if we stick together and don't let our past and our pain decide our action, we can move forward with fresh eyes and genuine hope."

"Easier said than done." Chrishtan tried to regain control of his emotions. He had to, for his brother. "But together, I know it will get easier. Thanks for not giving up on me."

"How could I?" Browden tried to force one of his goofy smiles. "You're my brother. Not to mention, I'm pretty sure you never gave up on me either."

"No." Chrishtan shifted his eyes to the blankets. "Just on myself."

"You're not alone," said Browden. "And you'll never be alone. We're all here with you now and we are all struggling with different things. But we're all here for you and you for us."

"Thanks, Brother." They embraced once more. "Now, it's time I get out of this bed. Where's Raelle? I'd like to see her if I could."

A look of apprehension came over Browden's plump face. "You can't."

Chrishtan threw the covers off of his body. "What do you mean I can't?" He tried to swing his legs over the bed, but nothing happened. A burning twinge of fear and regret surged through him. He recalled not being able to move his legs in the aftermath of Lochran's black lightning. He tried once more to make something below his abdomen move. *Come on... anything! A toe even!* But his toes remained motionless. "No..." A hurricane of despair swept through him along with the all too familiar agony of grief. "No, no, no. This can't be happening. Isn't there any way to fix it? A cure of some kind. A remedy? Magic? Anything?"

Browden looked with compassion at Chrishtan, then at his

immobile legs. "We don't know yet. Oleevar said he would do everything in his power to create a cure. But he can't do anything until everyone is rested, healthy, and back in Ellios. He, Cohlen, Raelle, and Samuel have been through quite an ordeal as well."

A chill from the cool temperature of the room caused Chrishtan to shiver. He swiftly threw the covers back over his lifeless legs as he mourned their tragic death. His life had become a never ending cycle of loss and destruction. *The Architect has cursed me. How is it that I have offended him so? I am no one.* The touch of Browden's hand on his shoulder shifted Chrishtan's despairing gaze upward.

Browden did his best to keep an encouraging expression as he spoke. "We *will* get through this. I know it. But right now, is there anything I can do? Something to make you feel even the slightest bit better for the time being? "

"Yes," said Chrishtan as he wiped the tears from his face. "Raelle, I'd like to see her. But... I'm not so sure she wants to see me." Chrishtan recalled her anger within the Verge and the strange lucid dream of what he thought was her kissing Tonz. Surely Raelle had found comfort in him after Chrishtan had abandoned her. The thought tore him apart inside. But he could not blame her.

"I'll see what I can do." Browden assured him as he left the bed. "She's always had a soft spot for me." He winked, trying to lighten the mood.

"Thank you, Brother," Chrishtan said and Browden left the room.

Left by himself, Chrishtan's mind began to race. He was a warrior. A fighter. A general of the mission troops. Without the use of his legs, he was nothing and no one. Plus, what would Raelle think of him? He was no longer the strong warrior she needed. Now he was a weak, injured invalid. *He* was the one who needed saving. As emotions ran wild within him, Chrishtan recalled how Raelle's fists had pounded into his chest and tears streamed from her eyes. He had betrayed her trust. Chrishtan's heart sank. After everything, she had every right to hate him. He had not told her about Volshira and he had done it on purpose. He wanted to forget about Volshira. Pretend that she had never existed. But she had. He had lied to himself, and he had lied to Raelle. And now, he had lost them both. He had lost everything, even his own flesh and blood. Chrishtan's recalled the Lyre connection with his unborn offspring inside Volshira's belly. He heard the slow beating of its heart as its life slipped away. The memory broke Chrishtan's soul. He clenched his fists as hard as he could and did his best not to let the despair that roared within him exit his mouth. Tears pours from his eyes as his grief told him that he had failed. He had failed not only himself, but everyone around him.

***

Raelle gently knocked on the door of a closed Samissian bedroom chamber.

"Who is it?" She heard Samuel's voice on the other side.

"It's Raelle," she answered. "May I come in?" She pressed the lever on the door handle and poked her head inside.

"Yes, please." Samuel waved her over to where he sat on a bed next to the black-haired woman they had rescued from the Abequan dungeon.

Raelle quietly shut the door behind her. From there, she tiptoed across the cool stone floor. "I went to your room, but you weren't there. One of the guards told me I could find you here. Couldn't sleep?"

"No." Samuel shook his head.

"Me either." Raelle sat down on the bed next to Samuel. He held the woman's hand and softly stroked it. "Who is she, Samuel? Will you tell me now?"

Samuel took in an incredibly large breath and then slowly released. "This..." He looked in Raelle's eyes. She could see the hesitation in his as they darted from her to the woman and back again.

"Please, Samuel." Raelle took his other hand. "You can tell me."

"This is..." He let out another breath. "This is *my* mother."

Raelle swallowed the lump in her anxious throat. "*Your* mother?"

"Yes," Samuel explained. "And *your* aunt. Her name is Patrilla."

"You mean…" Raelle's stomach turned and twisted. "You're *not* my brother?"

"No." Samuel calmly shook his head. "Not technically. But, in every sense of the meaning of the word *brother,* I am. And I always will be."

Raelle's mind began to connect the dots. A horrible feeling gnawed at the pit of her stomach. "And *your* father?" She couldn't bring herself to say what she was thinking. It hurt too much.

"Yes." Samuel harbored a look of deep pain. "Lochran *is* my father."

Raelle covered her mouth with her hand and tears trickled down from the corner of her eyes.

Samuel pulled her in close to comfort her. "I'm sorry, Raelle. I swear, I'm nothing like him. He tricked me. He lied to me." He turned toward his mother. "He cut out her tongue, Raelle. He tortured her for years," Samuel sobbed. "If I had known what a monster he was, I never would have—

"I know…" Raelle wept into his shoulder. "I know." She could feel the truth of his regret and sincerity of his love. "I know you've probably been through a lot since leaving the valley. And I want you to know, I don't blame you."

"He promised me we'd come back for you." Samuel's wet eyes reflected Raelle's image. "I never would have left you there otherwise. Never, ever. I swear it." The tears began to come faster.

"I know." Raelle embraced him once more. "I know, little brother. I don't blame you."

Samuel released their embrace and wiped the tears from his somber face. "Thank you." He managed a grin through his quaking lips. .

"You will always be my brother, Sam." Raelle mirrored his expression. "No matter what."

"No matter what." He hugged her once more. "Through everything."

"Yes," Raelle said and looked across the room. On the opposite side, the ravaged auburn-haired woman lay in her own bed. "And who is she?"

Samuel took Raelle's hand and led her to the woman. He sat down on her bed and put the woman's hand inside Raelle's. "This…" He held back his tears, but his face still trembled. "This is *your* mother, Raelle. Queen Shellere Jowellia of Huronus."

Raelle did not blink as she sat down next to her comatose mother. No doubt Lochran had been torturing her for years as well. He had been the one to remove her eyes. A stampede of emotion trampled Raelle. She buried her face in the woman's chest and began to bawl. The loud sobs bellowing from her throat were barely muffled by the covers over her mother's body. Raelle continued to weep until she had nothing left. When it was over, she felt a pang of relief and comfort. Her rage had been quieted and her love had been reignited. She sat up and wiped away the mucus and tears from her now tranquil face.

"So, those people who raised us," Raelle queried. "Who were they?"

"They were supposed to be our mentors." Samuel answered, his head heavy with shame.

"Did they take us, or…?" Raelle didn't know how to finish the sentence.

"That's what Lochran tried to make me believe. That they kidnapped us. But I don't think they did." Samuel furrowed his brow. "I'm not exactly sure, but I think they were supposed to take us and keep us safe. Maybe train us? But I'm not sure. Once they wake up and are healthy enough, I'm sure your mother can tell us everything we want to know."

The thought of speaking to her real mother for the first time both excited and frightened Raelle. She was happy to have found her mother, but at the same time angry that she let Raelle go. And what about her father? Where was he?

Raelle bit her lip. "Do you know anything about my

father?"

Samuel pinched his mouth to the side. "I'm not positive, but I think he was killed. I believe Lochran murdered him because he was a—a—

"A what?"

"He called him a *scrub.*"

The word hit Raelle like an insult, though she had no idea what it meant. "What's a *scrub*?"

"Someone born without Lyre blood. A normal human. Your father was a half-blood, which makes your blood tainted, unpure. Or so they say."

Raelle pursed her lips. "What does that mean? Am I weaker?"

"I don't know." Samuel ran his fingers through his own hair. It was something he had always done when he felt frustrated. "I don't really know much at all. And everything I thought I knew was a lie."

Samuel's familiar habits made Raelle feel at home. "Same here. I know nothing of who I am anymore."

"I think it's safe to say we the people we used to be, are long gone by now," Samuel said with a sigh of defeat.

"Samuel, look at me," Raelle said as she swallowed her doubts and reached for confidence. She could no longer waste any more time feeling sorry for herself. She had to be strong for her little brother. The person she was becoming had a duty to her people and her family. Who she *was* before no longer mattered. "Who we *were*, we will never forget them. We will relish in their happy memories. The awful things that have happened to us, we will not forget that either. But we also cannot let them destroy us. The things we've had to do to survive, they've made us stronger. I *know* who you are, Samuel. And I *know* who you will become. Who *we* will become— leaders and saviors to our people."

Samuel leaned in and hugged her. "I've missed you, Raelle," he whispered. "I hope and pray you're right."

Raelle did her best to crack a smile. "Of course I'm right. I'm always right."

"Yeah, yeah." Samuel grinned and stretched with an enormous yawn.

"Why don't you go try and get some rest." Raelle yawned along with him before pressing her feet to the floor. "We can talk more tomorrow."

"All right," said Samuel. "See you in the morning."

"See you in the morning." Raelle paused at the door. "Love you."

"Love you." Samuel pulled his mother's covers up over her shoulders. "And thank you."

"For what?"

"For understanding."

With a final smile, Raelle closed the door behind her. For a moment, she stood in the hallway against the wall and attempted to collect herself before heading to bed. A few doors down, she heard another door shut and Browden exit from it. *Chrishtan's room.* As angry as she had been with Chrishtan, she still cared for him deeply. She still wanted him to be okay. He was still her friend. After all, if it weren't for him, she would most likely be dead.

"How is he?" Raelle called quietly down the hall.

As soon as Raelle met Browden outside the door he answered in a whisper. "He's... he's devastated."

Raelle's heart thumped loudly. "He's awake?"

"For a moment," Browden sighed. "Long enough to find out he can no longer walk. I let him know that Oleevar is going to figure it out as soon as we got back to Ellios, but..."

"But what?"

"He's suffering, Raelle." Browden finally looked at her. "And I know things aren't perfect between the two of you, but he truly does love you. And he's dealing with a number of issues right now. Maybe it wouldn't hurt if you just went and sat with him. You can't be mad at him forever."

"I know that." Raelle exhaled. "I just... Things will never be what they were before."

"No, you're right. They won't. But now that we're all

together, maybe you two can find yourselves again. You can do it together. With all of our support. No one is asking you to marry him right now. No one is even saying you have to be in love with him. But what *I am* saying is that he needs you. He needs all of us." Browden rested his hands on her shoulders and looked her straight in the eyes. "And whether you like it or not, Raelle, *you* need all of us, too. And that includes Chrishtan."

Raelle could tell that Browden knew more than he let on. She had never heard him so serious. But she knew he was right. They all needed one another. And as much as Raelle reveled in her new-found independence, she also knew that distancing herself from the people in her life whom she had come to care for was not going to make her stronger. And holding a grudge against Chrishtan for his mistakes was not going to make her tougher or happier. It only made her more bitter. For some reason, she had convinced herself that her love for him had made her weak. That his love for her had made her dependent upon it. But she knew that was not true and it was not his fault. *I chose to lean on him. I let him love me. I wanted him to love me. I wanted all of it.*

The realization hit Raelle like the arrow that had once struck her heart. Why had she felt the need to pretend? Had her anger toward him simply been a wall of protection? A way to stay strong and train as hard as she could while he was away? If she was angry with him, then she couldn't miss him. There was no need to grieve his loss. If she did not care about him, then she could focus her energy on getting stronger. Believing that she did not need him, allowed her to do it all without him. Because after all, she had no other choice but to do so. *What have I done?* Raelle's heart sank and he mind rattled with conflict.

"Go, Raelle." Browden stepped away from the door. "It's not too late. It's never too late."

Raelle nodded and grasped the door handle. "Thank you." She flashed a somber smile and opened the door. "For everything. For saving us. For never giving up. For this."

After stepping inside Chrishtan's room, Raelle quietly shut the door. Instantly she felt the temperature drop. In the corner of the small stone-walled room, a dying fire struggled to hold on inside the fireplace. Raelle tiptoed over and threw a few more logs on top.

"Raelle?" Chrishtan called softly from across the room.

"Hey," she said tenderly as she made her way to his bed. "How are you doing?" She felt silly asking, but it was all she could think of. In a way, her guilt made her feel nervous.

"I'm better now that I get to see your face." He faked a smile. His shirtless chest and arms still harbored the marks of the dark lightning. It looked as if someone had drawn red veins outside his skin.

"You don't have to be strong for me anymore, Chrishtan." Raelle sat down on the bed. "I can take care of myself. I know you're hurting. You don't have to pretend anymore."

"I—I'm not. I—

"Chrishtan, please." Raelle rubbed her face with her hands. She could see the truth of immense suffering in his eyes. *Is he doing this again? I need him to be completely honest with me, for once.* Chrishtan's attempt at *pretending* to be all right only vexed her.

Chrishtan must have seen the frustration in her eyes. "I'm sorry." He dragged his fingers through his hair, pulling hard on the fibers. "You're right. I'm horrible. I'm beyond horrible, I'm... I don't even know. I can't explain it."

"Please, try," said Raelle. She wanted so badly for him to open up. It was the *only* way they would ever be able to make it together. "I want you to know, I'm not angry with you." She tried to ease his mind. "I was, but... I'm not anymore."

"I'm not sure I deserve that," Chrishtan said glumly. "I understand why you were mad at me. I don't want your forgiveness just because you feel sorry for me. I—

"That's not why." Raelle shook her head. "I'm just trying to understand things for what they are and move on. You didn't technically do anything wrong. What happened in your past has nothing to do with me. And whatever Volshira did, that wasn't your fault. I know what she did to you. And I'm sorry that you had to go through it."

"I'm sorry, too." Chrishtan gazed into her eyes. "For everything. For not telling you about her. For trying to pretend that my past didn't exist. For being too protective of you. If I had just let you come that day, maybe you never would have gotten shot. Maybe things would be different. I just—you symbolize so much to me. And, I wanted to protect that. You were all that was good and untainted in the world. But it's far too much pressure to hold someone to that. And I was selfish wanting to keep you hidden. Maybe if the Huronian army had seen that you were alive, things would have been different. And I know Samuel and I would have never fought."

"That is a load of shite." Raelle smirked as she shook her head.

Chrishtan raised his brow high. "What?" He had never heard Raelle talk like that.

"I mean, you can't say those things. We have no idea what would've happened had I just gone with you. Maybe I still would have been hurt or killed. You did what you did to protect me because you care for me. You can't live by *maybes, would haves,* and *could haves.* And we definitely can't take it back now. Dwelling on what you should have done or could have done is not going to help *us* to move forward."

"Us?" Chrishtan squeezed her hand. "Is there still an *us?* Do you want there to be?"

"I think... I do." Raelle paused. She thought of Tonz, and the relationship she had built with him over the past three months. It was something she had not intended, but had needed, even wanted. Tonz had been nothing but supportive and honest with her. He was more than deserving of her love, but at the same time, Raelle also loved Chrishtan. Their connection was unexplainably powerful and deep. It made her feel things she could not explain. But at the same time, she did not want to compete with his past, his pain, and his insecurities in order to have it. She was not ready to make any decision just yet.

Raelle continued in a firm tone. "But for us to move

forward, you've got to learn to be open and honest with me. You've got to face your pain head on. I don't want you to pretend anymore. I know you think that's being strong, but it isn't. Trust me, I know. I've been doing the same thing over the past few months. It's only a short-term solution, not a long-term one. And it tears you apart inside."

"I know… I know." Chrishtan closed his eyes. "You're right. And the truth is, I've been doing that my whole life. But I will do whatever it takes to make things right between us. To make myself better and stronger. I'll do anything for you, Raelle… for *us*."

"See, that's part of the problem. You can't just do it for me, Chrishtan. Or for anyone else. You have to do it for yourself. Or don't do it at all. And you can start by telling me, or someone how you're *truly* feeling. You need to get it out. You've been through so much I don't even know how you're so calm."

Chrishtan closed his eyes and clenched his jaw. Along with his lips, his hand trembled like that of a scared child. "I'm devastated." He opened his eyes and tears streamed out. "I feel like I've failed. I've lost everything all over again and more."

"How have you failed?"

Chrishtan tried to wipe his tears. "It's not so much how, but *who*."

"Well, then *who*?"

"My Abequan people, you, Shira, and my…" His lips shook violently and the tears flowed like a raging flood.

Raelle softly stroked his hand. "Take your time. It's all right."

"M—my unborn s—son."

Raelle swallowed her dismay. "Son? Wha—what are you talking about?"

"Sh—Shira." Chrishtan closed his eyes and pressed his lips together. "She was pregnant. With *my* child."

Raelle suddenly felt sick with grief. She had already known Volshira was pregnant, but she thought with the child of the demon. As much as it pained her to hear that Volshira had been carrying the child of the man she loved, she knew he was hurting much more. He had been manipulated, raped, tricked, and murdered by this succubus. And to make matters far worse, she had been carrying his illegitimate child? *She truly was a monster...* Raelle leaned forward and cradled Chrishtan's head against her chest. She gently stroked his hair as he wept into her bosom. "I'm so sorry." Raelle shed tears of empathy. "Truly I am."

After a few long moments, Chrishtan began to recover from his sorrow just enough to speak once more. His face twitched and trembled as he looked into Raelle's eyes. "She was pregnant with twins."

"Twins?" asked Raelle. Her shook with alarm. "I thought you said, *son.* Singular."

"I did." Chrishtan swallowed. "The other child was not mine."

Raelle moved closer to him. "The other child belonged to the demon, Azmodil then?"

"No," Chrishtan whispered and looked away.

"Then who?" Raelle took a moment to let the thought sink in. "Oh, my Architect... No..." Her heart shattered into pieces. *Samuel...*

"Samuel," Chrishtan whispered. "I'm sorry Raelle. I take it he doesn't know."

"No." Raelle wept softly. "I don't think so."

"Are you going to tell him?"

Raelle felt sick inside. She did not want to tell him. Samuel had already been manipulated and tortured by both the succubus and his own father. To tell him would surely be the death of his soul.

"I don't know." Raelle shook her head. "I don't want to keep anything from him, but at the same time... Like you, he's been through a lot and I don't know what this will do to him."

"Well, you don't have to tell him right now." Chrishtan gently grasped her shoulder. "You can take some time to think it over."

"Yeah..." Raelle looked down at her fidgeting hands.

"Raelle?" Chrishtan lifted her chin and looked deep into her troubled eyes.

She peered back at him, but felt at a loss for words.

"I love you." He managed a sincere grin. "And I'm here for you."

It was the first time he had ever said it in real life. And although Raelle had gone back and forth many times over the past few months about whether she truly felt the same, in that moment, the truth fell upon her lips. "I love you, too."

Chrishtan pulled her close. He pressed his warm lips to hers. Raelle welcomed the familiar feel of his lips and tongue. It felt like being home again, in the comfort of her own bed inside the valley. She was safe and warm. It was more than just kissing. It was more than just a physical need. It was love.

Raelle gently pushed him back into his pillow and straddled his hips. Chrishtan continued to caress her face, hair and body as Raelle used her hands to memorize each and every peak and valley of his muscular frame. She wanted so badly to give herself to him. To show him how much cared for him. But she knew he was injured and unable. It didn't matter. She could wait. Nothing would take away from this feeling. In that moment, nothing could tear them apart. Raelle knew what she wanted. It was time to stop pretending.

# CHAPTER 30
## FOR VILGARE

The sound of someone knocking on the door made Raelle completely aware of how chilly it was in Chrishtan's room. After she had fallen asleep on top of him, she had never gotten up to refuel the fire.

"Just a second!"

Raelle stretched and pressed her feet into the cold floor. She squinted in the light of the morning sun that shined through the waterfall curtain outside the window. Outside, tiny droplets of water fell from melting icicles that clung to the vines that grew all around the circular window. Raelle dragged her feet on her way to stir the fire and added a few more small cuts. She blew on it a few times to reignite the dwindling flame. As she did, she heard Christian yawn and stretch loudly behind her.

"Good morning beautiful." He smiled.

"Good morning." Raelle smirked. She knew that he knew full well how compliments made her feel awkward. But she also knew that he would never stop doing it. "You clearly don't know what beauty is." She winked.

"I think I'm aloud to think of beauty any way I see fit." He tilted his head. "Is it not in the eye of the beholder?"

"Yeah, yeah…" Raelle wiped her bark-covered hands on her leather pants and went to the door. She opened it to find Browden on the other side.

"Good morning, Sister." He smiled his goofy smile. In either hand, he held a hollowed out piece of wood containing meats and fruits. "I thought you both might be hungry, and I figured you might want a little more alone time before we head back, so I brought breakfast. Everyone else is in the dining hall."

"Yes, we're definitely hungry, thank you." She took the wooden bowls from him and smiled. "Well, aren't you chipper this morning."

"I am alive." Browden popped up on his toes and then

back down. "You seem pretty sprightly yourself."

Raelle took a moment to eye his white feathery wings. They would take a bit of getting used to. "Today is a new day." Raelle grinned. "And though we have a great deal of hardship ahead, I know that together, we can do this."

"See." Browden smiled. "Told you!"

"Oh, hush," Raelle joked before returning to Chrishtan's room. It had grown a couple degrees warmer since answering the door.

"When you're finished eating, we'll get packed up and head out," Browden called from the hallway.

"Sounds good!" Raelle replied before gently kicking the door closed.

"Breakfast in bed?" She carried the bowls over to Chrishtan.

He used his arms to pull himself upright. "Yes, please." He smiled.

After finishing their meals in the joy of one another's company, Browden returned and helped Raelle to dress Chrishtan in warm leather and furs for the ride home. Samuel joined them and helped Browden and Raelle in carrying Chrishtan down to the dining hall where the others were finishing up their breakfast. When they first walked in, Raelle saw that Karaleste was still dressed in her beautiful gown and cloak, eating fruit and engaged in conversation with Oleevar. On her other side sat Tonz. Raelle could tell by the disappointment on his face that he knew she had spent the night with Chrishtan. She did her best not to let it bother her and her mind took her back to just before she left for the Lantern Forest.

*You don't need to worry about that right now,* Tonz had told her. *When the time comes, we'll work it out. No one is asking you to make those kinds of decisions right now. And whatever you decide, I will respect it. This is mainly my fault. I shouldn't have...*

Raelle shook the memory from her mind and returned to the present moment. *We'll talk later.*

379

"Chrishtan!" Oleevar smiled as he wiped his mouth with his napkin and stood. "My favorite meddlesome warrior. You're awake!" He walked around the table to greet him as Browden and Samuel set Chrishtan in an empty seat.

"I hear you're going to be the one to save my ass and get me back on my feet." Chrishtan embraced his elven brother with an enormous grin.

"Wouldn't be the first time I've saved your precarious arse." Oleevar winked and patted Chrishtan on the back. "It's good to have you back, General Vilgare."

"We've missed you, Brother." Cohlen leaned in for a hug.

"It feels good to be back." Chrishtan glanced over at Tonz who stood at attention. "At ease, Lieutenant. Good to see you."

"Fantastic to see you too, Sir." Tonz relaxed and moved around the table to Chrishtan. He made no attempt to look at Raelle. It was as if he was ignoring her completely. "I'm glad you were able to make it back to us. Abequa needs you now more than ever."

It hurt, but Raelle did her best not to let Tonz get to her and left the boys behind to chat while she went outside to pack her horse. Samuel followed shortly behind.

"Raelle!" he called after her as they walked out into the snowy forest to the enormous tree that had been hollowed out and turned into a stable. "You all right?"

"Yeah." Raelle approached the only horse that had not yet been packed. "I'm fine. I mean, as fine as I can be anyway. Why?"

"I don't know." Samuel shrugged before helping her blanket her mare. "You just look a little flustered."

"It's fine." Raelle rolled her eyes and shook her head. "Nothing to worry about."

"Does it have anything to do with a little love triangle you seem to have gotten yourself into?" He smirked as if it were funny. *Typical Sam.*

"You know what?" Raelle threw a cloth saddle over the horse. "I don't need you giving me a hard time about this. I'm going to work it out. It's going to be fine."

"Who would have thought, my big sister only out in the world for a short time, already breaking hearts," he laughed. "But I trust you've got it under control."

"Damn you, Sam." She threw a canteen at his head. "Now I kind of wish you were back in that dungeon."

"Oh, you missed this and you know it." His crooked smile incited hers.

It was true. She missed it terribly. Even in the valley, it had been years since she had seen his sense of humor. Today was the first day in years that she and her brother had connected in the same way as when they were younger. Raelle knew that it was Browden's return that had brought the glint back to Samuel's eye. The thought of telling him about his unborn child tore her up inside. She knew it would surely destroy his new-found hope.

"Yeah, yeah." She continued to pack. "Just help me with this so we can get back to Ellios."

"Right," Samuel replied. "And after this, I've got to pack up that sleigh." He pointed to a wooden luge in the back of the stable. "With your help, of course."

Raelle assumed that was how they would transport their mothers back to Ellios. "Oh, all right. Just stop messing around and get this done."

Samuel jested. "Yes, Milady."

"So, have you and Brow had a chance to talk yet?" Raelle finished up her horse and walked to the back with Samuel.

"Yeah, for a few moments." Samuel said as he began blanketing the sleigh. "He came in after you left last night." Samuel glanced at Raelle with a look of clarity. "He's Chrishtan Vilgare's brother."

"Yes," Raelle replied with a grin. "Yes, I know."

"I almost killed him." He looked down with a frown. "For my father."

Raelle approached him and squeezed his shoulder. "But you didn't know that."

"And you getting shot." Samuel peeked up at her,

shamefaced. "That was my fault too."

"It doesn't matter now, Sam." Raelle patted his back. "That's over now. We have to focus on the here and now. And look forward to the future. With so many truths finally out in the open, we now have a real shot at making things right again. We can't dwell on all the lies and manipulations that trapped us in a real life hell. Yes, we've all been through more than anyone should ever have to and we've all definitely made mistakes along the way, but we can learn from them, right?" *Tonz taught me that...* Once again, Raelle felt the dissonance pulling her heart in two different directions. *We'll talk...*

"Yeah." Samuel shifted his gaze downward again. "Yeah, I suppose we can."

"I missed you, Brother." Raelle hugged him. "Welcome back."

"Thanks." He cracked a half smile. "I missed you too." He then looked away and nervously twiddled his fingers. "We're taking Shira back with us to Ellios."

"I figured as much." Raelle dropped her arms to her sides. The memory of what Chrishtan had told her popped into her mind. She still was not sure whether she should tell Samuel about his unborn child. Deep in her heart, she knew he had a right to know, but the thought of sending him back into his dark depression made her heart hurt. She decided she would wait until they returned to Ellios. She would wait for the right moment. Whatever that meant she did not know, but it eased her mind for the moment. "I know Chrishtan wants to give her a proper send off as well." Raelle could tell her expression was less than approving.

"It wasn't entirely her fault, Raelle." For whatever reason, Samuel felt the need to come to Volshira's defense. "The demons poisoned her mind."

"Did I say anything?" Raelle retorted. "But since we're one the subject, *she* poisoned yours. I'm sure she had it out for you from the beginning. She hates us and our family." She shrugged. "I understand why, but she hurt a lot of people. What she did was no better than what Lochran—

"Yeah, I got it, Raelle," Samuel cut her off. "Let's just get this sleigh ready to go."

"Sure thing."

As soon as they were all packed and the sleigh attached to Samuel's horse, the group took off through the Roeesar forest toward Ellios. Still, Tonz refused to look at or speak to Raelle. She figured that the sight of Chrishtan's arms around her as they rode together on horseback didn't help the situation. But Chrishtan was unable to sit up on his own and needed to use her as a prop. After all, had he not done the same for her not that long ago? Raelle loathed the thought of Tonz hating her. She cared deeply about what he thought of her. And in truth, she owed him an explanation. But right now, Chrishtan needed her more than ever and she wanted more than anything to be there for him. She and Tonz could talk after they got home, just as he said they could before Chrishtan's return. She hoped Tonz would be mature enough to hear her out. He had promised her he would, but now Raelle was not so sure.

After hours of riding along the snow-covered trails of the Roeesar forest, the group came out of the trees at the back of Ellios city. The only way inside was through the secret back entrance of the palace grounds another eight kilometers ahead of them. They kept a steady pace as they made their way along the untouched snowy isthmus between Lake Bithle and Lake Eachyros. As they approached the back ingress of the fortress, Raelle saw something in the distance flying toward Ellios from the south.

"Are the air raiders only now returning to Ellios?" Cohlen shielded his eyes from the sun. "That doesn't make any sense."

"No." Oleevar shook his head. "You're right. It doesn't."

They paused just outside the wall to look and listen. Each one of them focused their Lyre to get a better sense of what was headed in their direction. Raelle closed her eyes and honed her senses. As she listened, she could hear what felt like a stampede. Her ears picked up the screeches of something she had heard only once before. And the shrieks were accompanied by the scent of something she had only once before smelled.

383

"Dranogites!" she and Chrishtan called at the same time.

"Oh, Architect." Oleevar began to hyperventilate. "It can't be. Not now." He turned to Raelle's brother. "Samuel, do you know if the Warlocks are cooperating with Lochran? Did he ever mention the Ornz people?"

"Not that I know of." Samuel shrugged and shook his head.

"Karaleste?" Oleevar turned to the Jassokian princess. "Have you?"

"No." She did the same as Samuel. "I know nothing. I only just arrived at Lochran's palace a couple of days ago. He hasn't spoken of any other allies to me."

"I'm sure Zeell has already seen them and is sending out reinforcements to the front." Oleevar swiftly opened the back entrance and they fled inside the walls. "We need to get out there and see what's going on."

"What about Chrishtan and the women?" Cohlen glanced back at the sleigh carrying Shellere, Patrilla, and Volshira.

"Samuel, take them inside," Oleevar directed. "Set the women up with their own rooms so that Karaleste can start working on them straight away. Tonz, go with them and help them get Chrishtan safely to his room."

"I'm not going anywhere," Chrishtan protested. "I'm going out to the front with you."

"Chrishtan," Oleevar rebutted. "There is no need to do that."

"I agree," Browden chimed in. "You're in no shape to go out there right now and you know it. Don't do this."

"We're wasting time arguing about this," Oleevar raised his voice. "Chrishtan, your stubbornness has no place in this matter," he snapped. "I am king and *I* say what goes, understood!"

Raelle had never seen Oleevar so authoritative. It actually frightened her, because surely it meant that they were in some serious danger.

"Raelle, trade places with Tonz," commanded Oleevar. "Tonz, take Chrishtan, Samuel, and the women back to the palace.

They are going to need your clearance to get in."

"Yes, Sir," Tonz replied as he hopped off his horse.

Raelle did the same and Oleevar helped Chrishtan to stay upright. "This is behemoth shit," Chrishtan griped.

"Shut your mouth," Oleevar snapped. "We already lost you once."

Tonz turned to Oleevar. "Once the women are all settled, we'll meet you at the gates."

"Bring me some *real* daggers," Raelle requested.

Tonz nodded briskly to acknowledge her request and he and Samuel headed off toward the palace.

Still on horseback, Oleevar, Cohlen, Browden, and Raelle raced toward the Ellios front gates. Raelle felt bad leaving Chrishtan behind, but she knew it was for the best. When they reached the bronze walls of the entrance, they hurried up the stairs where they found Zeell at the top with a lineup of sentries armed with ranged energy rifles.

"Your majesty," Zeell greeted Oleevar with open arms. "You've returned just in time. I'm glad to see you alive."

"Thank you, Zeell." Oleevar hugged his friend. "What's the status?"

Suddenly, they all felt the ground quake. The stampede Raelle had felt in the distance was now in sight. Hundreds of mounted Ornz combatants rode up along the path through the Emeralz plains on the back of behemoths and enormous serpents. Overhead, a small group of air raiders rode atop the backs of dranogites of all shapes, sizes, and colors. As the dranogite air force landed just outside the Ellosian force field, their mounted soldiers paused half a kilometer behind them. From where they stood atop the Ellios gates, Raelle saw the lead dragon rider signal something she had learned in training. They wanted to speak to the person in charge.

"I'm coming with you." Raelle grabbed Oleevar's arm.

"So am I," Cohlen spouted off.

"I'll be circling from above," Browden asserted. "Keeping an eye out on *everything*. Just signal if you need me." The warrior in white armor put on his helm, flapped his wings, and took off into the sky.

"All right, let's go." Oleevar stepped away from the wall and swiftly made his way back down the row and to the stairs. At the bottom, he mounted one of their hovercrafts and opened the gate. He did not wait for Raelle and Cohlen to mount their horses behind him.

As they got closer to the dragon riders, Raelle saw that a female elf led the flock. She looked to be about the same age as Samuel. As the young warlock jumped down from her green-scaled dranogite, she removed the hood of her heavy amber cloak. Raelle ogled her long green hair and dark skin and thought that she may have been one of the most stunning women she had ever seen. Her bright purple eyes almost seemed to glow in the shade of the enormous cloud that now covered the sun. She was clothed in uniquely crafted animal skin armor decorated with amber colored stones along with animal skulls and bones. Like Karaleste, her face was tattooed with majestic designs and decorated with small amber gems. Thin metal piercings stuck through the center of her brow line and went down to the center of the bridge of her nose. The last thing Raelle wanted in the world was to have this young woman as her enemy.

Oleevar left his mount and walked through the snow toward the edge of the force field. He used his Chocaz stone to create a hole large enough for the young warlock to fit through. Once she was inside, Oleevar removed the stone and the hole resealed itself.

Raelle stayed atop her horse and listened for Oleevar and the beautiful Ornz warlock to begin their discussion.

"Who are you?" Oleevar asked in the sternest tone Raelle had ever heard him use. "What business do you have bringing trouble to my doorstep?"

"I am Meerya of Ornz. And our business is not with you, elf. It is with the one they call Vilgare." The striking warlock answered him in an equally confident tenor. "We have come for him."

"You must be joking." Oleevar retorted.

Raelle's heart sank. *No... no... no, no, no... They'll have to get through me first. I'm not letting him go again. Not now!*

# BOOK III
of the
## *ON THE VERGE*
Series

# COMING 2017

Want to stay up to date on R. J. Jojola's upcoming book release dates? SIGN UP for RJ's Mailing List at

**WWW.RJJOJOLA.COM**

Also receive FREE *On the Verge* related CONTENT.

# THANK YOU FOR READING

If you LIKED *FROM THE VOID*

Please RATE IT and/or LEAVE a REVIEW

at amazon.com or goodreads.com

# ABOUT THE AUTHOR

RJ Jojola is a former middle school English
and science teacher using her passion for all things menacing
& fantastical to create worlds of
epic fantasy and horror.

## TO FIND OUT MUCH MORE ABOUT
## R. J. JOJOLA & HER BOOKS, VISIT:
## WWW.RJJOJOLA.COM

To Keep Up With Her On
### SOCIAL MEDIA
### LIKE HER at:

facebook.com/rjjojola
facebook.com/ontheverge
instagram.com/rjjojola
twitter.com/rjjojola